Blood Enemies

Volume Four

THE DECEIVER SAGA CONTINUES...

Blood Enemies

Volume Four

R. J. Machado De Quevedo

Blood Enemies

R. J. Machado De Quevedo, Author
P.O. BOX 1505 | Elk Grove | California 95759 USA
www.RJMachadoDeQuevedo.com

Cover Design by Karen Phillips

Biblical scripture references are taken from the New King James Version.

Published in the United States of America

ISBN: 978-1-947932-04-3
1. Fiction / Thriller / Suspense
2. Self-Help / Christian Life / Spiritual Warfare
19.03.03

DEDICATION

Losing someone you love is like waking up from a deep sleep
and discovering that while you were dreaming, the world around
you crumbled and dust and ash lay where only hours before green
pastures grew in luscious groves, adorned with a colorful flourish
of wild flowers.

To the loving memory of my oldest sister, Esther Marie.
Your life was taken from you on August 25, 2015.
You couldn't outrun that moment in time Death chose for you.
You simply ran out of time.
We all ran out of time.
I will always miss you.
I will always love you.

"We must develop and maintain the capacity to forgive. He who is devoid of the power to forgive is devoid of the power to love. There is some good in the worst of us and some evil in the best of us. When we discover this, we are less prone to hate our enemies."
—Martin Luther King Jr.

CONTENTS

AUTHOR'S NOTE

hen I received word in January 2017 that the traditional publishing house I had published the first three books in *The Deceiver Saga* through was closing, Tate Publishing and Enterprises LLC, I was upset. Well, truth be told, I was more than upset. I was angry, frustrated, and nearly in tears. All that time and effort I'd poured into getting these books off the ground seemed to have been wasted. And the promise of publishing more books felt as though it was being stolen from me.

But then I felt the Lord whispering a gentle reminder into my heart. It wasn't for nothing. It wasn't in vain. I had been given the opportunity and the privilege to publish three books the "traditional way". I'd learned a lot about being an author and experienced the production process of publishing three books. I had knowledge I could draw from.

I decided then and there, rather than let the bad news devastate my dreams, I would use what I'd learned to republish these books myself. It was a hidden blessing; an opportunity to take more control of my future and the destiny of my books.

It has been a tremendous amount of work but it has been worth every second. And I am proud to report that I re-released and self-published book one in *The Deceiver Saga*, *The Deceiver*, in December 2017. Book two, *Broken Seed*, in November 2018. Then book three, *Sanctuary of Fire*, only a few months later in January 2019!

During the last two years, I also finished writing, editing and now, self-published this forth book, *Blood Enemies*! Hallelujah! I am so relieved to have this long-awaited book finally out for all of you to read!

Once again, I'd like to say to all my faithful fans reading this, THANK YOU from the bottom of my heart for your support and patience. I appreciate you more than you could ever know. God bless you.

Prologue

atherine stood at the living room window, shifting slightly from left to right, wringing her long dark auburn hair with her elegant hands where it lay draped over her right shoulder. She pulled back the curtains to see the street as she waited, her anxious start-and-stop breathing making a foggy glow on the cold glass.

She glanced to the left then to the right of their quiet street that still lay in deep slumber at this godforsaken hour. She inhaled deeply, realizing she'd been holding her breath again and hastened to wipe away a tear that had found its way to her cheek once more.

The call from her niece Helena kept replaying in her mind, haunting her. Her voice had been a whispered rush of desperation, pleading for them to take her in. Her husband wasn't who she'd thought he was. He was a monster. He'd beaten her, hurt her. Done...things.

What was Katherine supposed to say? "No, Helena. You can't come here. Your Uncle Frank isn't one for unexpected company.

Can you wait until the weekend so I have time to soften him up to the idea?" Absolutely not. This was her niece. Her *only* niece. Her sister Gloria had died three months before. She'd never forgive herself if she turned away Gloria's wayward daughter now, after all this time.

Katherine heard a shuffling behind her as her husband came back into the living room for the second time that hour. "Kitten, she won't be here for at least another hour or more. It isn't a quick drive. Come back to bed, darling. Get some rest," Frank said through a large yawn.

"I can't. I just can't. What if she broke down on the side of the road and he caught up to her? What if she never made it out of the house?"

"Katie, don't do that, honey. Don't start thinking about everything that might have gone wrong. It's a long drive from Redding. She may not even know her way around Elk Grove. She's never been to our new house before, so she'll have to find us. Give her time."

"I know that Frank! But you didn't hear her on the phone. She was so scared! It just all reminds me of that night when Gloria showed up on our doorstep and, and—" Katherine turned around to meet her husband's eyes, her words failing her, her own eyes wide and frightened. At the sight of his beloved wife nearing meltdown, Frank idled over and wrapped his arms around her shoulders, pulling her into a tight hug.

"Shh, now. It'll all be okay. You'll see. Just hang in there, Kitten. She'll be here soon. Shh," he soothed, patting her gently on her back as she buried her face into his neck.

"Oh Frankie, Gloria would be so devastated to know her daughter was having to run for her life from that man. I'm almost relieved she isn't around to see this," Katherine started to sob.

"Shh, shh," Frank whispered. "It'll all work out." He gently pulled her away from the window and led her to the sofa. She sat down, still embraced in his arms. There they sat silently and waited. Katherine closed her eyes, resting her face into Frank's broad shoulder.

Nearly two hours later headlights lit up the dark street. The sound of an old pickup truck rumbled louder as it approached their house. Katherine stirred from her light doze on the living room couch and rubbed her face, blinking into the bright light now flooding into the window past the open curtains as the vehicle turned into their driveway.

Frank had gotten up to man the window, his arms crossed, his forehead creased in a serious frown. He turned to Katherine and nodded with a look that told her he was ready for whatever they were about to get involved in and he'd support her no matter what she decided.

Katherine quickly rose from the couch and slipped on her thick white robe as she headed to the front door. "Come on Frankie. She might need help." Frank slipped in silently behind her, his hand touching her back briefly in support as she exited through the front door.

A hunched silhouette was visible behind the wheel. The large light blue Chevy's engine continued to idle with an offbeat rattle. A chill went through Katherine as she took it in, as if the very sound it made held the cries of many sorrows and the agony of many lives. She didn't understand the eerie feeling that overtook her and it scared her. Who was the man who owned that truck? What had he done to her niece?

The engine shut off and the driver switched off the headlights. The door opened slowly with a creak. The thin woman inside gingerly got out and reached in to grab a small bag. She looked up at them; her face had been brutalized. The dried blood along her cracked lips and along her eyebrows sat like some kind of absurd makeup on her delicate face in the darkness, the faint glow from their front porch light doing little to erase the look of desperation still on her face.

"Oh dear God!" Katherine's momentary fear vanished in a rush of shock and concern. "Helena! Oh child! What did he do to you?" She rushed over to her niece and took her face in her hands, tears spilling down her cheeks in response to the young woman's pain.

"Auntie Kate. Oh, Auntie Kate," Helena burst into tears and she wrapped herself around Katherine, nearly sagging into her arms.

"Frank! Frankie, come here. Help me! The poor girl's nearly exhausted."

Frank hurried over, catching Helena around the waist just as her knees gave way. He swooped her up in his arms and her head flopped forward onto his chest. Her weak sobs of relief and distress made her body tremble against him, the stale adrenaline void of power to keep her upright now that she had finally arrived to her safe haven.

Frank's eyes were wide as he looked back up at Katherine in angst, "She needs a doctor."

"No. No doctors. Can't trust anyone," Helena's voice cracked. "Please, no hospital."

"Come on Frank, we need to get her inside," Katherine said as she bent down to grab the small bag that had slipped out of Helena's limp hand. She paused, looking at the bag. "This is a diaper bag?"

"My ba-babies...side seat," Helena whimpered, trying to point to the truck.

"Wh-what did you say?" Frank sputtered, his eyes growing in panic. Frank and kids didn't usually get along. Babies down right terrified him. As if the idea of one in the house was bad enough, more than one was enough to make him want to tuck tail and run away himself.

Katherine rushed around the truck and opened the passenger side door with a *whoosh*. Her mouth opened and words failed her as she took in the baby's car seat tightly strapped down on the passenger seat and then a pale little girl who was still sleeping soundly, curled up in a tight ball on the floor in front of the bucket seat. The little girl's tiny clothes were faded and worn, her cheap tennis shoes splitting along the sides from her feet outgrowing them. Her arm was smudged with dirt and her black pony tail frizzy from sleep.

The baby was wide awake. Peering silently up at Katherine with haunted blue eyes, her matted red hair making her look red all over, but thinner than what Katherine thought a baby should be. *Shouldn't they be plump and chubby at this age?*

Katherine gathered herself and reached out to the baby. The baby took her finger and pulled it toward her wet toothless mouth, gumming it, looking for a meal.

"Frank, she has two little girls here." Katherine announced in a hurried whisper, not wanting to wake the neighbors.

"Let me take her inside then I'll come back and help you," Frank answered quietly, shifting Helena in his arms for a better hold. He walked back to the house and used his foot to open the front door wider as they passed through. He set her gently on the couch where she slumped, barely awake now, having spent all of her energy just trying to stay alert in case they were being followed.

"Thank you," Helena mumbled, wheezing as if she'd just ran the hundred and eighty miles rather than drove them.

"Rest now. Just rest. You're safe here," Frank answered, reaching over to turn on the table lamp to bathe her in a soft glow of warm light. The light made her squint and shy away, hiding the mess that was her face. The bruises and welts on her cheek looked a sickly green and purple in the light, exposing a pattern of several days' worth of back to back beatings.

Dear God, what has this woman endured? Frank wondered, feeling sick and helpless.

He wasn't sure how to comfort a woman who wasn't his wife. Helena had been around since she was small, but he'd always kept his distance having been uncomfortable around children, and even more awkward around loud, laughing young ladies. He was out of his element and felt the distance between himself and his niece more deeply than he ever had before.

As worried as he was to have this bleeding and battered woman slumped on his couch, he was also angry about it. He felt intruded upon, inconvenienced. If it had been up to him, he'd have told her to go to a women's shelter or something. He and Katherine barely knew Helena anymore. She hadn't talked to her aunt in years and thought she could call up at one o'clock in the morning and ask to come stay with them? But Frank could never really tell Katherine no. Not when something was important to her. Especially not after watching her heart break and her eyes fill with helplessness when she hung up the phone and told him who had called and why.

As Helena looked up at him, her face drained of any spark of life, he scolded himself for his lack of compassion and callous heart. His harder nature had always been softened by Katherine's kind and gentle spirit. She had taught him how to love, how to give. She'd changed him in remarkable ways with her patience and unconditional love throughout their many years together. This broken young woman was a part of *her*. Perhaps the closest thing they would ever have to a child of their own.

Helena was still so young. Maybe twenty-four? Twenty-five? He studied her swollen face, the dried blood and the frighteningly dark circles beneath her eyes. No woman deserved to be treated like that. He couldn't even imagine striking Katherine. His beloved Katherine...How could any man possibly hit the woman he claimed to love? How could they possibly justify such a thing? How could they forgive themselves if they lost their temper and even did it once? Let alone again, and again, and again?

Frank felt himself bristle, a protective anger replacing his selfish one. He took one of Helena's hands in his, and gently placed his other hand on top of it, kneeling down in front of her, giving her something she probably never received at home, respect.

"Helena dear, I'm so sorry for what you've been going through. Your aunt and I are going to help you. All three of you. You'll be safe here."

Helena began to cry large unstoppable tears. He hastened to get up and sat beside her and wrapped his arm around her shoulder while she cried, her small body trembling weakly.

Outside in the dim light, Katherine stared in helpless panic as the baby blinked up at her in expectation, gumming her finger eagerly. *Where is Frank? I need his help with these girls! Poor Helena must be in pieces in there. Oh God, I hope Frank is being patient and kind to her!*

Katherine gently pulled her finger out of the baby's mouth expecting her to cry but she didn't even fuss. She just tapped her lips together and licked her little pink tongue across her empty mouth, asking for food but not making a sound.

Maybe she already learned that silence was safest? Katherine cringed at the thought then wrinkled her nose as she got a whiff of the baby's messy diaper.

"I need to get you inside and changed little one."

She couldn't wait for Frank anymore. She *had* to get these girls out of the cold and inside. Katherine bent down and gently tapped the delicate shoulder of the little girl still sleeping on the floor. She stirred and mumbled but didn't wake, so Katherine rubbed her tiny chilly arm. The poor thing didn't even have a coat on.

"Come on, honey. Wake up. Your mama's waiting for you," Katherine whispered. She didn't even know their names! She hadn't even known Helena had any children! She felt her eyes prickle with tears again. No, she had to keep it together. She might scare the kids if she lost it. They needed to feel safe, not to pick up on the adults' fear.

"Honey, come on. Wake up," she rubbed her arm gently again.

"Mama?" the little voice asked confused.

"Your mama's in the house, honey. Come on with me. I'm your great auntie Katie. I'll take you to her, alright?" Katherine tried to speak in her softest voice, not wanting to frighten the poor child. God only knew what she'd witnessed. She doubted she would trust many adults, let alone a perfect stranger.

"You're my gwate auntie?" The little girl asked, sitting up and rubbing her wide startled eyes. They were striking, like a clear tropical sea. She was such a beautiful little girl with her black hair, seascape eyes, and pale skin. She turned her face up squinting to see Katherine better in the dim light. At the sight of the large purple bruise on her cheek, Katherine's stomach twisted. Who would ever want to hurt that precious little face?

"Y—Yes, I'm your auntie. You're going to be staying with me and your Uncle Frankie with your mama and little sister for a while. Is that okay?" Katherine asked her kindly.

"Okay," The little girl said in a small voice and got to her feet. She reached over to give the baby her finger. The baby sucked happily on it, gripping her big sister's hand fiercely.

"You take good care of your sister, don't you?" Katherine asked, amazed that this little girl would seek to check on her little sister as soon as she woke. She couldn't be more than five or six, and already carrying the weight of the world on her tiny shoulders.

"Mama needs my help. Father doesn't like it when she cries. I help keep her quiet," she whispered, biting her lower lip and shifting her feet to look nervous at last.

"Your father gets angry when she cries?" Katherine tried to sound casual.

"Yeah," the small voice answered timidly.

"You want to come inside the house with me honey? Your dad won't be there."

"Ahuh." The little girl stepped out of the truck, blinked, rubbed her eyes again and then frowned. "Where are we?"

"You're at our house. We live in Elk Grove. Are you hungry?"

"Ahuh," she reached back in the truck, stretching to grab a little blue blanket that had slipped onto the floor by the driver's seat. "This is Melanie's. She has to have her blanket, okay?" The little girl stuffed it onto the baby's lap and Katherine helped tuck it in around the baby.

"Your sister's name is Melanie? That's lovely."

"Yeah. Melanie Olivia Bishop."

"And what's your name sweetie?"

"Vivian. Vivian Katherine Bishop," the little girl took a few steps away and looked around at the large house looming up before her, her eyes wide. "This all yours?" she asked in a small amazed voice. "You have kids?"

Katherine swallowed. Helena had named Vivian after her? She hadn't expected that. She felt her eyes swimming with tears again. The little girl turned around at her silence, having expected her to answer her questions. At seeing her auntie in tears, she rushed back over to her.

"Don't worry Auntie Katie. Don't cry. I'll take care of you. Want me to sing to you? It helps my mama when she cries. Helps Melanie when she cries too." Vivian's little face was covered in concern. She reached up and took Katherine's hand in her tiny one.

Katherine dropped down to her knees and Vivian embraced her. Those thin little arms tightly wrapping around her neck and she began to sing to Katherine in her sweet voice of innocence.

"Somewhere, over the rainbow, skies are blue. And the dreams that you dare to dream really do come true. Someday I'll wish upon a star, and wake up where the clouds are far behind me—"

Frank stepped around the truck, his face softening at the sight of them, the child's little song of misguided hope stabbing him in the heart making him feel more sadness and sympathy than he'd ever felt for any human being hovering around three feet tall. His eyes met Katherine's. Their silent conversation a promise that they would do whatever they could to protect these three young ladies. They'd have to. For if not them, then who?

Truth or Dare

Chapter One

*T*he cool water should have tasted refreshing, but it wasn't. It tasted bitter in my mouth and was too weak to wash away the acidic sizzle that was permeating my palate and burning its way down my esophagus. I felt cold and clammy. The fresh T-shirt and jeans I'd put on only eight hours before felt as dirty and contaminated as my mouth and mind did now.

I'd been in the bathroom throwing up and breathing heavy for a few minutes. It had taken every ounce of strength I had to force myself to walk, not run, *without screaming*, from the living room. Instead, I'd silently set down the file I'd been looking at and walked in a daze to the hall bathroom, unable to answer my friends' calls of concern at my abrupt departure.

I'd managed to gently close the door behind me. Locked it softly. Then I bolted to the toilet with two lunging steps, dropped to my knees, threw the lid up (because two women live in my house and we always put the toilet seat down), and stuck my head down into the hole just in time to lose every ounce of food and drink I had left in my stomach.

I don't think I can do this.

Those images had been harder to look at than I'd expected. Not that I had expected it to be painless or seemingly flat colorless photos. But seeing the bodies of my mother and sister dead, warped, broken, and in various stages of decay and putrefaction had *not* been what I'd imagined. My memories of losing them had not all been pleasant, but those images were going to cast shadows of a different kind of horror that my nightmares couldn't even shine a light on. How had I not expected that? I already knew they had both been found weeks after my father killed them.

I'm such an idiot! They weren't found right away! You knew this already! Of course the forensic photos would be like this. You should have known what to expect!

My mind swarmed with the images of my mother Helena and sister Vivian. Then as if jealous of not being remembered, and with an intensity that made me bow over, the colorful memories of Mastema and Verin's demonic rebirth that happened the night before overtook me. Their dead bloody bodies had been animated for a short time after I'd killed them. They'd following me up to the top of Mount Moriah seeking to destroy me before they'd been stopped by the Lion. It had emerged from my palm and erupted with a roar, chasing them down.

During the final death of their animated bodies, their true form had been revealed. Their demon spirits had emerged. It had been a horrific sight. A living nightmare in which I had to fight back, run for my life, and finally stand my ground. It had been the scariest thing I had ever seen. Killing them had felt like the right thing to do, the only thing to do. It was a battle of life and death after all. A battle for the future Savior's path to redeeming us all through the first sacrifice by Abraham and his son, Isaac. I hadn't thought I'd ever kill anyone let alone giants. Did that make me a killer too? Was I somehow like my father?

You're not a killer Melanie, don't be silly. Well, you're not a trained killer. And you don't enjoy killing.

I winced at the internal admission. Killing giants with a four-thousand year old sword handcrafted from God and infused with the Holy Spirit's power didn't really make me a killer too, did it? I'd been fighting for my life at the time. I don't even hunt! I'm not a soldier nor prepared to see the aftermath of battle with the sight of brutalized bodies. David was. David had. And I'm sure Liz knows how to kill someone, too, with all her extensive knowledge of martial arts and weapons training.

Has she ever killed anyone before? I caught myself holding my breath at the thought. I had never asked her that. *How have I never asked her that? I have no idea if she's ever had to take a life.*

Do you really want to know if she had? Would you respect her any less or simply accept it like you have of David?

"Oh, God," I breathed. *Would they think differently of me if they knew what I'd done back at Mount Moriah?*

This line of thought wasn't helping me feel any better.

My best friend Liz, real name Elisabeth Becker, worked as a consultant with several government agencies for her profiling expertise and her deep understanding of complex religious factions and what drove them. She also spoke several languages, specializing in dead languages such as Aramaic, Biblical Hebrew, Latin and Coptic.

Her undercover partner, Agent Bradley Carter, doubled as her boyfriend and colleague at Sacramento State University. They were both professors there and moonlighted as government consultants and were occasional operatives when called upon. I'd known of Liz's involvement with the government but had only been suspicious of Bradley's up until about eight hours ago when he'd busted in on my long deferred make out session with David.

Brad had arrived with a satchel full of files. But not just any files. They were *my* files. Or rather, files that pertained to the most devastating and horrifying moments of my life and those individuals who had either done the crimes or been the victims. My own files were among them having been one of the victims on more than one occasion, not the criminal.

These case files also held the details of the brutal murders of my mother and sister, complete with crime scene photos, autopsy records, witness statements, you get the gist. Basically, the entire investigations.

Other files were still "active" or "live" files. As in, they were what the government kept in-house about the criminals and suspects that happened to be in my life. Not because I was worth protecting, but because my path had unfortunately crossed into theirs and they were the ones being looked at. I just happened to be a common denominator in their criminal history and victim of choice.

Ooh, lucky me.

These files contained information on their backgrounds, current and former whereabouts, known aliases, and arrest records. They also contained some of their genealogy, both ancestrally and progressively, known hangouts and affiliations, memberships, tax records, property records, income sources, credit history, bank records and an extensive forensic level recording of their expenses including spreadsheets with their recent credit and debit card history. I suspected some of those were little added bonuses personally requested by Liz or Bradley. I didn't think the government even cared about some of the stuff in there, but as a profiler, Liz would.

I tilted my face under the faucet again and did my best to cleanse my mouth once more with the cool water. It felt futile, lacking any real cleansing power.

"Oh, God, I don't know if I can do this," I croaked again to myself, sucking a big breath deep into my lungs. I felt almost a little light headed. All these years of wanting answers, wanting to know the truth and I was buckling. But these investigative files into my mother and sister's murders seemed to just stir up more unanswered questions. It didn't make sense. The evidence gathered at the scenes didn't make sense!

My father's interviews by the police were in both files. The police bought his imaginatively spun stories, his lies. Somehow, they believed my mom ran off with a lover and abandoned her family, getting herself killed by the mysterious lover, her dead body being found in a ditch, off Gas Point Road, just outside of town. They never identified the lover or the killer. Imagine that.

About my sister; her file said they had suspicions that she was attacked and killed by a teenage stalker from another school. My father claimed Vivian had confided in him that a boy named Steve had been following her. She'd met him at a game and he had become obsessed with her. The only problem was there were about seventeen Steves in Shasta county from various high schools who were around her age and, of course, my father didn't know what he looked like or which school he went to. They had interviewed boys for months and spun their wheels looking at innocent kids when they should have been looking at my father.

Why didn't they see it's him!

I grabbed a new tooth brush and the tooth paste from under the sink we kept for guests, not that we ever had any over. I brushed and scrubbed my mouth out, trying to remove the taste of vomit and in a way cleanse myself of all the horrible images and descriptions I'd been looking at for the last eight hours.

I caught a glimpse of myself in the bathroom mirror. The light-green T-shirt I had on did little to brighten my sickly colored face.

I plunged my face into the running water once more, trying to clear my head but the images of my mother and sister's dead bodies kept floating to the surface.

Why can't I turn off my brain? Stop it. Stop it!

You're not used to seeing death and decay. Of course it will affect you! You aren't looking at enemies dead on the ground. You're looking at your mother! Your sister! You loved them!

I let out a whimper as I tried to force myself to swallow the knot and stifle the sob constricting my throat.

A soft knock at the door made me jerk my head up and I yelped. Water spilled across my face and ran down my neck, dripping onto my light green T-shirt and onto the sink counter. I pushed my long sleeves back up and reached over to unlock the door. I'd already thrown up everything there was to expel, it should be safe to let someone in. I drew in a long breath and braced myself for whoever was out there.

"Caught up to you finally, did it?" Liz asked gently as the door opened. She stood there, back straight, shoulders square, ready to see this through.

"Ah, yeah," I managed to say, my eyes dropping to my fuzzy pink slippers. They had instantaneously lost their ability to make me smile. I couldn't find a drop of joy to cling to at the moment and I felt the realization deepen my devastation.

I cleared my throat and wiped my watering eyes with the back of my hands. "All the sudden I just couldn't hold it in anymore. It was like everything we've been reading out there and all the pictures we've been looking at, just crashed down on me like an eclipse, Liz. I just couldn't see anymore. I'm sorry, I lost it. I thought I'd be stronger with this stuff after what I saw and did on my...on my recent *trip*," I lowered my voice into a corrected whisper right at the last part and gave her a meaningful look.

"About that. We seriously need to talk. You still haven't told me what you meant when you said you were glad the angels were able to clean off all of the dirt, blood and body parts," she whispered back, taking a quick glance down the hall to make sure one of the boys hadn't followed her back here.

"Well, it's not like we've had time! You called Bradley over, remember," I said a little too defensively.

"I know Mel. But he came over *early*. David stopped by too unexpectedly right after dinner if you recall, right when we were supposed to talk," Liz whispered back calmly.

"Then why—"

"Mel, you've had your plate pretty full for a few days. Maybe we should call it a night. You're clearly exhausted and at your peak with this. We can keep dissecting these files but there is only so much we can do in one setting and it's getting late." Liz stepped into the bathroom with me and closed the door behind her.

I took a step back to make room for her. "I want to keep going. I *need* to keep going."

"I know you do. But you need to pace yourself. This is going to be a marathon Melanie, not a sprint. Pushing yourself when you are already exhausted won't help you see things any clearer. It'll just make you feel more overwhelmed and your thoughts even more disconnected. Exhaustion does not a good research partner make," Liz took my shoulders in her hands and looked down at me, her face full of understanding. I met her emerald eyes and nodded.

"You're right, Yoda. I was in here thinking to myself how none of this seems to be answering my questions. Well, other than confirming that my mother's maiden name was O'Hair, daughter of Gloria, sister of Katherine, wife of Frank Gable! Which means I really am Frank's niece! But aside from that little bombshell, I'm just more frustrated than anything! All this is doing is making me sick and angry. Oh, Liz. I am so angry!" I dropped my head and I felt her forehead touch mine as if she was trying to share her mental strength and clarity with me.

We stood there in silence for a moment, then she pulled away with a soft smile. Her hands gripping my shoulders gently in sign of support.

"You're not alone in any of this Melanie. We'll be here with you every step of the way."

"I know. And I appreciate it. My circle of friends is growing," I said with a weak smile. "But so are my enemies, Liz," I reminded her, my face dropping to a serious, humorless scowl.

"*Our* enemies, Mel," Liz corrected me.

"And my...my blood enemy," I added mostly to myself, my anger flared making the words come out strained and warbly with the extreme tension and deep-set emotions I was barely able to contain.

"I know Melanie. I know. But—"

"This is going to take forever! I could barely make it through eight hours of reading, research and discussions! Did you see those files? They hardly investigated their murders, Liz! It was like...like they weren't even worth their time! How can I possibly believe they will apply themselves now, even if my father—"

"Melanie, don't give into the frustrations of police protocols and politics. It's as much a game of strategy as it is of wits whenever finding justice and administering the law are concerned. You need to prepare yourself for the long road ahead, and yes, for some pretty hard resistance. If we find any mistakes made, past or present, those who made them won't be happy. The more we dig, the more we'll find, and that can add to our enemies too. You have to prepare yourself mentally for the challenges ahead."

"But the longer this takes the more people my father has time to hurt! He's out there somewhere right now, Liz. And he's already proved he's smart enough to elude the police and the FBI. He's been getting away with rape and murder for decades! *Decades*, Liz! He could teach classes on it!" I snarled. My hands flying up in the air, gesturing wildly.

"He could...teach?" Liz said slowly, her eyes focusing on a point far above my head and her face getting that look of dawning revelation as her eyes grew larger. She always got that look when she had a breakthrough.

"Liz? What is it? What did you just think of?" I asked, gripping her shoulders now and almost shaking her.

"Teach," Liz said unhelpfully in a singsong voice as if mesmerized by her own genius.

"What about teaching? I was just kidding. Being flippant. I didn't really—"

"How did he get so good at eluding the police and avoiding capture all these years, Mel? You said it yourself, he's been doing it for decades! I need his file...I need to see if he..." Liz turned abruptly and rushed from the bathroom leaving me with my hands held out where her shoulders had been, the air from the flung open door *whooshing* past me.

"Okay," I said to myself, confused. I rushed out of the bathroom behind her.

Why can't you complete your sentences at a time like this!

When I entered the living room, I found Liz already crouched at the coffee table reading through one of the folders again. Her face hard and focused. Her eyes zipping back and forth, her hands flipping page after page.

"Melanie," David said as he leapt to his feet to come to me. "Are you okay?"

"I'm trying to be. I really am," my voice was a little weak.

"I don't want to press you with a bunch of stupid questions and state the obvious, but I know this has to be hard for you. This is your family. There can't be anything harder than reading about their murders and looking at these photos, being reminded so vividly of what was done to them. You loved them. There isn't any shame in taking a break or being done for the night. We can't fix everything all at once anyway," David said gently.

"I know, you're right. Liz and I just talked about that. But then she reacted to something I said and ran back out here."

I pointed to Liz, lost in her own world through the thickest file. It must have been my father's file. His was the thickest one in the pile.

David and I walked back over to the living room together hand in hand and stood behind Liz to look down at the file she was paging through. Brad sat quietly on the couch directly in front of her, leaning forward, watching her, holding his face in his hands, his attention captivated.

God, he's so in love with her; it's sickening. And sweet. Very sweet. I'm glad she has someone like Bradley loving her.

"I never get bored watching her when she gets like this," Brad said glancing up at David and me as we entered the room. "It's like watching an ant build a tunnel, focused, driven, fifty times stronger than it should be, and so adorable," Brad smiled as he said it, a light in his eyes at watching the woman he adored barrel through the mass of papers clipped to the file, her eyes darting from side to side as she speedread it.

Liz glanced up at him annoyed, "An ant?"

"A-huh," Bradley smiled wider, delighted she'd paused to acknowledge him.

"Humph," Liz huffed, looking back down with an eyebrow raised to strengthen the look of severe disapproval on her face. "Keep smiling like that at me boy and I'll be an ant alright. An African army ant. And I will devour you."

"Do you promise?" Brad remarked teasingly.

Instead of answering him, Liz held out her hand, "Laptop," she demanded.

Brad ran over to the kitchen, snatched up his laptop, and rushed back over, handing it to her without question. Liz hit some buttons and I saw a blue and white logo pop up briefly with an eagle on it before Liz shot me an apologetic look and slid the laptop to an angle, blocking David and I from seeing the screen. She did some quick typing and navigating around, her eyes scanning the page at lightening speed, her face growing frustrated.

"Did you find porn? Cause it ain't mine," Bradley feigned embarrassment and wiggled like a kid in trouble, trying to get Liz's attention again.

That stopped Liz in her tracks. Or at least I thought it had. She flipped to a certain page in Dwayne's files and blinked at it, her face going slack. Her body too still.

"Liz?" Brad and I asked together.

"I found it. A lead. A place to start," Liz turned her head to look up at me. Her eyes dim, rather than light with the exhilaration I'd expected. She was usually animated and excited when she discovered something everyone else missed.

"What is it?" I squatted down in front of her.

"According to this, in 1971 your father went to truck driving school when he was nineteen, shortly after his parents died. He got his commercial driving license, class A. It allows him to drive almost anything," Liz informed us.

"I know. I mean, he used to talk about all sorts of trucks and different kinds of cargo he pulled once in a while. Like we were supposed to be impressed," I huffed. "But what does that have to do with teaching?"

Liz's eyes lit up. "He worked for a solid four years for the same trucking company and according to his tax records, he was making some pretty decent money for the '70s."

"News to me. We always ate food scraps and bought outdated canned goods on sale," I complained bitterly. "Cornmeal and powered milk were the worst," I made a gagging face by sticking out my tongue.

"What happened at the end of the four years?" David asked, gently leading the conversation back on track.

Liz smiled at him gratefully, "He quit. There are no employment records for him again until August of 1978," Liz said with significance.

"Okay," I frowned.

"Well, don't you see? What if he went off the grid because he was perfecting his craft? Studying with a mentor, like a *teacher*," Liz's voice was alight now with conspiratorial wonder.

I was suddenly exhausted with disappointment.

"Isn't that kind of a stretch?" I questioned doubtfully. "A three-year gap could mean a lot of things. What if he just ran off to Tijuana to rape and pillage or something? Who says he was hanging out with a mentor or um, a master serial killer teacher?"

"But he could have! It might even make sense if—" Liz defended her train of thought.

"My father would *never* follow anyone, Liz. That's like...unfathomable," I couldn't keep the cynicism out of my voice.

"It may feel like that Melanie, but misery loves company, and even in the world of the sick and twisted, like looks for like," Bradley chimed in. Was he defending Liz or was that just a fact?

"You don't know my father," I countered, still reluctant to accept Dwayne would bow to anyone.

"I'm not going to assume I know your father better than you do Melanie," David intercepted Bradley's response, "But anyone is capable of swallowing their pride for a time to get something else they'd rather have. Look at me," David's voice was gentle and he placed a hand on his own chest to signify the point he was going to make.

"Do you think it doesn't hurt my pride a little bit to be going to a community college or working at a restaurant as a waiter? I'm a soldier. A Pararescue Jumper team Pilot. An Air Force Captain. A cross-military trained, Joint Special Operations soldier. A decorated Officer. A helicopter pilot. But here I am," David smiled kindly down at me, "completely changing the direction of my career at thirty-two years old. I had everything in the Air Force, but what I wanted...no, what I *needed* was to get out. If restarting my life means going to a college full of people more than ten years younger than me, or sitting under professors who know less about real life than Kermit the Frog so I can have a chance at a normal life again, then I'll swallow my pride every day until I have something new to be proud of," David said clearly, his point sinking in.

"Oh," I said feeling a little sad for him. "That I can understand. You were *The Sentinel*, right? Someone who was respected and trusted. Now, you're stuck going to college with little miscreants like me," I smiled at him then quickly grew serious. "I just can't picture it for my father. But, maybe I'm biased," I shrugged. "You guys could be right."

"Elisabeth?" Bradley said her name like she was a little girl caught telling a fib. "Your idea is more than just an idea. I know you. What have you connected in your mysterious tricky brain that you haven't explained to us cavemen yet?"

"And cavegirl," I corrected him, trying to lighten things up.

Liz hesitated, looking all the more like a little girl about to tell a secret.

"Do tell," Brad teased and Liz shot him a slightly unfriendly look edged with a little humor.

"All the things I read when I was a girl about the pocket communities in Redding and in Shasta County, the ones with the most law enforcement activity, started replaying through my head as I reread your dad's file." Liz placed her hand on his file possessively.

"A girl?" I asked. "How old were—"

"Comparing what I recall of the cold cases I had read, the ones they were never able to solve, I found a few familiar locations of where the victims' bodies were dumped," Liz spoke over me, growing exicted. She looked almost manic and started to breathe heavier.

"What do you mean? Familiar locations?" David asked before I could.

Liz looked at me briefly then back at David, her eyes widening, "The ditch off Gas Point Road outside of town where they found Helena's body, Melanie's mother, had been used previously as the dumping sight of a Caucasian woman named, Maggie White, back in 1963. In 1964 a young teenage girl, named Jamie Schwartz was found in a field. Years later in 1981, that same field was rezoned to build the Cottonwood High School. Your sister's body was dumped there in the summer of 1999 in the groundskeeper's shed out behind the baseball field. It was nearly the exact spot where Jamie's body was found."

"Oh my God," I breathed, nearly silently.

"Coincidence?" Bradley speculated.

"Not likely," Liz paused as if waiting for one of us to realize something she already figured out. No one said anything so she continued.

"What I'm thinking is it's possible Dwayne knew of these locations because he knew the person who had used them *before* him. It's possible he's been reusing the other dump sites for years. All we need to do is get the cold case files from the '60s and start comparing like we did with your mom and sister's. It might be a long shot, but if we see the other dump sites were reused, it could mean Dwayne was marking his territory, like he's trying to erase his old mentor and reclaim the kingship!"

"You don't think he just read about them in the paper and chose two sites that were convenient for him to leave my mother and sister?" I sounded like the forever critic. I wasn't trying to. I just wasn't seeing everything she was seeing.

"Maybe, Melanie. You could be right if it wasn't nearly impossible. Because here's the thing; your father was only eleven and twelve years old at the time and furthermore, the two cold cases I mentioned were never reported by the media and never in the newspapers," Liz refuted.

"How do you know all those facts and what was or wasn't aired on the news in the '60s? That wouldn't have been in any file," David asked, with a slight frown.

"She's got an eidetic memory," I answered.

"Really? That's impressive," David nodded to Liz with admiration. "There's just one thing, she wasn't born yet," David shook his head now, looking at Elisabeth again but with curiosity.

"Then you read about it sometime later when it was released? Or saw it on an old episode of *Forensic Files* or something?" I guessed wildly.

"Actually, it is from seeing it, but not from watching it on television. I read the cold case files. My grandfather was trying to make Detective in the 1970s in the Redding Police Department. He thought that if he was able to solve some old cold cases, maybe he'd get promoted. He'd been trying to make connections on a handful of unsolved murders but never managed to figure out more than the detectives who had been assigned to the cases. Since he knew my mind didn't work like other kids, he tried to inspire me and encourage my analytical thinking by letting me read his old solved case files. When I got bored of those, he agreed to let me read the cold cases he hadn't been able to solve. I'd try to help, but didn't see anything he missed. I can't even imagine what my grandfather will say now if we were to help him solve—"

"You never told me that!" I burst out in surprise. "I didn't know you ever reviewed cases with Grandpa Billy! And if you could have solved them, that would have been cheating!" The words came out too sharp and accusing. I bit my lip, embarrassed I'd scolded her in front of the others.

How has she never told me this?

"No, Mel, he made Detective all on his own well before I was ever old enough to read his case files. And besides, we stopped discussing his cases all together after he got promoted to Captain, when I was about eighteen, *before* I'd even met you. He said the nature of his responsibilities had shifted and he was privy to confidential information no longer suitable to discuss with his granddaughter and too political in nature to expose me to. We hadn't done it in years up until I met you," Liz shrugged, unashamed and undeterred by my hasty pounce to judgement and my irrational hurt feelings.

"I'm just surprised you never told me you two did anything like that," I said, my voice sounding a bit whiny and I cringed. I caught David's eye. He was smirking a little, a twinkle in his eye at having heard me whine like a little girl.

Liz smiled patiently and shrugged, "You might say meeting you and seeing the pain you were in was enough to soften him to the idea of opening up his files to me again."

"You started up again after you met me?" I repeated back at her, her words dawning on me with a new sort of uncomfortable revelation.

Liz got up to her feet, the tension in my voice making her want to distance herself from me slightly. "Yes. I asked him for your mom's and sister's files a long time ago Melanie," Liz looked down, finally ashamed that she'd kept it from me.

"Wh—what?" I croaked out. "You what?"

Liz drew in a steady breath and wet her lips, her eyes starting to shine. Liz never cried. Well, she did. But usually only with empathy for me when I cried. But she was close to tears now and I felt my chest grow cold.

"I've reviewed their files before, Melanie. Years ago. And I...I couldn't find anything they missed at the time! I read them all, over and over! I wasn't able to find a damn thing! Not a single loose thread to pull and unravel any of the lies or the mysteries," Liz said, pacing back and forth, her hands on her hips.

She had already read their murder cases and hadn't told me!

I felt betrayed and lied to. I felt my hands start to shake so I stuffed them in the pockets of my jeans and glared at her.

"And how will *now* be any different?" I seethed, my anger rising.

"Now we have your emerging memories to fill in the timelines before your mother and sister died. We have your testimony! Now that he's shown his true colors with a clear attempt and intent to harm you, his *own* flesh and blood, it won't be a big leap for a jury to imagine the other horrible truths about him. Violently and repeatedly raping your sister while you were forced to watch since you were eight years old! Killing her a few years after he killed your mother. And those are just the murders we *know* about. There has to be more!"

I blanched and glanced at David. He paled at the news that my father had repeatedly raped my sister, forcing me to watch. I blushed, a vivid humiliated red. But Liz pressed on, plowing right through my difficult moment to the point she wanted to drive home.

"You aren't the same frightened child anymore Melanie Olivia Bishop. You're finally ready to take him down, to fight back!" Liz made a fist in front of her, her face fierce. "All of those elements combined put the evidence into a different light. But honestly, now that I'm older as well and have more training and experience of my own to contribute, I'm sure I'll catch what I missed when I was twenty-two," Liz drew in a deep breath, determination on her face with a certainty that she would figure out this puzzle once and for all.

"You read these when you were twenty-two!" I jumped up to my feet, the realization crashing into me even harder, stunning me. "You had access to these and didn't share them with me? Elisabeth! How could you do that to me?" I shouted, hurt, angry, and shocked.

Liz shook her head, hands out to try to calm me down. "I wanted to help! It was too much of a coincidence to ignore, you losing *both* your mother and sister to murder. I suspected that your father may have been involved after I'd seen the way he'd hurt you. But you never said anything! I didn't want to be the one to accuse him and be wrong! Or even worse, to get your hopes up unless I found something to prove it, Mel. You were only sixteen years old when I gained access to these files the first time. You couldn't handle looking at them then! You can barely even handle looking at them now! You just threw up in the bathroom!" Liz responded urgently, pointing behind me to the hallway.

"That is *my* mother! *My* sister! You had no right to keep those from me! No right Elisabeth Abigale Becker!" I shouted senselessly, pointing at her belligerently.

"I wasn't even supposed to have them Melanie! Please understand that! I couldn't tell *anyone* I had them. My grandfather could have been fired!" Liz tried desperately to make me see reason.

"I wouldn't have told!" I shouted at her.

Liz hung her head and blew out a breath before looking back up at me, true pain in her eyes. "Melanie, I wasn't about to give you false hope of exposing their killer and delusions of finding justice if we had no possible chance! I couldn't do that to you! I would never forgive myself for breaking what was left of your spirit or your hope. *Never!* I'd never do that to you, Mel. I don't regret keeping this from you, not for one second! I'd make the exact same choice if I had to do it over again because it was the *right* call. Once you have a chance to think it over, I know you'll agree with me!" Liz insisted with a mix of pleading and confidence in her voice.

I turned my back on her and started pacing. She was so damn logical! So infuriatingly right!

Then why do I feel so betrayed!

I spun back around, angry tears filling my eyes. Liz was there, right in front of me, and I took a step back, startled by her silent and quick movement toward me.

"We have a chance now, Melanie. I *know* we can bring their killer, *your father*, to justice! I'm not giving you false hope now. I'm offering you my help, my resources, my protection, my friendship. I didn't lie to you Melanie! I *didn't* betray you. I simply didn't tell you what I'd spent month after month doing, night after night because I didn't want you to know I was failing you! You'd been failed too many times before. I didn't want to be someone else who failed you too! I didn't want to break your heart all over again—" Liz's words cut off abruptly and she swallowed hard. Shame and disappointment in herself came rushing into her face and flooding her eyes with tears.

I felt my anger fizzle out with a puff, my selfish childish perception dissolved by the truth of her heartfelt words. She'd been trying to help me. She felt like she had failed me. She hadn't wanted to hurt me with hope just to have it destroyed with failure and dead ends.

"You didn't fail me, Liz," my voice was softening and I blinked away the tears that threatened to spill past their thresholds.

"I wasn't able to do it then. Maybe because I wanted it too much or was too inexperienced. Or maybe because I didn't have the right perspective. I just don't know. But I do know this; I will not let you down again, Melanie. We have a chance here. A real chance. Please, don't hate me for keeping this from you. Please don't let this keep us from finishing this!" Liz took my hands and squeezed them briefly then pulled away, wiping her eyes.

I reached out and pulled her back to me. We hung onto each other for a moment before I was able to speak without my voice threatening to break. "You didn't fail me Liz. You've never failed me. I get it. I understand why you kept it from me."

What was it about a trusted friendship that chases away heightened emotions and brings rationality back with such ease?

Liz pulled back and wiped her eyes once more, a small smile of thanks that I'd dropped my offense toward her on her open face. I think I was probably the only person, other than her grandfather, that could make her cry. I wasn't proud of that fact. But it did solidify to me without a shadow of a doubt just how much she loved me.

"Well, you're failing me," Brad chimed in with a dry humorous lift to his voice. "You promised to devour me. What gives? I am feeling utterly failed and disappointed over here." Bradley shifted his weight to toss out a hip and posed his hands on his hips very femininely to mock our chick moment. Leave it to Bradley Wayne Carter to break up an emotional female exchange with his unique brand of humor.

Liz turned to Brad laughing. David was chuckling too, eyebrows still up slightly at having watched Liz and me go at it for a moment with a full gamut of emotions in less than three minutes. He seemed intrigued by our relationship and complex history.

Oh, you just wait hot stuff. You have so much to learn about us.

I went and sat on the abandoned loveseat and patted the spot next to me with a tight smile up at David. He wandered over and sat down, his hip touching mine and he put his arm around the back of the loveseat to rest along the top. Hugging me but not hugging me. Giving me space but still being close. It was sweet and so exactly what I needed. I smiled at him before looking back at Liz.

"I'll start making calls in the morning to get those cold case files," Brad said in a sudden yawn, and went up on tiptoes for a long stretch.

"Call Stewart, will you?" Liz suggested.

Brad paused in mid-motion of reaching for his satchel. "Stewart? Um, our Central Intelligence tech?" He half whispered.

"Yup. I think he can get us more than what's in these," Liz pointed to the slew of case files and papers on the coffee table. "Mind asking him to run these names for us?"

Brad reached over and squeezed Liz's shoulder. "Good idea. I wasn't sure if we should tap into *those* resources or not," Brad said a little elusively glancing at us.

"If you get asked why, have him call me," Liz said quietly. Brad just nodded, a silent exchange passing between them before she nodded very slightly at something he'd been asking her with only his eyes.

"I thought these already were the public files and the *non-public* files," I inquired trying to grasp what I was missing.

"They are, but there are even deeper layers we can go," Liz almost whispered.

"Oooh," I let that sink in for a moment.

How deep can it go?

"Calling it a night?" David asked the group, recognizing the signs and reading the unspoken communication of his fellow covert operation specialists in the room.

Everyone except me. How do I know these people again? I asked myself wryly.

"Ooh, good call bro," Brad said with a chummy smile.

"Yeah, I think we should. I need to step away. It's pretty late and I don't want to overload Mel anymore. But honestly, I need to workout. I have so much adrenaline pumping right now at the thought of catching the man who might have mentored him or maybe figuring out who he is, I couldn't sleep even if I wanted to," Liz said quickly.

"You can take it out on me if you want to," Brad teased again, wiggling his eyebrows.

"You two need to just get a room," I laughed.

"I've been trying! She isn't dumb enough to follow me in," Brad pretended to pout.

"Knock it off, you goober," Liz laughed and smacked his shoulder.

"So, there isn't anything else we can do tonight? What about these?" I gestured to the files on the table before me. "What's the point of all these?"

"Finding connections and making intuitive leaps," David answered nodding to Liz. His face showed respect for her intelligence and appreciation for her loyalty to me.

I glanced at my best friend and studied the look between them. I was feeling a whole range of emotions directed at her right now. I wasn't sure if it was classic transference or just the overwhelming shock of it all. I was appreciative, awed by her intelligence as well, but I also held onto a little sizzle of anger at her. I still felt betrayed and something else I wasn't sure how to describe other than...suspicious.

What else had she been keeping from me all these years? What else was she still hiding from me deliberately? How did I know this was all there was? Had she asked Brad to strip the files of anything specific before he brought them over? He'd obviously had them to himself before he'd come here. For how long? It had been weeks since my father got out and attacked me. How long had Brad had the files?

"Research. Digging for clues. Insights into the killer your father is, try to identify more victims and add it to his profile," Brad offered, pulling me from my observation of Liz and David.

"Don't you mean *killers*?" I retorted dryly.

"Well, yeah. Dwayne's theoretical serial killer mentor —"

"No, not him. Don't forget, Jill's gang is another issue here. Police Chief Wales has been harassing us. What about his connection to Jill as her uncle? The one who used to rape her with her step-father like some kind of sick sporting event. When do we dig into that bit of cheery news?" I asked sarcastically. Anxiety hit me as the laundry list of filth we had yet to sort out expanded in my mind to take over the momentary feeling of murky insights I hadn't had time to absorb.

"All in time. We haven't forgotten about them," Brad said again before Liz could answer me. She was studying my face and body language, reading my instability and mood swings. I had to be about as colorful as a strobe light right now. Each emotion was pinging around inside me, making me dizzy.

"Chief Wales used to rape that girl Jill, right?" David asked me, his face shocked all over again. I felt bad for him, he was having to catch up on a lot tonight.

"I recorded a conversation she and I had recently and she talks all about it. I'll let you listen to it later. It was a doozy." I sighed.

"It might feel insignificant, but we've made excellent progress tonight, Melanie." Liz chimed in. "We found proof of the link between Chief Wales and Jill. We have somewhere to start as far as why he'd been protecting her and railroading you. We *may* have found a link between your father and another serial killer which could blow the lid off of his carefully covered crimes and leave them *both* open to exposure. We've made a dent!" Liz said reassuringly. "A significant one."

"Sure, I guess you're right," I said with little conviction. "It just feels so thin. I don't know, theories and—" I stopped and closed my eyes taking in a deep breath. Trying to release my frustration, my anger and my feelings of betrayal.

"What else?" Liz asked me, her voice gentle.

I opened my eyes. Feeling the emotions draining out of me once again at the concern in her voice. My brain started working and I started to find words to the other feelings in my gut.

"I feel like we were close to something else important, but I have no idea if we found it already. I can't help feeling like we're not seeing it. Something right in front of us! I feel like...like when you know you're forgetting something important or that something means something else but you can't decipher it. It's bugging me!" I looked down at the coffee table covered in files, photos and case logs. It was almost a blur.

Information overload is right.

"When can we start again, tomorrow?" I pressed, looking around at everyone, trying to draw a commitment from them for more.

More? Melanie, look at these guys. Look at what they are doing for you. Risking it all for you. You want more from them?

"Mel, aren't you supposed to meet up with Doctor Eugene Picard again tomorrow?" Liz reminded me, then glanced at David until he met her eyes. David perked up, seeing what she was really asking of him, not me, and looked at me curiously.

"Doc? Umm, yeah. Day two of introduction to firearms and some self-defense. Stuff like that to get my CCW. I'm supposed to meet him at ten o'clock tomorrow morning. But I can cancel. This is more important." I wasn't really sure which priority should take priority. Learning to defend myself, or finding a way to stop those who wanted to hurt me in the first place? It was a cyclical math problem I wasn't sure how to solve.

"No, you should go," Liz advised. "These files aren't going anywhere and you can't let this take over your life. Trust me Melanie. I've been helping to track down monsters and predict their behavior for a long time now. You can't stop living while you do it or you'll lose yourself in the quest. There's enough here to sink our teeth into and absorb. Our subconscious minds will be working in the meantime. Your subconscious never stops processing information. And sometimes, it finds solutions before you're aware of them consciously."

"Shit. I just...I just want it over."

"I know Melanie, but we have to do the research and build up evidence to have a convincing case. We have to be patient and do this right. If we rush too fast, we might overlook something that could cost us the case. Go see Doc tomorrow. Learn all you can from him. That is something you *can* control," Liz said wisely.

"Mind if I come along?" David asked me, his eyes boring into mine.

"That's not a bad idea," Liz answered for me.

Like you weren't in on him asking to come with me with your telling eyes.

"You know the situation even better now than what he described to you," Liz continued to say to David. "I'm betting Doc might even be relieved at the revelation that you know and care about his student being that Melanie was the one he wanted you to help him protect anyway. You two might come up with a more efficient self-defense training program for her if you collaborate. I've shown her some of the basics over the years, but she needs to face that internal fear of facing a man so she can learn to not freeze up and push through it to really fight back hard. Hey, maybe you could—"

"Um, Liz?" I interrupted, my hand waving hello to remind her I was right here.

"Oh, sorry, Mel. I just really think it would be a smart play if he helped," Liz said apologetically.

"I agree," I answered back quickly so she'd know I wasn't upset about her speaking for me. "I was going to say yes. It's just that...well, I feel like a dork. I know the basics about guns and self-defense from what you've shown me and from what Doc showed me earlier today, or rather yesterday," I said glancing at the grandfather clock against the far wall. "It's just that I...I don't want to embarrass myself in front of David—again," I said shyly, glancing at David and then at the floor, feeling like an idiot for even admitting it out loud.

Liz's face showed understanding but then she looked at David. Clearly telling him with her eyes to jump in and put me at ease. She needn't bothered trying to signal him, he was already there all on his own.

"You couldn't ever look like a dork to me, Melanie. I'm a part of this now," He gestured with his hand, pointing around the room to include us, and all the files and photos. "I want to help however I can. As long as you want me around, I'll be here for you. And, it would be great to see Doc again. After we talked this afternoon, I told him I'd come by in the next few days anyway. It's been too long. At least three months. Far too long to make excuses since we're both living in the area."

"You are helping, David. You have no idea how much it means to me that you're here," I said with feeling.

"Would you mind if I came with you?" he asked me now, letting me decide for myself.

"Y...auh..." I stammered. In a flash my mind was flooded with all the reasons I should say no causing my "Yes" to be drowned out in my throat.

Was I really afraid of embarrassing myself in front of David? Yes. Did I feel unsure and dorky handling guns from lack of consistent and repetitive practice? Absolutely. Was I still humiliated that David learned about my past from a third party and from what he'd personally stormed in on and saved me from six weeks ago? Duh, most definitely. Was I concerned that I might have another hormonal rush of young-girl-crushes-on-older-buff-daddy-figure moment and turn beet red in the face in front of David? Again, duh! Hell yes I was! But did any of that really matter now? Was my pride, humiliation and insecurity really a sound excuse to turn away help from the most trusted man I knew? No, no it was not.

"Yes, David. Yes, please come with me. I could use all the help I can get," I finally said, surrendering to the inevitable and to what needed to be done. I shifted my feet, my anxiety about tomorrow already making me squirmy.

"Are you sure? You hesitated a while there," David asked lightly, lacking any offensive tone or expression. He was simply making sure I was okay with it.

I reached up and grabbed his collar, drawing him down to me. "Yes, I'm sure," I smiled up at him. "Besides, he's the first buddy of yours I know. Maybe I'll learn a little more about *you* watching how you interact with your old compadre." The thought made me smile, the first pure smile I'd had all evening since we cracked open these files. "It'd be like seeing into your past."

At the mention of me witnessing his interactions with his old friend, he seemed to sober but readjusted his face quickly into a smile. "Sounds fair. Would you like me to drive?"

"Sure. I have to be there at ten."

"Pick you up at nine-thirty? Then afterwards we can swing by the restaurant and start putting the final touches on the place.

Frank asked me to give him a call when we can make it in to help. That okay? Or too much in one day?"

"Frank? Oh crap. I forgot all about the restaurant! Poor Frank!" I exclaimed. I felt horrible! I'd promised the old goat I'd help him clean up the place! I was mostly responsible, sort of but not entirely, for the place being wrecked and the police shutting it down after that insane snap from reality all the customers and staff experienced over six weeks ago.

Wow, November was a really bad month for me.

Liz had said not to worry about any of the household bills either until it reopened. I'd taken her up on her offer since I had been healing from my attack. And with the media beating down the door or following me around for a follow-up story, I hadn't been in a rush to return to work anyway with my face plastered all over the news next to my father's. Everywhere I went was like having dozens of eyes watching my every move. It had lessened over the past couple weeks, but I still caught the curious glance or muffled inappropriate remark.

"Hey, it's okay. Frank said he's not opening for at least another week, but we really should get in there as soon as we can to get a start on it. Will you be okay now that you know for sure he's your great uncle? Are you ready for that? I don't want to push you into dealing with more too soon," David said, looking truly concerned.

"No, I'm ready. He doesn't know I know. And I don't even know for sure if he knows. So yeah, I'm okay with going to set up. I don't think I'm going to tell him yet. I want it to happen naturally if possible. Maybe try to get to know him a little better first. I'm not really sure when or how I'll tell him. But I think I should someday. Anyway, we can go help him straight after training tomorrow," I agreed.

"Sounds like a plan," David nodded his head in assent.

I looked around the living room with the files, photos and papers scattered about. "But, when can we start looking at these again? I didn't get to read everything yet."

"We will, Mel. Don't worry. It won't be forgotten. I promise," Liz assured me. "Don't stop your life, remember?" She smiled encouragingly at me.

"Okay, Liz. I'll try." I gave David a brief kiss on his cheek, making his eyes go all deep and slightly unfocused again. He looked at my mouth and studied my face. I recognized that look from earlier tonight when we'd finally given in and kissed each other for the first time. He made me nervous to see that much passion and desire in his eyes. I swallowed loud enough that I could hear it and felt my face turn red.

"Looks to me like it's you two who need to get a room," Bradley laughed and cat called.

Liz snarled at him. "Bradley Wayne Carter, I will kick your butt, not that you have much of one, if you so much as tease Melanie about getting it on one more time."

"One more? She got it on before?" he said giggling, and then ducking as Liz snatched a cushion off the chair and flung it at him.

David stirred beside me glancing down at me and away with a sideways smile on his mouth. He had the most beautiful mouth. Full heart-shaped lips that were so kissable. And now I knew what an amazing kisser he was too. He'd stolen my breath away, literally, when he kissed me earlier. He had made me feel more alive and desired than I knew anyone could. It had felt so wonderful it could've been a dream.

David must have felt me watching him and he looked back down at me, his face going serious and his chest hitching up a notch as his breath caught. Our eyes met, intense and seeking. Then reality smacked into me and I blinked, looking away and to Liz for help.

Not ready to entertain the idea of more than kissing. It was too soon.

We'd finally started seeing each other in a more-than-just-friends capacity. Um, just in the past eight hours actually! He'd come over around four o'clock last night and I'd finally confessed to him how much I cared about him. It was just past twelve o'clock in the morning now. And as it was, we hadn't even had the official "let's be boyfriend and girlfriend" talk, or even a first date for that matter! I was much, much too inexperienced to leap ahead of myself. This was already a really big step for me.

One slow steady step at a time. That's how I need this relationship to go. Not that digging through your mother's and sister's homicide files is exactly a relaxed startup conversation. Yeah, Doctor Phil wouldn't even know what to do with that.

I looked back up at David to find him still watching me, burning a hole right through me and I felt nearly powerless as I fell into the passion of his eyes.

"I'm going to head home. I know when I'm not wanted anymore," Brad whined playfully, causing David and I to glance at him and finally breaking our locked heart pounding gaze. I hadn't even been aware of when I'd returned my eyes to his or how long we'd been lost in our own world.

This is bad.

"Fine get out of here," Liz said dismissively, winking at him.

"Walk me out?" Brad asked with a hopeful expression, grabbing his laptop and sticking it in his satchel. He didn't bother with the files.

"Hell, why not," Liz retorted and followed him to the front door.

"You know, you promised to devour me my little African army ant," I heard Brad tease again followed by a loud *smack.* Brad was laughing and then I heard Liz mumble something low making him laugh harder. "Okay, *that* will be worth the wait. I'll hold you to that little woman."

"Excuse me?" I heard Liz say through a giggle, her voice fading behind the front door closing behind them. Then there was silence.

I felt David stir next to me one brief moment before his hands suddenly wrapped around my waist spinning me around and I found myself being half lifted, half swept up into him. He pressed me to him, one hand at my waist, the other at the side of my face, sliding to the back of the base of my neck and into my hair to hold me tenderly. His mouth found mine, his lips parting my willing lips, his tongue tasting me hungrily. His passion stole my breath away once more. I swooned, my knees gone and my body completely passive in his arms, surrendered and trusting. He was firm but gentle. Demanding but tender. Yet there was still a careful respectfulness in the placement of his hands and the coaching of his mouth on mine. He let go of me pulling away slowly, our lips the last of our bodies to part. I inhaled speechless, blinking to refocus my eyes on his face, feeling nearly drunk. My body tingled all over.

God, he's a magnificent kisser. Not that I had a lot of experience to compare it to. Okay, I had none actually.

David seemed lost for words too. He was breathing heavier and he tucked his hands into his pockets as if to keep himself from reaching out and grabbing me again, almost afraid to touch me.

"I need to go...right now," he said in a hoarse whisper.

"Yeah, it's been a long day. I think we're all pretty tired."

I tried for meaningless small talk hoping he wouldn't see my internal battle. I was trying to keep myself from leaping at him or dragging him to me again. It wasn't a spirit of lust this time like it had been in Turin, Italy. No, this was far different. It was simply him and me. Us. A human surge of hormones, perfectly matched chemistry, and that deep desire to be close to someone. No, to be close to *him*.

David wet his lips and drew in a slow breath. "I'd stay and help you pack these up, but I think it'd be safer if Liz did it with you," he admitted unabashed.

"Right," was all I could say.

"Good night, Melanie Olivia Bishop. I hope you can get some rest. If you can't sleep, call me. I'll leave my phone on if you want to talk. Otherwise, think of me holding you as you drift off to sleep. Kissing your cheek. Whispering...I love you."

He stepped up to me again, the last of his words whispered to match the fantasy he'd described.

"I, um," I stammered.

"I know you can't tell me the same thing back yet, but I hope that someday, I'll prove to you I can be worthy of your love. Let me prove it to you. Don't run away from *us*. That's all I ask," David implored, taking my hand and kissing it softly, almost adoringly.

I nodded, once again speechless to his confession of love for me and his ability to read my apprehension so precisely. It made me so incredibly happy to hear him say that to me. *He loves me!* But it also made me afraid that I'd ruin it somehow. Happiness never seemed to last long for me.

Stop thinking stuff like that Melanie! You are blessed, not cursed. You can have happiness.

"Night, Bishop," David winked, and headed to the door.

I watched him as he left, his wide shoulders and narrow waist carried straight with confidence. He glanced back at me looking torn, his military training still evident in the power of his walk and air of alertness that even now, settled over him and brought his head back around to the sound of Elisabeth's footsteps as she headed back inside the house through the front door.

"You're off too?" Liz observed with a nod of thanks and a small smile.

"Yes Ma'am," David paused to let Liz pass into the entryway. "Actually, may I speak to you for a moment outside please?" David said quietly.

"Sure," Liz answered casually, her eyes searching his face. I watched as her face grew serious as she read his tells. She glanced briefly at me in acknowledgment before following him outside, her hand grabbing the doorknob to close the door securely behind them, blocking them from my view.

And from hearing their conversation.

"Tsk," I clicked my tongue to myself disappointedly. "Wonder what's that about?"

Oh, I got it. Maybe he wanted to apologize for not staying to clean up the files? Or maybe he wanted to ask her more about her own evident government connections and how she got all that intel on him and admitted to having their own "central intelligence tech"? Or maybe, he just wanted to ask her what my favorite flowers are?

I smiled to myself at the thought. *Yeah, that must be it. He wanted to get dating tips from my best friend about how to impress me and woo me.*

"Aw, sweet man," I whispered contently to myself, letting out a small chuckle of delight. I hadn't expected to feel delight at the end of this evening. But there it was. David was the delight of my life. What a curious thing to realize. David truly made me happy.

Lord, please let me keep this happiness with David. Please don't let it get consumed with the darkness that surrounds my life. Bring us all through this, Lord. I prayed silently but earnestly to God.

And please don't let me ruin it. I added as an afterthought.

Helena

Chapter Two

*a*s far as men went, Dwayne Bishop was truly a gentleman. Having always treated Helena with respect and kindness since the day they met, he made her feel like she was the only woman on Earth. One who was worthy of love and adoration. Something she always doubted about herself having never known her father.

Dwayne never missed an opportunity to make her feel beautiful, graceful, desirable, and above all, needed. Why then was he suddenly changing before her eyes? Every day a little piece of him seemed to dissolve slowly away like ice melting in the hot sun only to evaporate before her eyes. He was becoming unrecognizable. A stranger. She feared that underneath the surface of the fading mirage hid a monster, caged, waiting to get out. Could her mother have been right all along? Had she been blinded by love, or what she had thought to be love?

Helena didn't understand the transformation she was witnessing. She knew she'd gotten married fast, even by modern standards. Maybe too fast. They'd only known each other a month when they started dating. They'd met in Biology class at Sacramento City College and started partnering up in the Lab. She'd been drawn to his bad boy charms and romantic gestures. He was older than her by a few years but still within an acceptable age to be starting college. In fact, he was on their baseball team and was one of their star hitters while he was there. Not only was he charming and intelligent, he was hot. Really hot.

She didn't know what it was about him, but any other man would tuck tail and rush away with a mere look from Dwayne if they approached Helena. She liked feeling safe around him, protected, like an important treasure.

Six months later they'd run off and gotten married up in Tahoe. Every day since then had been like a dream. Making love in the mornings and the evenings. A chaste kiss between classes. A flower left on her pillow to find when he'd slip away in the morning to get to a class that started before hers. He'd leave inappropriate notes in a text book to make her burst out laughing in the middle of a boring lecture, making her have to apologize to the professor, again and again. She never knew when or how he would surprise her with a trinket or token of their love. He was simply romantic.

Yet now, the flowers stopped showing up, the notes were forgotten. The lovemaking had become demanding and often too rough, uncomfortable and, at times, made her feel used and dirty, despite the fact that she was his wife. Even if she wasn't feeling well or was sore from the roughness of the sex the night before, he'd manipulate her into feeling guilty about denying him. It had become just sex, lacking any of the tenderness or affection he had shown before. He no longer cared about fulfilling her needs. It had become selfish and hollow. Hurtful, not only physically at times, but emotionally.

Dwayne stopped trying to make her laugh. Stopped taking her out on dates. Stopped making her feel beautiful. Stopped making her feel loved or appreciated. He would even snap at her when she'd try to surprise him with a practical joke, attempting to bring laughter back into their lives. If she made a mistake like failing to make his favorite dinner recipes perfectly, he'd push the plate away complaining loudly how neglectful and careless she was. Accuse her of clearly not loving him enough if her cooking was any proof.

Last night he even called her useless for not pressing his shirt the way he liked it. She'd cried for an hour. Hurt and confused. Questioning herself, wondering what she'd done so wrong to lose his love and respect so quickly. Shouldn't they be closer now that they had a baby, not more distant?

Hadn't she already done what he'd asked and quit school so they could start a family? Hadn't she already moved away from her hometown and up to this God forsaken hillbilly town so he could live in the home his parents had left for him? Hadn't she practically given up all of her friends when she came here? She was even estranged from her own family now because of him!

Her mother Gloria had acted irrevocably hurt when she found out that Helena had run off to get married without telling her. Helena had refused to see her mother for the past year, never returning her calls or her letters, a punishment Dwayne convinced her was appropriate for rejecting her new husband. When she finally did read her mother's letters, Gloria had insisted that any man who'd whisk her daughter away to wed and make her walk away from her college education and her family, wasn't a good man at heart. Helena was starting to wonder if her mother had been right. Had she made a terrible mistake?

The last time she'd spoken to her mother was the day she told her she was married and moving away. It was more of an emotionally charged fight than a talk essentially. A complete disaster. Helena wiped a tear away at the memory. She had gone to her Aunt Katherine and Uncle Frank Gable's house for a Fourth of July barbeque. Her mother Gloria had been there as well. It had become one of their family traditions. The four of them celebrated most of the holidays together.

Since Helena had been told that her father had been a one-night stand, she never knew him and didn't care to. In fact, she wasn't even sure if her mother knew who he was. All she really had in the way of family was right there at that barbecue. Her grandparents were already deceased, so it made for a small family gathering. Frank, her aunt's husband, didn't have any extended family in the area to invite either. From what she knew, they all still lived in New Orleans where he was from.

Her aunt and uncle weren't able to conceive children. At least that's what they told people who'd ask. Helena thought that more likely, the truth was, her Uncle Frank was a bit of a hard ass and too serious, stubborn, and selfish for parenthood. Her aunt though, she would have made an amazing mother. Sometimes Helena even wished she had been her mother instead of Gloria.

Her Aunt Katherine used to take her and her mother on little weekend getaways. She said it was to spend time with her girls, but really, Helena thought it was her way of creating the feeling for herself that she had a daughter of her own. Katherine would stay up all night talking with Helena when they'd go camping. Counting shooting stars and playing practical jokes on Gloria together. Always laughing so hard they were afraid they were going to bust a gut or pee their pants.

Dwayne had come with Helena that Fourth of July. It was the first time her family had ever set eyes on him. Helena had kept

Dwayne a secret at his request. Believing in the romantic idea of having a secret passionate love affair. Ideas that Dwayne had introduced early on in their relationship. When she arrived at her aunt's house, she introduced Dwayne as her husband and informed them all that they'd run off and got married three weeks before in Tahoe. It was a rough visit after that.

Her mother was furious she'd been blindsided. Katherine ushered them to the back patio to eat, trying to be the polite hostess, but unable to keep the crease from her brow.

After they were seated and begun eating, focusing awkwardly on their plates instead of talking, Helena decided to just rip the Band-Aid the rest of the way off.

"Mother, I dropped out of school. We're moving up to Redding next weekend. Dwayne inherited his parents' house. It'll be a fresh start for us. It's free and clear so I won't have to worry about working when we're ready to start a family." She smiled, hoping for a pleasant response to the other half of her big news. She wanted to tell them that she was already about eight weeks pregnant, but Dwayne had asked her to keep that a secret too for now. He said it was *their* news to share when they were *both* ready. He also had said on the way over that he didn't think four big shocks all at once would be a very considerate way to deliver the news.

After telling them they were moving, Helena waited for someone to say something but everyone was silent for a few seconds more. Katherine, who had been watching Dwayne carefully since their arrival, was the first to speak since it was obvious Gloria wasn't ready yet, having stopped chewing her corn on the cob mid bite. She swallowed and took another large bite. She just chewed and chewed, glaring at her daughter and new son-in-law, her eyes jumping between them both. Shock, disgust and then rage switching over her face like changing the colored lens of a spotlight.

"What's the rush dear?" Aunt Katherine asked. "Don't you think you should finish your college education first? You've only just begun after all. Why can't you start a family here, near *your* family?" Katherine's voice was gentle but her words were direct enough.

"We want to move now so we can start trying right away," Helena lied. "I want to be able to help pack and get us situated in Dwayne's house before a baby comes along and slows me down," Helena explained, glancing at Dwayne for support. He smiled and took her hand, kissing the top of it while he eyed the table. He was being a quiet man today, and it wasn't like him. He was usually the life of the party, never without the right thing to say. She wished he'd be himself so they would see why she fell in love with him.

"But you'd be without any family support all the way up there in Redding, sweetie. Marriages for young couples are hard enough these days. What will you do when a baby comes? You're going to need all the support and help you can get. And what about your college education? Your mother worked hard to save for your schooling. That's not easy for a single mother you know. Will you be continuing your studies at a community college up in Redding?" Katherine asked anxiously, leaning forward to be closer to Helena who sat with her hands in her lap now across the patio table, leaning back in her chair.

"Um, well. No. We think I should stay home and raise our children," Helena looked down, then with some effort, looked back up to meet her aunt's searching eyes.

"We?" Gloria finally spoke, her voice flat.

"Yes mother. *We.*" Helena said, a stubborn defiance infiltrating her voice to make her sound like a rebellious teenager.

"With him? This stranger?" Gloria stood up, face contorted and hands squeezing her hips.

"He isn't a stranger to me Mom. He's my husband!" Helena stood up as well and gestured to Dwayne. He was sitting back in his chair now, arms resting comfortably behind his head looking far too relaxed. His smile didn't seem to match the tone of the conversation. He seemed pleased.

"And what exactly are you smiling about, *son*?" Gloria snapped at him.

"Stop it mother! Don't you start! You've never liked any of my boyfriends. Ever! And you wonder why I didn't bring him home for you to meet before we got hitched?"

"That man," Gloria pointed at Dwayne, "isn't a gentleman! He didn't even have the decency to ask me for permission to marry my only daughter! No man with *good* intentions acts that way. Forcing you to walk away from your college education like this? That was your dream! To become a teacher! He isn't a good man at heart Helena! Don't you see that? Now he's dragging you away to Redding and stripping you for your dreams *and* your family! What could possibly make you do this? Are you already pregnant?" Gloria stormed.

Helena was glad she hadn't told her mother she was pregnant now. Dwayne had been right to ask her to keep it a secret. He'd been so right. Her mother couldn't handle any of this.

"Don't talk about him that way Glor-i-a!" Helena seethed out her mother's name.

"You aren't going anywhere Helena! I forbid it!" Gloria's voice broke, her eyes wild.

"That man is my husband mother! You can't forbid me from doing anything anymore! I'm a grown woman! I'm his wife. Which is more than you ever were to anyone!" Helena shot back spitefully.

Gloria's eyes filled with tears. "Yes, I was Helena." Gloria whimpered.

"What are you talking about?" Helena said with disbelief. "You're a *liar*," she accused and glanced at her aunt for confirmation.

Katherine shook her head, her eyes saying her sister was telling the truth.

"I married your father. He was...he had nothing but darkness inside him. I see that same darkness inside of this man you call your husband. I recognize what he is! Helena, please...please don't go with this man." Gloria pleaded.

"You're lying!" Helena spat again, pointing to her mother. "You told me my father was a one-night stand! A drunken mistake. You said you didn't even know his name! You never said *anything* about marrying him!"

"I didn't want you to try to find him! He's a monster! A predator. I had to protect you." Gloria's eyes were streaming nonstop tears.

Dwayne sat up a little straighter. He hadn't anticipated Helena not knowing who her real father was. He figured the excuse she'd given him about her father being a one-night stand had just been her attempt to hide the truth out of humiliation and shame. This was turning out so much better than he had planned.

"Liar!" Helena repeated venomously, looking around at the others again for confirmation of her mother's deceit. Knowing stares of shame at having helped her lie coated their faces instead.

"No...I...I was just trying to protect you! Like I am now. Please believe me. This man is a monster! I can feel it in my bones. Don't—"

"You'll say anything to keep me from being happy because you were never happy!" Helena trudged on, refusing to accept the truth. "You were always depressed and sulky," she seethed viciously, "Always afraid to live! Always so controlling and protective, treating me like I couldn't make any decisions for myself. Well not anymore!" Helena shouted.

Katherine stood up, her hands out to try and calm them into peace. "Helena. Gloria. Please! Yelling isn't going to resolve anything. Let's just take a moment to catch our breath and then talk this out—"

"Auntie, you should know. You're my mother's only real friend. Was she ever married? Is she telling me stories? Is she?" Helena shot a look of confidence at her mother that she'd caught her in her lies.

Gloria looked desperately at Katherine. Her eyes large and her mouth trembling. She started to shake, her shoulders quaking. Helena watched her mother's pain and fear in confusion. Was this fear of being caught in a lie or fear of something else?

Gloria nodded to Katherine and sat back down, her head hanging and her sobs rattling the table where she leaned upon it. Katherine nodded in acknowledgement, agreeing to share whatever secret it was they were both protecting.

"Yes, sweetie. My sister was married once. He charmed her, romanced her, and seduced her. When she got pregnant, he convinced her to marry him and run away. That's when it all changed. He confined her to their home. Stripped her of her dignity and treated her with less respect than a servant should have received. He was violent. Sadistic. Abusive. I didn't see my sister for two years, Helena. *Two* years! I couldn't even find her." Katherine had broken into sobs. "She was seventeen when she ran off and married him. Two years later I came home one night to find her at my door, with you in her arms. You were only a few hours old. She'd left the maternity ward in the middle of the night to escape him. All she had was you and the clothes on her back. It was the only chance she'd had in two years to run." Katherine put her hand on her sister's shoulder.

"I...I don't believe either of you," Helena sputtered.

"Helena, dear—" Katherine tried.

"No! You don't even make sense! You said he got her pregnant, then took her away! How could I have *just* been born when you saw her two years later?" Helena accused, pointing wildly toward her mother as she glared at Katherine, not stopping to consider the obvious truth.

"Your...your brother died...your father," Gloria's voice broke as pain filled her eyes, she couldn't finish.

"Helena, your father had taken a wooden spoon to your brother. When she tried to stop him, he hit her hard enough to knock her out. When she woke, he had already beaten your brother to death. He had been sick and had only been crying from his tummy ache. He was just a baby—"

"No! No! You're both liars!" Helena spat.

"It isn't the truth of your father that you don't believe. It's the truth about *him* that you refuse to see and that you don't want to believe. You can feel it in your heart. I'm telling you the truth. And you know, somewhere deep inside you, that he's a monster," Gloria said with as much strength as she could muster. She stood up again, pointing at Dwayne with the butter knife in her hand. "You leave my daughter alone. I know what you really are. I see through you," Gloria hissed.

Dwayne stood up slowly in response. A cold calm seemed to rest on him. He was unfazed by all of the shouts and accusations. He gently placed his arm around Helena and turned her to face him. He wiped the tears away from her face with a gentle finger. A small smile one might give a little girl to comfort her and reassure her that the monster wasn't real, was resting on his face to placate her. It must have looked kind to Helena, for at the sight of it she softened. To Gloria and Katherine, his smile was derisive and manipulative.

"Don't worry about any of this, Firefly. We're stronger than blood. We're soulmates. I love you no matter who your father is. I promise, I'm going to spend my life loving you. You'll never have to be afraid of anything if you spend your life with me. I'll always take care of you," Dwayne hugged Helena to him, and she melted into him, crying softly on his shoulder. He looked at Gloria, Katherine and Frank while her face was turned away. It was a look of someone who thought they'd won. An air of superiority and dominance made him look hard and arrogant, confident that their words had fallen on deaf ears. He smiled at Gloria. A widening smile mocking her.

Gloria inhaled, fear striking her gut anew. She recognized the look in his eyes. She'd lived with a man who had possessed it for years, or rather, was possessed. She let out a gargled cry, panicked and strangled, unable to form words in her desperation.

Helena lifted her face at the unnatural sound coming from her mother. She released Dwayne and walked around the table to her. She hugged her mother's trembling body to her tightly for a moment before letting go. She didn't understand her mother's reaction to Dwayne. It seemed far too exaggerated and irrational. Was it her way of trying to manipulate her? Helena decided that her mother would have to be the one to surrender, and admit whatever lies and games she was playing. In the meantime, perhaps the best approach would be to just ignore it all for now and let time bring perspective back to her mother.

"I'm not you, mother. And Dwayne isn't my father. Whoever you say he *really* is. I'll call you when I get settled, okay? We can talk more then. Love you." She pulled away and went to hug her aunt and uncle. Her hugs were brief and robotic, lacking any of her usual warmth and heartfelt goodbye. They'd treated her husband so badly. They'd accused him of being a monster like the man they suddenly claimed was her father. It all seemed too convenient of a story to her. And no one had stood up for her or her husband. They were all betraying her.

"Come on honey, let's go," Helena held her hand out for Dwayne. He made a show of shifting uncomfortably and smiling as if embarrassed. He nodded to Frank, who was still silent and watching all of this like he was at the circus. Dwayne walked around the table from the opposite side and offered his hand to Frank. They shook briefly and then he reached for Katherine.

"No! Don't you touch my sister or my daughter!" Gloria screamed. Stepping in between them and lunging at him with the butter knife.

Katherine let out a startled yelp at having been shoved aside by her sister. Frank finally stood and quickly rushed forward to attend to Katherine and had intended to intercept Gloria as well, but Dwayne had already seized Gloria's wrist, extracted the knife from her hand, and tossed it aside. He held out her wrist and grabbed her other hand to pull it away as she screamed inaudibly and tried to claw his face. He watched her struggle, a look of amusement on his ruggedly handsome face.

"Gloria! Oh Gloria!" Katherine cried.

"Mother! Stop it!" Helena begged in horror.

"Mom," Dwayne said, his voice an even placid tone. "You're my mom now, Mrs. O'Hair," He said "Mrs." With a mocking tone. "Please try to see the best in me. I'll take good care of your little girl. I promise," He bent down and kissed her cheek. She snapped at him, like a caged animal trying to bite, her wrists still pinned easily in his hands.

"No! No! I won't let you take her! No!" Gloria cried powerlessly.

"But I already have her," Dwayne whispered softly into her ear. He released her wrists and walked away, joining Helena. He offered her his arm as any good gentleman should. He turned back around to face them all, Helena on his arm trying to look dignified, though inside she was trembling and shaken with confusion and uncertainty. She hadn't expected any of this and was already regretting the cruel words she had spat at her mother. She had never talked quite that way to her before.

"Perhaps when the shock of our marriage has had sufficient time to wear off, we can try this again. I look forward to getting to know each of you more intimately. I regret to say, I've been without family since I was nineteen when my parents died in a car crash. I'm hoping to find that again with Helena and with each of you." Dwayne smiled and then turning abruptly, escorted Helena out toward the side gate at a slow but purposeful speed. She glanced behind her in farewell to her family.

Her mother had dropped to her knees sobbing. Her aunt Katherine stood like stone watching them leave. And her uncle Frank, well, Frank was Frank. He was already grabbing the butter knife from where it had dropped in the middle of the lawn, and dipped it in the butter to lather on a second piece of corn on the cob.

Revelation Ride

Chapter Three

Sometimes the idea of a family depressed me. Why wouldn't it? After all, I'd had most of it stripped away from me one piece at a time. Each blow covered by lies, deceit and unimaginable pain. I'd chosen to believe that family wasn't just about blood ties, but that family could be created out of loyalty, trust, and the love of true friends.

I would be going to see Frank later today and now that I knew for sure that he was my great uncle, I wondered if it made me the liar to keep that from him? Part of me wondered if he knew who I was. If he hadn't known, had he made the connection now that my father had been plastered all over the news? He would have known his name, right? Assuming my mother even introduced her husband to her aunt and uncle before she died. The problem was, I wasn't sure what he knew or if he'd even known my mother as an adult. The pictures I'd seen in his office were of my mother Helena as a little girl, her mother Gloria, and my great aunt Katherine. Frank hadn't been in any of the pictures with my mother.

Unless he was the one taking the pictures?

The doorbell rang and I reached over to tap the digital picture frame next to my bed to see who was at the front door. The upgraded security monitoring system Elisabeth installed a few weeks ago sent live footage to four different disguised monitors throughout the house and we could also view them from our cell phones, and, of course, watch from a computer if we wanted to. This digital picture frame was one of the house monitors.

I looked at the screen and smiled to myself. *Right on time.* It was nine-thirty sharp and David was standing at my front door with two Peet's to-go coffee cups in his hands. I sprang to my feet and grabbed my small purse. I'd downsized it for convenience today. I was wearing my dark green sweats and a lime-green tank top underneath with a pink sports bra since Doc was going to show me some more gun handling and self-defense moves today too. I didn't really care if the sports bra made me look even flatter in the chest than I already was. A woman can't worry about such things when her life is on the line. Okay fine, I still thought about it. But it wasn't like I was "worrying". And besides! A padded push-up bra didn't do me much good anyway, nor was it even practical today.

I sighed at my reflection in the mirror and my now flatter chest, snatched my matching sweat hoodie off the back of the chair, and slipped it on as I jetted down the stairs. I slung the purse strap over my neck and across my shoulder to secure it to me and also to keep my hands free.

Last night, Elisabeth had come in from speaking with David and found me sitting on the floor next to the living room coffee table. I was hugging my knees to my chest, forehead resting on them, sobbing. I'd tried to return to the pile of files and in my stubbornness to keep going, ended up breaking down into sobs all over again. It was just so much to process, to *see*. Elisabeth had rushed over and squatted down in front of me. She looked at the files I had reopened and dropped haphazardly to the floor all around me, then quietly brushed them aside and lifted my face with her hands.

"These can wait. They aren't going anywhere sweetie. Don't try to solve all of this in one night, remember?" Liz kissed the top of my head as if I was a little girl and started cleaning up the files while I sat there nearly motionless, my silent sobs barely trembling my shoulders anymore now that the last of my energy was spent.

Liz put the files neatly in a box that she must have grabbed from somewhere. I hadn't even noticed she had left the room to get it.

I watched her weakly with blurry focus as I continued to cry. She grabbed the files one at a time and placed them in a certain order as she stacked them inside the box. She replaced the scattered reports, photos, diagrams, and random loose pages that had ended up on the coffee table, floor, or couch cushions into the proper files without hesitation. Her eidetic memory allowed her to recall with perfect accuracy which document went into which file and in precisely the correct order.

"My heart hurts," I said, my words breaking between slowing sobs.

"I know it does. You're going to make it through this. I promise," Liz said softly.

"When?" I asked, not even knowing how to ask or what I was even asking anymore. I was exhausted and full of sorrow after having looked at my mother's and sister's files again. I'd been sitting there alone for the past twenty minutes looking at them while David and Elisabeth talked outside. It had been longer than I'd expected them to talk and unfortunately, more than enough time for me to give into the horrible magnetic field of the files we'd left abandoned and unattended.

Liz looked at me, her eyes remorseful. "I'm sorry it took me so long. David just...a few things came up that needed to be clarified.

I'm sorry I left you alone with these, Mel." Liz put the last file in the box and came over and embraced me tightly. I melted into her, my heart seemed to pound in my chest, the ache was so great it was crushing.

In the silence of our embrace, I suddenly felt as though I was a small child again, losing my mother and sister and feeling so isolated and alone, frightened and hopeless. I knew the emotions had to be a lie. I wasn't alone and I didn't have to be afraid anymore. God was working this out for my good, right? I didn't have to feel hopeless anymore. We were at the beginning of proving my father's guilt. The beginning of bringing justice. It would happen. It had to happen!

"Come on now. Time for bed. Come on," Liz coached and half carried, half walked me up the stairs to my room.

Now, as I rushed down the last of the stairs to let David in, I glanced at the living room almost expecting to see us all huddled there, concentrating hard on the files in our hands, passing photos around, and discussing the significance of it all. But the box of files was gone. I spun around quickly, they weren't anywhere in sight.

Hmm, maybe Liz locked them in the safe after I went to bed so they wouldn't be sitting out exposed, tormenting me?

I opened the door and David stood there smiling down at me. He looked tired, but still as handsome and strong as ever. His jet-black hair and honey brown eyes never looked so inviting.

"Honey, I'm home," David teased as I smiled up at him.

"David," I whispered, and wrapped my arms tightly around him.

"Morning," he said into my hair as he rested his chin on my head. His warmth soaked into me and I found myself gripping him, trying to take in his strength and his comfort. He must have felt me pulling the life out of him because he simply held me and let me cling all the harder to him, pouring into me his love and security.

I finally pulled away and looked up at him again, "One of those for me?" I asked seeing the coffee cups still in his hands.

"Oh, yeah. Here you go." David offered me one and studied my face. He reminded me of Elisabeth a little bit as he did it. "You doing okay today?"

"I guess. I didn't sleep very well. Dreamt a lot about my mom and sister...and *him*. He was always there in the shadows, lurking, waiting, laughing at me." I shook my head and then took a big sip of coffee. I didn't usually drink coffee but this wasn't half bad with its creamy sweetness coating my tongue and heat making it's way down my throat to warm me. I let out a sigh and took another sip. I needed a caffeine boost after my late night and restless sleep. This was perfect.

"Ooh, this is really good," I hummed, pleased.

"Glad you like it. Ever had Peet's before?" David asked.

"Nope. Don't usually drink coffee."

"Oh," David sounded disappointed.

"But don't worry, this is delicious and I can use all the pep-up juice I can get," I touched his arm in thank you. "Liz always says it's hard to beat Peet's."

"You can tell me if you don't like it; we can stop and grab you something else if you want. Doc won't care if we're a few minutes late," David suggested kindly.

"I don't want him waiting for me after he's being so accommodating. This is perfect. Honest! Shall we?" I asked gesturing to his tricked out black Jeep Rubicon next to the curb.

"Yes, let's. I have your breakfast in the Jeep. Do you like ham and cheese croissants?"

"Like them? I love them! Were you getting tips from my bestie last night?" I asked teasingly.

"Maybe," David said with a tight smile then averted his eyes, stepping back out of the house with a welcoming wave of his hand to indicate ladies first shall pass.

I followed him then locked the door behind us. Elisabeth was already gone, having gotten up earlier than me to go for a run. She was probably still out there right now, jumping bushes, dodging cats and showing up the wannabe marathon runners. Not on purpose mind you. It just happened naturally.

I watched as David slipped back into soldier mode, checked the street left and right and took my free hand to lead me safely to the passenger side of his Jeep. I'd never been in his Jeep before. In fact, I'd never been in any vehicle with him. I felt my heart miss a beat. Not too long ago I was afraid of confining myself in a small space with him from fear that I'd molest him like I had tried while under the demonic influence of Jared in the walk-in cooler at work. Well, actually, Jared was a demon. Or so I thought he would be once he died, being that Liz and I believed he was one of the Nephilim. Either way, he seemed to embody an evil spirit of Lust and had sent it out to attacked me, nearly consuming me that evening. Only by God's grace and David's prayers did I manage to resist it.

"I've always loved this Jeep," I said in way of small talk to distract myself from my growing nervousness and the uneasy guilt trying to broadcast itself on my face at the thought of what I had almost done.

"Me too," David winked at me and opened my door. He offered me his hand again to help me climb in. It seemed taller than I had expected with it's all terrain mud tires and rugged design.

"Maybe you can take me for a spin on your motorcycle sometime too," I said without thinking as I slid my legs in and grabbed the seatbelt. "Shoot, that was a stupid thing to say. I'm sorry David," I gushed, my face heating up and turning red.

David was gracious, and smiled patiently. "It's okay. I—"

"No, no it's not. My father ran it over with that flower delivery truck he stole. I'm so sorry I brought it up. I don't know what I was thinking. I'm such a—"

"Beautiful, kindhearted woman," David said cutting me off. "When I get a new one, I'll take you for a spin."

"You're too kind to me David," I said embarrassed.

David leaned in and took the seatbelt out of my hand, leaning over me to secure it in the lock for me instead. His height of six-foot made it easy for him to reach over me. He paused there, half over my lap, his face eye level with mine now that I was sitting high enough.

"If I knew you wanted to ride on the back of my motorcycle, I'd have cashed the check from the insurance by now and taken you with me to pick out my new one," David said smiling from ear-to-ear.

"Really?" I said matching his smile with one of my own. I was so relieved I hadn't bummed him out by mentioning the death of his motorcycle at the hands, or truck, of my father. Dwayne had purposefully backed into it, knocking it over before running over it with the delivery truck so David couldn't chase after him the night he'd stopped my father from raping me.

"Definitely," David said, his face drew a little closer.

"Why?" I added curiously and smiled bigger. David's honey brown eyes bore into mine. At this close distance, I felt my stomach flutter and my mouth go dry. He made me so nervous, he was so handsome.

David laughed, a rich masculine sound. "Well, if I'm being honest with you...which I always want to be, it would've meant you'd be straddled behind me, your arms holding tightly onto me, as I whisked you around town, showing you off. What more motivation do I need?"

I felt my face turn bright red all over again and I dropped my eyes, embarrassed at his directness. I hadn't thought of that. Well, I'd thought of that, but I hadn't known he would have thought of it that way too. I swallowed hard.

"Melanie?" David said my name softly and I glanced up at him and bit my lip. I felt my eyes a little too huge and my pulse racing. I was sure he could see my pulse beating it's way out of the side of my neck.

"I didn't mean to make you uncomfortable. I'm sorry if I embarrassed you by being too forward," David said, cupping my chin gently in his hand and looking deeper into my eyes, making me even more nervous. "Maybe I shouldn't be *that* honest with you just yet?"

Get a grip woman! Kissing David might be the best thing that has ever happened to you, but you have to take it slow. Take a breath. Breathe!

I followed my own advice and inhaled until my lungs hurt. "No, it's okay...I...it's just that I, I didn't mean to hint about...well, something like that," I said awkwardly. "I only meant that it would be fun. Um, to ride on one!" I added in a stumble. "I've never been on a motorcycle before. Liz has offered, but I've always been too afraid and—"

David leaned in and kissed me tenderly, a gentle comforting kiss that silenced me and calmed me all at once. When he pulled away, he whispered to me, "Melanie, I know you weren't. I'd never assume that of you. I'd be honored to take you for your first ride. It will be fun. I'd make sure of it."

I burst out laughing. "I think we should stop before we both dig the holes any deeper."

David joined me with his deep chuckle, his eyes going big now. I think I'd taken his offer naughtier than he had meant to this time. "Deal," he said laughing again and kissing my cheek. He walked around the back of the Jeep to the driver's side, slipped off his black leather jacket and tossing it in the back seat as he climbed in.

"Hey, you wanta drive the beast?" he asked, amusement on his face.

"Me? Oh, no. Not today. Maybe another time though. How about where there's mud and I can't hurt anyone else," I teased.

"Mud kind of girl, huh? I like." David wiggled his eyebrows at me like Bradley had to Elisabeth the night before and I burst out laughing.

"I just think I'd be safer in a field of mud than around other cars or pedestrians trying to tame this beast for the first time," I added with a giggle and an eyebrow wiggle of my own.

David chuckled and buckled himself in. Grabbed his too-cool Ray-Ban sunglasses and slipped them on, making him look like he was ready for the sexiest soldier of the year photoshoot. He was wearing all-terrain tiger camos and a solid tan V-neck T-shirt. He was looking very Air Force today, minus the leather jacket and the fact that he was wearing dark tennis shoes instead of combat boots.

"Here's the rest of your breakfast," David said with a sideways smile handing me the wrapped ham and cheese croissant off of the dash board.

"Yummy, thank you!" I said taking it from him and starting to unwrap it. I took a bite of the sandwich. It was delicious. "Oh, David. This is soooo good."

David watched me chew, his eyes lingering on my mouth, "I'm finding that I can get drunk just watching you enjoy something," David's voice had grown a little husky.

"Um, so do you know where Doc's training facility is?" I asked, bringing us back on track to our morning appointment and away from dangerous waters. I could feel it heating up again and I wanted to dash it with a splash of cold before we were both consumed by *it*.

That's a dumb question Mel. Of course he would. They're friends.

"Yep, been there a few times before. What'd you think of it?" David asked, effort to follow my lead making his voice sound too casual. He started the Jeep and checked his mirrors, turned his head and pulled out onto the street.

"It was bigger than I thought it'd be inside. That gun range downstairs is badass. I'd never seen so many guns except at a gun store. And those rooms off to the side of the hall looked pretty interesting too. I only glanced at them as we walked past and didn't get to explore much. Do you know what they're for?" I asked, hoping he'd have information to share and keep us talking about something unrelated to us.

"Yeah, one is for hand-to-hand self-defense and combat training. You'll probably get to be in that one a little bit today. I call it the "wrestling room" but Doc calls it "going to the mats". There's also the main classroom—"

"I've been in that one," I interrupted. "Doc had me answering questions in there as to why I wanted my CCW."

David glanced at me. "I'm sorry you had to go through that. I'm sure it wasn't comfortable for you. I know how private you are," his voice was sincere and his face concerned.

"Well, he said he wanted assurances my reasons were just and not about seeking revenge. I guess I don't blame him really, I think most people would want revenge," I said, my voice shaking a little from the rush of emotions I'd felt at having to divulge such secrets to a perfect stranger and explain why I was afraid of my own father. And then, to try and explain why a group of ex-cons were out to get me, it had been a rough day.

"Uncomfortable isn't a strong enough word," I added as an afterthought.

"That's one of the things I love about you Melanie. You're not consumed by hatred, even with all the horrible things you've been put through, you don't want to live your life full of fear or hatred. I admire that. A lot," David reached out and patted my knee then returned his hand to the wheel and checked his side mirrors, turning his head as he concentrated on merging north onto Highway 99.

I took in a big breath. Then I took another bite of my breakfast sandwich and then another. I needed a moment to gather my thoughts. My afternoon with Doc felt like forever ago. Technically it was just yesterday. But after having been transported four-thousand years in the past and stuck there for four days, it seemed like an eternity ago. Here at home, my absence had only been a matter of minutes whereas the reality was, I'd been gone for days. That was just one of the mysteries of God. He worked outside of space-time and could pick you up and plant you anywhere he wanted you along the timeline.

Marty McFly, eat your heart out.

Of course, I couldn't tell David any of this. I hadn't even had a chance to tell Elisabeth the details yet. We'd been interrupted when I had tried. I had to remind myself that talking to David about "yesterday" meant it was *his* yesterday, not mine.

"Yes, it was hard. I never talked to anyone about my past before, other than Liz. Now, there's you and Bradley. It's rough. Honestly, it's absolutely humiliating. It makes me feel vulnerable and exposed, like being naked in a dream with a crowd looking at you, seeing all your flaws and weaknesses. And now that my father and I have been plastered all over the news, it's even worse. I don't feel like I had much of a choice in any of it," my voice was sounding as vulnerable as I felt. I was proud of myself though, I hadn't cried. I was just sharing with him the facts about my feelings.

"I know it's been hard Melanie. But I agree with Elisabeth, I think God wanted Doc and I to know. God's in control of this. I trust him," David said softly.

"It didn't take me too long to feel like it was okay to tell Doc, even if it was sort of a requirement. I trust him. I trust you and Bradley too," I added to make sure he knew I felt that way about him as well.

"I hope you know that Doc's one of the most trustworthy men I know. You can tell him anything. I hope you don't feel too betrayed that he asked to talk to me about it, even if you didn't know it was me at the time." I watched David's face as he said it, it was contrite.

"He really scared me when he first asked. But I chose to give him my permission because I felt it was the right thing to do. He didn't try to pressure me into it. Now I know what I felt was right, because it would mean you would finally know the truth about me and my family. It was painful but...but he broke the ground for me by telling you the truth. It's kind of a gift from a certain point of view." I meant every word.

"I'm glad he called me. I know there is more to your story. I'll let you tell me on your own time, alright?"

I smiled up at him, "And I will. In time." I looked down at my lap. We drove in silence for a minute. Not an uncomfortable one, but just quiet, thoughtful. Both of us thinking about all that had happened in our lives that we had yet to share with one another. I was sure he had many stories to tell me too about his family, his military career, the war.

To break the silence, I finally asked, "So what else does he use that big room for? The one I was in with the white boards and 70-inch flat screen TV on the wall?"

"He teaches the legal side of the concealed carry course and also does some police officer training courses in there," David said, pride for his friend showing on his face as he glanced at me. "He runs a bounty hunter instructor school, did you know?"

"That's right! He's some kind of DOI approved instructor, right?"

"Yep. The white board is to teach them laws, tactical plans, strategy, research and investigation methods, and whatever else they might need to know. I've been in there when he'd showed them footage of takedowns and arrests gone wrong. Trying to scare those fellas, and ladies, into not making the same mistakes."

"Sounds interesting."

"I bet he would've been able to point out what I did wrong if it'd been filmed," David sounded ashamed.

"What do you mean?" I asked confused.

"Um," David glanced at me. "When I let your father get away," David's face tightened and I could see the anger he still carried at himself because my father got away that night. He glanced at me and away.

"David. That wasn't your fault. You know that," I said immediately.

"I know, I know. I just keep replaying it in my head. His strength wasn't natural," David sounded sure.

"That's because it wasn't. It was demonic. And he never was right in the head. Crazy and possessed make for a bad combination. Trust me," my voice was a little shaky.

"Melanie, I'm sorry. Of course. You'd know better than me. I didn't mean to—"

"I know. I didn't take it badly. Just don't blame yourself for it. You did more than enough that night. You stopped him from..." I couldn't say the rest out loud.

I looked out my window at the cars we were passing as we zipped along in the fast lane. David let me leave it there, he knew what almost happened. I didn't need to finish the sentence.

"So, what are Doc's other rooms for?" I said to break the silence again.

David seemed eager to let me change the subject and answered quickly, "Well, he's got his own sound proof interrogation room and two jail cells tucked away back there too. As you know, the other side of his business is bounty hunting so sometimes he catches and holds for a little while if he suspects the perp might lead to a bigger catch. It isn't exactly normal protocol for a bounty hunter, but with his military background and connections, and since he's technically considered law enforcement as well by being on call with SWAT, as long as he reads them their rights, he can hold them a while. He's granted more flexibility than most."

"Wow, he has a cell there too? That's crazy. Is that legal?" I was truly surprised. I hadn't expected that.

Maybe he can find my father and keep him there so I can ask him a few questions of my own.

"It's like a mini police precinct in a way," David chuckled as he looked at my surprised face. "It's all been made official so he can't be accused of wrongful imprisonment."

"Cool. I wonder if the Feds ever ask him to hold someone for them. Like a high-profile terrorist or something. You know, for the government?" I turned in my seat a little excited by my theory. "You know, to keep them out of the spotlight or hidden from other foreign agencies or something," I said all conspiratorially.

"Umm...well. I wouldn't ask him that if I were you," David said a little too seriously.

I blanched. I had just been kidding. *Was I right? Holy cow. Maybe Doc's been looped into secret stuff like Liz. Oh, that's just awesome!* Then a sobering thought hit me. *But then why would David know about it?*

"He also has his office and a state of the art workout room with cardiac machines, martial arts props, weights, pull up bars, benches, stuff like that," David said putting the conversation back onto safer ground and pulling me from my mischievous thoughts.

"Nice! What else?" I asked, getting a little too excited to poke around the place today. Maybe it was my nerves redirecting into another form of energy, but I'd rather feel excited and adventurous than nervous or intimidated.

Or like an idiot mishandling weapons and getting my butt kicked in the self-defense lesson today. The thought of being pinned to the matt by Doc made my stomach clench. *Will I freak out or have a flash back and think of when my father pinned me down, hit me, shoved his hand into my blouse and molested me? Tried to rip my pants off to rape me?*

Stop it! Stop it! Just stop it!

I was breathing a little hard and took a big sip of my coffee. I focused on the heat and taste of it. Forced the images of my father looming over me out of my mind. Forced the sounds of the demons laughing around me out of my thoughts too with my urgent prayer up to God.

Lord Jesus, help me. I rebuke the power of those thoughts and their hold on me, in Jesus name!

David was looking straight ahead and oblivious to my internal battle.

"Let's see," David replied, "Doc put in a locker room, two bedrooms, each with two bunk beds and some lockers, a couch, and extra clothes. He set them up in the back wing. And there's a little kitchenette in the breakroom area." David's tone changed to sound a little uncomfortable which made me look away from the road and up at him.

"Bedrooms?" I asked, a little breathy. I was still recovering from the mental flashback of my father. I hoped David didn't take it wrong. "Why?" I carefully added more steadily.

"Um, mainly for keeping an eye on the prisoners I'd assume," David wet his lip and studied the road a little too hard.

"Does he have showers too then, for anyone having to spend the night to keep guard?"

"Yep, there are a few in the locker room," David nodded. He glanced at me with a small smile then back at the road, his body slightly stiffer and his hands readjusting on the steering wheel, almost nervously. Something was suddenly off. And this time, it wasn't the silent battle going on in me. Something was going on with him.

"David? You okay?" I asked, placing a hand on his forearm.

He looked down at me, his smile drifting away making him look kind of sad. Then he looked back up at the road. He took a second to answer, checking his mirrors again. I gave him time to answer, seeing him remembering something or looking for words.

"Do you remember when I ran into you at the courthouse because I was visiting a few courtrooms for my criminology course?" David finally answered.

"Of course," I replied, not sure what this had to do with anything.

"I told you I'd been in the Air Force as a pararescue jumper helicopter pilot, remember?"

"Yes, I remember," I answered softly, encouraging him to continue.

"I told you about those poor boys I'd known coming home from the war just to be tossed to the side. PTSD in full swing, unable to adjust back into civilian life. Lost," He paused and swallowed. David glanced down at me. I could see that he was leading up to something.

"I remember. It's horrible. So sad. After everything they gave," I said wholeheartedly.

"Last night when I told you I was in a dark place when I got home from the war, consumed by all the guilt, shame, and remorse…Well, like those boys with PTSD…that was me too, Melanie. I was overcome by all the horrible things I'd done in the name of war and duty. There are things I've done that if you knew—" David broke off, a look of pure anguish on his face.

"I'd understand, David," I said urgently, leaning over to be closer to him. "I mean, I'd try my best to understand. I know it couldn't have been easy making life and death decisions every day. Killing people to save others."

David nodded and swallowed. "I killed many people, Melanie. Even—" David's words choked off. He paused a minute, deciding something. I waited patiently, unwilling to rush what I could see was very difficult for him to explain.

"When I got back I was pretty messed up. I was in a bad way. I knew Doc retired shortly before I did. He had already started up his business and got this place downtown," David said quietly. I remained silent, letting him speak.

David cleared his throat. "Well, one night, I didn't know what to do. I was scaring my parents. My sister Leilani couldn't even calm me down. The nightmares were horrendous and I hadn't truly slept in weeks. I was exhausted, angry, lashing out at them, ducking when I'd hear a car backfire, even packed my gun when I went for a walk in the park with my sister and Rose," David choked up. "I really scared Rose," David said, his voice full of regret.

"Who's Rose?" I asked softly.

"She's my niece. She was only three at the time. I freaked out in front of her and she started bawling. My sister yelled at me for it. Told me to get my shit together or she'd knock the shit out of me. Then it was me who was bawling. I literally couldn't move as I stood there crying in the middle of the park with families walking by. I was paralyzed. I felt so horrible." David cleared his throat again and shook his head, a deep crease contorting his face as he relived the emotions of that day.

"My parents didn't know how to help me. I was really lost, Melanie. Accidentally scaring the people I loved. Frightening my niece...I was losing myself. I felt like a broken man. A broken soldier. I hardly recognized myself anymore. Finally, I put my pride aside and called Doc and begged him to help me. He picked me up and brought me to his downtown facility, where we're going. He spent all afternoon and most of the night talking it out with me. Helping me cope. Reassuring me that I wasn't a bad soldier or a bad person. I was a human being with a big heart and when people care as much as I do, they...they sometimes lose hope because of the evil they see and are forced to be a part of." David glanced at me. I sat silently, just listening. David's eyes returned to the road and he did a thorough mirror check as he gathered himself a little to continue.

"Doc pulled out a fold-away cot he had stuffed in the basement and told me to get some rest. He put his AK-47 on his lap and said he'd keep watch. That was the first time I slept through the night in months. When I woke up around eleven o'clock the next day he was still sitting there, weapon ready in his hand, back facing me, watching the door. He hadn't moved all night. Even though he knew with his rational mind that there wasn't a threat, he did it anyway...for *me*. When I returned home later that day, my parents were besides themselves with worry. They thought I'd gotten arrested or worse, run off to kill myself. So many of my buddies had already given up and ate their gun—" His voice broke and he forced down the emotions threatening to overflow into sobs. I saw the tears pooling in his eyes then he sucked in a deep breath through his nose and collected himself again.

"Oh David!" I whispered, tears prickling my eyes as well.

"The next day my parents ambushed me by inviting over our family pastor. Pastor Matthews. At first, I felt betrayed that they invited him without my permission. I'd been avoiding church. Couldn't seem to feel worthy to walk through the front doors. I could hardly pray anymore. But he was kind and loving, and the Holy Spirit spoke through him directly to my heart that day. He prayed a prayer of deliverance over me. I felt the Lord cast out the fear, the anger, the self-loathing, the night terrors—all of it gone. I still struggled afterwards from time to time but not to the same degree. The strongholds had been broken and what was left was the natural healing of my mind and of my spirit." David smiled then, a gleam in his eye of triumph and hope.

"That's wonderful," I smiled back, truly happy for him. I knew exactly what that kind of freedom and deliverance felt like.

"I followed up with Doc and told him about all of it. He ended up turning two of those empty back rooms he had into bedrooms. Told me that whenever I needed to get away from my parent's house or just needed to hang out with someone who really understood what I was going through, to make myself at home," David glanced down at me, his eyes weren't wet now but I could see that the memories still troubled him. He took my hand and held it to his heart as he drove.

"Doc really helped me out. He and my pastor really looked out for me. They even met up to come up with a strategy to help me. If it wasn't for them, and the Lord, I don't know if I'd be sitting here with you right now, Melanie," David smiled, half his mouth lifting. "Of course, my family's support meant a lot to me. It wasn't their fault they couldn't help me all on their own. No one who isn't a trained professional is really equipped to handle a trained special ops soldier who can't talk about his missions and has a severe case of PTSD. Thank God for Doc who had clearance for me to talk to. And thank God for my pastor who understood prayer and the spiritual warfare I was in. Not everyone understands strongholds and deliverance. The two go hand in hand. One healing the mind, one the spirit."

His chest under my hand was hard and full, the muscles tight, his heart beat strong and fast. It took me a second to find my voice, "Doc means a lot to you, doesn't he?"

"Yes. He wasn't only my commander, but he's like my second dad. I trust the man with my life," David said certainly. "Which is why I'm so glad you went to him for help."

"Actually, that day you ran into me at the courthouse was the day I saw a judge about getting an emergency no contact order issued against my father. I'd just found out he was getting released from prison because he'd left me really frightening messages. I still don't know how he managed to get my phone numbers. They are unlisted! After Judge Graham approved the emergency no contact order, he gave me Doc's card and said he would help me. Later, Doc told me the judge was his cousin."

"Ah, Arty Graham. Yes, I know him. Another good man," David lifted my hand off of his chest and lightly kissed the tip of my knuckles.

My eyebrows went up. So that was how he knew that cases in that specific court room couldn't be for anything good when he'd caught me coming out of it that day. He knew the judge. Huh, and I had been so scared he'd heard everything.

Not that it matters anymore. I'm glad he knows now.

"Doc gave you a place to feel safe when you got home, to fight your demons?" I asked gently, still wanting to hear more about him. In fact, David was still a pretty big mystery to me. Yes, we cared about each other, but we really didn't know that much about each other except for our experiences together at Kate's Café where we'd witnessed the best and worst of one another's character, or in our philosophy class at Cosumnes River College. What we'd learned most about each other was during the last six weeks since my life did a tail spin and David got caught in the ensuing cyclone. But given that I'd avoided him for weeks after the attack, it really wasn't very much exchanged in the way of new insights.

Except for Doc telling him all about my troubles and for the files we all gawked at last night.

"Yes, Doc really helped me out. But I'm not the only one. He's been trying to help vets ever since. When I'm done with my psychology degree, I plan on working with him. We've discussed it a lot and really see the need. We want to open a clinic downtown just for Vets to help them rehabilitate and deal with their PTSD. I want to help them enter back into society again rather than feel estranged from it," David said, his voice going a little hoarse as the emotion surrounding his new calling hit him.

"I think that's a wonderful idea. You'll touch so many lives, David. I'm so proud of you," I praised him. "You've come a long way and gave up so much for us, for this country. Thank you. Thank you with all of my heart," I had started to tear up and couldn't stop it. The emotions flooded me and spilled over to run down my face. I wiped the tears away with the back of my sleeve.

"Thank you," I whispered again. "For everything."

Like a Virgin

Chapter Four

he low rumble of the truck's idle vibrated the steering wheel underneath Dwayne's hands. His fists clenched the wheel harder as another surge of unsatisfied desire washed through him like the guttural withdrawal cravings of a heroin addict, desperate and nearly unbearable. Dwayne let out a huff of hot Budweiser breath and shifted in his seat, adjusting the crotch of his pants.

His mood darkened as he took another chug of the beer and carelessly crammed it back in to the center console. His longing grew stronger as he studied the focus of his attention a mere two-hundred yards away. He rubbed his tired eyes and turned off the radio with an agitated jab to shut up Madonna's whiny voice as she sang her newest hit, *Like a Virgin*, before he switched off the engine.

Dwayne had been further down the street a few minutes ago, parked quietly underneath the big oak tree that loomed out like the hand of God on the corner lot. He'd slowly inched the truck up closer and closer every few minutes over the past half hour, unable to resist the compulsion for a better look. The need to get closer growing louder and more intolerable along with the voices in his mind.

The ominously twisted oak tree he was parked under now concealed the light blue Chevy into the void of its powerfully dark shadow. Given the distance at which he was parked, it gave off the impression that his truck belonged to the visitor of someone else living on this friendly neighborhood block.

Dwayne had been watching Mr. Lebarre's sixteen-year-old daughter, Stephanie, for the last half-hour. She was only a teasingly four houses down now and he watched with an urgent hunger as she grabbed a fresh towel off the pile she'd brought out with her. She unfolded the towel and leaned over the hood of the family's new maroon, 1984 Thunderbird. She turned back around and started to wipe off the beads of rinse water trailing down the side of the car. With each rushed wipe of her towel, water splattered onto her T-shirt and short gym shorts to drip down her short muscular legs. She was barefoot and stretched up on tiptoe to reach the center of the car's long hood, thoroughly soaking the front of her T-shirt in the process. She straightened up, shock on her face as she pulled the clinging shirt off of her tight young breasts.

Dwayne swallowed the audible growl of longing as it escaped this throat and wet his lips. He felt his pulse speed up and he slid down in his seat a little, wanting to hide his excitement from the world as if it might suddenly stand still, face and watch him. He could almost taste the water on her sweaty skin and he closed his eyes, inhaling deeply, imagining the smell of her sweat mixing with fear. It'd been a long time since he'd seen true terror enter the eyes of woman at his hands. He'd been playing it safe for a while now. He missed it. The longing was growing like a dry forest fire within him. He didn't know how much longer he could suppress his darker cravings. He missed it so much.

Dwayne figured Stephanie was still a virgin which made her even more tempting to him. She might just be enough to push him over the edge and break his "fast". She was still too naive and unaware of her own body to *not* be a virgin. Hell, she still wore pigtails half the time and would turn bright red whenever a cute boy her own age would try to talk to her. He'd been watching her for a few months now and had seen how shy and reserved she was. Her body screamed virgin. It was practically begging him to break his fast and change that.

Stephanie's father was one of those church going, religious types. Dwayne had first seen him and his family entering the same Community Church where Dwayne permitted his wife, Helena, to go a few Sundays a month. It was there he had first laid eyes on Stephanie Lebarre. She was laughing with her friends on the front steps of the church and had captured Dwayne's attention right away. He could hardly keep his breathing under control as his wife Helena took her time unbuckling their little girl from the back seat and gathered her up in her arms to attend the service. She'd leaned in to kiss him good-bye and he nearly slapped her as her thick red hair swung forward to block his view, reminding himself at the last millisecond he was supposed to be a loving husband and devoted father. After all, she hadn't known she'd blocked his view from the young and supple Stephanie Lebarre. He'd kissed Helena and forced a smile as she left, their black haired, blue eyed daughter Vivian on her hip to make a perfect picture of a happy mother.

Helena stopped as Stephanie reached out to pinch Vivian's rosy cheeks and giggled as Vivian shyly tucked her face into her mom's shoulder. They had talked a few moments before they went inside to join the service. Helena and Stephanie lingering at the back of the late comers with bright smiles and laughter on their faces.

Dwayne had watched Stephanie with blood pounding excitement. She was perfect. She had been Richman's type. Young, blonde, blue eyes, soft bodied and sun kissed skin and the look of innocence in their faces. All their nights of watching, waiting and then taking, flooded back like an addict seeing and smelling heroin boiling in a spoon a mere foot away. He had to have her. She was going to be his. It was just one more reason for Dwayne to let Helena go to church.

He would drop Helena off with their three-year-old daughter, Vivian, right before church started at nine o'clock in the morning. He made sure to come pick them up as soon as it was over. Since the Community Church had precisely timed services, he was never late, and she never had a chance to linger too long. He didn't want her to have the opportunity to get chatty or share anything too personal. It was too risky. She might make friends again and he did *not* want that. He needed to be her entire world, her only friend, her only support. He wouldn't share *his* wife with anyone. She was meant to be his and his alone.

He knew if he kept her from being seen by certain members of the community she had met since they'd moved up there, they would come calling on her to make sure she was okay. Not everyone was as blinded by Dwayne's charms as Helena was. He could see it in their eyes and the subconscious reactions in their body language; they suspected he wasn't a good man and they were afraid for her. They watched him too closely whenever he was near them, as if they were afraid he might suddenly rob them or steal their children. If he pulled her from their church, they'd notice. He didn't want them looking into their life, into him. If they did, he'd have to take care of it. And he wasn't willing to take a risk that big. *Yet.*

One day he would orchestrate a full separation from her church and her acquaintances. She didn't have any friends left. She'd chosen him over them, even over her family. He'd managed to manipulate wedges between them all and move her to Redding to take her away from them. After all, his wife belonged to him. Her time and friendship was his. Her life belonged to him as well. She just didn't fully understand that yet.

He could tell she was starting to see past his fake smiles and forced laughter and had peered into the darkness within him on several occasions. He'd tried to keep it hidden from her, to suppress it, but it was getting harder and harder to hide the truth from her. He'd caught her watching him a few times, pensive and troubled behind her eyes as the hidden truths began to seep out of him and sink into her.

Having a little girl hadn't helped any. Somehow, her purity and insufferable giggles brought out the darkness within him. He just wanted to stuff her away, put her in a hole and get rid of her. Breeding with Helena had been an accident. She had been so excited that he had just played along to keep her happy and the inevitable at bay. He tried to act like the loving husband. But the games were getting old.

Dwayne grunted and forced the thoughts of Helena and their stupid little brat, Vivian, out of his mind. They were mucking up his fantasy. It'd been a long time since he indulged himself like this. He'd been so strong, so incredibly patient. He'd been playing it safe for a long time now but the dark cravings were starting to become almost too much to resist any longer. Soon he'd have to give into them or they'd drive him mad. But the truth was, he *wanted* to give into them. He was exhausted with the fight to resist.

Dwayne felt his abdomen tighten as his excitement grew with the idea of releasing his dark desires after all these years. He focused harder on Stephanie as she took a few steps down the body of the car, drying it with her moist towel. She pressed her body fully against the car again and slapped the towel across the roof, reaching ever higher to try and get the last of the water off. She struggled, her face intent as she did her best to wipe the water away. When she stepped back, she turned her back on him, struggling with her clinging shirt trying to free it from her body. He wanted desperately to see. He felt his frustration peaking, driving him all the more mad.

"Ooh," Dwayne complained, leaning forward to try and see, his breathing growing heavier. He resisted the urge to take matters into his own hands as his body reacted to what he could only imagine were perky breasts and water-soaked shorts, clinging to the surfaces of her body. He couldn't afford to get caught. He had to be smarter than his body. He had to regain control. He *always* had control.

He leaned back in his seat and finished off the beer with a new determination. Then crushed the empty can in frustration, letting out a breath, willing his body to relax. He leaned his head back and closed his eyes, taking a slow breath in and out, but the image of Stephanie's wet, perky body flooded into his mind. He couldn't take it anymore. He gave in and he let his mind wander for a moment, imagining sneaking up behind her with no one around. He would crush her body against the car with his own, while covering her mouth with his strong hand. He'd press himself against her tight firm ass, allowing himself a small taste of what was to come. He'd hiss in her ear to be quiet or he'd kill her. Then he would drag her away to his truck and force her inside. He'd take her to a quiet place where no one could hear them. He'd drag her out and throw her to the ground. She'd cry and whimper, too afraid to move as he'd pin her to the ground, forcing her legs open as he'd unzip his jeans. Then she'd understand and the all-consuming fear would enter her eyes. She'd shriek and struggle and kick! Fighting with all her useless strength against him, bucking and clawing as he'd pin her wrists—.

"No!" Dwayne rebuked himself with a sharp hiss. "Not here. Don't think about *that* here. Stay in control!" he whispered harshly to himself.

Though stalking Stephanie alone was a new experience, raping her on his own would be also be a new experience. He could hardly wait. No more sloppy seconds. He would be her first and her last sexual experience. A cold smile slid across his face at the thought.

Like a god I will possess you, and like a god I will end your life.

Dwayne's eyes narrowed onto Stephanie once more as she bent over to grab the tire brush out of the soapy bucket and began scrubbing the hubcaps. He wondered when she would remember to clean those.

Typical stupid female. No clue how to wash a car.

He closed his eyes again, leaning his head back once more. "Never get caught in your prey's neighborhood. Remember what you were taught. Don't leave connections."

I should go. I've been sitting here too long.

After Dwayne's "mentor", Roger Richman, got arrested in 1979 for possession of an illegal substance with the intent to sell, Dwayne hadn't been involved in a hunt to help stalk, kidnap, rape, and kill anyone. He had learned a lot from Richman. But Richman wasn't around anymore to tell Dwayne what to do. Richman always told Dwayne if one of them was caught, to cut off all contact. No calls and no letters lest a connection between them be established. And most importantly, stop all of their "activities" for at least five years to ensure that any suspicion of a partner die with the investigation, should there be one. Dwayne had remembered the rules. And even though Roger Richman had initially been arrested on charges *unrelated* to kidnapping and rape, he knew the risk that his other crimes might come out, and so he'd have to play it safe just in case.

For Dwayne, stalking someone on his own was a new experience. He had always followed Richman's lead and done what he was told. It had been hard at times following instructions. Dwayne thought himself much more intelligent than his mentor, but still, he had needed the old man to show him *how* to do what he'd been craving and not get caught. After all, Richman had been at it for nearly thirty years and had never been caught—until now.

Dwayne had done what the police couldn't, he'd uncovered his identity and tracked Roger Richman down. He had suspected the killing rapist had once been in law enforcement. He very carefully and masterfully tracked the killings he suspected belonged to the unknown killer. He put dots on a map of California to see where he killed the most. It wasn't long until he noticed a pattern between how often a victim was found and that groupings of them were more frequent in the Redding and Sacramento area.

Dwayne fixated on murders closest to his home town of Redding inside the Shasta County perimeter and narrowed in on the killer's preferred hunting ground. Dwayne's instincts told him he would frequent bars in the heart of his kill zones where young girls looking for an adventure and thrill might happen by and become easy prey. It's what he would do. Dwayne went to every bar in Redding during the times he estimated the killer would be back up his way, after tracking his killings and the timing between them. In silence from a corner, he carefully watched every man who entered and left, waiting to *feel* his kindred spirit speak to him.

One night, after months of searching the bars, he spotted him. In walked a tall black-haired man with a precisely trimmed mustache over thin lips. His eyes were dark, almost black with cold calculation. Dwayne knew it was him. Something about the man excited him. Made him almost giddy. He collected himself and approached the man and started casual conversation with him about the best beers here and how hot the bartenders, Besty and

Josie, were. They ended up drinking the night away and played a few rounds of pool. He befriended the man over the course of five months and slowly earned his trust.

Dwayne knew if he shared with Roger his darkest fantasies, Roger would eventually admit to him how he'd already lived them out. After a while, Roger didn't disappoint. He let it slip he had dabbled in rape a time or two. With Dwayne's encouragement and adoration, he manipulated him into telling him more. Finally, able to brag to an adoring fan about his conquests and all that he'd managed to get away with for the past thirty years, they were taking fishing trips so Roger could tell him all his secrets with no one to hear.

It took very little effort for Dwayne to convince Roger how badly he wanted to indulge himself on those stupid, unwilling, useless women that roamed blindly around them. Since Roger had already opened up and bragged about his conquests, he invited Dwayne to come along one night to get a taste for himself. It had gone without a hitch. Dwayne played the perfect audience and patient participant. He let Roger give all the orders and did everything he said to the letter.

By the time Dwayne introduced the idea of Roger bringing him on as a partner, someone the older man could mentor and pass on his legacy to, Roger's ego was so primed, he agreed without hesitation. He'd played right into Dwayne's hands. After Dwayne felt he'd learned all he could from the man, he made an anonymous call to the police about the stash of drugs Richman always carried in his truck. It had been Richman's own habits that had made him so easy to destroy him. He used the drugs sometimes to subdue his victims and when he was between hunts, they helped him relive his conquests. Dwayne had used them to become the bars that ultimately kept Richman from them.

Fool. Stupid idiot. I always knew I was better than you. Now this is my playing field. Are you ready to watch my conquests hit the news? Will you see me from hell you bastard? I'll be sure to dedicate my first to you. Then you'll know your legacy is complete.

He'd been longing to go out on his own to experiment and find his own victim type but Richman had insisted he wait, he wasn't ready yet. So that's when Dwayne decided to get Richman arrested.

Though the initial charges had been for illegal possession, it hadn't taken the cops long to link him to the rape of a young teenage girl who'd come forward a few weeks before his arrest. She had been the only one of Richman's victims to have gotten away, and she'd given a detailed description of her attacker to the forensic artist, including a very specific description of a tattoo matching the one Richman had on his left forearm. It wasn't until Richman was in custody awaiting his arraignment on the original charges of illegal drug possession, that the detective made the connection.

Richman had been careless. He'd grown arrogant in his old age. And it had been one of those late nights after too many beers when Richman stumbled out of a bar and was approached by two teenage girls asking him to buy them some beer from the liquor store across the street. He'd obliged. Telling them to meet him in the back alley and he'd pass it off to them.

He'd sucker punched the chunky pimply-faced one, knocking her out cold. Then grabbed her frightened and surprised friend and viciously raped her. She'd finally gotten away only after someone snuck up behind Richman and knocked him out with a bottle and ran off. She never seen her hero's face. She found another empty bottle nearby and smashed it over Richman's head again, before rushing to her friend who was waking up. They'd ran for it, too afraid to call the police out of fear of getting into trouble themselves. It wasn't until the girl's mother found her trying to cut her own wrists a week later that the truth came out and she reported the crime to the police.

Dwayne had followed Richman that night and had seen an opportunity to get him arrested. But it hadn't worked. The girl hadn't stayed to call for help or call the police. She'd ran off like the little coward she was.

Dwayne had no idea she'd gone to the cops later. He learned about the connection the police had made like everyone else, on the local news. He'd been perfectly delighted. With the additional charges of possessing illegal drugs with the intent to sell and the rape of the teenager, he'd go away for even longer. What great luck!

Roger, that old devil, had thought he was infallible. He had sure tripped himself up and fallen right into a hole of his own making. But as long as he didn't take Dwayne down with him, it'd be all good for Dwayne.

Unfortunately, Richman hadn't lasted long in jail. Richman had sent Dwayne a letter after he was arrested telling him the date and time he'd call him and which payphone to wait at, breaking their code to cut off all contact. Dwayne still wasn't sure how he'd gotten the letter sent without raising suspicion and Dwayne was pissed he risked exposing him like that but he couldn't resist. He had to know what the old man wanted to tell him.

Richman called Dwayne as scheduled and told him in a low whisper, "I won't let them take my secrets from me boy. I won't give them back my women. They're mine. Mine! Don't you ever leave one alive. You hear me? Those bitches can't keep a secret. Bitches talk. Don't you ever leave them breathing! Or you could end up like me."

"We always finished them off," Dwayne said, feigning surprise. "Who was left to talk?"

"I don't always take you on every hunt boy. Sometimes I just want one on my own. I don't always want to share," Richman answered coldly.

"I figured you were, but I thought you'd tell me," Dwayne accused, trying to sound hurt.

"Boy, you're good. Real good. But I've been doing this for decades before I found you and sometimes lone wolves need to hunt alone. Don't take it personal, boy. It's not personal."

"Yeah," Dwayne grunted. "But you told me not to hunt alone," Dwayne couldn't keep the sulk out of his voice.

"That was for your own good, boy. I know you're ready to be on your own now. You've been ready for a long time. But I enjoyed mentoring you. It was selfish of me to keep you so close and not let you do it on your own. But I need you to listen to me one more time. Promise me," Richman whispered urgently.

"What is it?"

"Promise me!" Richman demanded, his anger and dominance echoing through the receiver.

"I promise," Dwayne submitted unwillingly, playing his role one last time.

"Promise me you'll take a break boy. Don't try to do it on your own yet no matter how madly you want to. Just let things quiet down first. Then...then I want you to do it for the both of us!" Richman paused, taking in a deep breath and glancing around to make sure none of the officers or other inmates were listening to him.

"Find yourself a wife. Build a life, a family. You can hide in plain sight if you have a normal life. I did it for years, it works. Just don't make my mistake boy. Don't get into the hard stuff, the drugs. That shit's why I got arrested. Be smarter than me. I'm relying on you to carry on our work. Can I count on you boy? Can I trust you to carry on without me when the time's right?"

Dwayne stood in cold silence inside the phone booth, his anger burning through his blood making his jaw lock. How dare Richman think he could tell him what to do anymore! Dwayne wanted to tell him how he'd found *him*, not the other way around! Roger Richman still didn't know Dwayne had tracked him down and manipulated their entire relationship right from the start to get what *he* wanted and now that he was done with him, *he* had gotten him arrested.

Dwayne smiled at the irony and swallowed back his silent humorless anger. He bit back a furious laugh, knowing that now, everything was on the line. The police had connected Richman to one rape. Could they connect him to more? What if he told Roger he had found him, befriended him, manipulated him and gotten him arrested? Richman might talk out of revenge. What if he cut a deal anyway and told them he had a partner? Now he'd have to wait before he could go hunting for a victim of his own. Now he'd have to keep pretending to be this man's "boy" and prove his loyalty to keep him silent. Why hadn't he thought of that before he got him arrested? Damn it! This witness was messing everything up!

"You hear me, boy?" Richman hissed.

"I hear you. I promise. Umm...What did you tell them about me?" Dwayne asked, his voice barely able to hide his duplicity, the anger and the joy a strangled mix.

"Nothing. I'd never do that to you, you should know that. You're like my own son, boy. You don't have to worry. I'm not gonna be able to talk to anyone after tonight."

"Why? What's happening tonight?" Dwayne asked suspiciously.

"I'm gonna leave this body and take over Hell. I'm gonna rule from the underworld."

"No! No, that's not fair! I still have questions. I still have things to learn from you!" Dwayne yelled, the realization that his mentor was about to kill himself turning his anger into worry, not for Richman, but for himself. What if he couldn't really do this on his own like he thought? What if he messed up and got caught? Richman had been doing this for over thirty years and had only gotten caught because he'd been into drugs, giving Dwayne the perfect set up to stab him in the back. He'd managed to not get caught for decades as he traveled all across California raping and killing women. Dwayne had learned a lot of his tricks but he knew there was still more he could learn from the man. He had wanted a chance to have Richman admire *him* for a change, waiting longingly for details of his conquests on the outside.

Richman coughed and lowered his voice more, "Take a break son. Take a *long* break. Don't give them anything to link you to me. Burn my house. Burn my truck. Burn my trophies. Go find a wife and hide inside a family."

"I don't want any fucking wife or any damn kids," Dwayne snarled.

"I know boy. Those sows are only good for two things. But you *have* to. Just listen to me one more time, son. Be smarter than I was," Richman's voice cracked and he cleared his throat.

"Roger—"

"Good-bye boy. It's been a true pleasure teaching you. You'll be fine without me. And when the time comes, do it for the two of us," the line went dead.

"Roger?" Dwayne hissed into the phone. "Richman?"

Dwayne found out a few weeks later from talk at the bar that Richman had committed suicide in his cell by slashing his wrists on a jagged edge of the metal cot.

If there was one thing Dwayne hated more than anything else, it was not getting what he wanted. Yes, he had wanted Roger Richman in prison. His mentor had become an obstacle that needed to be removed so he could be free to take who he wanted, as he saw fit. He hadn't planned on Richman killing himself after his arrest. He hadn't wanted the bastard dead. Not yet anyway. In his own way, Dwayne still wanted the man's approval. He'd planned on showing him how much he'd learned by spending the next several years of Richman's incarceration sending him gifts and notes to comfort him whilst in prison. A gesture of generosity to share his victims with him, like a good "son" should.

Dwayne had only experienced the feeling of thrilling satisfaction that the student had become the master for a few short days before Richman had killed himself. He had wanted to make the master starve for the life he would have, waiting desperately, torturously for the next scrap he'd toss to him, knowing that he would forever have to live vicariously through Dwayne, through his pupil. But Richman had taken that away from him when he killed himself. Richman had won! He didn't even know he'd been playing Dwayne's game since the very beginning.

After Richman died, Dwayne Bishop spent months getting into bar fights and kicking around any stray dogs he'd come across. The last thing he anticipated was for Roger Richman to kill himself. Even though he had been angry that his ultimate plan to show off his crimes to his mentor had fallen apart with his suicide, a part of him felt bad a little about that. The man had been his mentor after all. They'd been close. Well, as close as two psychopathic serial rapist and murders could be. Their bond had been forged with blood, sweat and semen. They respected the art of the crimes they committed and the guts it took to perform them.

Now Dwayne was being forced to abstain from his darker cravings, letting time pass to cover up any patterns that might lead back to him. Damn it! It wasn't fair! The idea of marrying some sow to hide in plain sight was intolerable. Dwayne had never had a relationship. Never a lasting one. He'd tried dating in high school, but found the girls too closed off, emotionally driven, flighty and protective of their precious virginity. The very idea of faking his way through the dating stages and getting married sounded nearly impossible. He wasn't sure if he was up to the task.

Richman had told him about his own marriage and how badly it had fallen apart. His wife had suspected something was wrong with him and had ended the marriage very publicly, ensuring her life and crippling his ability to rid himself of her completely lest he be suspected of the crime.

He'd told Dwayne they'd had a daughter that his wife had taken with her when she left and changed their last names to her maiden name, O'Hair. He had finally tracked down his daughter only a few years ago. Kept a picture of her hidden under the lining of his dresser's bottom drawer. Her name was Helena and she lived in Sacramento and was attending a city college there. Studying to be an artist or something like that.

He found out his ex-wife had moved there to be near her sister a few years before. Had he known, he would have tried to find his daughter sooner. But his ex-wife Gloria had been careful.

Marriage had never been something Dwayne ever wanted and even in his hour of need, he resisted the idea. But Richman's last advice wouldn't stop echoing in his mind. If he was going to have any chance at a long-lasting satisfyingly dark life, he'd have to be smart about it. Then it struck him. Richman had a picture of his daughter at his house. What better way to honor his mentor than to use his own daughter to hide behind. What sweet irony. Oh, that was perfect.

Dwayne had snuck into Richman's house, using the key he'd given him. Found the picture and barely glanced at it as he stuffed it in his front pocket. He rummaged through his closets until he found the dark cedar box Richman kept his most precious possession in, the tokens from his killings. Rings, necklaces, watches, lockets, even one of their retainers, a ribbon with hair still twisted in it, press on nails ripped from some of the women's bodies, even a prosthetic hand.

Dwayne slammed the lid to the box. His heart was racing. He would add them to the collection he would make from victims of his own. He'd match Roger's kills and see them tenfold. He knew Roger wanted him to burn his trophies, but he wanted them for himself. Many of them he'd earned too. He wanted what should now be his. An inheritance.

He went to the kitchen and turned on the gas to the stove before he left. He went out the back of the house, stuffed a greasy rag into the top of one of the many empty beer bottles Roger had tossed outside, lit it, then threw it through the back door. The house exploded and Dwayne ducked for cover behind the broken-down pickup in the back yard.

Later that night, Dwayne broke into the tow yard that was holding Richman's seized pickup truck. He unscrewed the gas cap, stuffed another greasy rag into it and lit it with his lighter. Then he ran for it, darting over the back fence only moments before he heard the *BOOM* of the truck exploding behind him. He'd kept his promise to his friend. He burnt down his house, he destroyed his truck and any evidence that might be left in it, and now, he'd keep his promise and find himself a wife.

Once he stopped running, Dwayne finally pulled the picture out from his pocket. His breath caught. She truly was beautiful. The soft face with large blue cat eyes seemed to pull him in. Her voluptuous dark-auburn hair made her look like that actress, Maureen O'Hara. He could do this. She'd make it easy. The glint of innocence and morality was like an aura around her even through the photo. How he'd love to tarnish her, blacken her soul with sex and lust for him, making her writhe while he possessed her, and her wanting him too.

Dwayne caught his breath. This was the first time he'd ever imagined sleeping with a woman who wasn't being forced, wanting it. He contemplated this new fantasy. If merely looking at her face could invoke this new wave of desire and hunger in him, then maybe it was fate to take her as his wife to hide behind. Maybe it was meant to be.

Fate had never been a consideration for Dwayne. It was a myth the weak minded used to justify their pathetic powerless existence. But perhaps it was, in this instance, a sign from the universe that he really was a god among men, and that his superior mind and craft was meant to be. He was chosen to rid the world of those too weak to fight him. He was the taker of life. The one chosen to prove who had a right to live and who should die. If they couldn't conquer him, then their life was not meant to be, his was. He would gain the power over them and with it, take their rights, their choices, their existence.

He'd have to think this through carefully. Maybe hiding in plain sight at the college would be a good way to start. Maybe he could play baseball again like he had in high school. After all, he needed to leave Redding to distance himself from Richman's crimes. Since Richman's daughter lived down in Sacramento, all he'd have to do is find out which college she went to and start attending there. Find a way to get to know her and somehow convince her to marry him.

Lucky for Dwayne, Richman had written his daughter's name on the back of her photo. Helena Scarlet O'Hair. Her mother had loved *Gone With The Wind* and had inflicted it upon her daughter. He found Helena enrolled at Sacramento City College by sweettalking some blonde idiot admissions clerk into checking their enrollment lists. He even charmed her into giving him a list of her classes.

The day Dwayne met Helena, she'd caught him off guard with her honest smile and genuine kindness. She'd been nice to him, even offered to help him study for their anatomy exam. Much to his amazement, somehow, he'd found himself looking forward to seeing her, even talking with her a bit. She wasn't too stupid for a girl. She even seemed witty, her quick humor and easy smile made him wish he was normal for the first time in his life. She didn't seem to mind his quiet demeanor and awkward presence when he wasn't pushing out the charm. She seemed drawn to him. So, he decided to keep trying. Could he be a boyfriend? Was it even possible? Was he even capable of feeling those kinds of emotions? Or was he just calling himself into character to reach his goal, to hide in plain sight within a nuclear family.

Dwayne hadn't hunted in nine months. He'd resisted the urge with every ounce of self-control he had, trying to play it smart. He realized with a sudden disbelieving shock, that he hadn't even thought about it in at least a week. Helena had been all he'd thought about. Maybe there *was* a way to hide in plain sight. Maybe Helena could be his camouflage. For the first time in his life, he wanted to forget his dark cravings. He wanted Helena.

After only dating a month, he knew. He wanted to keep her. He'd even respected her desire to hold off having sex until she got to know him better. It thrilled him to have to wait like this, making his hunger for her grow with each passing day. Depriving himself of her body made him feel in control, dominating his own impulses. A master of his needs.

He got even more than he had expected out of his relationship with Helena. She made him feel things he'd never felt before in his whole miserable life: accepted, loved, and appreciated. Those pure wholesome feelings had made him feel so good—at first. Almost like being high but on the love of another person. When she finally succumbed and gave herself to him willingly, it was clear she had wanted him just as badly. Truly wanted him, needed him, and had hungered for him as he had hungered for her.

But he knew the truth was, she only *thought* she knew him. He knew she wouldn't even want to look at him if she knew who he *really* was and the evil things he had fantasized about, planned, and done, over and over again. He hoped she never learned the truth about what he was or he'd have to dispose of her like he had others. The thought made him flinch. He didn't want to hurt her if he could help it. But how long could he keep that part of him dormant. *When would it come back?* He knew it wasn't gone, merely slumbering lightly in its den.

Dwayne had honestly thought that getting married to this voluptuous redhead would've been enough to silence his darker cravings and maybe even wash them away for good, but it hadn't. Helena found out she was pregnant about six months into their relationship, and since she wanted to keep it, he knew he'd have to convince her to come away with him back to Redding where her family couldn't continually try to intrude upon their relationship. He had inherited his parent's house when he was nineteen after they'd both been killed in a car crash, which was perfectly fine with Dwayne. He would be able to brag to Helena that he already had a home for them to start their new life in, a home full of love, just like his parents would have wanted. It would make it all the easier to convince her to move.

Dwayne came to with a start. His neck had a kink in it and he moaned rubbing it as he squinted out the truck's dirty front window. He had fallen asleep? *Fuck. Damn beer.*

Stephanie Lebarre was no longer outside. Her dad's car was once again clean and shining like the pristine new Thunderbird it was. The shade of the large oak tree he was parked under had shadowed him nicely while she'd worked and the stupid little twit hadn't even seen him. *What a clueless little whore.* But he'd seen *her* all right. Oh, yes, he'd seen plenty of her.

Dwayne started the engine and put the truck in drive. He slowly rolled down the street and glanced at the Lebarre's blah-tan house as he passed before speeding up to exit the neighborhood. He'd be back. He'd wait a few months so anyone who might have noticed his light blue truck would forget it. Then he'd come back and take Stephanie Lebarre with him. Two more months.

You better make good use of the time you have left, kid.

He rounded the corner and shifted into third gear then accelerated into fourth. A smile came over his mouth.

"My time of fasting is over, Roger. This one's for you. Your type and everything. I'll be sure to do her good," Dwayne said out loud. He laughed, a boiling excitement rekindled in his core, the blood lust and physical lust rushing through his veins with an addicting surge. He sighed. He'd missed this. The thrill of the hunt was back. He was coming back alive. Two months...he could wait. Two months and it would all begin again. Two months, and his dark cravings could finally feast.

Strawberries and Cream

Chapter Five

*W*e pulled up to Doc's bounty hunter training facility right at ten o'clock. With all of the heavy conversation on the way here, I don't think either one of us realized just how fast David had been driving. It was a miracle he hadn't gotten a ticket. But every police car we saw along the way already had another car pulled over to the side of the road.

Sometimes I think it's divine intervention.

I gathered my little purse and started to open my door when I saw David jogging around the back of the jeep and up to my side door. He beat me to it, opening the door and offering me his hand again to help me down. I let him help me, loving the way he made me feel, delicate and feminine, valuable and special, but also respected—as an equal.

I hardly ever felt delicate or feminine on my own. I always felt like a *pretend* woman with my too round butt and hips and unappealingly flat chest. I felt plain and simple. Clumsy and unsure of myself. My self-love had been getting a lot better since I had rekindled my relationship with God. Plus, having a man in my life all a sudden, who looked at me the way David did, made me feel loveable.

David's warm hand in mine was strong and firm, but careful. He always touched me so perfectly, with so much thought and caution, able to sense my needs and what might spook me or hurt me.

I hopped down and smiled up at him, squeezing his hand in thanks. He closed the Jeep door behind me looking down at me with a smile of his own. I still hadn't let go of his hand. It felt so natural in mine that I'd forgotten to release him. He led me to the sidewalk still smiling down at me.

"One second okay. I need to pay the meter," David said with a little humor in his voice as he glanced at my hand.

"Oh right!" I giggled, embarrassed that I'd been hanging on to him so tightly.

He walked over to the parking meter and paid for the two-hour maximum. "Can you please remind me to come add some coins if we go over two hours?" David asked me.

"Sure. Hopefully I remember," I said with a small chuckle. "Not sure what Doc has in store for me in the second half of today's lesson. Honestly, I'm a little nervous about it," I admitted shyly.

"He's a great instructor. Don't worry, you'll learn a lot from him. And he'll take it at whatever speed you want. He'll be watching you for comprehension, absorption of the information and techniques along the way. He might change the pace too if needed. But he'll also push you hard and expect your best effort or he'll lay into you a little bit too. Verbal motivation you might say," David rambled out almost automatically.

"Sounds like you've said this before?" I half stated, half asked.

"Oh," David laughed. "Yes, actually I have. I used to talk some of the soldiers down from frozen-freak-out mode when Doc would show up for cross military combat tactical training in the field."

"Soldiers freeze up during training, too?" I asked totally surprised.

"Yeah, sometimes. Some people aren't good under pressure, no matter what you put them through or try and prepare them for. Unfortunately, when you take gentle or timid personalities and try to press them into the shape of a tough guy, you might just get cracked stone. Not the solid pressure resistant fortified men you hoped for. After some time in battle, those kinds of men start to break down even further. It's hard to repair what was already a weak foundation. Does that make any sense?" David asked me, his forehead creased.

"I think so," I thought about it for a second and added, "and the military thought it a good idea to cross train those soldiers with even more stuff?"

"It was a matter of upping the odds of their survival. It had to be done," David answered with a drop of sadness in his voice.

"I see," I was feeling a little sad again too. I walked to the front door of Doc's building thinking about what David had said, that even soldiers froze up sometimes during training. It didn't really make me feel better like I think he had intended. Instead, it made me so sorry for those men and women who had gone through that. They had suffered day after day in the war. They had probably joined thinking it wouldn't be that bad, that somehow the world and advances in technology and science would protect them from the brutal realities of war. Then it was too late. They were thousands of miles from home and had nowhere to run. And if they did run, they'd be deserting the men and women they'd sworn to protect, and who had sworn to protect them, too.

Can't just hang up their camos and quit if they change their mind either. They'd go to prison for desertion!

I must have been in a daze, standing there swaying, lost in my thoughts, because I heard David jog over to open the door for me. My hand was slowing making its way to clasp the handle. I wasn't sure when I'd left him behind. He smiled down at me, looking so proud of me.

"What?" I asked skeptically.

"I still feel like I'm dreaming. You here with me. *Willingly*," David laughed a deep husky sound. "You really are my dream come true Melanie."

"I know what you mean. I still can't believe it either," I said quietly, glancing down and then back up at him, feeling shy at the sudden change of excitement and joy spilling out of him.

David ushered me in through the open door and into the lobby. I glanced around quickly and located Doc's massive body behind the reception desk. He was bent over writing something down. He glanced up at us and lifted his chin in way of a hello, his head tilted to hold the phone to his ear, pinning it with his shoulder. He was still one of the biggest black men I had ever seen. Although comparing him to some of the Sacramento Kings basketball players, he'd be eye to eye.

Ooh! Maybe David and I could go to a Kings game sometime. That'd be fun. We never did get to use his Monster Trucks tickets.

"Right," Doc said sternly in his deep baritone voice, projecting too much volume into the phone. "I wouldn't if I were you," he growled.

This sounds interesting.

David walked up to the reception desk and peeked over. He read upside down whatever Doc was writing on the notepad and I watched his eyebrows go up. It must not have bothered Doc that David assumed he could butt in and read his notes because they made eye contact and Doc rolled his eyes. David chuckled and stepped back to join me once again.

I looked away and glanced around the lobby. I actually took the time to slowly look at it all this time. I hadn't really had a chance to take it in four days ago, oh wait, "yesterday", being that Doc had been hiding behind the door and scared the living crap out me. In my nervousness, I hadn't noticed him. Somehow, I'd missed the six-foot eight-inch tall, ripped black man standing behind the plant next to the front lobby door. I mean, who would have missed that? He is enormous! The other reason why I'd hardly noticed what was past the other doors "yesterday" was because I'd been so shocked by his size; he was all I could focus on as I followed him down the hallway in a daze to the classroom and then later down to the basement's inside gun range.

"I don't take threats lightly," Doc roared into the phone and I spun around, started by his sudden temper. There was a long pause as he listened and stood up to his full height. His chest swelled and his hand gripping the receiver flexed. I feared he'd crush it. I saw a little reddening in his face and knew someone was really getting under his skin.

"You of all people should know I don't take orders from *anyone*. Especially *you*! Why can't you get that through your thick head by now?" Doc shouted into the phone making me jump. He shot me an apologetic look, his furious face softening a bit. "I have to go. I have a student," Doc said coolly. "No. Not today. Don't you dare." He slammed the phone down.

"Not much has changed, has it?" David asked with a wicked smile on his face.

"Can it boy, before I throw you right back out that door," Doc said looking pissed.

Doc walked around the desk and looked down at David. Yes, he looked down at him. Doc made David's six foot even frame seem tiny in comparison. Seeing the two of them side by side, face to face like this was a little unnerving. I wasn't quite sure if Doc was teasing or actually pissed at David, he looked at him with such a formidable glare and even puffed up his huge chest even more. Of course, I couldn't see his huge chest, not really. It was covered in a tight dark-grey Jack Daniel's T-shirt.

Stop it right now Melanie. I scolded myself and dragged my eyes off his impressive torso.

He's impressive like a Clydesdale is. I told myself. *Powerful and able to crush you with one hoof. Or send you flying into the next corral with one kick.*

David looked back up at Doc, face straight, unemotional, eyes locked onto his until Doc's face slowly cracked a smiled. Then slowly, a huge, larger than life smile formed, filled with pure joy.

"Aw, come here, boy!" Doc said cheerfully and grabbed David into a fierce bear hug. They laughed heartily together. "Good to see you soldier! Where you been hiding these past few months?" Doc asked smacking David on the shoulder as he released him.

"Working. College. Wooing this fair maiden," David replied gesturing to me and giving his friend a very manly smile of conquest.

I walked up to them, my shoulders visibly dropping now that I was certain no one was about to get hurt, or worse, die. "Hey Doc, what's up?" I asked, my voice actually squeaked and I grimaced.

"Strawberry, good to see ya," Doc said and extended a fist for me to bump with my own. I bumped his fist and smiled up at him.

"Thanks for the extended training lessons. I really appreciate it," I gushed, the nervousness kicking in again making my stomach knot.

Relax woman. Relax. You're with friends. Big muscly, protective friends.

"Small world the Sentinel here being your...um, what exactly is David to you anyway?" Doc said, eyeballing David playfully.

Funny, I'd been wondering the same thing on the way here. It isn't exactly defined yet.

"Umm...well. We're good friends. And...and we're," I glanced at David, hoping he'd fill in the blank.

"I'm whatever she wants or needs me to be, for as long as she'll keep me around," David finished for me, looking deep into my eyes. His eyes seemed to connect to my soul and I shivered. He wasn't upset at my lack of ability to "title" us. He was going with it, wherever I led.

God, I love you.

"Thank you, David," I whispered. "You're amazing," was all I could really think to say at the moment.

"That's even better than boyfriend if you ask me, bud," Doc remarked. "She's smart enough to take her time figuring it out, which means when she finally does, it'll stick. Hopefully it's in your favor," Doc boomed out a laugh. "And considering the fine lady hasn't kicked you out or pushed you away yet, she must be willing to put up with your ugly mug for some reason." Doc elbowed David in the ribs breaking our eye contact.

"I think so too," David said with a masculine chuckle.

"So, did you already know everything I told you yesterday when I called ya, or was that a whistleblower moment on my part, man?" Doc asked David, his voice serious now. He looked at me for confirmation of how awkward he might have made things for me. Doc seemed to understand how hard it had been for me to tell him about my past to begin with. And with how reluctant I'd been to give him permission to discuss it with his mysterious and confidential advisor, the Sentinel, a.k.a. David Abramson, unknown to me, he probably knew he'd already pushed the boundaries of my ability to trust.

"No, no, I didn't. Well, not all of it. The only part that made sense was when you said a young lady you were training was attacked by her father and was afraid he was coming back to get her," David's voice was somber. "In that moment, I knew you were talking about my Melanie."

"How this whole thing slipped past me on the news is another mystery," Doc said more to himself than to us. "I've been so busy I hadn't been watching it much lately."

"If you had, you would have seen us both on the news on different nights trying to avoid their invasive improv interviews," I grumbled. "Those sneaky suckers even showed up at my school!" I complained.

"Kid," Doc said to me softly and I looked up at him, feeling the weight of his look on me, making me squirm. "God works in mysterious ways, Strawberry. And right there is the proof," Doc said pointing to David with his long finger. "Hang onto this man as tight as you can, you hear? He's a good boy. He'll do right by you. 'Cause if he don't, and I mean this now," Doc said giving David a hard squinty glare again, "I'll hunt him down and skin him alive for ya," Doc winked at me, but somehow I didn't think the warning look to David had been a joke.

"I'll do my best," I smiled back up at him and took David's hand in mine. David's fingers intertwined in mine and I blushed. It wasn't our first time holding hands but it felt so intimate in front of Doc.

Thank God, Doc hadn't seen our first time.

My brain was in hyper-loca-mode making small things bigger and big things smaller. A self-defense mechanism, I think.

"Doc must like you a lot to threaten to skin me. I've only heard him make that threat to his daughter's boyfriend," David said cheerfully.

"Dude, your facts are outdated. Jasmine married that punk. Can you believe it?" Doc said sounding gloomy now.

"For real?" David responded, shocked. "I thought she broke up with Tyler."

"So did I. Then I got a call three months ago saying they'd run off to the courthouse and gotten hitched. I just about wet myself." Doc shook his head and placed his hands on his hips reminding me of a huge black Mr. Clean.

"Should I call you Pops again?" David jabbed, with a smirk.

"Pops?" Doc's eye's narrowed.

"Affirmative, Sir. A new son-in-law means you're a new dad! Congrats," David ducked as Doc swung a fast open hand out at his cheek to smack him one.

They both laughed as Doc lunged at him and chased him to the door, grabbing him around the waist, effectively picking him up into the air in a rib crushing squeeze and flung him over his shoulder. David laughed as his air was puffed out of him, then he did a fancy twist flip and launched himself off of Doc using the top of his shoulders to swing himself back down to the floor.

It reminded me of something I'd done when I'd been fighting the giants at the bottom of Mount Moriah. I'd been infused with Holy Spirit power at the time and been wielding the sword of the Lord, so I was doing things only a trained warrior would know how to do. Don't think I could do that here and now unless I got hit with the Holy Spirit again. I just wasn't coordinated enough.

"Come here you squirmy little runt," Doc laughed as he turned around and made another dash for David. It felt like they were showing off for me. Or maybe this is how two grown men act when they forget they're in their thirties and fifties? Like little boys on a playground without supervision and untamed.

I burst out laughing seeing them act so childish. Their friendship sparking the resemblance of Elisabeth and I having food fights or towel smacking wars and roughhousing in the kitchen.

"Oh, hell no!" David laughed, running behind me and pretending to hide like a scared little boy. He placed his hands on my waist to maneuver me in front of him and block himself from Doc with my body. Well, as much as a big strong man David's size can hide behind a five-foot six-inch, one hundred and thirty-five-pound woman.

With a big ass and no chest. I signed internally.

Doc walked up to us looking mischievous. "Come out here boy," Doc chortled. "Come out from there before I come and getcha!"

David tucked himself in closer behind me, hands still on my waist, his face emerging over my right shoulder in my peripheral vision. I felt a shiver go down my neck and all the way down to my, well, my butt cheeks as his breath tickled my ear and neck and the warmth of his body radiated against the back of me.

Then I yelped. An annoying, undignified sound of surprise as Doc snatched me with one strong long arm around the waist and right out from David's gentle grasp. He swung me around, my legs flying out into the air making a wide arch as I clung to him, shocked into a death grip around his neck. Doc was laughing, unaware of how he had shocked me and scared me with the suddenness of his playful act.

"Auh!" I yelped again.

"Eugene!" David's voice was hard and authoritative.

Doc was still laughing as he spun me around and placed me on my feet behind him, successfully removing the body that had blocked him from his target. My eyes were large and my pulse was racing, my mouth still dropped open in a dumbass look of surprise. Doc turned back to David and stopped laughing instantly as he read David's expression. It was far from amused. He was pissed.

"What the hell man?" David burst out, stepping up into Doc's personal space, his eyes on fire. I stepped back and to the side as Doc actually took a step back, his face displaying his own shock now at David's aggression.

"We were just playing kid, calm down," Doc said affronted, his shock being wiped away now that he'd gathered himself. He reclaimed the step he'd retreated bringing him back toe to toe with David. They just looked at each other. Something passing between the two of them I didn't understand. It wasn't like before when they'd pretended to be serious. There hadn't been any real emotion behind it, just games. This instantly felt different and my pulse sped up with uneasiness.

After what felt like forever, though it was probably only a few seconds of standoff silence, I couldn't take it anymore. "What just happened?" I inquired tentatively, coming to stand in line with the two of them but staying a safe four feet away.

"Something I thought I'd never see," Doc answered before David could. David just glared at him harder.

"And what's that?" I asked confused.

"Well, Strawberry...your boy here's a tad green with jealousy," Doc said glancing at me to look disappointed.

"What?" I said, disbelievingly. I glanced at David, his face had darkened and he still wasn't smiling. He didn't even look at me to tell me with his eyes or his expression that Doc was wrong. He just glared at Doc, his face growing harder.

"Ain't that right, boy?" Doc asked, releasing the tension in his body and giving David a very casual "come on and admit it" sort of look.

David lifted his chin and swallowed, then turned away. He walked to the front window peering out at the street, his hands on his hips. He stood there quiet. I watched him in silence as his shoulders rose and feel with breaths that seemed too hard and too deep. I didn't understand how they'd gone from playful to ready to fight for real in a matter of half a second. What was I missing?

I looked at Doc, waiting for him to explain more, but he didn't. He just took in a slow breath and went to lean on the front of the receptionist desk, hands behind him, and crossed his feet as he leaned back. Doc gave me a small silent smile. He was waiting for David too. Maybe he understood something I didn't.

Okay, this isn't exactly how I expected today to go. What the hell was wrong with these two?

I slowly walked up behind David, tired of being in the dark. "Are you okay David?" I asked quietly. I placed my hand on David's back. It was physically hot to the touch. "David?" I asked again, even quieter.

I stepped up to his side and peered up at him. His face was troubled, his eyes haunted, lost. I didn't think he was really seeing anything outside the window.

"David, what is it?" I whispered now, my voice was careful and growing concerned. He looked down at me and the troubled look seemed to shatter, his eyes seeking mine desperately.

"I...I'm not—" David tried, but his words seemed to lose more volume with each try.

"Spit it out!" Doc ordered, sounding more like his old commander than his friend.

David spun around, nearly knocking me over with the side of his arm, completely unaware that I'd stumbled to keep my balance. He was so angry at Doc, focused on him. "It's not what you're thinking," David shot back in a hiss. "I'm not jealous, Eugene!"

"Right, and I'm not black," Doc retorted sarcastically.

"Why is it you think you can speak for me?" David growled, his hands balling into fists. He was making me nervous.

"Well, you ain't sayin' much. Why not narrate for you?" Doc shrugged contemptuously.

David took a step forward. I wasn't liking the tension building back up. I matched his step and took his hand in mine. David stopped in his tracks, my touch bringing him back to me for a moment. He looked down at my hand on his and back up at me, his face burdened with a weight I'd never seen on him. My heart broke for him and I drew myself up to him, holding his hand to my chest with both of mine.

"David, please talk to me," I begged him. I shot Doc a look of warning all of my own.

David took in a big breath and let it out slowly. "I'd rather talk to you about this alone," he said quietly to me.

"Like hell you will," Doc cut in furiously. David pulled his hand away from mine and took another large purposeful step toward Doc. Doc's apparent attempt to reclaim his old domination as David's commander was not settling well on David in his present state of mind.

"David, don't! Please," I begged him, afraid of what he might do.

"Look kid, you've never treated me with this kind of disrespect before in all the years I've known you. There's no way in Hell I'm letting you walk out that door without explaining yourself to me. Why, huh? You're either the ugliest shade of jealous-green I've ever seen in my life or you're, you're...Oh. Oh shit. I'm—" Doc switched gears midstream. He waved his hands in the air as if to rub away the last several minutes and drew in a big cleansing breath.

"You're what?" David poked senselessly.

"I'm an idiot. Damn, I'm a fool," Doc hung his head and a hand went up and wiped his mouth as if to reset the words he'd been about to shout at David. Doc dropped his hand and looked up at David, pressing his lips together tightly, looking bothered. He seemed to be choosing his words carefully before he spoke again and was glancing between the two of us as if he was strategizing his next approach.

"Talk kid. Now. You know the drill. You need to expose the wires that lead to the detonator before you start cutting or you risk triggering a full-blown explosion. Let it go. Let it out. Talk to me kid," Doc's tone had completely changed. He was sympathetic but firm, a fatherly tone replacing his angry one.

Much to my relief, David seemed to deflate a fraction. I saw a little bit more of his self-awareness return to his eyes. It started to click in my head. David had just been telling me on the way here how war had affected him. Perhaps this little bout of fun we'd just had paralleled something else from his memories overseas and had sparked a small relapse into the post-traumatic stress disorder he'd warned me about.

"David?" Doc asked gentler now.

"I don't want to go there, man. Not today. Today isn't supposed to be about me," David said, his voice sounding weaker than I'd ever heard it. It hurt me to hear him like that, struggling for strength, for self-control.

"But you are *with her*," Doc said pointing at me. "This is as much about her as it is about you," Doc repeated and walked up to David and me, his steps slow but purposeful.

"It's...it's not something I've wanted to talk about yet," David countered, looking down, then back up, continuing to resist.

"Then it's time," Doc suggested.

"No. No, I can't," David swallowed hard. His eyes betraying the true depth of his pain fighting to get out.

"It's your duty," Doc said, a mere three feet away now, his hands at his sides unthreateningly. "It's your duty to the people you love to exorcise every last piece of evil from the desert that entered your mind. Don't give the horrors their dark corners to hide in son! You've come too far. You've told me almost everything else.

Why would this be any different? Why try to hold onto this one alone. What don't I know?" Doc pressed. "Is it about —"

"I *can't*," David repeated, shaking his head, his face struggling to stay cold and stubborn.

"Hold it in today, and risk losing control tomorrow. You know I'm right, David. Talk to me, son," Doc moved a step closer. David stiffened. Doc took that last step, toe to toe once more, but this time not in anger, a standoff of wills. One dead set on helping the other, one resistant to the help.

"You didn't even notice that you almost knocked this sweet little lady over when you came at me just now," Doc continued boldly. "What happens the next time this trigger sets you off? You strike her thinking she's someone else? You don't want Strawberry here to get creamed now do ya?" Doc challenged.

"Melanie?" David asked, looking at me with wide panicked eyes. "Melanie, I'm sorry, I didn't mean to—" David's voice broke and he reached for me, then drew back his hands, looking at them like they were something dirty.

"I'm fine. Really," I lied quickly resisting the urge to rub my arm. My shoulder and upper arm were actually throbbing. I was going to have a big bruise; I just knew it.

"Talk," Doc ordered David again, bringing David's attention back to him.

David's eyes finally lost the battle, and they dropped down to somewhere around Doc's chest, unable to look his old friend and commander in the eyes. A single tear ran down his face and passed over his beautiful dimple, making my heart hurt for him. I wanted to wrap my arms around him and make him better. But he was scaring me. I'd never seen him like this before. I didn't know what to do.

"I can't," David said defeatedly.

"You *will*," Doc demanded again, grabbing David by the shoulders and giving him a little shake. David looked up, there was no anger in his face at being man handled, only agony. "You will!" Doc repeated again with more force.

In that moment, I got it. Doc was David's "Elisabeth". As she looked out for me, almost maternally, using tough love when she needed to or patient reassurance in moments where a stronger voice wouldn't have worked. Doc felt the same of David. He loved him like a son. I could see it now. They were probably best friends, but Doc loved him. Enough to piss him off and push him hard for his own good.

Just like Elisabeth has done to me lately.

"We're supposed to be training Melanie today. Come on, let it go, please. I'm not ready to talk about this," David implored.

"When are we ever ready, son? This is still a kind of training for Melanie. It's my understanding that she's just begun to talk about her past and is learning to trust. Why don't you show her how it's done and give her something back of yourself to hold in confidence for you? Isn't that what friendship and building a loving relationship is all about?" Doc said wisely.

Oh yes, he was definitely reminding me of Liz now.

"But—" David tried again.

"No buts!" Doc insisted.

"But it's about...about *her*," David whispered, a tear breaking free and betraying his resolve.

"Melanie's right here. She's okay, David. Her father didn't get to—" Doc was saying calmly but his attempt at smoothing over David's last apparent argument was interrupted abruptly by David.

"No, not her," David glanced in my direction, not meeting my eyes this time. "*Her*," he said meaningfully. I was lost. Her who, if not me?

"Double damn," Doc said taken aback. "For reals?"

David nodded. Their eyes met and a history passed between them I didn't understand. I glanced from one to the other, waiting.

Who the hell are you two talking about! I screamed inside my head. What I said very softly out loud instead was, "Her? Um, her who?"

David drew in a breath and finally made eye contact with me looking like a kid caught by the teacher passing a note to another girl across the room. That was probably just my mind's worst-case scenario trying to kick in, but who was this "her" damn it!

"Danielle," David's voice was rough with emotion. "Her name was Danielle," He said looking truly sorry. "She...she was my wife. And...and she," David broke, a sob tore out of him, bowing him forward before he had time to catch himself. He straightened up, ever the soldier trying to fight the pain, fight the overwhelming battle of emotions that marched over his heart, trying to smash his spirit.

"Wi-wife?" I croaked out, stunned.

"Slow your roll, kids," Doc encouraged, placing a hand on each of our shoulders.

"You need to start at the beginning, son," Doc said to David, gripping him a little harder so he'd look at him.

David broke eye contact with me to look up at Doc. I was sure he'd seen the confusion and betrayal in my eyes. I couldn't help it. I just couldn't believe it!

He'd been married! When? How did I not know this!

"You can do this. It's time, kid," Doc said again.

David nodded, surrendering. "Roger that."

"Where you wanta talk, kid? Here or in the back?" Doc asked, nodding to David in acknowledgment of their rebuilt understanding. David just stood there, unable to respond, risking a look at me again and seeing the growing betrayal and anger building in my eyes. He glanced back at Doc and tried to mouth a word, but nothing came out.

"I know. Your old room," Doc offered helpfully, his voice gentle now.

David's face melted into a look of complete helplessness. I knew what the room had been to him before. His safe haven. A place to go to escape the confusion of civilian life and to hide from a family that didn't know how to help him. But Doc had helped him. Doc had been his anchor in the storm and his guide back through troubled waters.

"Yeah. My old room will work fine," David said softly. David bravely took my hand in his and squeezed it. I pulled away, unable to be touched right now. I didn't understand. David looked at me, hurt flooding into him at my rejection. I saw a new level of panic and concern hit him and his delicate self-control struggle to keep him together.

"Take his hand. Don't let him go through this alone. Let him explain. It isn't what you think," I heard the voice of the Lord speak into my heart.

But he was married! I screamed bitterly to the Lord in my mind. I felt so betrayed. Lied to!

I know I'm innocent and inexperienced compared to him, but not that inexperienced! What was I thinking? How could I really expect a thirty-two-year-old man to be a virgin?

Melanie, you've been so naive! I yelled at myself in my mind. I was such a fool!

"Melanie, let him explain," The Lord said firmly again into my heart. *"Know him."*

I looked into David's face and I saw his worse fears becoming realized. A rush of his feelings seemed to penetrate me and I gasped. God was giving me a soul to soul intimate discernment into his heart and I saw it so clearly. He had been so afraid of always being alone. Never being understood or finding someone who would love and accept him entirely after what he'd done and had been forced to become. How could anyone ever accept him? His past included. Finding love again with me had been unexpected, a miracle in his eyes, even an answered prayer. He was afraid to lose me. Afraid I'd be taken from him or leave him. I felt his heart breaking, the anguish ripping into him, tearing his heart to pieces.

My mind flashed back to when I'd been in the hospital after my father's attack. Elisabeth had caught David sneaking into my room to be with me. I had pretended to be asleep and had heard their entire conversation. She had asked him if he had ever been in love before and he'd said yes. I had thought she knew I was really awake. Had she already looked into him and known? Was that her way of giving me a head's up but not intruding into the beginning of the delicate relationship we'd been building? I felt my heart soften toward David and took a step toward him.

He hadn't been lying to me. He simply hadn't known how or when it would be the right time to tell me. I knew what that was like. I'd been caught off guard and forced to divulge my secrets to him so much sooner than I'd intended to. I hadn't felt ready either and had expected him to run away from me too.

A word of knowledge hit me, and I suddenly just knew.

"Danielle? Danielle, is she...is she dead?" I whispered, taking his hands in mine now, and searching his eyes. David's chin trembled as the relief that I'd taken his hands again washed over him just as the horrible truth he was about to say out loud collided like a ten ton truck within his body.

"Yes," his voice wobbled. "Danielle...Danielle is dead. She died on...on my last mission. In Afghanistan. She was...was killed," David croaked out. "It was me. I...I was the one who killed her," He amended in a rattling whisper, his struggle to control himself finally abandoned and he began to sob, his wide shoulders convulsing and his knees threatened to buckle. Doc rushed to steady him and I dropped his hands.

Doc wrapped him up in a fierce bear hug, the larger man unashamed of comforting his friend, despite their very masculine careers and tough-guy training. He smacked his back affectionately, his own face displaying the pain he felt for his friend.

"You'll be alright, son. You're going to be alright," Doc said confidently, his strong voice carrying the complexity of their relationship; part commander, part father, part friend. "We've got ya." He held David tightly as he wept.

My heart was pounding in my chest. My mind threatening to go numb. I had to keep it together. I had to see this through so I could understand what the hell just happened. Yet as hard as I tried to remain strong, I felt myself slipping. Slipping into doubt, fear and distrust. It had taken me years to let my guard down with David and now this? Why now?

Hold on Melanie. You haven't heard him out yet. Maybe it isn't what you think. Isn't that what the Lord just told you?

But David had been married! He killed his wife? Had it been an accident or on purpose? Have I been blinded by what he wanted me to see in him? Is he nothing but a liar? I just found out he's a killer. That's different than being a soldier. Am I dating a monster like my father?

It's not too late to see the truth! I don't have to stay destined for heartbreak or worse... end up dead like my mother.

No. No. That can't be true. It just can't be!

The darkness of these powerful spiraling thoughts stole my breath away. My body went rigid with the fear that these thoughts were answers to truths yet spoken. Warnings of my instincts to run.

Run? Run away when I haven't even heard him out yet?

Was I going to lose the only man I'd ever thought of as truly good and worth risking my heart to? The only man I ever felt this way about?

"Come on. Let's talk in back. Melanie, you comin'?" Doc asked me, his eyes boring into mine knowingly.

I nodded. I didn't trust my voice to answer him but I knew my stunned face was betraying me. I was relieved David didn't look up at my silent response.

"Good," Doc confirmed, giving me a look of encouragement.

Doc gripped David's shoulder and turned him toward the hallway before he could glance my way. I think Doc was trying to give me a minute to collect myself. I felt weak and shaky. I was probably a grotesque pale white and blotchy red all over.

Just like smashed strawberries and cream. Or like my heart.

Yup. That's what my heart felt like. Smashed.

Hope Box

Chapter Six

 followed David down the hallway at a safe distance. My thoughts were still racing, replaying what little facts I had.

He had been married.

He had killed his wife.

He was a good man, wasn't he? My heart told me he was good. Elisabeth even thought so.

So how could this be true? How? There has to be an explanation to all this!

I also needed to understand why he had a PTSD level reaction to his friend simply playing around with me a moment ago. How had it been triggered? It seemed like such an exaggerated reaction. Illogical and unbalanced. The complete *opposite* of David. Why now? What was causing this? What was really going on here? Was PTSD so powerful if could change a good man in such a way at the smallest provocation? Was PTSD why he killed his wife? Would that mean he could hurt me too? I rubbed my sore arm absentmindedly.

I watched Doc and David as they walked down the hall. David in a daze, almost robotic. He stopped mechanically at the closed metal door, his trembling hand reaching out for the handle and took hold but he didn't turn it. He just stood there, his head hanging down and his shoulders curved in. I'd never seen him so defeated. He looked utterly broken. My heart squeezed at the sight of him and I momentarily forgot my own distrust, doubts and fears of who he was. I felt like I was looking into his past; seeing him after he'd returned home from the war, a broken man. A man lost and drowning.

David had never displayed any signs of PTSD. Well, not around me anyway. I knew he must have gone through something extreme having been a soldier in the War Against Terror for six years. The day we talked at the court house, I'd seen the pain and torment lingering within his eyes as he talked to me about his fellow soldiers. Their struggles here at home to get the proper treatment they deserved weighed heavily on his heart. He'd explained that was why he wanted to be a psychologist, to help out his fellow soldiers. But I hadn't known he had also been talking about *himself*. For some reason, that realization hadn't really sunk in. I knew he had suffered somehow, but I didn't think it was this strong. Even on the ride over as he casually talked about some of his experiences, I still hadn't really understood the significance of what he was trying to tell me.

Was I naive to think he was somehow too magnificent and too strong to be affected this way? Had I made him out to be Superman in my mind? After all, he had always done the right thing by me. He'd always been gentle, polite, romantically insistent but not creepy or perverted. He hadn't even given in when I hadn't been myself and tried to seduce him in the walk-in cooler at work.

He literally was my hero! He had come to my rescue when my father had tried to rape me, risking his life to defend me. He'd stayed with me, covered my body back up, tended to my wounds, and held me, comforting me afterwards until the ambulance arrived. He even gave me space but made sure I knew he was there for me if I needed him when I had continually brushed him off and relentlessly ignored him out of humiliation for weeks on end afterwards. Now, he was helping me investigate my father and his crimes to further protect me. He was immersing himself into my life, as crazy and dangerous as it was, because he cared about me. Because he wanted to protect me. Because he loved me. Was losing the idea of having found a "perfect man" the real reason I was freaking out inside? Or was it simply too much, too soon?

I felt the necklace around my neck suddenly grow warm and tingly, and I reached up to touch it. Little sparks danced on my fingertips as the necklace grew hotter. I felt tears prickle my eyes and I swallowed. I wasn't being fair to David. I had to give him a chance to explain. To redeem himself.

Hadn't I also given him too much, too soon too? My past and my present were twisted and full of darkness. Despite all of my issues, he still right here, by my side. Shouldn't I hear him out at the very least before I considered bailing out on him? Didn't I owe him that much? Didn't he deserve at least that much grace and mercy?

"David," I said his name carefully, not wanting to spook him, but at the same time, I needed him to reconnect with me. "David, baby," I whispered again, approaching him slowly. I'd never called him that before. It slipped from my mouth naturally, and I didn't try to stop it. I needed him to trust me, to know how much he meant to me even if inside I was struggling. I needed him to tell me what was happening in that beautiful mind of his.

David looked up at me, his eyes still wet and red. His head dropped further, as he struggled to maintain eye contact with me. Shame, fear, and pain blinding him from recognizing his true allies. I took that last step so that I was in front of him and I reached up to take his face in my hands. I lifted myself on my tip-toes to touch my forehead to his. If his head hadn't been hanging so low I never would have been able to reach it. He closed his eyes, tears silently trailing down his face.

"David, you are the bravest man I've ever known," I began, then pulled my face from his to watch his face, seeking eye contact. "I know this is hard, but you can do this. It seems as if you've carried this all alone since you came back home. Is that right? Just you and the Lord?" I asked gently.

"Ye-yes," David breathed. "Too hard to talk about."

"It's time now baby. Don't get me wrong, God is the best source of strength and healing there is. But he also gave us others to share our burdens with. I know I'm one to talk, but I've finally started to accept that simple truth as fact. We can't carry everything all by ourselves, David. We just aren't strong enough. Let us help you. Let us be your support. Let us carry some of this for you so it doesn't feel so heavy," I whispered the last, using the gentleness of my words to draw his eyes back to me.

When he finally looked at me, I wrapped my arms around him, squeezing his torso firmly with my arms, trying to pour all of my care and sincerity into him, hiding my own fears and doubts down deep so he wouldn't feel discouraged by them. I rested my head on his chest and just clung to him. He released the door handle and returned the hug, his heart breaking my heart, his pain clinging to my own pain. We stood there for a few minutes, two broken souls pouring into one another. Sharing untold tragedies and losses, our souls intertwining like two vines seeking substance and strength from the other.

"Yeah, man. Strawberry's got it right. We're here for you. You don't have to be brave all by yourself no more," Doc added, patting David on the shoulder hard enough to shift our position a little bit. "We care too much about you to let you stay where you're at right now. Darkness ain't a good place to dwell. Let us be your guiding light through this one."

David slowly straightened up as he released me and made an effort of squaring his shoulders. He peered down at me, his face still full of hurt, but the flicker of determination starting to catch fire within him once again.

"You're right. You're both right," David said quietly and he turned and opened the door.

He silently led us in. Doc was the last, giving David and I space to enter well into the room before he closed the door behind us. David took several steps deeper into the room than me and stopped, his breathing picking up slightly and he tucked his hands into his front pockets to keep them from shaking. I hesitated. Unsure as to how much space we should give him before we pressed him again to talk this out. I decided to give him a minute to reacquaint himself to the room and gather himself for what was about to happen. I stepped back for a moment to allow him time to find his peace again in the safety of this room.

I slowly and casually paced the floor, looking around curiously. There were no windows. It was secure from all sides, save the entrance we'd just come through. The room was long and spacious with small neat furnishings arranged to give the illusion that there was more breathing room than what there was. The cream-colored walls made it warm and not too bright despite the overhead florescent lights shining boldly.

There was a card table in the front left corner with four chairs pushed in around it. A fluffy brown leather loveseat was angled away from the entrance and toward the back half of the room as if someone might stay sitting there overnight keeping watch over the men who sleep restlessly within these walls. I walked up to the couch and ran my hand over the back. The leather was soft and gently worn. A slight sagging in the right-side cushion and armrest told me someone large and heavy had indeed spent a great deal of time right there, keeping watch.

Two sturdy oak bunkbeds stood in each rear corner with crisp white pillows on top of tightly tucked forest-green wool military blankets. The couch was angled toward them. The floor was concrete except for a large oval rug that lay between the bunkbeds. It was splattered with neutral tones of various greens and tans. It took me a second to realize it was mimicking the colors usually found on military uniforms. A nice touch of "home" to a soldier. Something to help put them at ease.

There were four tall black lockers on the right-hand wall next to the entryway with a filtered water dispenser on the left. A long iron bench stretched out in front of them with a built-in rack underneath for shoes or boots. It presently held a pair of worn out black combat boots. The sides dusty and scraped. I wondered whose they were? Or why Doc had left them there. They were too small to be his. But looked about David's size. A current tenant perhaps?

I continued to survey the room. I counted six posters on the walls, each with an inspirational phrase or word of encouragement beneath a peaceful calming or majestically uplifting picture. A bible was on the card table next to a stack of playing cards. The shelves along the far wall between the two sets of bunk beds held board games, puzzles, weights, a stack of paper, pencils and pens in a cup, clean T-shirts and pants, men's boxers, tightly rolled socks, a radio, along with extra blankets and pillows.

The room wasn't musky like one might think it should be having been closed up. I looked up to find two large square air vents overhead. Plenty of circulation of air into a room this size to keep it's guest from getting too claustrophobic. It was slightly cool in here too but didn't feel chilly. It was fresh and smelled of metal and clean linens. The room was cozy and clean. I could only imagine how familiar and comforting it would feel to soldiers struggling to adjust to civilian life again or for those fighting the demons that came back with them from war.

David walked into the middle of the room toward me, spinning slowly, taking it all in again. He seemed to be feeling it as much as seeing it. Taking strength from the familiar surroundings. He closed his eyes and breathed in slowly, his shoulders lifting then dropping, releasing his tension and some of his anxiety.

He opened his eyes and turned to speak to Doc who had been waiting against the closed door, still giving us both space.

"You feel okay stepping back in the Hope Box, soldier?" Doc asked him kindly.

Hope box? Interesting name for it.

"Yes, sir. I feel safe here," David admitted.

"It will always be yours when you need it," Doc reminded him.

"I know. You're a good friend to me Eugene. The best," David's hoarse voice held gratitude.

"Can't help myself. I like you too damn much boy. For some strange reason, I just do," Doc said jestingly.

I wandered away to wait silently along the side wall to give David space and start talking on his own. Doc was encouraging him enough now. I didn't want to add too much pressure by continuing to push him. I didn't want to learn the truth about his wife that way. Forcing him or making him more uncomfortable talking about it wouldn't help either of us to get through this.

Not that I had been given a choice when he found out about me.

Melanie this is different. Don't focus on that now, it doesn't change anything.

Besides, I didn't want him to resent me later. I already knew how easy it was to fall into that mindset once certain truths about you came out before you felt you were ready to share them.

Like what has happened to me my whole life. I grumbled to myself internally.

Geez, Melanie. Come on. This is about him *not you. Knock it off with the victim mentality.* I scolded myself, disappointed with my own internal attitude.

My mind was trying to back track on me. I'd have to work on snapping it back and away from focusing on the unfairness of it all and not let the negative thoughts take root. They would be nothing but destructive and I knew they were just a distraction from what was really important in this very moment. David.

Oh, Lord. Help us to help David through this. Please God. Give him strength to keep going and let this out. I don't want him suffering alone...or at all. Please, give him grace Lord.

"I've given this memory...this secret, too much room in my life," David started up on his own. I guess giving him a little space had been the right call.

He ran his strong fingers through his beautiful jet black curly hair and sighed. He looked around, finding me against the far wall, keeping a respectful distance away. "I've kept it pushed down," he said to me. "Hidden. Tucked away into the darkest corner of my soul, wishing it would just fade away and that one day, I'd simply notice it was gone, having forgotten all about it," David drew in a big breath and looked up at the ceiling. A tear slid down his face and I fought my longing to run to him and hold him once again. I didn't want to distract him from finally letting this out. I didn't want to be a distraction from the breakthrough he could have.

Or keep him from telling me what really happened so I'll know without a shadow of a doubt that I am with a good man and not with a hidden monster like my father.

"Oh Lord," David cried up to God suddenly, startling me from my thoughts with the urgency and volume of his prayer. "I *know* you set me free from strongholds of violence and the terrors of war. I *know* your presence was with me in battle and that you never, *never* left my side! You gave me discernment! You anointed me to lead my men and rescue the lost amongst us!" David shouted it to the ceiling, placing his hand over his heart, his other in a tight fist at his side, beating against his thigh rhythmically.

"Lord, I *believe* you healed my heart *and* my mind from all the destruction and evil I saw, said, or did, in the name of war and in the name of my country. Take the rest of this darkness and agony far from me, oh my God. Take the weight of my sins, the weight of my actions, this overwhelming guilt, and cast them far from me lest they crush me, Lord Jesus, my Savior," David was speaking now with passion and boldness up to the Heavens. He lifted his hands up to the ceiling, beseeching God. Demanding an audience with the Creator. Demanding his true Commander-in-Chief to hear him.

"You did not leave me to die nor did you leave me to waste away in my sorrows and my pain. You lifted me up and carried me! You surrounded me with your presence and covered me with your wings. Oh Lord, my Rock and my fortress! You have been my ever-present help in a time of trouble! Do not depart from me now. Please...please, oh God. Help me once again! Take this burden from me. I give it all, all to you. I surrender my will to you. I give you my everything. Once again, I give you my life. I am yours," David had dropped to his knee, his hand once again over his heart, the other still in a fist, knuckles locked to the ground holding himself up. His head was bowed and his eyes were closed. Tears streamed from his eyes as he surrendered all that he had left of himself to God.

I couldn't help it anymore. I had to go to him. I hurried to him, dropping to my knees in front of him, placing my hands on his head, soothing him. I hadn't even known that I'd started crying silently too, but I was. I was feeling his every word of his prayer strike me in my heart as if they had been my own. His prayer so close to my own heart's cry, that I knew the words more intimately than I knew him.

David didn't raise his head as I gently petted him, he just kept praying, quieter now, and in another language. I thought perhaps he was praying in Spanish at first, until I realized I didn't know what any of the words were and I should have known a few since I'd taken two years of Spanish in high school.

Is he speaking in a heavenly language like Michael the Archangel had told me about? I wondered to myself.

Just the other day when I had slipped in between space-time with the Archangel Michael, he had explained to me how some people are given a gift from the Holy Spirit that expresses itself as speaking in the tongues of men or of angels. He said it was another way to pray for things that we can't find words for or know how to express. Essentially letting your spirit talk to God's spirit without your human words or thoughts getting in the way. It seemed to me that David was doing that right now. Pouring his heart out to God with all that he was, his spirit saying what he couldn't with his human mind or human words.

But I understood now that it was a *gift*, like having the gift of discernment, a gift of music, or even a gift to acquire wealth. Not everyone has it or gets it. But Michael also said, the greatest gift of all was love, so not to feel left out if you can't speak in a heavenly language. It didn't mean you were less than someone else. But it was a gift you could ask God for, and God answers those who diligently seek him.

After a few minutes of concentrated prayer, a peace settled over David. He physically changed as his breathing became softer and slower, his body relaxing. He was no longer tense or weeping. His eyes were still closed as he slowly rose to his feet, straightening up to his full height, standing firm.

I had released him as he had began to rise, stepping back to give him room once more, unsure as to what he was doing or if he intended to move, walk or even talk. David opened his eyes and looked at me, his face softened and his eyes sympathetic. Why was he looking at *me* that way? This was about him not me.

"Melanie, I'm so sorry that I've put you through this today," David said remorsefully, his eyes boring into mine.

"You haven't put me through anything today, David," I said, thinking I was telling the truth but then realizing he was right. Only moments ago, my thoughts had been full of fear, doubt, hurt and distrust.

"But I startled you. I think I even scared you. I knocked into you and didn't even notice and I broke down in front of you," David glanced down, ashamed. "I wanted you to know you could trust me and count on me, not lose it out of the blue like this. I thought I was past these kinds of moments. I never wanted to be the one to frighten you."

"You have nothing to be sorry for, do you hear me?" I said sincerely. "Yes, you startled me. And yes, you scared me, but *not* because I'm afraid of you, David Jonathan Abramson. It's because I finally saw the depth of the pain you still hold inside of you and I'm concerned for you. I care about you. I care... deeply. I was scared of what you've been going through all this time, alone. I was scared that you were resisting our help. I was scared what that would mean for you and for *us* if you shut me out," my voice broke and I realized my eyes were tearing up again.

Damnit! Don't cry you sissy! Be strong for him. He needs you to be strong right now!

"I would never shut you out. Never," David reassured me. "But I don't want to cause you more pain or harm either—ever. That is one thing I won't allow myself," David turned to Doc. "If I talk to you both about this, it will harm her. Not physically, but it will break her heart. I don't know if I could bear that," David turned away from us both and started to pace the room.

"Now you listen to me," Doc said sternly. "We just went over this boy. And you just prayed it out. Are you telling me kid that you would intentionally step back into the shadows with this secret tearing away at you after you just stepped out and got your first breath of fresh air from it in three years? Is that what you got out of that prayer?" Doc's voice was growing impatient.

"No, that's not what I'm saying—"

"Well what the hell are you saying then?" Doc spoke over him, his huge hands on his hips and his muscles bulging in agitation.

"Melanie," David turned his back on Doc and looked at me, "I'm just saying that it isn't in my heart to ever hurt you. And what I need to share *will* hurt you—immensely. I *know* it. I can feel it already. I know I already *have* hurt you just with the little I've said. I told you before, I won't ever let anyone hurt you and I'll always protect you. Even if it means protecting you from me," David turned to look back at Doc then back to me again looking pained but resigned. "Even from me," He repeated.

"Are you...are you breaking up with me?" I asked, my own face showing pain and disbelief. I felt my eyes enlarge at the thought. I hadn't considered that.

After all this? After finally trusting someone with my heart, he's breaking up with me? Is that what he's saying! What had I done? Why?

"No, no!" David rushed to me, taking my hands and holding them against his heart. "I'm giving you a choice."

"What kind of choice?" I warbled, my chest squeezing, and my breath catching.

"A choice to choose *when* you're told," David answered carefully, swallowing hard and pressing his lips together.

"When?" I asked.

"We can stay in this room and you can hear the truth," David replied, his voice strained. "And I mean *all* of it. Every detail, knowing full well that it *will* cause you more pain. You may not be able to look at me the same way once you know. You may even want to take a break from me for a while to sort it out. I'd understand if you did. Or…Or I will come back and talk to Doc about this later. Alone." He glanced at Doc who now was pacing around the two of us slowly like a stalking animal.

"Just him and me," David continued. "You won't have to hear about Danielle. You won't have to know the details. Not until you're ready to know. Even if that means waiting until after your father has been apprehended and brought to justice. Or, waiting until the threat against you with that gang has been neutralized. You get to choose *when* to add to your burden by *choosing* when you hear about mine. Then I promise, when you tell me you're ready, I *will* tell you everything. Whenever you want. I'm giving you a choice to reset the day. We can continue with your training, as we intended. We can set my issues aside and focus on *you*. After all, that's why we're here. To teach you how to protect yourself. To look after *your* safety. You're the priority here, Melanie. You will always be my first priority," David whispered the last, his heart pounding under my hands.

I took my hands back and grabbed his face, bringing his lips down to mine. I kissed him hard and long. When I released him, he was slightly breathless and searching my eyes, trying to figure out what I'd been trying to tell him with my kiss. I saw Doc in my peripheral with a little smile on his face. I'd forgotten we weren't alone.

Oops. That's not embarrassing at all or anything.

"Thank you for the offer," I said to David and pretended like it didn't matter that Doc had just watched me kiss-attack my boyfriend.

Ooh, my boyfriend. I like the sound of that.

"Thank you for putting me first and looking after me. Thank you for always doing what you think is best for *me*, David. But I need to look out for *you* right now. I'm not going to let you go through this alone for one more second. You need to talk about this, and I want to be there for you like you have been for me," I reassured him.

"Just knowing you care about me this much is more support and encouragement than I can even tell you Melanie," David said softly.

"It's more than that too," I admitted. "Whatever it is you have to say, we'd need to talk about it at some point anyway. From where I stand, I'd rather know now than always wonder the who, how or why. I'd rather know about...about who else had captured your heart, so that I won't have the constant struggle inside of wondering what she was like or what went wrong and if I'm making the same mistakes she did. I don't want to wonder if I'm somehow less—"

"You're nothing like her, Melanie. *Nothing*," David said firmly. "You have nothing to worry about. You are even more beautiful than she was, not only on the inside but the outside. Since I'm being honest," David glanced at Doc apologetically. I didn't understand that look, but David continued, and I let it go. "You have a pure heart and are genuinely kind to others, even those who don't deserve your compassion. Once I tell you about her, you will understand just how different the two of you are. But the facts will still be the facts, no matter when you learn them. Please, don't be so eager to hear this out of a misguided sense of insecurity or concern for me. I have never loved another woman the way I love you. You are...you are what I've waited my whole life for. It's like you were created from a blueprint designed just for me. You are already a part of me. I feel whole when I'm with you," David whispered.

"Then let me in. Share this part of yourself with me. I can take it. I can take more than you think," I whispered back.

"I think she understands what she's asking and what it will mean when she hears it, boy," Doc interjected. "I called this room the Hope Box for a reason."

"He's right. I do understand," I added. "It's your time to let us help you."

David nodded, accepting my answer, believing me. He walked to the end of the room and sat down on the bottom right bunkbed, his feet spread apart and his elbows resting on his knees. Doc and I ambled over to join him. I took the bottom bunk on the left, sitting on the edge of the mattress facing him. Doc sat in the worn leather loveseat just as I knew he would. He assumed the position of guard, advocate and trusted advisor. His face was serious, his eyes only seeing David.

"Start at the beginning boy. You know the drill. Best to squeeze the wound until it bleeds to get all the infection out until fresh blood seeps out. Clean the wound thoroughly, otherwise, you risk another infection settling in. Take us through it, one step at a time. You can do this," Doc counseled.

"I remember," David answered in agreement, nodding and pressing his lips together.

"If you find yourself hesitating, trying to decide if you should say something or not, that just means that you *should* say it. It's your mind's way of cluing you in on where the biggest triggers are and what has the deepest hooks in you. Don't hold back or you'll only do yourself a disservice," Doc further reminded him gently.

"Yes sir," David affirmed, then glanced at me. "But...parts of this intersect with the classified mission I was on at the time of her death. There will be parts I cannot fully get into," David added looking at me directly instead of Doc now. "It will seem like I'm being purposefully vague or avoiding certain truths, but it isn't because I want to keep it from you deliberately. It won't be because I *want* to avoid it, Melanie. It will be because duty requires me to be vague in those instances. Even if you weren't in this room right now, I'd still have to avoid certain details because Doc wasn't a part of that particular mission. Do you understand?" David asked me carefully, his eyes deadly serious, a slight frown on his face.

"I think so," I answered honestly. "You'll have to skip over details that might give away secret military mission details or compromise your oath, right?"

"Precisely. I know it doesn't seem fair to you. You've been so open with me and told me everything that's come up so far without holding back, even at your own humiliation," David said softly looking disappointed in himself. "And here I am telling you up front that I can't—no, that I *won't* tell you everything. It isn't fair. I want you to know, I *know* it isn't fair. And I'm sorry. Truly, I am."

"I suppose I can understand that. It's like, um," I glanced over at Doc then back at David. "It's like my other friends that you met. They can't talk to me about certain things they have had to do either," I said not as cryptically as I had hoped. It sounded better in my head.

Darn it! I bet Doc will figure that one out. It isn't like I speak Latin.

"I will do my best to tell you everything else I can. I swear. Even if...even if it's hard," David's voice choked up a bit and he cleared his throat. He rubbed his hands back and forth along his thighs. I think it was a self-comforting yet anxious gesture all mixed up into one.

"I trust you. Just share what you can," I said reassuringly.

Don't worry David. I've been on a few of my own secret missions you don't even have a clue about yet either. So, in that way, I guess we're even. Sort of.

Memories rushed through my head of being stuck between the folds of space-time on the haunted streets of Turin and began to flip like a picture book through my thoughts. Climbing over teetering piles of antiques and artifacts. Discovering the hidden door behind the elaborate hanging tapestries. Finding the mysterious celestial book conspicuously buried in a pile of dusty books and scrolls beneath the window in the lost room. The images sped forward, placing me in the dry, sun piercing wilderness of Israel's predestined lands. Demon's clambering up the hillside trying to snatch me from the arms of the Archangel Michael. Barbaric giants trying to kill me. Angels and demons engaged in a fierce battle at the base of Mount Moriah. Picking up my sword and defending myself.

"Where did you go just now?" David asked me tentatively. "You seemed a thousand miles away."

If he only knew.

"Just reminding myself what a good man you are and how hard this must be for you. I'm ready to hear whatever you can tell me." I forced a smile and briefly gripped his hands still rubbing back and forth on his thighs.

David smiled a small smile of appreciation at me for my understanding.

"Doc, can we all get a glass of water before I start. I know I'm going to need it. I think it might even help Melanie to swallow what I have to tell her," David mentioned, his tone significant and his eyes locked on Doc's.

"Sure thing kid," Doc got up and walked over to the water dispenser by the lockers and started filling up three wax cups.

David got up and knelt before me, taking my hands and holding them to his lips.

"Thank you for doing this for me," He half whispered against my knuckles. "Whatever I share, please know, it is in the past. A part of my history. Something that, in it's own way, changed me, in both positive and negative ways. It's the negative aspects that I struggle with. Please...don't...don't give up on me as you listen. Try to stay present and really listen to all of it before you let it sink in

140

too deep and shut down your ability to *hear* me," David finished, his face earnest.

"I promise to do my best," I whispered back and leaned over to kiss his cheek softly.

Despite nearly shutting down in the lobby at the first utterance of killing his wife, I thought I was doing remarkably well. I was still here wasn't I? I wasn't sure what was going to be so bad about what he had to share. I know listening to him recount his life with his wife wasn't exactly going to be enjoyable for me. I hadn't ever thought about him being married to anyone but maybe myself someday if I was being truly honest. I wanted to know everything about Danielle as much as I *didn't* want to know anything at all. Especially the "he killed his wife" part. That was sure to be a doozie. But if we were ever going to have a chance, I needed to keep it together and hear him out. Had he meant like in an accident or something? The difference between premeditated murder and manslaughter was huge. Whichever it was, I could handle it though. Right?

David's worry and apprehension about my possible reaction was starting to make me even more nervous about hearing him out. What could possibly be so bad if it was done during a time of war and was necessary?

Gosh Melanie. Can killing ever really be necessary?

Then I remembered the giants ready to kill me, Eliezer and Jehu, so that they could get to Abraham and Isaac. It was either them or us. I chose us. And I had killed them.

I guess killing can be necessary. Who am I to judge David? His act can't possibly be as bad as mine. Can it?

Heart War

Chapter Seven

"Reporting as ordered, Sir," Captain David Abramson said to Colonel Quinton Lewis in a clear strong voice. He had shaken off the heaviness of his troubled sleep and bounded to his feet almost instantly when Lieutenant Colonel Mario Oscars came to rouse him a few minutes earlier, informing him that Colonel Lewis wanted him to report immediately.

It hadn't really mattered that he had been summoned only three hours after his head hit the pillow. He hadn't been sleeping well anyway. He had too many disturbing thoughts running through his mind. His dreams had filled him with anxiety and restlessness causing him to feel as if he'd spent the last three hours running uphill.

The day-to-day monstrosities of war and witnessing the evil men were capable of was enough to make any soldier question their real purpose, even David. But witnessing firsthand the impact of the evil deeds of men, and the seemingly endless bloodshed, weren't the only things troubling David lately.

David's commanders had come to respect and appreciate David's dreams. It had taken them a few times to begin to accept the fact that when he gave a warning, they should listen.

Recently, David had been invited to participate in a top-secret joint military meeting in which he conversed over an encrypted video conference call with Colonel Quinton Lewis, a head Air Force Intelligence Analyst, an Air Force Lieutenant General, and the Assistant Director of the CIA. David was asked to attend several of these meetings after extensive interrogation and vetting had taken place, giving him the necessary clearances.

It wasn't standard protocol to have an Air Force Captain present, but the reputation of his "intuition" or "revelations" had preceded the confides of his squadron and commanders. In fact, it had never been done before, if military records were to be relied upon. Rumors of his "special gift" had made its way to D.C. After a thorough investigation into him was conducted, his value became evident. The potential benefits of using someone like him were too rewarding to ignore.

Eventually, it became routine for them to include him on discussions of a sensitive nature. Some inside even labeled him the "military's clairvoyant" rather than *Holy Spirit* filled. However, after David's protests, he was assigned the code name "Sentinel". Doc had actually been the one to nickname David *The Sentinel*, and it had stuck, all the way to Washington. Doc said David was their own Angel of Mercy, sent by God to act as a guardian and watch over their soldiers. David had tried to dismiss the nickname, but it had caught on like wildfire. It was a little hard to persuade the other soldiers not to call him that after he saved so many of their lives.

David rebuked anyone who teased him about being psychic or used that word on him, even Colonel Lewis once. David wouldn't let anything get the glory for what God had done. He told them flat out that he was a man of faith and he believed the dreams and words of warning he'd heard in his heart were from God and God alone, not some a cultic psychic power.

That day, what they shared rocked him to his core: They believed they had a traitor within one of their U.S. Afghanistan military bases feeding their secrets to the enemy. This time however, he didn't have any discerning words of knowledge or revelations to share. It was as if he had a block in his spirit, keeping him from entering into prayer and hearing the Lord.

There had been too many coincidences for it to not mean something. How was it that the smiles and momentary looks on his own wife's face kept swarming his thoughts every time he heard a rumor that military secrets had been slipped to the enemy? And again, when he heard reports that another one of their military bases had been attacked? Her face had flooded his mind yet again, as news of secret classified covert operations reached him.

The image of Danielle wasn't because he longed for her or was missing her while she was stationed out at Camp Bastion in Helmand Province where they'd met. The thought of his new bride's face should have at least brought him joy or longing, should it not? But lately, when her beautiful face consumed his mind, it brought with it an inexplicable dread that sat and spun into a clawing knot in the pit of his stomach. It was as if God was trying to tell him, through his deaf ears and blind eyes, "Look closer. Listen to me." But why? He seemed deafened lately to God's voice. As if he'd blocked him out and could no longer listen, even when he *strained* to hear him.

He couldn't say he knew Danielle inside and out. They'd met at the military hospital at Camp Bastion only five months ago when he had delivered several runs of badly wounded soldiers in need of specialized medical treatments there. She made her interest in him known the first day they'd met. Since his squadron was given some recoup time before being sent back out to the ISAF Coalition Base in Kandahar where they were stationed, he found himself spending most of that time with her.

It felt good to have female companionship again. He was especially close to his older sister Leilani, and even though he was friends with several female officers on his base, he didn't confide in them and purposefully didn't get too close, other than professionally. He had managed to stay focused on his missions and not jump into every cot a warm-bodied woman invited him into. He was invited quite often too, but had politely refused. He'd remained steadfast on not using anyone or being used. But there was something about Danielle that captivated him. To have a woman like her express interest in him had been too much to resist. She was strikingly beautiful, alluring, highly intelligent, mysterious, provocative, and projected a wild energy that both drew him in and made him feel cautious at the same time.

She told him she'd been reassigned from a base in Kabul and sent to work in the hospital at Camp Bastion because they were short staffed with surgical nurses. She also doubled as an ICU nurse when not in surgery due to their limited staff and never-ending need for medical support.

At first, he thought her brave and fearless for enlisting to serve her country knowing she'd been sent to a medical facility in the dangerous Middle East to work in a hospital and an operating room that would probably be under-budgeted, low on medical supplies, lacking in staff, and filled with the worst kind of carnage. But the more he listened to her talk over the past four months since they'd been married, the more he saw the truth inside her heart.

She hadn't actually enlisted because she'd wanted to serve her country or even cared about people at all. She'd done it because she'd burnt every bridge she had stateside and wanted to go somewhere she felt free to be herself and prove them all wrong. She adamantly refused to discuss her family back home. She claimed they were overbearing, controlling, and didn't allow her to be herself.

Ironically, the military wasn't where you were encouraged to be yourself. You didn't belong to "you" anymore. You were technically, the property of the United States Government. Taught to act with honor and integrity and expected to hold a certain belief system that reflected the ideals of the Constitution of the United States of America and its way of life. You were forced to obey and follow orders and encouraged to follow strict ethical protocols.

Danielle wasn't really into any of those things. She thrived on defying even the most basic rules at every opportunity and despised being told what to do. It once thrilled him to give into her and indulge her little rebellions after living by the rules, always doing the right thing, and being obedient. But now, it only concerned him and made him feel disappointed in himself.

David knew Danielle wasn't "the one" even before they got married. He never believed they were meant to be. He knew it was foolish and reckless to rush into marrying her when he knew this in his heart. Especially after only knowing her for four weeks at the time *she* proposed to *him* and he accepted. They'd gotten married the next day by the base chaplain. David was constantly running back and forth from one base to the next on pararescue missions, which allowed them to spend only a few days or hours together during those first few weeks. That was part of the thrill and adventure of it all. Her wild and mysterious nature was intoxicating. At first.

Every time he was around her, he had a rush of exhilaration, recklessness, and was consumed with a lustful hunger. He knew in his heart of hearts that something was off about it. It wasn't the right way to build a lasting foundation for their love. Love? David wasn't so sure anymore if he had ever *really* loved her. She had pulled lust from him, giving him an escape from the horrors and duty of war for the moments they managed to steal away together. She was a rule breaker, defiant, and stubborn with a will of iron. She made him feel reckless and wild. He'd never felt that way before. He'd never allowed himself to be anything but a responsible, respectful, sensible, and an honor-bound man.

Even though David had faith God would get him out of the Middle East alive, he'd seen too many of his friends who believed the exact same thing get blown to bits and sent home in body bags and coffins. David didn't want to die without ever really letting loose for once in his life and sticking it to the rules or that damn sense of obligation and responsibility he'd carried on his shoulders his whole life. He wanted to do something illogical for once, like marry a free-spirited, breathtakingly beautiful woman who stirred him in ways he had never allowed himself to experience before.

Danielle wasn't just about living. She was about finding ways to break every rule and rebelling against even the simplest things. She enjoyed getting away with it, and no one ever knowing. It gave her a sense of superiority and power to do what she wanted right under their noses. At first it had been exciting to start breaking the rules with her; it hyped up the thrill of their sexual encounters and gave him a rush. But now he was starting to see it as something else, a trap, a path littered with rebellion and sinful lusts. He felt ashamed and sickened at his own behavior. He'd been acting disgraceful. Her being his wife for most of the time they'd known each other hadn't even made it feel okay. The whole thing just felt wrong.

"Rebellion is as the sin of witchcraft," David remembered reading in his travel size Bible back in his barracks. Was that why he hadn't been hearing God's voice lately? Was that why so many things had been going wrong on their latest missions? Had he rebelled from God and what he knew was right? Had he chosen lust over his love and fear of the Lord by refusing to listen when he felt God telling him not to pursue her in the first place? He had done it anyway even after literally hearing God tell him, "David, she isn't the one."

God had warned him about so many ambushes and attacks against his squadron and others at their base and at times, even other bases or moving military transits. God had revealed to him the plans of their enemy in dreams and spoke to him moments before atrocities were about to happen, saving his life and the lives of his fellow soldiers countless times over. God's voice had been why his commanders and their superiors had taken notice of him and started including him in on classified discussions and briefings seeking his counsel. But for the past couple months since he married Danielle, he hadn't heard God say anything! Or had he?

The dreams were getting bolder, and the message louder, "Look at her!" But why? What did Danielle have to do with any of this? What did she have to do with the attacks and their recent casualties?

Only moments before Lieutenant Colonel Oscars had come to rouse David, the dream had come again. A black *niqāb* falling away from Danielle's face to reveal shimmering eyes full of wicked delight, smiling triumphantly as she raises her hands, blood and bits of human flesh slowly dripping from them, and wet streaks of dark blood trailing down her elbows. Then she looks down, and beneath her is David. His eyelids are melted shut, his ears torn off and the skin left behind pinned down over the gaping holes sewn to his skull. She has ripped his heart out and left it beating on top of his chest while he sputters bubbles of blood from his lipless mutilated mouth, trying desperately to breathe. His body is lying on top of a mound of uniformed soldiers from every branch of the military; the gory carnage of David's most recent fallen comrades, the men he hadn't helped save. The voice in his dream thunders this time, "David! Look at her!"

David had only told one other person about *these* dreams he'd been having recently, his best friend Doc. Part of David knew it probably wasn't fair for him to call Doc up and put this on his shoulders, but he *had* to talk to someone about it. He was afraid Doc may not be able to be objective about Danielle since it turned out she was Doc's step-daughter, a fact David gained knowledge of *after* they got married.

David had called up his best friend to tell him about his new bride. After describing how they met, her occupation and finally stating her name, he found out who she was. She had been using her mother's maiden name *Touch*, pronounced *too-ij* in Cambodian, as she had described her heritage briefly to him as African, Cambodian and European. She had never once mentioned anything else remotely personal about her parents including Doc's last name *Picard*. David had been clueless.

She hadn't even told Doc about David either. In fact, all the times David had talked about Doc to her, she just smiled and listened, never saying anything, or asking anything about his friend. She had only ever been curious about his missions, and always looking for ways to get David to share more or give up the classified details. He never did, which seemed to irritate her. She'd pout and claimed he didn't trust her or love her if he was going to keep secrets from her. David brushed it off and didn't cater to her pouty moods so she soon knocked it off and stopped playing that angle. He simply rationalized her behavior as testing the boundaries. Another sign he chose to ignore in retrospection.

After David broke the news to Doc, and Doc broke the news to him, David asked Danielle why she'd never told him Doc was her father. She just laughed and said, "I enjoy my silly little secrets, David. Don't you know that by now?" Then she sauntered off, looking back at him and tossing her head back again, mocking his confused expression. Why was she allowed secrets when she'd accused him of not loving her enough to tell her about classified military secrets? It had bothered him a lot. But once again, he had rationalized it as Danielle just being Danielle: elusive, mysterious and sensually dangerous.

Doc told David in later conversations that he had told Danielle about his trusted up-and-coming Pararescue Pilot before they'd met. He confessed he told her what an amazing Special Ops Officer he was too, how devoted he was to his PJ's, and how he hoped she would find a man of his moral character someday to make her happy.

Learning that Doc had told Danielle about him before they'd even met had changed David's entire perspective about their first encounter. Danielle, letting the other medical staff rush off with the wounded to the medical facilities while she lingered behind to flirt with the pilot climbing down from his helicopter from a long 22-hour mission. It started to feel to David like maybe she had been waiting to meet him, planned to seduce him, maybe even to marry him. It had all been her idea from the beginning. But why? To get one over on her step-father whom she seemed to hate? To prove she was smarter than him. To take pleasure in her "silly little secrets?"

Much to David's relief, Doc hadn't taken it badly or been offended upon hearing about their marriage. He proved yet again what an objective man he was when David shared with him later about his recent dreams, even as gory and disturbing as they were with Danielle portraying the wicked woman of blood lust.

When David told him about the dreams, Doc simply remained silent a few heartbeats. Then he had said very calmly and clearly, "You know, you don't have normal dreams boy. You never have. I don't think this is newlywed jitters. I think you need to be askin'

God what he's trying to tell you, kid. And do it quick. I think it's a warning."

Doc's openness and response had been all the confirmation David needed. He knew he'd made a terrible mistake marrying Danielle. But there was more to it than that. Much more. He could feel it. The problem was, every time David tried to pray about it lately, he just felt full of rage.

Rather than surrendering and asking God to open his heart and ears again and let him see the truth, he found himself hissing at God, "You're not doing enough to end this war. Too many good men and women are dying. What's the point to any of this? Why are you allowing this? Why did you put me here? To watch my friends die? To watch good men and women get blown to bits and not be able to save them? What do you want from me? Why can't I be happy and take something for myself for once? Why don't you want me to have her!"

David had felt his heart quickly hardening. He hadn't really meant to let it happen. He felt ashamed and grieved that he was starting to adopt Danielle's ideas and callous attitude. It was like she had slowly poisoned him. This wasn't him. This wasn't who he was. What was wrong with him?

As a helicopter pilot and Pararescue Recovery Specialists, their motto was "These things we do, that others may live". It was a selfless career choice. A *calling* to be one of the "Angels of Mercy," as they were nicknamed. David had taped a bible verse up in his helicopter when he'd first hit the ground in Afghanistan six years earlier in October 2001. It read, "Greater love has no one than this: To lay down his life for his friends. John 15:13." That was *who* he was. That was *what* he was. Why did he feel so contaminated and guilty? Was his affair with Danielle, their marriage, their relationship, so wrong? Was it so wrong to want an emotional and physical escape from the pressures and horror of this war? To not feel so alone all the time? To hold someone? To have someone hold him?

Yes, it is wrong. Because she isn't the one. You used each other. You don't really love her the way you thought you did. The two shall become one, remember David? You cannot be unequally yoked as you are. You've pulled yourself off the path of righteousness. She's led you off course. And you willingly followed her!

Your soul tie to this woman is rooted in rebellion and intertwined with the darkness she has in her heart. There's more than darkness there...something evil resides within her. You know it to be true! You can feel it! Rebellion is as the sin of witchcraft. Witchcraft is just another way Satan can claim a foothold. Curses and deceit. Lies and lust. That's why you're becoming hardened toward God! That's why she's influencing you. You're sharing in her spiritual contamination as one flesh. The familiar spirits she has agreements with are now tormenting you, trying to get you to be in agreement with them too. David, you know how this works! What were you thinking?

What was I thinking? That's why I've become deaf to God's voice. Blind to the truth! But what truth am I not seeing? Is this truth what will rip out my heart? Did I open myself up to this, Lord? How many soldiers have died because I wasn't steadfast in my convictions and run from temptation instead of running to it? To her? Oh, God... tell me! What am I not seeing? What have I done? Lord forgive me for not listening to you. How do I make this right?

The thoughts swirled in David's mind, one after the other, after the other. He stood before Colonel Lewis not really present, almost swaying on his feet. His physical exhaustion, grieving heart, and clouded mind making him feel ineffective and disconnected. He stood before the Colonel, half awake, consumed with his thoughts, knowing full well that he was moments away from being sent on yet another emergency mission, or given a verbal browbeating for not paying attention to what the Colonel was telling him at this very moment!

"Captain Abramson? Did you hear me?" Colonel Lewis asked David, some concern in his voice, rather than berating.

"No, Sir. Sorry Sir! I'm still waking up Sir!" David answered as clearly and attentively as possible, puffing out his chest and snapping back to attention with a little shake of his head.

"I can see that. And I'm sorry to wake you after only three hours of sleep Captain, but we received reports of another military base being attacked at O-three hundred," Colonel Lewis informed David. "I know your squadron is running on fumes, but I need your boys to gear up and get out to Camp Chapman in the Khost District immediately. I want Angel One up in the air in ten! Live fire is still a threat. Incoming reports of casualties and severely wounded. We need to get our wounded out of there!"

"Sir, yes, Sir!" David confirmed, the urgency of the mission igniting some energy within him from some secret reserve he had in his soul.

"I need you to be clear that your secondary mission here is the wounded, Captain. We're sending Cherub Six and Seraph Seven to assist with the rescue op. Your *primary* mission is securing the prison if it's still compromised when you arrive."

"Prison, Sir? I thought Chapman was a Forwarding Operations Base, Sir?" David interjected.

"Officially, it's an FOB. But unofficially, it is a temporary holding site for some select prisoners we recently captured. The enemy's ground assault appears to be after our war prisoners Captain. They caused a distraction at the far end of the base with suicide bombers then sent in their fighters to liberate the prisoners. Our soldiers on the ground are holding and keeping them at bay. We believe the fight is almost over but just in case, you have the clearance level to be informed that we have three high-ranking

Taliban officers being held in that prison awaiting transfer to a CIA black site. We believe they have valuable information about where Osama bin Laden is hiding and his most recent plans. We *cannot* let them escape! We need a chance to extract the information. You're clear to go in hot. Collateral damage may be inevitable. But Captain, do us all a favor and try to use restraint near the *kalats*. We don't need another headline about excessive civilian casualties. Do you understand your orders?"

"Yes Sir! Primary objective, secure the prison if it's compromised upon arrival using selective fire. Secondary objective, assist Cherub Six and Seraph Seven to bring home the wounded," David summarized. David was used to having more than one objective asked of him and his squad. As Pararescue Recovery Specialists, they were special ops, but his team was also trusted with other classified information, often working with secret missions and objectives of the CIA or International Security Assistance Force, or ISAF, as they preferred to call it.

"Have you had any dreams that might help us tonight Captain?" Colonel Lewis asked quietly as if someone might be listening, though the tent was completely empty except for the two of them.

"Not lately Sir," David said, looking down and feeling the shame in his heart swell.

"Maybe you have your bride on your mind too much these days to allow anything else in, aye soldier?" The Colonel tried to tease with a wink, but the joke fell flat, the truth of his words striking David's heart hard. The Colonel wasn't a Christian, but he had become open to the idea that there was a God fighting with them and for them in this war. The Colonel had seen too many things to deny God's hand defending them and it was through David that he'd witnessed evidence of God's intervention time and time again.

"You're more right than you know," David acknowledged. "I haven't been myself lately Sir."

The Colonel stepped up closer to David and studied him for a moment. "I'm sorry to hear that Captain. Hopefully, after this last run, you boys can have a break for a little while. We're expecting another deployment of PJs to arrive the day after tomorrow. Perhaps you can rest up a bit then. *God* willing," The Colonel said "God" with feeling this time and David met his eyes.

"Yes. *God* willing Sir," David nodded.

"Dismissed!" The Colonel declared.

"Yes Sir!" David acknowledged, turned on his heel, and jetted out of the Colonel's tent.

David jogged to his barrack and clapped his hands together several times sending *cracks* through the room, his voice boomed as he shouted, "Gear Up! Let's go! Critical Mission! Up! Up! Up!"

The men jumped out of bed obediently, responding to David's orders without question or resistance, even in their sleep-broken state. David filled them in on their primary and secondary mission as they geared up. Within ten minutes they were loaded into the helicopter and headed out to Camp Chapman.

Not So Happy Ending

Chapter Eight

think David was right. I should have waited...oh God.

I was doing it again. That thing that happens to me when I'm in overload. My head felt light and my fingertips were tingling. I could feel my pulse in the pit of my stomach, surging.

THRUMP-THRUMP-THRUMP.

Auuh. What had I been thinking?

I hadn't truly known what I'd been asking David to do when I'd encouraged him to share that part of his past with me this early in our relationship. He'd been right. He'd been *sooooo* damn right. It had been hard for me to hear all of it, about her. I'd had to force myself to stay present in my thoughts, bearing every detail. I'd tucked my knees up only a few minutes into his story and held them to me, not only to keep myself focused on squeezing something other than my hands into the blankets on the bunkbed, but to keep myself from plugging my fingers in my ears.

I'd asked for it. Literally. He'd understood the pain it would put me through better than I had. He'd known.

I should have trusted his judgment. I should know better by now! I reprimanded myself.

I hadn't expected the truth to hurt this much. My mind was reeling, spiraling into the uncharted murky territory of co-mingled hurt, anger and even disgust. And beneath that, was an even more confusing layer of betrayal, jealousy, and a selfish longing to be his only love, his only lover.

Not that I'm anywhere near ready to be that!

My emotions and my thoughts were bounding recklessly between the different fragments of his story about Danielle and what my own imagination was concocting in between the lines with details he hadn't been able to share.

Or had purposefully withheld like he said he would.

What he had shared had been terrible enough without my imagination making things worse!

Oh Lord. You better help me make sense of this and handle these emotions because right now I think I'm going to be sick. Or explode. Or just plain lose it.

I leaned against the long hallway wall outside the Hope Box, the door closed behind me. I needed to step out as soon as David had confirmed he was finished sharing his story. It was almost more than I could accept. The story he'd told was conflicting with every personal impression and idea I'd ever had of David. Logically, I'd known such things went on in war. Logically, I couldn't blame him. Logically, it all made sense. Why he'd done what he'd done. And why he had killed her.

Oh, but what horrible things he had done. How could he? How?

I felt a surge of acid rush up my throat and I bolted back up the hallway to where I'd seen the lady's bathroom sign near the front lobby. I ran inside and right into the nearest stall. I barely made it! My neck reaching out to place my head over the toilet just in time. I puked up every ounce of my breakfast. I was crying when I came up for air and I slumped against the stall door, sliding down to rest on my butt, my arms wrapping around my stomach as I cried for the horrible reality of war and what it made good men like my David do.

My mind swirled with the images of my own past. My father beating my mother and sister to death right before my eyes. Blood everywhere. The constant never-ending violence. The sound of flesh hitting wet flesh and bones snapping and being crushed. That had been my reality too. My warzone was my entire childhood. The nightmare of my life was only outmatched by the nightmares I used to have at night.

Then images from just a couple days ago rushed in to mix with my distant past. Wielding a celestial sword, cutting down giants and beheading my enemies. Their blood spilling or squirting onto the ground. What I'd done had been almost worse.

But that had been different, hadn't it?

Yes, it's different! I wasn't killing human beings, like David had. I'd been killing Nephilim. Those angel-human hybrids whose bodies encase the immortal evil souls of demons. I was fighting for my life! I was fighting evil.

Actually, Melanie. Be fair. David was fighting for his life too and David was fighting evil encased in human form, not Nephilim.

"Ah!" I clasped my hands to my temples and squeezed my eyes shut. "No. No. Stop." I was trying to get the images out of my head of the blood and body parts I'd seen firsthand, and of the images my mind was creating to fit in with David's descriptive story. The sobbing started up again as hurt, anger and confusion rushed in to fill every last gap of reasoning in my mind making me feel a deepening hollowness and detachment even from myself.

I ignored the soft tapping at the door. It just seemed to blend into the pounding of the blood in my ears and was drowned out by the sounds of my own sobs. I hadn't meant to rush out of the room as I had, but I needed some air badly. I felt like I was suffocating, the walls closing in on me. The sorrow and pain in David's voice as he'd recounted his experiences with Danielle had flooded the room with a tangible ache.

Or had that just been from the enormity of my own feelings? I hadn't known I'd react that way. I thought I would be stronger than this. More of a help to him. More of a support. David must feel so abandoned in there right now. He's probably thinking the worse of me. I'm reacting just like he'd feared. Oh God. Poor David.

"Strawberry, you in here?" Doc's kind baritone voice called out as the bathroom door opened slowly and the tapping on the door stopped.

I couldn't answer him. I was too busy trying to get some air into my lungs having almost sobbed myself into a state of hyperventilation.

"Baby girl?" Doc repeated softly.

"I'm here," was all I managed to croak out.

I heard Doc's large footsteps approaching, lighter than you'd expect of a man his size, and I wiped at my face.

Like that's going to fool him you idiot. You're sitting on the floor in front of a toilet. He can see your ass under the door. Like he won't figure it out.

I was so mad at myself now. Had I been a coward to run out like that rather than finish what I'd pushed David into starting to deal with?

"Are you alright?" Doc said gently. He squatted down on the other side of the door and placed his hand underneath it to rest gently on top of mine. He patted the top of my hand lightly, as if he was afraid to hurt me too.

"He doesn't blame you for needing to step out to process all this. I hope you know that. He knew you'd react this way. He even warned you," Doc reminded me, not with accusation but with kindness.

"I know he did, but..." I sniffed and swallowed a sob.

"But you hadn't expected the truth to be *that* bad or for him to have loved...or wanted to love Danielle *that* much?" Doc asked intuitively.

"Y-yes. And the things he's done..." I couldn't finish.

"He isn't an evil man Melanie. He isn't your father. Don't let your perception be colored by your own horrible past experiences. He isn't anything like Dwayne Randal Bishop. Not one bit," Doc declared urgently. "It wouldn't be fair to him."

"I know that! I know all that in my heart. I'm just having a hard time getting my mind to see it that way right now. I just need a little time to process it. To think it all through. To pray about it. I'm just—"

"Scared. You're scared you're falling in love with a man hiding a monster inside? Someone you may not know as well as you thought," Doc tried to guess.

"Not exactly. No," I denied, then realized I was lying.

"But you *are* scared," Doc insisted.

"Fine. Yes. I am a little. But I'm not sure *why* I am. I'm just...I just need time to think okay," I started to cry again and I tried desperately to stop myself which only seemed to make it worse. I was hiccupping out the words as I continued, "I...fe-feel so...so sad for him D-doc!" I wept.

"Come on out here baby girl," Doc half coached, half instructed me.

"W-why?" I sputtered.

"Just come on out here," Doc said again, but softer this time. I could tell he was trying to tone back his usual take charge nature and be sensitive to my situation.

I dragged myself up off the floor and dusted off my butt and hands. The bathroom was spotless. A perfect military shine on all surfaces. I doubted even the toilet had a solitary germ on the lid.

Well, now it does since I'd barfed and splattered my nasties all over it.

I felt a rush of hot red hit my cheeks on top of the flush my vomiting and hyperventilating had already caused.

I probably look as nasty as the bathroom smells now. Oh crap. I'm going to have barf breath.

I flushed to toilet and carefully opened the stall door and looked up at Doc who loomed over me with his hands on his hips. His face was sympathetic and he gave me a kind smile. "Thank you for opening the door baby girl."

I nodded and waited. I couldn't really get out of the stall with his huge body blocking the door. I guess I could if I squeezed past him but I wasn't comfortable with that either and didn't have the presence of mind just to ask him to step back.

I gasped out loud accidentally. A familiar formidable fear striking my core. We were alone. In a bathroom. Alone in a bathroom, in a building with just one other person who was probably still all the way down the hall in a closed off room that was nearly sound proof. I felt my pulse quicken to a dangerous speed and my mind rushed to the police report describing how my father had brutally beat and raped that young teenage girl in a park bathroom, only to be stopped by a police officer who'd happened by.

"Hey now," Doc said carefully, his eyes widening a little and searching my face. He took two big steps back, placing himself against the far wall. He put his hands out in front of him a little as if to show no harm. "Doc's not gonna hurt you none," He told me carefully with a tone I'd imagined he'd used with an armed psycho.

What was wrong with me? I'm acting like a spooked cat. This is Doc. He won't hurt me.

"I know. Sorry. I—" I stopped talking and rushed past him to the sink. I turned it on and used my hands to wash off my face and rinse out my mouth several times. I grabbed the paper towels and dabbed roughly at my face, trying to snap myself out of it. I looked up. Doc was still against the wall, unmoved. He was just watching me thoughtfully.

"I don't think it's just David that you're scared of now," Doc said sadly. "I can see it in your eyes. You and I've been alone before. You were nervous then, but you trusted me. This is different. I think David's story stirred you in ways you can't identify yet because it is hitting all of your buttons. The buttons that run down to the deepest roots of your damage. You're even distrustful of me now, aren't you?" Doc walked slowly to the exit door behind me and paused, waiting for me to answer.

I tried to say something to deny it. But he was right. My mouth opened and nothing came out. I might as well have been gagged.

"I'll give you ten more minutes to gather yourself. If you aren't ready to proceed with some training by then, we'll just call it a day, okay Melanie? We can reschedule later. After David sharing what he did, I wouldn't blame either of you one bit."

Oh no! No! I need this training. Please don't call today off. Please—

"Don't worry about disappointing either of us because you won't," Doc spoke over my thoughts and I realized I'd been panicking internally and not communicating verbally. "You decide what you want to do. Just please come tell me, don't just disappear, okay? Clocks ticking," Doc finished tapping his grungy-gadgety looking military green watch on his wrist. His voice was even and absent of any judgment or offense to my reaction to him.

Doc had been considerate enough but still a decisive man of direction and purpose. A no-nonsense man of action. I respected that. Even if at the moment, his commanding presence, potential power, and physical strength were making me cautious.

Not his fault. He hasn't done anything. He hasn't given you cause to be afraid of him. Get a grip girl. Get. A. Grip.

Doc let the door close on its own behind him.

"Umm, thank you!" I managed to blurt out before the door closed completely. I hoped he heard me.

Please don't kick me out. I need this. I need this!

I was once again alone. I felt my pulse increase again and my breathing become uneven. I think I was having a panic attack. My chest felt like it was squeezing and I could hardly form a clear thought through the torrent of images and ringing of David's words in my ears.

This is ridiculous. Chill out girl!

I turned back to the sink and gripped the sides, looking at myself in the eyes. The face that peered out at me had been much like the one from last night. Shocked, horrified, even afraid. I hated that look on my face.

Why am I hiding in another bathroom?

"I hate you!" I spat at myself.

No. I thought weakly.

"No!" I tried again but out loud this time, refocusing my energy into pushing out the self-loathing.

I don't hate me! I hate feeling this way that's all. Don't confuse one with the other.

I rinsed my mouth out again several more times and felt a small rush of gratitude as I spotted a bottle of mouthwash in the reflection of the shelf behind me. I grabbed it and did a mouth-burning sixty second swish and gargle when suddenly I heard an uproar of yelling. A woman's voice was blasting profanity at someone.

What the heck?

I quickly spit into the sink and dried my mouth with the back of my hand. I emerged from the restroom cautiously, my mind changing gears quickly to alert. This unexpected distraction from a possible intruder or infiltrator into our private little training party suddenly sparked a new flicker of bravery and curiosity. I peeked my head out from around the door just enough to try and see the last five feet down the hall to the lobby. The corner was blocking me. I silently tip-toed out.

"I don't give a fuck Eugene! I told you on the phone I was comin' by and you ain't got no right to keep me from this place!" The irate woman was yelling.

"This is not the time or the place Tristina. I told you I have a student today!" Doc counter aggressively.

"I don't care!" Tristina hissed.

"Look woman! I've asked you nicely. I've even offered to call you after I'm finished. You do *not* get to show up here and interrupt my lessons like this! You aren't my wife anymore. I don't have to answer to you or explain myself. Get out!"

"You do if you don't want your daughter knowing why we really got divorced," Tristina said snidely, stepping up into his face. She looked over and made cold eye contact with me.

Oh crap. I hoped I wouldn't be visible back here. Great.

I stepped out from around the corner as if I'd been on my way up, trying to look nonchalant, but I think the "oh shit" look on my face was giving me away.

"Student or your happy ending?" Tristina said nastily giving me the once over with a cold judgmental glare.

My mouth dropped open in shock. "Wha—"

"Not you bitch. Him!" Tristina jabbed her finger into Doc's chest and glared up at him accusatorially. "Well? What kind of floor mat exercises have you been pumping into this one?"

"Watch your mouth!" Doc ordered outraged.

"I don't take orders from you *Eu-gene*," She rallied, snapping out his name in two cold syllables.

"This young lady is my student Tristina!" Doc growled. "And you will show her some courtesy. She has nothing to do with our issues so you leave her the hell out of it!"

"Wait," Tristina stepped away from Doc and paced haughtily toward me. I watched Doc puff up and flex but decided against grabbing at her or blocking her.

Tristina was tall for a woman, maybe six foot, and almost too thin. Her smooth light-brown skin and narrow, almond shaped eyes told me she was probably half African, half Asian. Which "Asian" I honestly couldn't tell you. It was hard to pinpoint with her dark skin and ambiguous features. But she was beautiful in that stunning sort of way that would turn a man's head. Her long thick black hair was pulled back in a tight ponytail to tickle the top of her firm rounded backside. She was in tight black jeans and a loose fitting red blouse that did nothing to hide her curves. She'd tucked it into her thin waist so that the badge and Glock on her hip were very clearly visible. She saw me eye her badge and gun and smirked, a superior air to her lifted chiseled chin.

This just gets better and better.

I bristled but stood my ground, unsure as to her intent. If it was to intimidate me, then I wouldn't show her she was succeeding. I'd met too many bullies in my life and knew better than to give them the satisfaction of seeing me sweat, badge or not. If her intent was just to size me up as a woman, well, I'd probably lose pretty fast in the comparison anyway. I knew I looked like crap. I'd just balled my eyes out, was wearing sweats, threw up in the john...

Umm, maybe I shouldn't use that word if she thinks I'm a hooker.

I'd had a terribly restless sleep the night before too. I probably looked more like a junkie with my ratty hair and grungy clothes rather than a hired "happy ending". Not that I really knew what they usually looked like apart from the way television shows characterized them. And I knew I wasn't dressed like Julia Roberts in *Pretty Woman*.

Great first impression Mel. Hooker, junkie or desperate student – with barf breath no less. Either way, not so cool.

"Student huh?" Tristina asked me speculatively.

"Yes," I answered honestly, my voice a little hoarse from the throwing up and crying but I bet she thought it was from being afraid of her. "Yes, I'm a student," I tried again, letting my confidence finally come out. "My boyfriend is down the hall," I added the last part just to make sure she believed me.

Oh, boyfriend. I like the sound of that out loud and outside of my own head.

Tristina raised a too-thin eyebrow and gave me the once over again with an accusatory glare. I said nothing more, just crossed my arms over my flat chest and popped out a hip with a look of my own that clearly asked, "well are you done?"

She blinked long and dismissively, making sure I knew she wasn't impressed my with own little display of attitude before she turned her back on me completely and headed back to Doc, her long black ponytail slithering against her long narrow back and bouncing up and down off her backside as she added some extra swing in her hips just to prove she knew she was better equipped than me and knew it. And yes, better equipped physically as well as weapon wise.

Doc's arms were crossed over his chest tightly too. He wasn't trying to mimic me but I quickly changed my stance so the thought wouldn't keep teasing my brain. His face was fixed in nothing short of a burning hot rage that I could see he was barely managing to keep locked underneath his careful self-control.

"Satisfied?" His voice was frighteningly low, even for his naturally deep baritone.

"You never were capable of satisfying me Eugene," she mouthed off vindictively. "Call me later. We need to discuss our daughter. She needs her father. As pathetic as you are, she still needs you. She and I aren't getting along right now. She's too much like you." She pointed at him.

"I'll call you," Doc agreed, his voice cooling off to sound a tad more normal.

"You just better. Oh, and she's getting married," she added coldly, a malevolent twinkle in her eye.

"She's what?" Doc bellowed. "She's only eighteen!"

"No shit," Tristina mocked.

"To that deadbeat loser, Harold?" He actually paled.

"Yep," she said with a spiteful grin. "I think she's doing it just because she knows I can't stand him. You need to talk her out of it Eugene. I don't want her marrying that white-bread redneck piece of shit." She shot me another hateful look and headed to the door.

Um, is that white-bread comment for my benefit? I couldn't stop my frown.

Tristina stopped before the front doors to turn and glare at me with her iced over eyes. "He might seem all fun and flirty at first and you might think it's innocent, but don't be fooled. He's just a dog looking for a leg to hump. He doesn't really care what *color* it is. You might want to remember that the next time you think about spreading those chubby little white legs for him. You're just a notch on his military belt like all the others," she seethed, her eyes telling me I was a little white whore in her mind no matter what I had said.

"Pardon me?" I said aghast. "I have never—"

"Yeah, that's what they all say," her voice was dismissive and she started to turn back to the door.

"Out!" Doc yelled at Tristina, his fists balled. She turned towards him about to say something nasty but he cut her off.

"Get the hell out of here before I call your boss at the DOJ and tell him you're harassing me and my students *during* my work hours while I'm teaching a *private* CCW course! I think I'll let him know you aren't conducting any official DOJ business either! I shouldn't have to tell you that one more disciplinary action for behavioral misconduct will result in your suspension. Now get out!" Doc walked up to Tristina as he'd yelled and peered down at her, daring her to defy him again. "Out," he whispered in a growl as he pointed past her with his long arm, invading her space and intimidating her all at the same time.

"Sure Eugene. I'm going." She smiled extra sweetly up at him, the falseness of it making my stomach turn over. She looked past him at me again, her eyes narrowing. I thought I saw recognition finally cross her face for a fraction of a moment, and her mouth open as a thought seemed to strike her. She composed herself quickly and turned on her boot heel, storming out.

Doc swiftly locked the front door behind her and kept a careful watch on her until she'd climbed into her navy-colored Crown Victoria and sped off. She was looking straight ahead, her cell phone already up to her ear.

"My most humble apologies Melanie. She had no right to speak to you that way," Doc growled. "Tristina never was one to recognize reality or ask before jumping to the worst possible conclusions," He gave me an embarrassed glance.

"Why would she think that of me? Isn't this a place lots of people come for training?" I asked totally confused.

David said you were one of the most trustworthy men he knew!

Doc shrugged and shook his head, "She was always an irrationally jealous woman. Never listened to reason. And I promise you on my mama's grave, I never cheated on that woman. *Never.* She might be one of the most beautiful women I have ever meet, but she is one of the most insecure, envious, revengeful, stubborn-headed, infuriating—"

"Was that Tristina?" David's voice echoed up from down the hallway, his footsteps sounded heavy and tired as they neared and grew louder.

"Yep. Sure was," Doc answered callously.

"Does she know I'm here? Did she ask about—" David was saying as he rounded the corner, his speech and movement stopped at the sight of me.

Oh, that's not an awkward pause or anything. Great. I hurt him. I knew it! Damn it.

"Melanie?" David said my name questioningly, his eyes going to Doc then back to me to assess the mood we were both in and the atmosphere in the room, not only from what little he'd heard of Tristina's "docile" tones, but from our heavy conversation in the Hope Box only ten minutes before.

I tried to smile at him to tell him I wasn't mad at him or planning on running away from him when I'd rushed out of the room. I felt the smile quiver on my face. He started walking again right toward me. When he was only a foot away he stopped, looking down at me with troubled eyes.

"Are you okay? Was it too much?" David wondered.

"Um, it was a lot at first but I can handle it. I just need a little time to sort it all out in my mind that's all. But I'm okay. *We're* okay, David," I reassured him, wanting to believe it myself.

"You left before I could tell you one more important piece to all this," David wet his lips.

Oh God. What now? I don't think I can handle any more surprises.

"How big of a detail is it?" I asked skeptically, my stomach already dropping to somewhere below my navel.

"Um, well," David looked at Doc for help.

"I think I know what you left out so just spit it on out, boy. It won't get any easier, for anyone. Clean the wound while it's open, remember?" Doc suggested gently gesturing to me. "Strawberry can handle it. She's tough," Doc looked at me and nodded once, his eyes telling me it would all be okay and to trust David. "Aren't you baby girl?"

"Just tell me," I whispered to David, unable to agree because I didn't feel tough at all. I swallowed hard. My pulse was speeding up to match my racing thoughts.

"Danielle's mom...Um, is Tristina," David said, his voice nearly cracking.

"*That* angry accusatory woman was Danielle's mother?" My voice did crack, fully and embarrassingly to make me sound like a twelve-year-old boy. I felt my mouth go slack and my hands start to tingle.

Don't pass out. Don't pass out. Don't pass out.

David looked over at Doc and then back at me uncertainly. He blew out a breath and sucked air back in through his nose and pressed onward, locking his hands behind him like a soldier about to deliver unfavorable news about the battle front to a testy commander.

"She was never told I was the one who killed her daughter. She was given the same coverup story as everyone else on base. It was classified so...so she wasn't ever told the truth. She tried to get her daughter's records, but they were sealed and classified by the military. So she ran all the records she could find about me. She hates me because she never knew her daughter got married in the first place and there I was standing at her door, telling her my wife, her daughter, was dead. She went ballistic with grief and rage.

"I found out later she tried to access information on me with her DOJ clearance. She got blocked beyond the standard public record stuff. She tried to pull some favors to get my records, suspecting I had something to do with her daughters' death. Her instincts are right, but we can't tell her that. She ended up getting warned by her bosses to back off. They had gotten called by a certain colonel, telling them to have her back off."

"But he knew," I said pointing to Doc. "Was her dad allowed to know because of his military status?" I questioned, pointing to Doc.

"Yes. He had clearance. Um, Doc wasn't her biological father; he was her step-father. He adopted her when he married Tristina. Doc was kind of my father-in-law for the few months we were married," David said, a shrug breaking his locked stance momentarily.

"Father-in-law," I repeated back almost trancelike. That hadn't dawned on me. "Hmm."

"Too much information for one day, right?" he asked quietly, reaching out toward me but pulling his hands back right before he touched me as I staggered backwards toward the row of cushioned seats by the front window.

"Whoa," I breathed. I hadn't expected that tidbit either. "Well, crap."

"The daughter Tristina was just talking about was our other daughter, Joy," Doc chimed in matter-of-factually. "I don't want you confusing them. We had Jasmine and Joy a few years after we got married. Danielle was four when I adopted her."

"Oh," I croaked out. Trying to make this all fit in my head.

"There was always something a little off about Danielle. Something broken inside of her since she was a little girl. I'd tried with all my heart to mend her. Make her whole. Teach her about kindness. Bring an understanding about empathy regarding others. But she never really got it. I realized when she was a teenager she was faking most of her empathy. It wasn't genuine. But she masked her true feelings so well, I stopped pressing the issue," Doc cleared his throat, looking burdened with his admissions.

I glanced at David who was focusing hard on Doc, hanging onto his words as if this was the first time he'd ever heard this.

"When Danielle first expressed love for David I was thrilled! I couldn't have hoped for a better man to love my daughter. But I was also worried. Not for her. For him. She could snap and walk away from him in an instant if she didn't get her way. She could really hurt him. I didn't want that for him. I even talked to him behind her back, asking him to be careful. I tried to warn him that my daughter always had an angle. But it was war and under the pressure and possibility that your life can end at any moment, it manufacturers a lot of intense emotions and superficial attractions that soldiers mistake as love." Doc gave David a "well, I told you so" kind of look.

David nodded his head and gave a slight shrug. He looked embarrassed but open to the unspoken rebuke.

"Well, in the end," Doc's voice broke. He cleared it and tried again. "In the end, her motives were pretty clear and David had no choice but to do what he did." Doc came and patted David on the shoulder reassuringly.

"I wish I'd—" David tried to say.

"Boy, you did what was necessary and you saved a lot of lives in the process. I didn't blame you then, and I don't blame you now. I was just saying that war is the perfect environment for short-lived romances and revelations about one another. You sure as hell didn't expect what you got on either point where Danielle was concerned."

"Yes Sir," David whispered.

"Danielle was your adopted daughter?" I repeated, hearing my voice as if from a great distance. I was fuzzing in and out.

God, please don't let me pass out.

"Danielle is dead Melanie. Like I told you...I...I had to...to stop her," David added, sounding disconnected but struggling to reconnect to the here and now, using me as his life line.

"K," was all that came out of my mouth. *I need to sit down.* I stumbled to a chair and plopped down, my legs having turned to jelly.

David came and crouched down in front of me, his hands gently resting on my knees bringing my head up and looking right into his eyes. The sunlight coming in through the window was making the honey-brown color of his eyes almost translucent, full of warmth and vulnerability. He searched my eyes as I searched his. I knew my eyes were wet and large, the learned truths and confusion swirling within them.

I wasn't mad at him. Well, okay I was. I was mad that the perfect idea I had of him was crumbling. Not entirely gone, but the fascia was blowing away in chunky bits as his walls came down and he bared his soul to me. I hadn't even known he had any walls. He'd always seemed so open and honest to me. I supposed, he'd been as open as he could have been with me up until now. If he'd shared this too soon, he would have lost me before I'd even known I cared about him at all. He'd been right to keep it from me until we were closer.

"What are you thinking? Please tell me," David implored to me. He leaned in closer, his hands absentmindedly sliding up my knees to the sides of my thighs, resting midway up.

He's never touched my thighs before.

The random thought shot an unexpected thrill through me that felt entirely inappropriate to the present situation.

Seriously? Girl what is your problem?

"Melanie, I'm drowning here. Please. Please say something. Anything. Please don't shut me out." His voice went raw with emotion and his eyes filled with fragile tears.

"I'm," I choked. "I'm," was all that came out again as my words failed me and my voice abandoned me.

David waited, the tears he was holding building, threatening to spill over the rim of his eyes.

I sat up straight, effectively pulling my face away from his and ripped the rubber band out of my hair. I ran my fingers through my long strawberry-blonde hair angrily. I just needed a damn minute to think! I shook my fingers through my hair to loosen it, rubbing my scalp as I struggled to find words and make my paralyzed brain start thinking again.

"You're mad," David interpreted.

"No!" I accidently shouted. "Not really *at* you. But yes, *at* you! A little I guess," I tried for honest. I was suddenly way too hot. I pulled my purse strap off from around my neck and dropped my little purse to the floor carelessly. Then I ripped the sweatshirt hoodie off too. My lime-green tank top came up partly to show my pale white stomach and I yanked it down, frustrated.

David reached up slowly, his fingertips brushing my collarbone. *Oh God.* A shiver went through me. *What is he doing?*

His hand slid across my collarbone to my right shoulder and down to the top of my arm where he'd almost knocked me over earlier when he had suddenly snapped and turned on Doc. His thumb traced the red and purpling bruise that had already started to form there, gently circling it.

"I did this, didn't I?" David questioned in a small voice.

"You didn't mean to. I was standing too close." I swallowed down my shiver. Was this bruise going to add to his self-disgust? *Oh no.*

"No, you were trying to help me. I...I didn't feel it when I, when I knocked into you. I'm sorry," He whispered.

"It was an accident. I'm not mad at you about that," I placed my hand over his until he looked up at me.

"I'm so sorry," he repeated. His face was ashamed and afraid reminding me of a little boy who didn't know if they lit the match the curtain would catch on fire.

"I forgive you," I answered without thinking. It was true. I hadn't even thought about it since it had happened. Granted too much had happened since then anyway, but it was a small thing. He hadn't meant to do it and hadn't even known he had done it until Doc had pointed it out.

"I'll be fine," I added to reassure him.

David's tears did leak out then, escaping his control. The look of pain on his face was so great, I wanted to cry too. But I didn't. I held it in. I was still upset with him for the other stuff. Part of me knew it was irrational of me, but damn it! I had a right to feel whatever it was I had to in order to make sense of all this and process it.

Wasn't Elisabeth always telling me that feelings weren't right or wrong, they just are? It is what we choose to do with them and how we choose to react to them that make us either in the right or in the wrong. For once, I was going to allow myself to feel whatever the hell I needed to so I could work through this!

"You sure?" David asked in a small voice.

It took me a second to figure out what he was talking about. I had been so lost in my own thoughts again.

"Hmm? Oh, yes! Yes, I forgive you for it. I bruise so easy. Who knows what it's from," I tried to downplay it, not wanting to make him feel worse.

David tried to give me a little smile. It came out weak but at least he was trying. I think he knew I'd lied trying to make him feel better but wasn't about to let me give him any slack.

"No, Melanie. I know I did this." He shook his head, his face full of regret. "I am *so* sorry."

"Well yes, but—"

"No. No buts, Melanie. My PTSD is not an excuse or justification for hurting you. *Ever.* Don't let your care for me lessen the care you have for yourself. Always put your wellbeing first. *Please.* No one has a right to hurt you, Melanie. Not even me." David's face was earnest, almost desperate. "You've hid secrets of abuse too long to start again now."

I was speechless. His words striking me to my core. I hadn't even realized I'd be about to cover it up, even if I knew it hadn't been intentional.

Just like I had all my life. Wow.

It was too easy to slip back into old patterns and learned behaviors. The revelation made me pause. I'd have to be cautious and not let my childhood programing infiltrate this new and blooming relationship. I needed to talk to Liz about this. She'd help me make sense of it.

David studied my face. "You know I'm right, don't you?"

"Yes," I shook my head. What else was there to say?

"This is new," David's hand left my shoulder and slid down to pick up the delicate gold chain of my necklace to straighten it since it had been tossed about by the violent removal of my sweatshirt.

I forgot I had that thing on!

I was glad he'd changed the subject and wasn't dwelling anymore on his mistake and I watched his honey-brown eyes as they focused on the glimmering jewelry.

He let his hand slid to the end and studied the medallion that dangled from it for a moment. It was about the size of a penny, the surface glimmered and sparkled an almost translucent golden color from the sunlight shining off it. The medallion wasn't perfectly round; it had six straight edges. On one side was an elaborately carved flaming sword.

I glanced down in relief at it too as he looked at it transfixed, the medallions reflection of the additional sunlight shining into his eyes making them look piercingly clear and golden as well. His eyes had never looked more beautiful and I felt compelled to ask him what he was thinking but I refrained.

I tore my eyes from his as he continued to stare into the medallion, the pondering crease in his brow deepening. The sword looked suspiciously like the one I'd fought with back at Mount Moriah. My eyes narrowed as well as I realized it just might be the same one. I think I could see the tiny design of ram's horns on the hilt.

Had the necklace changed or have I just not noticed that until now! It looks even more detailed than before! I'll have to look at it under a magnifying glass later!

David slowly flipped it over and tilted his head to the side as if to try and see if the image would change along with it, like looking into a holographic picture. On the other size was a decorative cup overflowing. The liquid inside had spilled over and was pooling around its base giving the illusion that it was sitting on a mirror. Though the images were incredibly small, they were remarkably and magnificently detailed. A slight smile slanted David's beautiful heart shaped mouth up on the left and he looked up at me, his eyes shining with what I thought was both hope and sorrow.

"It's warm," he said almost to himself as he set it carefully back to rest on my breastbone.

That necklace has always had a warmth to it since the day Gabriel gave it to me. I thought to myself instead of speaking it out loud.

I'd never told David about my encounters with the Archangel Gabriel and Archangel Michael. He didn't know anything about that side of my life. *The good, amazing and uplifting side.* I'd only ever shared the spiritual experiences I'd had with Elisabeth. And I hadn't even filled her in on the last one yet!

I am getting so behind.

"Melanie, I know I've put the weight of a lot of difficult truths on you today. I just ask, no I beg you...have mercy on me as you think about the truths I've shared with you." He lowered his head to my lap, his forehead resting on the edge of my knees, his hands on the sides of my thighs again. "I don't want to lose you. But I can't stomach the thought of causing you anymore pain either."

How did he know Gabriel told me this necklace was to remind me of speaking truth, but showing mercy!

David's words meant more to me than he knew. Had God spoken to his heart to let him see the necklace for what it was and discern the meaning? Gabriel told me most people would not know it's true meaning. David saw it for what it was right away!

Okay Lord. I get it. David's got your blessing. He's in my life for a reason. I'll work really hard at not staying mad at him...or at this situation.

I looked down at his thick soft black curls and saw the rounded shape of his strong shoulders still carrying the heaviness and burden of those hard truths from his past. He'd been carrying them all alone for so very long. Just as I had been carrying my own.

The night he'd rescued me from my father flashed to my thoughts again like a sudden curtain being pulled back and flooding a darkened room. I saw it all over again. Him yanking my father off of me right before he finished removing my pants to rape me. The sounds of their furious struggles and the familiar thuds of violence as he fought him off, chasing him away. Something no other person had ever been able to do.

David had returned and picked me up off the floor where my father had beaten me to the ground. He'd set me gently on my sofa as if I'd been the most valuable and precious thing he'd ever touched. He'd locked his eyes onto mine as he pulled my ripped jeans back up over the curve of my hips and gave me back my modesty and dignity. He hadn't wavered and he hadn't tried to ogle me. He'd refused to look at what my father had exposed and had respected me more than fulfilling his male curiosity.

He'd lowered his head next to me, thanking God that he'd come in time and saved me. Then he'd gathered me tenderly in his arms and comforted me, protected me, and held me until help arrived.

David you saved me. You risked your life for me. You've always put me first.

The truth spoke through my thoughts and with it, mercy and compassion filled me. I didn't think. I just acted on what my heart whispered to me like a musical wind, interrupting the screaming of my thoughts and the thrumming of my emotions. I reached out and stroked David's hair ever so tenderly. I remembered touching it like this the night he'd saved me. The soft silky black curls slipped through my fingers and I felt any residue of anger and hurt slip away more and more like ice sliding off the hood of a slowly thawing car.

I felt the necklace around my neck grow increasingly hot where it lay on my chest until it began to burn, like the icy-hot of an invisible flame only I could feel. It pierced through my skin and into my chest where I felt it catch my heart on fire. I almost gasped as more compassion and love than I had ever felt in my entire life combined, poured into me. A holy love. An unforsaken love. True love. It was as if the last of my walls burned away, stripping me of restraint, fear, and my guarded inhibitions.

"David," my voice was a quivering whisper.

"It was one of the hardest experiences in my life Melanie—Having to stop...having to *ki-kill* her. My...my break down is proof enough of that. I know it was a lot to listen to. Almost too much to forgive me for. I can't even forgive myself." David kept his head down, my hand still stroking his silky hair.

"I know. I know," I soothed him. "I'm not mad at you. I don't think there is anything for me to forgive. You haven't wronged *me*, David. But my heart is breaking simply because...because I have to accept the fact that nothing is perfect in this world, not even you. Somehow, I put a childish, stupid girl's expectation on you to be the perfect Prince Charming. It wasn't fair. But honestly David, what breaks my heart the most, is knowing you've been in all this pain and you've been carrying it all by yourself for so long," I spoke softly.

"He pretty much did too," Doc confirmed. "I mean, I knew of course. She was my daughter, estranged as we were at that time," Doc cleared his throat. "But he knows I never blamed him. I understood what she was long before she became it. Long before someone had to stop her," Doc ended, his voice softening and his face finally showing sadness for the loss of his step-daughter, regardless of the circumstances.

"I've still felt alone in this," David whispered toward the ground, "We only discussed it twice before. The night I killed her when I called you after my debrief, and...and the day you came with me to tell Tristina in person her daughter was dead, once I was back home," he said miserably, glancing up at Doc. "I've tried to push it down ever since."

"I know, son," Doc whispered.

"Son". That word has a whole new meaning to me now. I realized it wasn't just a word of endearment but a title. An admission of a truth the two of them shared.

"But now I know too. And I'm here. I'm not going anywhere," I repeated his own words back to him that he'd said to comfort me the other night when he'd come over to confirm that I was the young woman Doc had been talking about.

"I can help you and support you just like you're helping and supporting me," I leaned forward and picked up his face in my hands. His eyes were closed once more, his shame and self-incrimination making him afraid to look at me.

"I don't deserve you," David's voice cracked.

"David, I—," I wanted to say it so badly! To tell him that I loved him. It was on the tip of my tongue almost struggling to get out of my mouth but I stopped it and pushed it deep down where I could manage it, learn to understand it first myself.

"I—".

I'd almost said it again! The words had almost poured out, a confession, sincere and devout. I would have meant every word. Instead I just tried to let that love flow through my hands to his beautiful mind and soak down into his heart as I stroked his face and hair with my hands.

I hoped he could feel what I was longing to tell him, what I was still too terrified to admit to him out loud. I felt silly that it had taken me so long to admit it even to myself. I think I'd known it already, but I'd been too afraid to acknowledge it. What I felt for him right now couldn't be explained any other way. I was madly and irrevocably in love with him.

I suddenly realized that my feelings for him had been slowly changing and growing for years. His patient kindness and gentleness had won me over long before I'd even consciously accepted how much I liked him. His constant attempts at wooing me had been sweet and endearing. He'd never been creepy about it, nor had he ever tried to take advantage of me. He'd shown me respect and consideration the entire time we'd known each other.

He'd never hurt me if he could avoid it. His resistance to talk about this hadn't been for selfish reasons; he'd been concerned that it was too soon into our "dating" relationship, showing me once again how much more he placed my needs ahead of his own. He was selfless and good. And I loved him for it. I loved him for all of it!

"David I—!" I tried helplessly again, "David I *care* more for you in this moment than I ever have. I need you. My heart needs you," I spoke louder, attempting to make my voice strong and full of certainty as the truth settled deep into my soul, empowering me. I know, I hadn't told him the "L" word, but I still felt like I had confessed something important to him, in a way I was ready for.

David's eyes shot open and he searched my face. Feeling the true meaning in my words and what I was too afraid to really say. I could see the relief and delight fill his eyes and his expression changed from sorrow and hopelessness to hopeful and amazed. Words seemed to fail him too. "You—?" David tried to ask but lost his voice, his tone said that he could hardly believe it and that it must be too good to be true.

"Yes! I am smitten with you Mr. Abramson. Do you hear me? This changes nothing except it brings me closer to you. You let me in past the walls of your most guarded secret and you trusted me. I won't abandon you. Admittedly, I still need to process all this but that's just reality, not a punishment. Okay? It will just take me time, but it's something I have to work through," I wished for him to understand me and accept my words.

"I understand completely. Thank y—," David could hardly get the words out before I covered his mouth with mine and kissed him long and hard, ending my kiss by covering his face with kisses, his cheeks, his chin, his forehead, the lids of his eyes.

The theme song from *Rocky* blared out of Docs pocket and he yanked out his cell phone looking a little annoyed as David and I broke apart, looking up curiously.

Crap! I'd forgotten he was here again! Oops.

"Now who is it?" Doc said aggravatedly. "I don't know this number." He scowled at his cell phone.

"Maybe it's important," David chimed in, straightening up at attention with curiosity as to who was interrupting us despite looking disappointed that our kiss had been broken up.

"Tristina, you crazy bitch. If that's you messing with me from another line I swear—" Doc grumbled to himself.

"No, you need to take it," David said knowingly. He had a look of absolute confidence on his face now. Doc eyed him briefly and an unspoken understanding passed between them.

The phone was still chirping out *Eye of the Tiger*, the phone repeating the song's bridge line for the third time.

"You need to answer that," David said again with certainty. I could tell from the look on his face he had a discerning impression that Doc must not miss that call. Doc recognized the change in David too. He had snapped out of the wounded warrior mode and back into *The Sentinel*.

I wonder why he hadn't listened to the warning inside about Danielle? I wondered confused.

David had told me he knew she wasn't the one and had even heard the Lord tell him so.

Maybe he just didn't listen because he wanted to be wanted, and he wanted what he wanted, regardless of the warnings going off inside. And ultimately, he was the one who had stopped her so maybe in the end he'd finally listened. Just in time too before she could...

"Hello?" Doc barked, not sounding at all friendly and cutting right through the beginning of my internal analysis of David's past dilemmas.

Dilemma? It was a whole hell of a lot more than just a dilemma!

"Yes, this is Eugene Picard. Who's this?" Doc said curtly. He continued to frown as he listened for a few intense moments making David and I wonder what was happening. Then suddenly his face light up into an anticipatory grin.

Doc snapped his fingers at us and covered the mic to mouth nearly silently, "Dwayne's been located!" He continued to listen intently, his fist making a pump in the air to say "yes"!

David and I looked at each other. Whatever he and I had just come through, it was going to have to wait. This was more than just he and I. It was about *him.* Our world had just changed dramatically and it was about to change again. I could feel the shift coming, like watching the shoreline while standing atop a boat, and the land looks like it's swaying. Left, right, left, right, right, right. But it isn't the land, it's you. Your boat is tipping over. And you? You're barely hanging on.

I felt my head swoosh and my gut clench with dread. This new shift was starting. *I'm sure glad I'm already sitting down.*

I felt my pulse quicken and my breathing stop cold mid-inhalation. *My father's really back? How close is he? How much time until...until he's standing in front of me again?*

Man Hunt

Chapter Nine

"Tell me everything you know!" Doc ordered. He raced back around the lobby's receptionist desk and shifted stuff about, finally snatching up a pad of paper and pen. He began writing furiously. It felt like forever as he listened, his face kept mostly in a tight frown, his hand writing, pausing, then writing again. "What! When?" He looked pissed.

"That'll take me at least forty to fifty minutes with my sirens blaring, assuming traffic even gives a damn and gets the hell out of my way! What's the quickest route?" He jotted down more notes.

"Is the park locked down yet?" He demanded to know.

Which park? Where? How close is he?

"Well, why the hell not?" Doc smacked his hand down on the desk so hard he made the little service bell jump off the front ledge to its death. It hit the carpet and bounced several times, piercing the air with a sharp *diiing, diing, ding, ding-a-ling*!

"Get it locked down *now*! Seriously? Call for reinforcements and get your choppers out there! Every extra officer you've got who's not already blocking the roads and combing the neighboring properties needs to be out canvasing those hills in a search grid with the K-9s. Who the hell is running the shots—" Doc stopped abruptly, the other caller clearly not willing to be scolded by someone they made a courtesy call to. Doc let the other person talk for a bit, his glower threatening to permanently turn the corners of his mouth upside down.

"Well, I'm not surprised Special Agent Nichols has told you all this already! So why isn't it done?" Doc shouted. "Do not let a single pedestrian leave that parking lot. Do you hear me?" Doc ordered, trying to lower his voice to sound reasonable instead of being driven bat-shit-crazy at their incompetence.

Doc started pacing behind the desk staying close to his note pad and looked down at his watch impatiently. "When was he first identified?" He looked at his watch again and almost snarled. "Lord Almighty! And it took you guys this long before someone thought to lock down the park? Oh wait, that's right. You haven't done it yet even though Special Agent Nichols told you that too," Doc said sarcastically.

Doc paced out from behind the desk looking so frustrated he could have stomped on his cell phone and hoped the man on the other end felt it.

"Right. I'm comin'! Get your men on it in the meantime. If the FBI show up before I get there, *please* tell your men to fall in line and just do what they're told or we could lose him if you haven't already." He glanced up at us, his lips tight. Then he stopped pacing and nodded in agreement to whatever he was hearing now.

"A-huh." Pause.

"Right." Pause.

"Couldn't agree more." He rolled his eyes.

What are they saying! The anxiety of this one-sided conversation was driving me mad!

"Okay, okay. Just get the dogs out there. We can't let this piece of shit outsmart us again."

Pause.

"I know you're doing your best."

Pause.

"Roger that. Call me with any developments, no matter how minor they seem."

He listened one moment more then said in his most cooperative professional tone, "Thank you for the call Sheriff. See you in forty."

Doc ended his call and slipped his cell phone back into his front pocket and let out an angry, "Shit!" He ripped off the top page of the note pad, folded it precisely into quarters and slipped it into one of his front pockets, then grabbed his car keys out of the desk drawer. He pulled out a chain with his badge dangling from the end and slipped it around his neck. Giving us a sideways glance, and looking like he was about to burst with both anticipation and frustration, he pulled his Smith and Wesson M&P .40 caliber out of the drawer, still in its holster and began unbuckling his belt. He slipped it onto the belt and threaded two double magazine pouches on the opposite side.

"It's about to go down," Doc said more to himself than to us.

"Dwayne's been spotted at a park," David both confirmed and stated, implying that we needed more information having only heard one side to this important conversation. He got to his feet to face Doc but remained standing right next to where I was still sitting. It was happening too fast. I couldn't breathe. I didn't trust my legs to stand on them.

"Affirmative," Doc confirmed. "I need to get out there to make sure they don't FUBAR this."

David nodded as if he understood that last part. He probably did. I had no clue what Doc meant.

Must be a military thing. FUBAR?

"I want him. That bastard isn't getting away from Doc! This hunt is mine!" Doc proclaimed.

David and I watched Doc as he turned around quickly to get to work. He reached up and tapped twice on the wall just to the bottom left of the large painting hanging on the wall behind the receptionist desk. The rustic scene of snow peaked mountains and tangled forest lining a dark rippling lake shifted about an inch to the right. He used his left hand and slid the painting over as if it was a sliding glass door. Behind it a mid-size safe was exposed. He placed his right palm on the biometric sensor and it beeped twice, the light turning from red to yellow. Then, just because it was Doc and he believed in overkill, probably literally, he pulled out his keys and thumbed through them until he extended out a small, odd shaped key and inserted it into the lock, turned it to the left, making the light turn orange.

I expected the safe to open. But then again, I'd never heard or seen a movie where an orange light meant a positive pacification of a locked system or safe. I was right! Doc leaned in and spoke five words very clearly, "Tristina, you're a real bitch." The security light turned green and the safe popped open with a characteristic *click.*

I stifled a giggle that nearly burst from me as his "magic words" struck me as absurdly hilarious in my air deprived brain. I had pretty much forgotten to breathe since he told us Dwayne was located. I tried to clear my throat to hide it, but I knew they'd already heard the strangled sound escape me.

Like clearing your throat will fool anyone Melanie. Get real.

David and I watched in patient silence as Doc pulled out a green camo bullet proof vest that was loaded down with what looked like a sat-phone, backup walkie-talkie, more ammo, and other pockets that looked full, but I didn't know what they contained.

I was just about to interrupt his soldier-make-ready-for-war dress up routine with a question about where they said my father had been spotted, because Doc still hadn't told us yet, when he reached into the safe and pulled out two more guns. He hefted his leg up onto the desk chair, strapped on a right ankle holster and inserted a gun. The second he put in a hidden pouch on the side of his vest. He grabbed out some handcuffs, three pairs to be exact, and slipped them into another pocket. He placed what looked like an electric cattle prod in a long cylinder-shaped pocket and secured the flap. A long-jagged knife appeared out of nowhere and he pulled it from the sheath and checked it on both sides, leaving the sheath on the desk. He turned and scrounged around in the safe for a moment before finding what he was looking for, a sturdy looking forearm knife holster. He smiled to himself and strapped it on, gliding the long, wicked knife home with a satisfying sound of *fthut*.

"Is that the knife I bought you last Christmas?" David questioned, rubbing his hands together and shifting a little from side to side. I could tell that David was getting anxious, waiting for more details just as I was. Or maybe David was hoping for an invitation from Doc to suit up and join him.

All I could think of was, *"Wow, three pairs of handcuffs? What are those for? Wrists, ankles and a link to tie him up like a hog? A knife to slit his throat?"* I felt the smile on my lips and I forced it away. *Bad Melanie!*

"Sure is!" Doc said with a broad smile.

See Melanie, his smile is appropriate. Yours is not.

I couldn't take it anymore. My breathing had sped up with mounting anxiety. I was either going to be sick, burst into a frantic scream "Would you tell me what is happening!" or continue to hyperventilate. Doc finally spit it out right before I lost it all together. I don't think he knew what state of mind I was in at the moment, since I still hadn't said anything.

Sometimes I think I'm going to explode, my feelings are too big for my body.

"Whelp, kids! I gotta run. Strawberry, they confirmed that your father was spotted in Hidden Falls Regional Park up in Auburn. Some poor trail jogger recognized him and ran down the trail to tell the Park Ranger he thought he saw that maniac from the news. Took them a while to figure out who he meant or what to do. Stupid lugs!" Doc seethed.

"I'm coming with you!" David nearly shouted, his own frustration peeked to its limit.

"Oh no, you won't boy," Doc denied swiftly.

"What? But why?" David countered confused.

"Your head isn't in the right space for a hunt like this today, for one thing, boy. It's been a long time since you've seen this kind of action and I won't have you getting hurt by making a silly mistake because of it. And second, you're not law enforcement," Doc overrode.

David scowled at Doc and was about to respond when Doc jumped back in to clarify, "I'm not sayin' you're not a good soldier, son! I'm sayin' it's too dangerous to go back into this kind of action when you're emotional and distracted and...drained. You know that," Doc walked over and gripped David's shoulders firmly.

"Yes Sir. But I can—"

"No, stay here boy. Stay here with your pretty lady. Focus on her. Focus on each other," He smacked David's shoulder and gave him a reassuring smile. He looked down at me with the same expression. I forced myself to stand to my feet still trying to process the one-sided conversation we'd just heard.

"My father's close by? Auburn? I thought for sure he'd left the area to hide out for a while," I said in disbelief. I didn't know what to hope for. Would they actually catch him today?

"Yep," Doc confirmed.

"With all his years as a long-haul trucker and all the creepy hiding places he must know about, why would he have gone up there?" I wondered aloud. It didn't make any sense.

"The Sheriff I spoke to said that a local rancher who lives near the park told him not too long ago he thought someone had been living in their barn. Found a makeshift bed and some food wrappers up in the loft but it looked untouched for a few days by the time he came across it. Sheriff dismissed it at the time as probably some local kids sneaking out to make out with their girlfriend or some such nonsense. They'd had similar reports over a few weeks from some of the other rangers and farmers in those parts. So it's possible he's been moving around up there a little while now. Hiding out and rotating," Doc explained.

"And he hasn't killed anyone?" I said surprised.

"Probably didn't want to draw unwanted attention by suddenly stopping what might be the frequent comings and goings of a rancher's business. Him not knowing the occupants of the ranch houses and all, he'd be really taking a gamble on how often they're expected to be seen. Sometimes just twenty-four hours is enough time to make certain neighbors or friends worry," David reasoned.

"Don't worry baby girl, we'll do all we can to find him. There's a lot of wilderness up that way but they're bringing in the dogs and two choppers. We'll find him," Doc tussled my hair like I was a kid, sending my already red frizzy mane into a disaster of directions. "Now you two stay put, ya hear me?"

I annoyingly tried to smooth down my unruly hair, my mouth opening to say something, but David beat me to the punch.

"Yes Sir," David consented, answering for both of us.

"Yep," I agreed easily, still wrestling with my hair. I wasn't going anywhere near my father. You didn't have to ask me twice.

"Shoot. I almost forgot," Doc rushed over to the safe again and pulled out another gun. This one looked different. Almost fake. He quickly slipped it away into the folds of his vest and locked the safe back up, sliding the picture back into place.

Hmm, you'd never know it was there.

"What's that one for?" I couldn't help but ask. It had looked strange with a two-tone odd shaped muzzle of silver and blue.

"Tranquilizer gun in case I decide not to pop his ass and actually capture him alive. Haven't decided yet," Doc winked at me trying to lighten things up. Or maybe just lighten me up. I'd grown completely stiff and serious, tingling with both adrenaline and dread coursing through my veins.

"How did they know to call you?" I suddenly realized it seemed odd they would call him, my instructor. As far as I knew he wasn't listed on any of the news flashes or bulletins.

"They didn't say, but from what I gather, when they called the FBI and got transferred to Agent Nichols, he told them to call me as back up," Doc said reasonably. "Nichols and I spoke yesterday after you left," Doc informed me matter-of-factly. "I wanted to know why he hadn't sent me the BOLO Alert about Dwayne. We've worked fugitive cases together before, being that I'm a bounty hunter and all." Doc pointed to his official badge hanging around his neck.

"He said BOLOs went out through all channels and when he didn't get my call at the forefront, thought I just wasn't interested or already be on a hunt for someone else. I told him I wanted in. I reassured him, I was. Turns out, he had already told your professor friend he liked my style. Told her my career spoke for itself so he promised to keep me in the loop if they got confirmation that things turned local. So, as a professional courtesy, we both agreed to keep the other in the loop of any investigative developments. I told him it wasn't about getting paid the bounty on this one. I only care about bringing the sick son of a bitch in for good and helping out this little baby girl I'd just met." Doc winked at me and this time, David didn't try to kill him.

Oooh, progress.

"Oh, okay," was the only intelligent thing I could think of to say. "Thank you," I added as an afterthought.

"Son, lock up for me before you two leave okay? You might want to take her down to the mats and show her some self-defense moves. Bring today back on track a little bit. Give you both something else to focus on. Think it'd be good for both of you, don't you?" Doc suggested friendly enough, but gave what I thought was a suggestive wink, directed at David.

"Sure, if she's up for it," David nodded and glanced at me to get my take on it. I shrugged to signify it was okay by me, my mind not quite processing everything at full speed.

"Okay, lock up after I leave and be safe you two," Doc ordered. I could hear the excitement growing in his voice about the coming hunt and potential apprehension of my father.

"We'll try. Be safe too, Doc. Don't let him get one up on you if you encounter him. He doesn't play by any rules. I think if he has any advantage, no matter how slight, he'll use it to the fullest," David advised grimly. "Try to partner up with another officer once you're out there since I can't come and guard your flank, okay Doc?"

"Hear you loud and clear kid," Doc hurried to us, smacking David on the shoulders as he passed with a nod, his face serious and mouth tight. He gave me a pretend tap on the chin with his huge fist, making me smirk a little despite my grim mood. "Keep your chin up Strawberry. Docs gonna get 'im."

He went to the door and unlocked it. His long stride breaking into a jog as he cleared the door and headed to his military-green and black Hummer parked across the street. There was an array of antennas on the top, a roof rack, light bar, winch, and I could also see a cage blocking the back seat for use when he made arrests. He even had undercarriage armor and the pushbumper on the front *and* back of the vehicle.

Two pushbumpers? What does he do, drive in reverse and spin someone? Ooh, I wonder if it's bullet proof too? Hmm, is this where David got his inspiration for his Jeep Rubicon he tricked out or is this a tough guy military thing?

My mind was spiraling and I quickly pulled my thoughts back. It wouldn't help me any to let my mind shut down out of fear. I wasn't going to give into that sort of nonsense anymore.

Get a grip Melanie! I ordered myself.

David swiftly locked the door behind Doc and turned off the lobby lights so the building would look closed, not open to walk-ins. He watched Doc making sure he made it to his vehicle and then turned to me. "This day is just full of surprises, isn't it?"

I nodded in agreement, still feeling slightly stunned.

Oh God. Help them catch that monster. Please. I prayed fervently. They had to catch him! They just had to. He wasn't that far away. Not really. Forty to forty-five minutes with sirens on? How much time had Doc lost answering our questions? My stomach dropped.

"Are you alright?" David asked me quietly.

"Mostly. Yes. No. Um, I think so," I guessed, sounding just as unsure as I felt.

"Come on. I'll distract you for a bit," David offered me his hand.

I gathered up my sweatshirt and little purse off the floor and slipped my free hand inside of his, feeling it's warmth seep into mine. His hand felt good. Strong, safe, and comforting. I felt myself relax a little more and I let his warmth and presence soak in. I couldn't afford to freak out any more today. That wasn't who I wanted to be anymore.

It isn't who I am going to be, darn it! God hasn't given me a spirt of fear, but one of power, one of love, and a sound, clear, focused mind!

I quoted the scripture in my mind, adding some clarifying points to further encourage myself. I was choosing to take hold of it. I wasn't going to be afraid of my father. I wasn't going to let him make me feel powerless. And I wasn't going to let the enemy torment my mind anymore!

Why do I keep having to tell myself this!

I was frustrated with my weaknesses. I was always slipping back toward the old habit of letting the fear and doubts spread throughout my mind to make me almost paralyzed with indecision and trepidation.

Well, not anymore!

Satan, you lose! I spoke in my mind with all the internal gusto I could muster.

God has already won! Satan was already defeated. Be strong woman! You can do this!

"Doc is great at tracking. He's one of the best I've ever seen. He's no joke when it comes to suspect take down and apprehension. That's why he decided to open a bounty hunting school and teaches this stuff. It's also why he's the one the FBI calls to help them catch their "Most Wanted" when they need extra manpower or need help hunting them down in the region. He's as good as they get," David reassured me, giving my hand a quick squeeze and started leading me slowly out of the lobby and back down the hall.

"I believe you," I smiled a little, thinking about how huge Doc was and how my father wasn't the tiniest bit intimidating to him.

Doc is also a father. Bet he was a great daddy, despite how that Tristina woman made him out to be.

There is such a difference in the idea of a father verses a daddy, at least to my mind. A daddy is someone a little girl will adore. Someone she makes her Superman, her hero. Someone she can trust to protect her, look out for her, take care of her. Even teach her how to dance or tell her she's pretty when she puts on a new dress.

I bet Doc had been that kind of daddy to his girls, even to Danielle, who wasn't his biologically. I was sure he wasn't to blame for what she chose to become in the end. How could he? He was so fervent about right and wrong, a believer of justice. He even spends his "retired" years seeking to bring the criminals to justice and apprehend them. Whereas she... she didn't have those same convictions. Doc had said she'd been broken from the start.

Poor Doc. He'd tried so hard.

I shoved the thought away of Danielle. I didn't want to think about *her* right now. That woman who had broken David's heart and to this day, the memory of her tormented him with guilt. She'd broken her daddy's heart too!

She didn't know how lucky she'd been to have David or a daddy like Doc! What a stupid selfish bitch! I hate you!

No Melanie. You can't hate her. I corrected myself internally.

Oh, but I do! She was the first woman David ever loved besides me. She had him first. She slept with him first! She married him first! She stole all the firsts with David that should have been mine!

I was seething internally. Infuriated! I had to rationalize things. I had to think about this differently.

Think about this girl. You can't hate a dead woman. You can't hate Danielle because David chose her before he met you. And it isn't fair to be mad at him either! He didn't even know you existed yet. He didn't even know you were alive! It's nothing but a waste of energy and effort to be mad at either one of them. So, knock it off!

Then it dawned on me that maybe Satan was trying to attack me mentally *again*. I'd rebuked the fear he'd tried to put into me only moments before and here I was, giving into another negative train of thought. Maybe I should rebuke these circular angry thoughts too just in case they weren't all my own.

I rebuke every thought that exalts itself against the knowledge of Christ in the name of Jesus! I take every thought captive that isn't my own or of God.

I took in a long cleansing breath to help straighten out my thoughts.

She didn't even know how lucky she'd been to have both my David and a loving daddy like Doc, I thought again, but with true sadness this time, not anger. *I guess that was my own thought.*

I'd never called my father my dad or my daddy. He'd always just been my "Father". The thing of nightmares. The cause of terror in every waking moment of my childhood. I knew the word *father* wasn't a bad word. After all, when I thought about God, I often thought of him as my Father God. It felt right and pure. He was my help, my protector, my provider. He was my hope and my salvation. But in the context of humans, there was no purity to the word for me. But "daddy"? Daddy was a word I had longed to be able to call *someone* as a child. And if I was being honest with myself, I still wanted "a daddy". Even now.

Doc is a daddy. I bet he misses his daughter. Even with her flaws. Is that what I was really picking up on when I felt drawn to him or confused around him? Was that the appeal? Yes, he is attractive for a man his age. But was it more? Some subconscious need of my own for a wholesome father figure? A daddy? Or was part of what I was picking up his *desire to make right what he couldn't for his own daughter, Danielle? David's wife? Do I remind him of her somehow?*

My thoughts were clearer, though still confusing in their own way, but at least it felt like they were starting to click into solid theories. The prayer had chased away the angry spiraling thoughts. It had also let me see clearly what I had been misreading in myself and possibly in Doc too. Bringing it all back into perspective.

Oh, thank you Lord! I get it now! I'm not a raving hormonal freak, I just want a daddy.

"You okay?" David asked me sweetly. I looked up at him and found him watching me, his face was inquisitive. He'd been watching my mind work and had probably seen every emotional response latched onto the jumping train of my thoughts as they had crossed my face, one after the other, after the other.

"Yes, just working some stuff out," I answered honestly, and tapped my temple to indicate it had all been in my head.

David smiled at me, a little sadness showing through the brave smile he had tried to project. He knew he'd caused me a lot of pain, heartache and mental anguish with what he'd shared with me about Danielle. But we'd already discussed it enough for one day, and I think he knew it wouldn't help our relationship a smidge if he were to press me and ask more questions about what I was thinking. Fine by me, I didn't exactly explain where all my thoughts had come from anyway. That would be awkward.

We'd strolled a few steps more in silence and then stopped in front of a big black door with a small glass windowpane in the center so you could see inside the large room beyond. As we had walked down the hall toward this room, my mind's rampage and internal discussions had been my only focus. I hadn't truly seen where we were going.

"We're here," David said with a slight lift to his voice. "I promise this will be a good distraction," David turned to me and gently pulled me into him, watching my face for signs of discomfort or anxiety.

I had meant what I'd said. I wasn't mad at him. I embraced him with ease, closing my eyes and smelling the musky sporty scent of his cologne. He still smelled fresh and clean and I resisted the urge to cling to him tighter or snuggle my face into his chest. I didn't want to spark something else. We were both too emotional, too raw, too vulnerable. I could feel it in the air between us; the potential for our own emotionally charged warzone affair. I didn't want our relationship to be superficially charged, inflating a love that should happen naturally. I wanted it to be real. I wanted it to last forever.

I gently pulled away and looked up at him. His eyes were a little moist again but he was holding himself together better now. I think the reality of our present circumstances and Doc running off to hunt down my father had helped bring him back to me and out of the past. It had triggered the soldier-warrior-protector inside him and somehow, brought back to him clarity, self-control and stability.

David smiled down at me, his eyes boring into mine, reading me just as I was reading him. Our silence was comfortable once more, though charged with a dangerous potential.

Is it because we loved each other so much and we just want to comfort the other? Longing to be close to wipe away the pain, erasing it with hugs, kisses, caresses and...

And don't go there, girl.

David wasn't moving. He seemed to be waiting for me to give him some sign that I was ready to enter the room and resume our training. Or was he waiting for something else? What did he want me to say?

I wonder how Liz is going to take it when I tell her about all this. If she doesn't already know. I thought wryly, realizing that with all her research into David with the unrestricted access she seemed to have to a lot of government records, she probably already knew about his short-lived marriage that ended with the death of his wife.

And how she died. I need to ask Liz if...Oh Shoot!

"I need to call Liz!" It dawned on me suddenly and I nearly shouted it in David's face. He startled a little, not expecting a sudden frantic burst of words out of me. He'd been expected something else. I still didn't know what. A rebuke? That I changed my mind and wanted him to take me home immediately? That I decided to never see him again because it was too painful? What? Or was he just looking for some reassurance that I really did understand him, understand why he had to do what he did, to accept him, and love him?

"I promised Liz I'd keep her in the loop if I heard anything, no matter what I'm doing," I said hurriedly, and in my regular voice volume, trying hard to not seem angry or crazy. "I can't believe I forgot! I'm sorry I blurted it out," I cringed a little.

"Right. Of course," David replied looking slightly embarrassed he'd forgotten as well. "Do you want to use the phone in the lobby, or—"

"No, I have my cell," I pulled my cell phone out of my little purse, unlocked it, and held down the number two speed dial for Liz's number. Liz picked up on the second ring. Before she could ask how my lessons were going I jumped in with the news about Doc getting a call and running out to help look for my father. I told her everything Doc had told us, as well as the part when he made us stay behind, David included, but I didn't tell her *why* he made David stay behind.

"I'm glad he had the good sense to make you both stay behind. I think David is too emotionally involved after seeing what Dwayne almost did to you. David might kill him if he gets his hands on him again. God knows I want to," Liz said confidently.

"You do?" I asked unsure if it was just something to say or something she says only when she means it. "Would you?"

Liz didn't answer me.

"You're not going to head up there too, are you Liz?" I probed, after she grew silent on the other end.

"Huh?" Liz said distractedly.

"Liz! You're not going up there too, are you?" I said a little louder. "Promise me you won't! I don't want you hurt. There's already a slew of people up there searching for him; the FBI, Doc, even the local police, and their dogs. They're on the hunt! They don't need you to—"

"No, I won't. Don't worry Mel," Liz cut in to stop my unnecessary lecture.

"Promise me," I insisted doubtfully.

"I solemnly swear," Liz answered me with her most sincere tone of voice.

"Okay, good," I sighed out in relief.

"You okay? News of your father shook you up I'm sure, but I'm sensing something else bothering you?" Liz probed perceptively.

"I guess. Yeah, I'm okay. David's with me," I deliberately avoided the part about something else bothering me. I looked up at David and let him see how much I trusted him to be with me, alone, and as my protector. I wanted him to know, that even though he'd shared his horrible experience with me, and what he'd been forced to do to stop his crazy deceased wife, I still trusted him and knew he'd never hurt *me*. "If you're not with me, David's the next best thing," I said, more to him than to her.

"Good. Glad to hear you feel that way," Liz said softly. I could tell by her tone she was picking up on the unspoken words between my words, and the part of her question I hadn't answered. I knew it. She was sensing something else had gone on today. Her tone told me she wasn't clueless but would allow me the dignity of telling her later, without David's listening ears to make me feel awkward, foolish, or embarrassed. She knew me so well.

"Keep training with David, okay. Get some use out of that facility today," Liz suggested.

"We will. We just came to a big matted room," I peeked through the window in the door trying to survey the room.

"Oh! Physical defense. Excellent! Remember what I taught you, but be open to whatever he has to show you as well," Liz advised wisely.

"I will," I shrugged shyly, then realized she couldn't see me.

I used to be too nervous to let Liz show me the really aggressive fighting moves. It wasn't because I felt completely uncoordinated and inadequate, but because the basic self-defense was all I could manage to get through. You'd think I'd be eager, but every time she'd tried, I ended up a mental and emotional mess. It just wasn't in me to hurt someone else. I abhorred violence against others. Mainly because I'd always been the victim. And even though Liz was my best friend in the entire world, I didn't even want to "pretend" to hurt her, even if it was only to learn to protect myself. My heart just wasn't in it.

I have to get over it! I have to get through this! My father nearly killed me six weeks ago! What am I waiting for?

"You ready?" Liz knew where my thoughts had gone. She knew how hard this was going to be for me. "Let it go. Let the panic out in the room if you feel it overwhelming you," Liz encouraged me. "Don't try to bottle it up. Let it fuel your aggressive reactions and defensive responses. But do *not*, and I mean it Melanie, do *not* let your emotions and your thoughts rule you! Refocus them into your will to live and pull power from your body by using the fear against itself," she finished, her voice very determined and instructional. I barely understood what she was explaining to me.

"You're the martial arts prodigy, Elisabeth Becker. Not me," I reminded her.

"I know, but you can do this. We've practiced before. This will just feel more real." Liz tried to take the edge out of her voice and replace it with reassurance. But I could feel her impatience with me. She'd been so eager for me to step up my self-defense practice with her, but hadn't been able to push me into doing it too much. After all, I'd spent the last six weeks recovering from my father's attack. He'd nearly killed me, hurting me rather badly. I had some cracked ribs, a concussion, fractured cheekbone, split scalp, and some pretty nasty defensive wounds. Oh, and let's not forget a healing bite mark on my neck from my father trying to mark me as his property.

What, more real? Oh...

"I think it will be different learning to fight against a man," I swallowed in agreement, just now realizing what she had meant.

I'd never had any practice learning to fight off an attack from a man in a safe and friendly environment. Every time I'd ever fought with a man, it had been in the midst of an aggressive and violent encounter where fear and terror saturated every fiber of my being. My very life or innocence had been threatened by "men" countless times in the form of giants, demons, Malachi, Damian and Pablo from Jill's gang, and of course, my own *father*. Of all the *human* attackers, my father had always been my greatest adversary. How was I supposed to separate those memories while sparring with David? Or with Doc! Doc was even bigger!

I looked over to David who was now checking the date on the fire extinguisher against the opposite wall, panic was settling into my core at the idea of having to ward off a man of his skill, strength, size, and power.

But you fought giants and demons and you won. Don't forget what you can do with the supernatural power of the Holy Spirit working in you and through you.

The reminder from the Lord brought some comfort to me. I knew I would be fighting not only David in that room, but my own memories and my own fears. I'd have to refuse to let my own learned behaviors of cowering or running far, far away, trigger the freeze or flight side of my instincts. I'd have to let the fight side take over instead.

Like I did when I fought off my father when I was eighteen, and again six weeks ago. And when I picked up the sword and fought off the giants, and actually killed them!

"You heading to Kate's Café afterwards or coming home?" Liz asked me, distracting me back to her and away from David who was done inspecting the fire extinguisher and was turning back to me. I quickly turned back to the door and looked unseeingly through the window. I didn't want him to see the panic and trepidation on my face.

Stop it. You need to do this! You need to face these fears! David won't really hurt you. He isn't your enemy. He is your ally. Today, he's your teacher.

"Mel?" Liz asked again, her voice growing concerned.

"Um, yeah. I mean...Yes. We're probably going to Kate's Café. Frank still needs our help," I said absentmindedly. That room was huge! It was pretty dark inside but I could still tell by the soft glow in a distant corner it was large. I suddenly wanted to get in there, my curiosity making me anxious to end the call and go face my fears.

Or maybe I just want more time with David to myself?

That too. There are comfy mats in there.

Bad Melanie! Stop it. Down girl. Bad.

"I'll let you go then. See you later Melanie. Stay safe," Liz requested.

Wait, did she mean safe as in physically or was she implying sexually?

"Yep. Bye Liz," I said, a trickle of shame intruding into my voice at my last naughty thought and I hung up the phone quickly before she could ask me about it.

She caught it in my voice, I know she did!

To the Mats

Chapter Ten

e entered the "wrestling room" as David called it and he flipped on the lights. This room was one door past the classroom I'd been in yesterday with Doc, off to the right. The black mats covered eighty percent of the floor. Now I understood why Doc called it "going to the mats". Skylights opened up high above us to let in natural light and make the room seem airier than it was. A row of mirrors hung flush against the left-hand side wall. In the far-left corner was groups of professional fitness center quality weight lifting equipment and large stretchy bands hung on the wall to help stretch out the students after their workout.

Unless they use them to tie each other up and practice escaping. Hmmm.

Off to the right side of the door was an open cubbyhole dresser for the students' personal effects with a long metal bench bolted to the concrete floor in front. Freshly rolled towels were in baskets on top of the dresser and a waste basket was on the floor to the left of it. A large blue door marked "bathroom" was cracked open in the far-right corner with a water fountain set alongside the entrance between the supply closet.

Wonder how often a student throws up in there? Or is that just me?

I looked around and then up at the six large skylights. "Why does the light switch have a dimmer on it?" I asked curiously. I was also hoping to take my mind off throwing up, the thought made my stomach surge in recent memory and I swallowed.

"Doc takes the advanced classes into dusk training. Dim light scenarios with rubber knives and fake guns. It's more realistic since many attacks happen at night while walking to your car, passing by alleyways, or entering a nearly dark house. He does complete darkroom attack lessons in here too," David said casually.

"Ooh, that sounds fun," I lied, my sarcasm uncontainable.

David chuckled. "Actually, it can be nerve-racking for the first-timers. Even the advanced fighters get pretty anxious when it comes time for those lessons, to be honest."

"Um, how can he teach darkroom attack training during the day with these skylights letting all this light in?" I pointed up to the one closest to me and walked underneath it absentmindedly.

David stepped back to the door and flipped open a little latched panel about six by eight inches in size next to the light switch, revealing a digital touch panel I hadn't known was there.

"Like this." He touched the blank digital panel. It lit up instantly and he keyed in a passcode. A block of icons appeared and he pressed one of the digital buttons. The skylights began to darken. I squinted up and saw solid black shades smoothly gliding between the two panes of glass in each skylight until they were completely closed and all the glaring light from the overcast sky outside vanished. He slid down the dimmer and the lights in the room diminished to near darkness.

"This is practically the dusk training setting. Just imagine the heightened adrenaline you get when warding off an attacker you can barely see," David spoke distractedly starting to pace the room a little, his hands rubbing together as if he was imagining a scenario just like that.

"Oh, I don't have to imagine. I already know." And I did. I'd been attacked recently by those big badass scary giants and demons. Granted there was a fire pit giving off a flickering reddish-yellow light at the time, but it was still quite memorable for several reasons.

"You do?" David asked, turning to me with concern.

"Oh, um...well y-you know," I stuttered. David looked at me quizzically and he took a few steps back toward me.

I wasn't going to share those adventures with him yet and I felt my face warm at having almost said something. My mind had flashed back to it so vividly for that brief moment that I thought I might spill it without a conscious thought.

Another real-life answer struck me and I quickened to supply him with an alternative explanation to avoid telling him my first thoughts. "Um, you know, all those nights of my dad stumbling around the house in the dark and never knowing if he was coming into our room to hit us or worse...Or the night Jill and her gang...Well, you've seen the file," I ended awkwardly, shifting my feet and glancing down. I hadn't thought of those other reasons until just then, but it was true. The thought of fighting in pure darkness made my palms start to sweat and I felt my heart speedup at the prospect of Doc trying train me in the dark someday.

"Of course," David said gently. He walked quietly back to the lights, turned them up, and reopened the skylight blinds as if by giving me back the light, it could chase away the scary memories.

Light chasing away the darkness.

"Those are pretty cool," I gestured to the skylights and smiled, trying to lighten the tone of our conversation again.

"Yay! I'm proud to say they were my suggestion," David smiled and ran his hands through his black curly hair and stretched upward. I felt my eyes roam over him while he was momentarily distracted and I looked away guiltily.

"Do you have any questions for me, Melanie? Anything else I can answer before we start?" Apprehension was in his voice and he sidled over to the stretching corner and took a grip of the bar above his head.

So much for him not wanting to ask me anything else.

David reached it easily and with his flexed muscular arms stretched up like that, showed off his beautiful physique. My eyes were pulled down to his narrowing waistline from his strong broad shoulders, the ripples of powerful definition making my pulse speed up. I felt my face heat up to a new shade of red and desperately wished for the darkness again to hide it from him.

"Well..." I cleared my throat and walked over to the water fountain and took a long slurp of water so I could think of something else to ask him other than the obvious. I dried my mouth with the back of my hand and twisted my long strawberry-blonde hair up, securing it into a knotted bun to hold it in place since I'd lost my rubber band somewhere. I turned to face him and caught him doing pull ups, his face in a slight frown looking straight ahead at nothing in particular as he pulled and heaved. His entire body was rigid, his back slightly arched to puff up his gorgeous chest, his ankles crossed and locked. Every muscle of his arms and forearms redefining sexy. I swallowed my instantly dry mouth and turned to take another quick sip of water.

"Well," I tried again, "Um, why did Doc make me tell him my reasons for needing the concealed carry permit?" I asked and idled over to him, not even knowing where the question had come from since my brain was melting along with my hormones. It must have just been the first thing I could think of other than anything related to our previous conversation. I wasn't going there yet. Not so soon anyway.

I hope I'm not sauntering. He looks so hot. God, you broke the manly mold with this one.

David's eyes fixed on me walking to him and he dropped back down to the floor and straightened his tan V-neck T-shirt. I noticed at the last moment that it had pulled up to reveal just enough of his well-defined abs and a very pleasant, and not overly hairy, happy trail that ended at the edge of his cargo pants. I couldn't help but slide my eyes a tad-bit lower and wonder what was just beyond what I couldn't see.

Bad Melanie! No! Noooooo.

I tried to look back at his face quickly as if I hadn't noticed and hadn't cared, hoping that he hadn't noticed me ogling him.

I'm a sucky actress.

I kept talking to hide the sudden nervousness I felt at the rush of attraction and curiosity. "Doc said the Sheriff would have asked me those questions if he hadn't. What did he mean?" I glanced away feeling shy, afraid my attraction for him would show on my too-easy-to-read reddening face. I didn't want to be thinking about David like this right now. I was still too raw and thrown by learning he'd been married. And we'd only just talked about it. It would be premature to move forward with any of that physical stuff. But I had to admit to myself that knowing *she* had gotten to partake of him *first*, was making me overly curious about what I had never had.

Get a grip on yourself woman!

"You know Doc works with the Sheriff's department and assists their SWAT sometimes right?" David asked, his tone saying he was a little thrown by the left-field question but was willing to play along.

He noticed me checking him out. I know it! Auh! That's so embarrassing!

"Yes," I said with false ease.

"Well, it's pretty hard to get CCWs in Sacramento County right now. They are highly regulated and nearly impossible to get. If Doc vets a few applicants for the Sheriff, and he clears them, they'll usually get it. He basically gives them his stamp of approval and conducts that portion of the interview for them. It's unofficial, technically. But there hasn't been a single applicant who's taken Doc's course and he whispered a good word to the Sheriff about that's been denied. I think he knew it was important for you to get it and wanted to make sure you would," David explained.

"Oh, really?" I answered pleased. "I hadn't realized that. Cool. Remind me to thank him for backing me up with the Sheriff," I smiled.

"Of course, if he disapproved of your reasons, he would have denied teaching you too. And, they'd probably find some excuse to deny you your CCW even if you got your certification from another weapons instructor," David added with a shrug of his big shoulders. "Granted, carrying concealed is a privilege not necessarily a right. People always think it's their right just because they finish the sixteen-hour course. But where they get confused is that you have a right to bear arms to protect your home, but to carry in public is under the jurisdiction of your state's Constitution. As such, people found to have questionable motives, mental instability, certain drug prescriptions, and especially a criminal past, are usually denied immediately, though the process may take some time to conclude. Due process and all that."

"I've barely chipped any time off of that sixteen-hour course requirement," I said aghast. "I only got a few hours in yesterday, and I don't think today even counts! We haven't even discussed guns or practiced in the downstairs range. We didn't even talk about the laws yet. And Doc left!" I wilted. "This is going to take me forever."

"It's okay, he'll squeeze the required training in somewhere, and soon. Don't worry. He knows how important this is for you. But keep in mind that even after you complete the course and he signed off on your certification, you still have to finish the application process. It can take several months to finish the entire CCW process."

"I already submitted my application and got my preliminary background clearance. Liz helped me start it a few weeks ago and I think she might have used a little influence to expedite it. I already bought my gun to list on the permit. A little Sig Saur P238. I'm going to pick it up next week once the DOJ's mandatory thirty days has passed. But I still need this CCW course and take the shooting exam with my new weapon, the *official* interview with the Sheriff Department, and the live fingerprint scan!" I huffed. "What if he doesn't have time? He cleared his calendar for me this weekend as it is. I'd feel bad if he had to do it again."

"I'm sure he won't mind. If it's a challenge for him, he'll let you know and refer you out to a colleague like he does sometimes when he can't find the time in his schedule. But I wouldn't worry. Doc seems pretty determined to train you himself," David smiled his lopsided grin at me and I felt my face warm up anew.

Darn it. He's so damn cute when he smiles. Stop smiling man. Stop. Smiling.

"So, um...What do you want to teach me in here?" I braved, forcing myself to move forward with our lesson plan.

"Well, I thought I'd show you some basics like how to fall and not hurt yourself. Tender places to pinch that will cause extreme pain to loosen an attacker's grip. How to bring down your attacker. How to get out of a chokehold. How to escape when you're pinned to the floor with your attacker on top of you, facing down or facing up," David looked a little nervous saying the last one.

Is he remembering finding me on the floor nearly unconscious with my father about to assault me? Or is he nervous about being the one on top, straddling me?

I hadn't thought of this before. David training me. Grappling with me. *Oh God.*

"Tho-those are the basics?" I asked, my voice cracking.

"Pretty much. But we can work our way from one to the next slowly so you don't feel overwhelmed okay? This will take time, practice, and endurance, but we can stop whenever you want." David was hiding his own nervousness again, his voice too matter-of-fact.

"Okay. It's just that Liz showed me some foot stomping and eye gouging stuff and how to buckle knees. She called *those* basics. Your list sounds harder," I sounded pathetic. "I'm not chickening out or anything...I'm just not very...very—"

David walked over to me and took my face in his hands gently, effectively shutting me up. He looked down into my eyes searching my face, my mouth, my eyes again. "Liz filled me in last night on what she's already shown you. She said you have those down and are doing great. We both believe it's time for you to learn more, step it up a notch. You can handle it. I'll be right here to help you through it," he all but whispered.

"Thank you," I whispered back, matching his volume. He was so beautiful. His hands so warm. His mouth looked so delicious. How was I supposed to concentrate when all I wanted to do was kiss him and hang onto him and comfort him?

"Now, I realize that it might be, umm," David looked up for a moment, struggling to find the right word, "Rather intense for you, being that after I show you the moves in slow motion, we'll speed it up to real-life speed, and it will start to feel much more real. It's natural to start getting waves of emotions tied to your past experiences. Like what happened to me in the lobby," David said with a note of regret and shame in his voice. "And...and being that it will start to feel more real, and being that I'm a man, you might even have a surge of fear toward *me*. Umm..." David wet his lips. "Does that make sense?"

"Completely," I said in relief. Good, he already understood where my mind had been before we'd come in here. "I'm scared," I admitted, looking down, both ashamed of my cowardice and regretful that I might be hurting his feelings by saying I might become afraid of him after I'd just told him and Liz I trusted him more than anyone else. It seemed so counter-logical. But I couldn't help it!

"I'm still *me* though Melanie. I'll just be taking on the role of your instructor and then your attacker. Both have a purpose. Both are for your benefit with my best intentions." He nodded to me as he spoke, willing me to hear him, understand him, and accept this as fact.

I nodded back, agreeing. He kissed the center of my forehead and released my face.

"Good. Now let's stretch and warm up so we'll be less likely to get hurt."

"Okay," I went and stuffed my sweatshirt and purse in one of the cubbyholes. "Shoes on or off?"

"On."

I turned around to see David doing pushups in the middle of the matted floor. His tight body looking even harder, his back muscles flexing under his shirt and his arms pumping with rippling muscles. And his butt...his glorious steel-like butt flexed into a rigid round mound.

Oh. My. God. Why do I want to bite him?

"Do you want me to do pushups too? Because I can only do like five," I teased, meandering over.

I'm meandering. Not sauntering. Me-an-der-ing. Plus for me!

"Oh no. I'm just pumping up to impress you," David said stone faced. I blanched, my mouth dropping open. David looked up at me and let out a hearty, very male laugh. "I'm kidding!" He chuckled, taking control of himself. "I'm warming up and I really am pumping up. But not to impress you. Though if I happened to affect you that way, I'll take it." He laughed again as I turned beet red.

"That isn't very nice," I whined. David laughed again.

"Sorry. I need to get my mind focused. I do pushups sometimes when I need to ready my mind and body. It's just a trick I learned," David jumped to his feet, still smiling his crooked smile, and straightened his shirt again. My eyes dropped automatically and I almost kicked myself. I laughed a small sound of embarrassment escaping me.

"We'll start easy," David took a stance with his legs shoulder width apart and arms loose at his sides. "I'll walk you through the warm up and stretches, then we'll get into the basics."

"K," I copied his stance, mirroring him.

"You might want to take your earrings out so they don't rip your ears. Oh, and that necklace so it doesn't get broken," David said as he reached out to touch it lightly with his finger again.

"Good idea," I said, jogging over to the cubby where I had stashed my purse to put my earrings inside. "But I want to keep this on," I amended. Tucking it behind my tank top. I didn't want to remove it. How could I even consider taking something off the Archangel Gabriel put on me?

"Well, okay. But it could get snagged or damaged."

"I'll be mindful," I smiled.

I don't think this thing could break even if I took an ax to it.

We spent the next ten minutes doing easy warmup exercise and stretching. Then David showed me how to take a fall from all directions; face first, backwards, rolling to either side. I understood now why we needed to warm up and stretch. It was hard work falling and trying not to get hurt.

As David introduced each new part of the lesson, he'd explain why the moves were effective defenses against unwanted touching or full blow attacks. He never just reached out and laid a hand on me. He always explained first, then would say, "I'm going to show you what the attacker would do now, okay?" Then he'd wait for me to acknowledge him before he'd take his place and slowly reach out, putting into slow motion what the attacker would do. Always deliberately slow the first several times, walking me through each counter move, for each layer of my defense.

I felt completely safe with his way of instruction and correction. His logical progression from one form of self-defense to the next felt natural and balanced. I nearly forgot that he was my incredibly hot and super sexy boyfriend as the lesson went on, transfixed on his every word and motion.

He let me try, fail and try again, until I could do each move almost flawlessly, escaping him or bringing him down to the mat. He'd only speed up each new attack-defense lesson after I'd mastered them slow. Then he'd bring them to full speed, him grabbing, me moving to defend myself, faster and faster, and faster still.

"You're a natural," David praised me when we stopped to take a short break after the seventh move had been taught and mastered.

I started gulping down the water from the fountain. "Hey, hey," David rushed over and gently placed his hand on my lower back. "Not so much," he said smiling. "You don't want to get a cramp or make yourself sick again with too much water."

I took one more swig and slipped him a smile, "You tired me out!" I playfully pushed him in the chest.

He smiled mischievously, "Oh, but we've only just begun my dear."

"Do you really think I'm doing good?" I asked, growing serious. I wanted to know if I would stand a chance in the real world.

"Yes! You're doing quite well. I'm impressed with how fast we're moving through the lessons. You're really getting this stuff down," David smiled at me proudly.

"I was so nervous. I didn't want to suck," I bit my lip.

David threw his head back and laughed, "You don't have to worry about that. You hardly suck. Really, Melanie. I'm very proud of you." He cupped my chin with his fingers and gave me a quick kiss.

I smiled up at him, biting my lip again, wanting another kiss, but not wanting to disrupt our lessons.

We'll have time for smooches later.

"Do you want a snack?" David asked me, glancing up at the clock.

"Sure!" I sounded a little too eager and I chuckled at myself. It wasn't like I was starving, but he really had worked up an appetite in me. My belly growled on queue. "But what about cramps?"

"Naw, these won't do that to ya." David reached into the top corner cubbyhole and pulled out a box. It was full of little snack size cracker packages and power bars. He tossed me a chocolate flavored power bar and started to open his own, sitting down on the bench, his legs straddling each side.

I came over and sat on the end, my legs together like the good girl I am, and not too close as to invade his space. The plastic of mine was giving me a hard time, and without asking, David reached over, snatched it from my hands, tore it open and handed it back. I reached for it, but then he snatched it upwards again just out of reach, his arm much longer than mine.

"Hey!" I giggled.

Oh God. I giggled.

"Want a bite?" He chuckled, dipping it down to my mouth and away before I could steal a nibble, toying with me.

"Duh," I laughed and then opened my mouth like a baby bird waiting to be fed. I blinked at him innocently.

David chuckled and brought the bar to my lips, letting me take a speedy bite, afraid he was going to snatch it away again. He watched me chew, his eyes alight with a playfulness I was starting to adore.

"More?" he crooned.

"Duh," I repeated making him laugh out loud, a deep heart stopping, masculine sound. My heart skipped a beat.

"Open."

I obeyed and he gave me one more bite, then swiftly stuffed the last half of the bar into his own mouth.

"Hey! That was mine!" I snickered.

David got up and ran to the center of the room trying not to laugh as he chewed the enormous bite. I jumped up and ran after him, still snickering.

"Bad boy!" I playfully scolded. "Very bad!"

David swallowed at last and laughed, easily dodging my playful takedown kick to the back of his knees that Liz had shown me. "Hey! None of that now." He laughed again and darted over to the water fountain.

God, he looks amazing when he runs.

I watched him from where I was, suddenly overcome with the wondrous realization that this remarkable, warmhearted, funny man, was in love with *me*. How had *I* gotten so lucky?

"Ready for the last few rounds?" David said straightening up and wiping the water from his lips. He turned back to me, his smile fading.

"What?" I said preoccupied. "Oh, yes. Let's."

"Okay, good. So for this one, I just want you to watch as I demonstrate. I'll be using a mannequin first to play out the scenario since I don't have another instructor or advanced student present to stand in. I want you to see what I'm going to do and what I want you to do, so you don't feel blindsided. Tell me if you aren't ready for these two moves and we'll do it another time. Okay?"

David had grown careful, which made me a little uneasy. His switch from humor to serious could only mean one thing. This was going to be the hardest of my lessons today. Whether due to technique or because of how it might trigger me in other ways. I couldn't remember what he'd said was coming. My mind was going blank.

"Okay," I said uncertainly, hugging my arms around myself.

David went over to a door labeled "supply closet", and went inside. He came out a moment later with a life-size mannequin. It's hand painted features were obviously female with the big brown eyes and long lashes. The lips were even red. It had shoulder length brown hair on it's head and a small padded chest to fill in the white country dress. Of all things for it to be wearing, why that?

"Doc uses dummies? I mean, mannequins to train with?" I remarked, confused. The white dress reminded me of the one my mother had worn the last time I'd seen her alive. *And seen her murdered in.* It even had a sash across the waist tied in a little bow, but it was red not blue like hers had been.

"Yes. Unfortunately, he doesn't always have a second instructor available to demonstrate the victim's role so he'll use the mannequins. He has male ones in there too," David said, gesturing toward the supply closet. "He won't ever use a student volunteer to play the victim for this one until they see what's involved. This one tends to upset some of the students. The women more than the men, for obvious reasons." David's voice was clear, but I could hear a trickle of sadness inside of it.

David squatted down and carefully arranged the mannequin on the floor in front of me, taking care to make sure it's dress was lying flat and tugged down to it's full length. He arranged the arms so that they laid evenly beside her. He looked at her for a moment, emotion passing over his face that he quickly corrected into a blank canvas.

"So," David said pointedly, still squatting down beside the mannequin. He looked up at me. "Sometimes, when someone is attacked, they may not be able to get away using the moves we've already gone through. They may even get knocked unconscious or stunned with a blow, and end up on the ground." He gestured to the mannequin. "I'm going to show you how to get away from an attacker when he has you pinned down on the ground. The man's height might work against you a bit, but since the average man in America is somewhere between five-seven and six-foot, this should still work. I'll explain more on that in a moment," David was watching me carefully as he spoke, making sure, as he had in the prior lessons, that I was following and ready for him to continue.

"What this lesson will do is empower you to throw off the balance and grip of your attacker, giving you the opportunity to shove them off of you and escape." David shifted and slowly changed his position, straddling the mannequin and grabbing the hands, moving them to above it's head, pinning them to the floor.

I felt my pulse speed up, my breathing becoming erratic, my palms started to sweat. It was all too familiar. My father straddling me, pinning me down. My father pinning Vivian down, night after night, raping her, over and over again—for years. My father lying on top of my mother in her white dress, beating her, strangling her, raping her...killing her.

"Melanie?" David said my name gently, concern saturated his voice but he didn't move off of the mannequin to come to me. "Melanie?" he asked again, his voice a little stronger.

"It's okay," I choked out, tears flooding into my eyes, my throat constricting. "Show me." I insisted. "I need to know this." I wasn't going to let my past stop me from surviving another rape attack or attempted murder and having a future. I wouldn't!

David hesitated, unsure if he should go on. "We can come back to this one," he both reminded me and advised, his voice soft.

"No! Show me! I need to know what we could have done to escape him!" I hadn't meant to shout or to include my mother and sister in my demand. But they were a part of me too. A part of my past and still waiting to be avenged in my future. They hadn't left me. Not really. I could almost feel them watching me, urging me onward. Calling out to me to not give up! Not to run away from this. To learn everything David was offering me here today.

"Are you sure?" His voice was quiet.

"Yes. Show me," I said again, a pleading in my voice.

"Alright," David turned back to the mannequin taking a renewed grip on its wrists. "The attacker might—"

"Can we call him Dwayne? Or my father?" I interrupted.

"I don't think that's a good idea Melanie. We should keep this as mechanical as possible to avoid overwhelming you or inhibiting your mind's ability to really absorb the instructions. The mind can set up road blocks to protect itself if we associate names or places in the lessons. The power of those memories and the emotions they invoke can be crippling. It will interfere with your learning process and retention."

"I watched my father do that," I pointed at him and the mannequin, my hand trembling but I didn't care anymore. "I watched him do that for years! To my mother, my sister, then to me! We never escaped him! He is in my nightmares David. He is the only one I fear," my voice was quivering and I wiped the tears from my eyes. "I need to call him Dwayne! I need to face my fear!" My last words coming out like a bellow. "Please," I whispered now, desperately.

To David's credit, he didn't get up to comfort me or try to calm me. He let me go through these emotions and find my voice, express my reasons, my need. He nodded, his face full of pain as he shared my pain with me, a true mate to my soul. Then his face grew harder, and he turned to the mannequin. He took a breath, readying himself. He was about to portray the role of my father. Not just give instructions and mechanically demonstrate the how and why. I was asking him to make it personal. More personal than it already was.

I could see the disgust flash across his face as this hit him and he had to deal with his own issues toward my father. I gave him a moment just as he had given one to me, so that he could shuffle his thoughts and feelings away in his mind wherever and however he needed to, so he could move forward with the lesson and become what I needed him to be.

David frowned slightly and cleared his throat. "It's important to remember, that being afraid when you're being attacked by your *father* or anyone else, is normal. It does *not* make you weak to feel fear. Fear is our mind's way of telling us that our bodies are in danger. Use it! Use it to drive you into action instead of letting it lock you up or cause you to freeze," David started, his voice full of emphasis and his advice sounding very much like Liz's earlier.

"If your father knocks you down and has you pinned like this," David pressed his weight forward on the mannequin, compressing what would have been her lungs, still holding her wrists over her head. "You can throw off his balance and tip him off by stretching your hands far over to one side," He demonstrated by moving the mannequin's arms over to the right.

"And simultaneously, lifting your hip toward the opposite direction you pulled your arms, up as high as you can, using your upper back and your heel to press and push off the ground. This lifts the attacker...I mean your father, up and over, making him lose his balance and effectively tipping him off of you as you shove. He won't expect it. You'll have to do it quickly and with a burst of power. Once you have him rolling to the side, pull your leg up and kick out with your foot, using his own hip joint as leverage to shove him away. Then get up as fast as you can. Kick him several times in the face, groin or stomach, and run!"

I was breathing hard like I was running already, having felt every word David had just spoke as if it was already happening. It was too easy to identify with this. It was so real.

"It seems too simple. Too easy," I said with disbelief.

"It's not. It takes a lot of strength and coordination, but it's a chance. A chance is all you need."

"I don't understand!" I shouted, almost panicked. I had to learn this!

"I'll go over it again," David said calmly, easing my panic back down with his calming tone and patience. He explained it to me again, breaking each step down even slower, demonstrating it in moment by moment actions, his words telling me exactly how and when to strike back. He even switched with the mannequin, propping her up on top of him to show me how he, as the victim, would pull his arms over to the side to make my father lean forward and off balance in one direction, while lifting the hip up swiftly and forcefully in the opposite direction to shove him off.

"Oh!" I exclaimed as it clicked. "Oh my God! I see!" I inhaled.

"Do you want to try it?" David got up and respectfully picked up the mannequin, straightening her dress.

"Yes," I forced myself to say, trepidation and adrenaline coursing through me like liquid ice.

"Alright," David walked back to the supply closet and put the mannequin back where he'd found her.

He walked back over and looked me over carefully. "Take a few minutes first if you need to. When you're ready, go ahead and lie down," He gestured toward the mats.

I nodded. My voice utterly failing me. I padded over to the water fountain and took a swig. I was having a hard time breathing.

You will not have a panic attack. You will not have a panic attack.

Breathe. In. One. Two. Three. Four. Out. One. Two. Three. Four.

I closed my eyes to regain control as I counted out my breaths a few more times. Once I felt more stable and grounded, I opened my eyes to face my fear. David was watching me patiently. His concern evident, but he knew that this was also a matter of life or death for me. It nearly had been and could be again. I needed this. He just didn't want to push me too hard too fast. But he was willing to push me hard enough to see this through.

I took another moment and stretched up and then bent down, letting my tight muscles pull then relax into the bend. I'd been clinging to myself so tight while David had explained this last move to me that I'd nearly cramped my arms up. I shook out my arms and feet, like a boxer getting ready for a fight. I rolled my ankles on the mat to loosen them up too and then came back to David, trying to make my gait purposeful.

Fake it 'til you make it.

"I'm ready. I can do this," I glanced up at him.

"You can," He kissed the top of my forehead again. "You will."

"Don't take it personally if I shout something nasty at you or look up at you like I hate you or something, okay? I really don't know what I'm going to say or do once I'm down there," my voice was shaky, as were my hands, but I figured they'd be shaking worse in real life so I ignored it all.

"I won't take it personally," David promised me.

"I know you're not *him*," I said more to myself than to David. "You're not him."

"I know," David reassured me.

"I know you'd *never* hurt me," my voice broke, and I stuffed away a sob.

"I would never," he promised me again.

"I know you *love* me," I barely made a sound.

"I do. I always will," David said confidently but quietly, no doubt in his mind that he would love me for the rest of his life.

I walked past him and slowly laid down on the mat face up, my body shaking despite my "fake it 'til you make it" pretend attitude. I closed my eyes and raised my hands above my head, accepting my fate. Tears started to stream down the sides of my cheeks and I left them there.

Let them come. Lord, let it all wash away. Please just wash it away.

I heard David take the last three steps toward me. I kept my eyes closed. I was almost whimpering but couldn't seem to stop, tears still streaming.

"Tell me if you want to stop," David said ever so softly.

"No, I can't. Keep going," I begged him. "Before I lose my nerve completely."

"I'm going to straddle you now," David warned me.

"Okay," I said, and blew out, trying to release my fear and settle my nerves.

I felt David's legs as they brushed against me, his knees pressing into the mat next to my thighs as he settled his weight above me. I was breathing heavier now, at risk of hyperventilating.

"I'm going to grab your wrists." He leaned forward, taking hold of my delicate wrists in his hands, his long fingers easily encircling them. He held them firmly, but not painfully.

I knew I was breathing like a runner, in and out, in and out. Faster. Faster. The tears running swifter and swifter.

"Melanie," David said my name softly. "Melanie, open your eyes." He asked me. It wasn't an order. He'd removed his instructor's voice and was using the one he seemed to save only for me.

I opened my eyes and looked into his, inches away. He was pinning me down. He was stronger than me. He could hurt me. He could force himself on me. He could rape me. But he wouldn't. Not really. Not *my* David. This was all for me. To protect me. To teach me. I had to remember this wasn't real!

"I want you to pull your hands up higher, and yank them to the right. You're right hand dominate, so I want you to push up with your right hip, using your right heel to press against the floor. It's your stronger side. It will give you the most power, an advantage," David was speaking slowly and clearly. "Do you understand?"

"Okay," I croaked out.

"I'll walk you through it, alright?" David said kindly.

"Yeah," I whispered.

"Okay. Now pull up and over to the right, really stretch." David let me pull my arms up and over slowly, in the same slow, mechanical, step-by-step action we'd taken on all the other moves while I was first learning them.

"Good." He was leaned over, a little off balance now, just what he said would happen to my father. His chest had been pulled forward and raised higher onto me as I'd pulled him, bringing his face both closer and effectively shifting his body weight more forward than back where my legs would be pinned, allowing me the smallest hint of more wiggle room underneath him.

"Now, still keeping me pulled up and over, lift up your right hip. Press hard against the ground with your right heel to carry my weight up and over to the left," David continued.

I did what he said, using all my strength to shove my hip into him, tilting my body to the left as my right hip came up to act as a lever and lift him. I felt him shift over to the left, sliding halfway off of me as his balance continued to be altered and gravity worked against him.

"Oh!" I cried out, thrilled to see what I was doing to him.

"Excellent, Melanie! Now, look, my hands are tearing away from you, because you've stretched me out too far and thrown my lower body to the side, now is when you rip your hands away and shove me off of you, using your foot to help, here in my hip joint." He was back in his instructor's voice.

I did it. I yanked my hands free of his slipping fingers and continued to shove him off of me with my hip, then brought up my right foot and pushed it against his hip joint to complete the motion. I did this slowly, with him instructing me every step of the way. I rolled away, finally fully unmounted.

"Now, get up!" David ordered me and I jumped to my feet, still breathing hard but feeling exhilarated.

"You would kick toward my face, stomach, or groin, as hard and quick as you can before I can get up to grab you. Then you'd run!" David finished, still laying on the ground where I'd shoved him. "You'd run," he repeated. "Do it! Kick out at me. Kick, kick, kick!"

I did it, three quick kicks toward him, not connecting to his body for this portion of the lesson.

"Great! Now run away!" David ordered, and I jogged away to the door.

"Okay. Okay," I breathed turning around. "Again!"

I rushed back over and got back down on the ground. This time I kept my eyes open as he mounted me, straddling my body securely with his. We repeated it all again, slowly, four more times, then David said, "Let's speed it up. You ready?" he checked with me.

"Yes, ready," I said, finally calmer and under control.

"I'm going to use more strength. And I'm going to drop all my weight on you this time," David warned me again.

I nodded and made to lay down. He did as he'd said. He dropped all his weight on me, letting his mass and strength show itself for the first time as he pinned my body beneath him. His body almost crushing me. His body was flatter on top of me this time, his knees barely bent to mount above me. Before I'd even adjusted to his weight, he swiftly yanked my arms up painfully, gripping my wrists securely in his hands, his grip was ironclad. I felt the panic try to creep up again and my heart raced, threatening to plunder it's way out of my chest. I could hardly breathe! He was being too rough. It felt too real.

David hissed into my face, "I don't love you. I don't even want you. You're nothing to me. You're only good for one thing," David hissed with malice.

"What—" I was overcome by confusion and panic.

"I'm Dwayne!" David growled. "Fight me off! Defend yourself! I'm going to rape you and tear you apart. David isn't coming to help you this time! No one knows you're in trouble! You're trapped in here. You're alone—with me."

"I—" croaked.

"I take what I want!" David snarled, his face contorting. My mind was racing. Panic driving me into myself, shutting me down. Fear and confusion ripping my heart, breaking my concentration!

"I don't understand wha—"

"Defend yourself!" David yelled at me, tightening his grip on my wrists even more, crushing them, his body pressing harder into me, suffocating me. For the first time, I felt how strong and powerful he could be. How intimidating and fierce. How...

Finally I got it! He was doing what I had asked him to do! Calling himself, my attacker, Dwayne. He was being my nightmare. Making me face my fears.

I heard myself gasp as I felt David's knees quickly shift and shove my legs apart, his hips painfully pressing into me, invading my space, my privacy.

"I said, defend yourself you stupid little bitch."

"No!" I roared, fury and hatred spreading through me like liquid fire. I yanked my arms up and over, ripping my wrists free of his crushing grip and simultaneously lifting my right hip up in a powerful motion of abnormal strength, spiked with adrenaline and fear. I felt him shift and I moved thoughtlessly to shove him off of me, kicking into his hip joint sending him rolling off and away from me. He made a grab for me and I shouted something inaudible, kicking him in the nose. Blood exploded into a spray across the mat and across my sweatpants. I kicked him in the stomach twice more with all my might and screamed, "No! I won't let you! Not again! Stay the fuck away from me!"

David was moaning, holding his stomach with one hand and the other hand out in front of him in submission. "Ouch."

I snapped out of it. Seeing him hurt and bleeding at my feet.

Oh, no! David!

I dropped to my knees in front of him. "Oh David! David, baby! I'm so sorry!"

"Oh, wow," David moaned again as he sat up, his hands to his nose now, catching the blood.

"I'm—I am *so* sorry! I thought...I mean, I flashed back to when...and you were...I just...it felt so real—"

"I know," David mumbled, tilting his head up and pitching his nose. "It's okay. Really," David stood slowly.

I ran to the basket of towels and grabbed him one. I rushed back over and tried to press it to his nose. He caught my hand and took the towel, holding it up to his face. I thought perhaps he was angry at me and didn't want me to touch him, but he didn't release my hand. His thumb created small comforting circles across the surface of my palm as he looked down at me, his eyes watering from the kick to his nose. Once he got control of the bleeding, he lowered the towel.

"How does it look?" he asked me, his voice void of any anger or accusation.

I let out a tense breath. "Busted," I said worried, biting my lower lip.

David let out a small laugh, "Good."

"Good?" I asked concerned. I hadn't kicked his head too hard and scrambled his brains, had I?

"Yes! Good! Great in fact! Melanie, you did amazing! You kicked Dwayne's ass!" David said triumphantly.

"Oh...oh I guess I did!" I said, joining in his triumph.

"I'm going to rinse this," David pointed to his nose and walked over to the bathroom. I heard the water running for a moment and the sound of him spitting. He'd probably swallowed blood from the nose.

"Did I break it?" I yelled through the door, feeling horrible.

"No, but barely," David said with pride in his voice.

"Sorry," I mumbled again.

Good one Mel. Don't kill your trainer. Geez.

David came out, his nose looking almost normal, except for the gash along the top and the bruising that had started to darken under his eyes.

"Wanna go again?" he asked, tossing the towel aside into the used towel bin across the room.

"Really?" I couldn't believe it. He was okay with me kicking him in the face and wanted to do it again?

"Yes! You've got this! You just need some more practice to really get the rhythm of the moves down. Just don't kick me for real next time, okay? Just make the gestures," David requested with a small smile and he winked at me.

"Okay," I bit my lip.

I laid back down and we practiced the move several more times until I was flawless. Each time, David used his weight, strength and an assortment of horribly vial and threatening words. He changed up how he would pin me or maneuver my body differently each time. He even showed me how to do it while laying on my stomach, which took more strength and was definitely harder to get out of.

He continued each round pretending to be a violent asshole like my father. He was good at it, although he lacked any true conviction when I looked past the snarled face and into the soul within his eyes.

After about a half hour, I could see how much playing a role like this truly disgusted him, even if it was just a lesson designed to save my life. Each time he seemed to grow angrier right under the surface. As my trepidation and panic lessened, David's disgust for how he was acting increased. Finally, I concluded that he needed the break more than me. I didn't want to make the suggestion if it meant he'd feel offended or that I thought him too weak to finish my lesson. That would be the last thing I'd want him to feel.

I need to look out for him too though. He's already gone through so much today. One more round and then I'll call it for today.

I laid down for one more practice run and David carefully and slowly climbed on top of me as he had each time before. He was about to reach up for my wrists when I felt overcome with gratitude and admiration for him. He had saved me for real already and now he was doing all this for me too; pretending to be a monster.

"David," I whispered his name and his face softened from the hard mask his role as my father demanded. His own open and concerned face peered down at me.

"Yes, Melanie?" David asked curiously, raising himself back up a little to look at me.

It took me a moment to find the words now that he'd dropped the pretense of being Dwayne. My fear was fully abated, leaving my head clear and focused only on him, my David. But it was still hard to explain where my thoughts had shifted to now.

For the first time, I was finally able to see *him*, really see him, my David, resting above me, his body lying on mine, his warmth penetrating my thin sweat soaked tank top and sweatpants. The closeness of his massive chest above mine with the feel of his heartbeat tangible through his stomach where his abdominal aorta pressed firmly into mine. His touchable hair, his honey brown eyes, those incredible heart shaped lips, those dimples...

God he's perfect and so beautiful.

My heart raced again, but not from fear. I wanted more of him. I wanted to feel his arms hold me as *himself*. I wanted his body on mine invited, not rejected. I didn't want to fight him anymore, even if it was pretend and just a lesson. A lesson designed to protect me, to keep me alive. I searched his eyes and found the heat that I was feeling was growing, mirrored in his eyes. It sparked a thrill of panic chased away with desire through me to ignite my body with a fire of passion for him.

"David, I—"

I hadn't been wrong. David must have felt the same thing I had and read it in my eyes as well because he slipped his hand into my hair to cradle my neck lifting the back of my head upward by his hand. He covered my mouth with his, the warmth and tenderness of his lips drawing hunger from me. He carried his weight on his other arm as he kissed me, careful not to crush me. I surrendered to him, totally willingly and wanting. Melting completely into him, his body pressing into mine, mine into his. His beautiful lips were so soft and warm, his tongue masterful.

I moaned. A sound of pure pleasure escaping me without a conscious thought and he tipped me to my side, pressing me into him, drawing me inward and upward. His other hand slid down to trace my back and found the curve of my hip but not trespassing further.

He rolled us, leaving me lying on top of him, giving me the position of advantage. Letting me decide how far to go, when to stop, *if* we stopped. He relinquished all control over to me, removing any threat or appearance of a threat that might still be in my mind. Offering me the dominating position. The choice.

I didn't want to stop. Though I knew we should. Instead, I kissed him harder, pulling my wants, my needs from his giving mouth. Letting him become mine. Giving myself to him in return. I wanted all of him, and I wanted him to know I was his.

Suddenly, he grabbed my hips, pressing me into him. He had grown hard and eager, the mass of him insistent as it found the front of me, and I gasped, a rush of want and passion stealing my breath along with his kisses. I moaned again, unable to stop myself, the surges of excitement and desire overwhelming me. I was both surprised by this, slightly embarrassed, and altogether thrilled.

I can't. We can't. We shouldn't.

Our clothes were our only barrier left to remind us of the distance we should keep. I traced my hands along his chest, feeling how hard his muscles were under his shirt. I gave in, my hands reaching underneath his shirt to feel the hot, slightly sweaty surface of his skin, risking what was left of my control to cross the thin barrier. His rippled muscles felt like heaven on my fingertips. I smiled into our kiss as the hair on his chest tickled my fingers, surpassing my expectations of softness and allure. I wanted to rip the shirt off of him. I wanted to drape my body over his and absorb him through my skin.

I didn't know I could ever feel this way!

"*Stop.*" I heard the Lord say to me.

I know we shouldn't Lord but I don't want to stop. God, he's amazing. He's beautiful. Isn't this natural?

David's breathing was heavy as his hands traced my hips, our bodies moving on their own accord as if perfectly familiar with the other's. He kissed me deeper and deeper as we moved, like a dance that only the music of our love could choreograph.

I felt my necklace begin to burn where it lay against my sweating chest just as I heard, "*Enough!*"

The words were loud and clear as if through a loud speaker! Audibly piercing the atmosphere with a *BOOM* that seemed to penetrate all dimensions. The light in the room snapped and popped as if sparks had ignited from nothingness. A surge of corrective power zipped through me, cutting through my passion like a sword through butter.

We instantly pulled our mouths from each other and looked around the room, a healthy respect and fear for the power of the Lord cutting through our carnal desires. I expected to see an angel or maybe even Jesus himself standing there, a look of frustration, disappointment and anger on their faces.

"I heard it too," David said, turning my face to look back down at him. He hardly seemed rattled by it, as if he'd heard such supernatural manifestations so frequently that they no longer startled or surprised him. He swept my hair back that had fallen loose during our tumble, and tucked it behind my ears. "I heard it too," he repeated softly.

"You did? Did you see it too?" I said, delighted that he experienced the Lord's rebuke with me, but then ashamed that we both had to have the Lord tell us to stop, literally shout it at us, because we'd gotten so out of hand.

"He already told me enough twice, but I just...I want you so badly," David admitted without remorse. "I haven't been with anyone since..." David glanced away then back at me apologetically.

"Me too. Wanting you, I mean," I climbed off him and sat there, my legs crossed, my arms hugging myself so I'd stop touching him.

David smiled. A big sloppy happy grin starting to spread across his face. "You blow my mind," David shook his head. He stood up and ran his hands through his own hair as he stretched to work out the last of his unsatisfied energy. The sight of him was impressive from my vantage point on the floor. His height and strength radiating off of him with the cut lines and rippling muscles of his body.

Lord, you're going to have to help me stay focused. Please, help me.

David touched every button I had been created to have as a woman. I was attracted to him like no other. A natural attraction that is. Pure human desire and the programed need to mate, seek connection, and become one.

David looked down at me, taking me in with his eyes as I had him. The passion was still there, a lingering evidence of his desire to have me, but it locked back into the restraints of self-control he kept it carefully secured behind. He offered me his hand. I took it and let him help me up.

"Are we going to go again?" I asked eagerly. "Practice any more *moves* I mean?" I tried to clarify, but it all seemed to have a double meaning now. "I mean, learn another self-defense move," I amended again, trying hard to not keep my thoughts from turning naughty so soon after the divine intervention.

David chuckled. "We should go to the café now, don't you think? I can call Frank to meet us there on the way." David suggested.

"Oh, yeah. Frank. The café," I said, almost disappointedly.

David chuckled. "The day's not over kid," David used Doc's nickname for me and I frowned at him.

"Kid?" I murmured, friskily.

"Compared to me, you're just a baby," he cooed and winked at me.

"Is that so?" I pretended to be stubborn and pouty as I put my hands on my cocked hips.

"Yes," David leaned down toward me. Thinking he was going to kiss me, I puckered up automatically, but he dodged my lips and planted a very tame kiss on my forehead instead.

That's your safe kissing place of choice today isn't it, Mr. Abramson?

I let out a huff of disappointment again and he laughed, a very masculine sound of conquestual delight.

"Don't get cocky," I scolded him playfully, unable to stop my automatic glance downward. "You didn't even get to second base," I blinked rapidly back up, my eyelashes batting to add to the innocent little girl persona he'd accused me of. David quickly reached out around me and smacked me on the ass, making me yelp.

"Just did!" He walked off laughing as my mouth hung open. "Coming?" he asked me, opening the door to the hallway beyond.

"Yeah, I'm comin'," I giggled, as I put my earrings back on and grabbed my sweatshirt and purse from the cubbyhole.

David held the door for me, smiling mischievously as I approached him.

"Some people's children," I mouthed off sarcastically and stormed past him, my chin thrust out, and my head held high like I was the Queen of England herself, so insulted. I couldn't help my shriek as he pinched my ass when I went by.

Untying the Knot

Chapter Eleven

Several hours after taking off from the ISAF Coalition Base in Kandahar to Camp Chapman to carry out their mission, David and his Pararescue Jumpers landed on the medevac landing zone at Camp Bastion, loaded to the brim with wounded. David's HH-60 Pavehawk Helicopter held three wounded American soldiers and the prisoners they'd been sent to secure, two high-ranking Taliban soldiers. Both prisoners were also wounded, getting shot during the siege at Camp Chapman. The third Taliban soldier held prisoner had been killed during the attack, details of which had not yet been relayed to David, and probably never would be.

Cherub Six and Seraph Seven landed nearby, a total of eleven wounded soldiers among them, some in critical condition, others stable but in need of emergency surgery nonetheless.

Angel One had arrived at Camp Chapman just as the enemy's reinforcements broke through the American soldiers' defensive line, infiltrating the southern part of the base that was subbing as a secret military prison, operated and controlled by the CIA.

David had made a low pass overhead, ordering his door gunners to spray a line of suppressive fire directly into the cluster of enemy soldiers pressing their way through. Those left alive fired wildly at the helicopter before being plowed down by David's gunners on the second pass. The assault on the enemy gave the U.S. soldiers on the ground the opportunity to fall back for cover before mowing down another large portion of the Taliban fighters during the helicopter's third pass.

Several stray bullets from the zealous enemy had penetrated the walls of the prison and wounded their own men inside along with some of the U.S. soldiers defending it. As soon as the area and surrounding perimeter was secure, David gave the order for his men to start retrieval.

David reminded his men of their primary mission on their way to the objective. Prevent the prisoners from escaping, and then carry home their wounded. After receiving confirmation, Cherub Six and Seraph Seven had all the critically wounded accounted for and were heading back to Camp Bastion's Military Hospital. David sent a secure message through their additional encrypted radio to apprise Colonel Lewis of the prisoners' status and transport to Camp Bastion. Most Pavehawk's were equipped with four or five radios. His was outfitted with an additional radio to be used only during covert operations that required his top clearance compartmentalization.

David had informed Colonel Lewis that two of the three prisoners were still alive but that they had both been shot. He advised him that to protect them from another attempted liberation, he brought them to Camp Bastion for medical treatment and for transport by the CIA to another site. The three soldiers they had picked up had been those guarding the prisoners, and all three were badly wounded.

As they landed at Camp Bastion, the Military Police and additional soldiers jogged over to meet them. The emergency medical responders were among them, pushing empty gurneys and medical supplies. David's wife Danielle was near the back of the pack wearing her green camo scrubs. Her long thick black hair was in a bun on top of her head. Flyaway hairs had escaped to blow in the violent wind of the helicopter's blades. If she had properly dressed with the tight regulation military bun, it would not have escaped so easily, even with the downwash caused by helicopter blades.

As David reported in once more to Colonel Lewis to let him know they had landed safely at Camp Bastion, he watched his wife approaching with the group. A shadow of dread began to grow inside him the closer she approached. Her eyes connected to his, up in the cockpit, cold and unfriendly. Her dark eyes looking darker than normal to David, despite the blazing sun directly in her face.

David felt a chill roll over him as he looked down at Danielle from the cockpit above. He nodded in greeting, a mechanical gesture void of any warmth, trusting that his helmet and the boom mic in front of his face would shield the majority of his emotions from her. He could almost feel the ice from her soul penetrate his being and he suddenly felt afraid of her. The last of his denial beginning to crumble.

Who are you? What are you?

The emergency responders were swarming around Cherub Six and Seraph Seven, helping to unload their wounded. As soon as they were securely aboard the gurneys, they rushed them off toward the base's hospital emergency bay entrance.

Staff Sargent Gary Callahan and the Base Military Police stood guard over the prisoners being unloaded from Angel One. Their weapons targeted on the war criminals, fingers alongside the trigger guard, ready for anything.

A couple of the wounded American soldiers not on gurneys were insisting that they were all capable of walking, though the other nurses were fussing over them, pressing dressings to their wounds and talking animatedly with them, trying to force them to sit in the wheelchairs they'd brought along to the landing zone. Four of the soldiers delivered by the other two helicopters were all on gurneys, fighting for their lives, the medical team buzzing around them, trying to stabilize them as they went.

David stayed in the cockpit alone, manning the helicopter and awaiting their next order. His co-pilot, Senior Airman Aaron Murphy, had climbed out to help the wounded soldiers they had transported and whisper reminders to them that they were not permitted to expose Camp Chapman's secret CIA prison to the medical staff. They had orders to explain the prisoner's presence simply as captured during the attack, to be treated and held for questioning as prisoners of war. *New* prisoners of war.

David squinted as a blinding reflection bounced off the glass of a passing military jeep and he almost didn't see Danielle glancing from side to side, carefully watching the doctors and nurses ahead of her and the military personnel passing by. She quickly tucked something into the back pocket of her scrubs as she rushed along the foot of one of the wounded prisoner's gurneys, none of the medical staff or other soldiers were watching her as they performed their duties rhythmically and automatically, rushing along toward the emergency medical bay entrance.

What had that been? David's suspicions grew.

"Look at her!" The voice of the Lord boomed within his spirit. It was so abrupt and cut through every other thought or feeling that he froze, midway through an inhalation.

"What Lord? What am I missing? What am I not seeing? What is she up to?" David grumbled in frustration out loud to the Lord.

"Angel One?" Colonel Lewis questioned through David's encrypted radio. "You getting one of those special hunches of yours again?"

Damn it!

David gritted his teeth. He'd forgotten the colonel might still be listening in during the ongoing mission considering they'd had important war criminals on board. The radio was designed so that it could be remotely accessed by those with the proper authentication codes for purposes of monitoring every detail of a special operation. David wasn't prepared to tell the colonel anything about the feelings or messages he'd been getting from the Lord about Danielle or his growing suspicions. She was his wife. Shouldn't he at least wait until he had some kind of proof?

"Angel One?" the colonel said a little more sternly, demanding an answer.

"Angel One has unloaded the cargo. All is secure," David answered instead.

"Who is *she* you're asking *Big Man* about?" Colonel Lewis redirected. He and the other commanders had started calling the source of David's hunches "*Big Man*" at Doc's suggestion as a sign of respect for David's beliefs and insistence that the dreams, words of knowledge, and feelings of warning he'd receive were from God and God alone, and not from some demonic psychic power. Whether they believed in God or not, they didn't want to offend their golden boy or discourage him from voicing anything that might help them gain a tactical or strategic advantage over their enemy. Especially if it meant saving American soldiers lives.

"I'm not prepared to say," David answered honestly.

There was a long pause. The colonel was not used to David being unsure about anything he felt God wanted them to know. "Why's that?"

"It...It's hard to accept," David all but whispered.

"What was *Big Man's* message? Maybe I can help you figure it out," the colonel offered, his voice losing some of its sternness to sound more reasonable.

"I'd really prefer not to say yet," David resisted.

"Sentinel. Please." The colonel had never said *please* to David before. It was always a direct question or order. David could hear his urgency, no, his desperation through the radio. He had called him by his designated code name rather than by their team callsign, reminding him of his other purpose, his other calling. "If it's so bad you don't want to say it, then I really need to know. Is it about the traitor?"

At the word *traitor*, David felt his stomach drop as though he was falling a thousand feet without a parachute, tumbling around and around, up was down, down was up, horizon nowhere in sight.

"Sentinel?" the colonel implored again.

"I think...I think it's my wife." David sputtered. "I think it's Danielle."

The long silence on the other end meant Colonel Lewis hadn't anticipated that answer and was considering the ramifications.

"You sure?" the colonel croaked out.

"No. Not one-hundred percent, but that's what my gut...no, that's what *Big Man* has been trying to tell me. I haven't wanted to listen. I didn't want to see it," David tried to explain himself, justify his delay in figuring this out sooner.

He had to try to make it right. His fellow soldiers had been compromised, ambushed, killed! All because he had been too caught up in his rebellion of responsibility and sexual exploration

with his wild intoxicating wife to stop and truly seek God and *listen!*
"It's all my fault," David whispered.

"No Sentinel. It's all on *her.* Do you know where she is now?"
Colonel Lewis questioned urgently.

David found Danielle in the distance rounding the corner behind
the group to enter the medical bay. "She's just entering in the
infirmary. She was part of the emergency medical response team
today waiting to assist the wounded. Something was off about her,"
David answered quickly.

"Park Angel One. Go see what's she's up do."

"Red Hawk?"

"Let's try to be quiet about this. I don't want an incident. We
don't need attention drawn to the fact that one of our surgical
nurses is spying for the enemy, passing along our secrets, or
betraying our boys to be slaughtered. They'd probably beat her to
death."

David felt sick. How had it come to this? "You want me to engage
her? Make a silent arrest for questioning?" David gripped the chest
straps of the restraint system still holding him in his pilot seat
trying to tether himself into the reality of this unbelievable
moment.

Lord, this can't be happening.

"No. Not yet. If someone sees you taking her in by force, it will
spur questions and speculation. She's your wife and you're known
for being a good 'ol boy. Someone will figure out she must have
done something pretty bad for you to do *that.* Let's avoid what
questions we can, shall we?" the colonel's words carried a second
message loud and clear.

David knew the colonel would want this handled as discreetly as
possible. That was why he was trusting David to keep an eye on her
and not enlist the base's Military Police or CIA visiting on site.

"How do you want me to proceed? I don't think I can act normal around her right now. I'm too—"

"Pissed off? Hurt? Full of hate for her?" the colonel cut in.

"Something like that," David said in a low cracked voice.

"Park Angel One and go check on your crew first. Tell them your orders are to stay the night and get some sleep. You've all been up for almost...what has it been? Thirty-six hours?"

"Forty-two. If you disregard the three hours of restless sleep I had right before this mission," David said, resisting the urge to yawn at the mention of it.

"Right. Well, then it won't be questioned or a surprise I've ordered my top PJ's to get rested up for at least twenty-four hours before returning home."

David started shutting down the helicopter, his muscle memory switching over into autopilot. Not something they encourage pilots to ever do in flight school, but he was so exhausted and at the same time, running on emotional adrenaline, he just didn't care.

"I can report in there in about five minutes." David forced himself into "mission mode" so he could see this through.

Look her in the eye? Knowing what I know? Lord, how am I going to manage this?

"Affirmative. Get one of those sedative syringes out of the onboard medical supplies to take with you. Hell, take a few. Don't forget to grab your portable encrypted radio so you can keep me apprised. Invite that wife of yours to join you after you *caringly* offer to stay and watch her work so as not to alarm her. Don't let her out of your sight. We have two high ranking Taliban soldiers left to question and if she is the traitor, we don't know if she will help them escape. I'll send a request over to her CO and ask them to do me a favor and give her some off-duty time to spend with my best pilot. Once you have her to yourself, tranque the bitch," Colonel Lewis ordered.

"But we haven't even investigated yet. It's a feeling, but—" David tried to appeal.

"Those *feelings* of yours have saved thousands of lives, Sentinel, including mine. To me, they are as good as evidence. The Patriot Act allows me to make arrests and ask my questions later. Get proof later. I'm sure once we investigate, it will all make sense. Missions have been compromised. Intelligence leaked. I bet it will all lead back to moments or opportunity for her. Now we have a direction to look, we'll be able to see the signs."

"I just want to make sure you don't start seeing connections that aren't there," David disputed. "Are you sure you're not just looking for a quick answer to push up the chain of command?"

David heard the colonel take in a sharp breath and went silent, filling David with a heightened concern that he may have crossed way over the line and just lost favor with the colonel.

The colonel cleared his throat and said with a rough growl in his tone, "Sentinel, I'm going to give you a pass for implying I wouldn't be fair in my investigation because I know she's your wife and I can empathize with how hard this must be for you. But do not *ever* question my intentions again, do you understand me?"

"Yes. I apologize," David paused but resigned himself to be bold despite his trepidation. "But you're asking me to deceive my *wife*. Sedate her, then do what with her? I've *always* obeyed my orders. I've done unspeakable things in the name of national security and this *War on Terror*. But you're asking me to assault my own wife, to—"

"Then, it's an order, not a request! Sentinel, if you need someone to blame for the action I am ordering you to take, blame *her*. Hell, blame me if you must. But once we prove this hunch of yours is true, you won't be sorry. You'll be relieved you acted and saved more lives and prevented more deaths by taking action *now*. You understand, Sentinel?"

"Affirmative, Red Hawk," David declared, his gut twisting into a sickening knot.

"Attaboy."

"What are my orders once I have her isolated and sedated?" David worked hard to keep the cold edge out of his voice.

"Radio me. I'll have the spooks on site come take possession of the prisoner quietly."

"No! *Please*. You know their interrogations of suspected traitors are...are...they will torture her! They will do whatever they have to uncover the extent of her treachery!" David exclaimed. "I can't give her over to them, knowing that. Please!"

"Calm down! I'll ask for restraint and considerations to be made since she's your wife. I know they value your participation with their previous interrogations and black book missions just as much as I do. It would be like hurting the family of one of their own. But it's the only way to keep her out of the Military Police system, and you know she won't last long under *their* watch. There's too much fire in the belly over this war. Having a homegrown traitor on base will just ignite a hailstorm of retribution, maybe even toward *you*. She's your wife and you didn't know? You didn't stop it? All your good deeds and your otherworldly reputation as *The Sentinel*, chosen by *God* to protect our troops, will all be washed away if knowledge of this gets out. Hell! They might even decide you were in on it and say that's where you get your inside information into enemy ambushes and hidden weapons caches. We can't let them destroy you too. I won't have it," Colonel Lewis said passionately.

"Please...please just ask them not to hurt her. Let me be the one to talk to her once she's in custody. I can do it. I can make her talk. I know her better than any of them. Please. Let me try." David was begging now, not caring how desperate he sounded. He may not really be in love with Danielle or even know her like he thought he did, but he couldn't let her interrogation include torture or other forms of violation. He just couldn't.

"I'll ask them. But I can't promise what I can't control," the colonel said honestly.

"All I ask is that you do your best," David swallowed back a title wave of self-disgust and repulsion.

"I'll pull every favor I have. For you, I will do this," the colonel's voice was empathic and sincere.

"Thank you, Red Hawk. Thank you," David said with feeling.

The colonel grunted in acknowledgment. "Alright then. Proceed with your mission, Sentinel. I'll call Camp Bastion's base commander right now to have them assign some bunks for your crew to rest up. And I'll call Danielle's CO. Once you radio me and tell me she's secure and unconscious, I'll call the on-site spooks in to assist you for a quiet transition back to our base. We'll set up a restricted area here for questioning. No one there will know we have her in custody for now. No one will know what your wife has done."

"*May* have done," David corrected.

"Yes, may have done," the colonel agreed halfheartedly. "Now get moving Sentinel. You need to get your eyes back on her A.S.A.P."

"Roger. I'm departing Angel One now. On mission. I'll report in as soon as I can."

"Affirmative. If I don't hear from you in three hours, I'm calling the spooks in to assist anyway. Understood?"

"Understood."

"Red Hawk, out."

David clicked off the radio receiver and unbuckled the five-point restraint system still holding him into the pilot's seat. He climbed into the back of the helicopter glancing around to make sure no one was paying attention to him. He pulled out four prefilled sedative syringes from the onboard medical supplies and put them in his cargo pants side pocket.

Four may be overkill but what if she sees the first one coming and knocks it away or some get damaged in a struggle. Best to be overly prepared.

He checked his uniform for the hidden encrypted radio he already knew was there but suddenly felt the compulsion to reassure himself it was on hand. It wasn't the standard issue radio for soldiers, pilots or PJ's, but it was standard for *him* given his clearance level and classified missions and intelligence he was privy to and directly involved in. They also wanted him to carry this radio on him at all times in the event he received a message or dream from *Big Man* that he needed to pass up immediately, bypassing the typical military roadblocks or the chain of command.

David double checked his Beretta M9 and chambered a round. He felt dirty doing all of this. But he was on task, on mission. He was following orders. He slid it back into the holster and left the security strip undone.

In case I need to draw quickly.

Oh, God. Lord help me. Three hours. I have three hours to secure my wife and radio in.

David climbed down out of the helicopter and walked briskly toward the infirmary. He felt disconnected from reality and this mission, like this was all a bad dream. He pulled his thoughts back in, forcing himself to focus on his orders, on how he would execute this mission.

What would he say to her? It would have to be something natural to them. Nothing to let on that he had an alternative motive. He could lead her to a hidden place to be alone just like she preferred, like they had so many times before. Maybe the back of the medical bay into that storage closet they'd snuck off to before. It was only ten feet away from the back entrance. Yes, that ought to work. He would sedate her once they were in the closet. Forcibly if necessary. Call Colonel Lewis. Wait for the CIA to come get her and take her away. Isolate her. Interrogate her.

Or me. Colonel's going to ask them to let me conduct the interrogation. God, I hope he keeps that promise. I hope they don't torture her!

David felt his foot falter at the thought of playing out his orders. He swallowed back bile rushing up his throat as his nerves kicked into overdrive. Nerves hadn't interfered with his focus in years. But then again, *he* never had to betray someone he thought he'd been in love with before.

What if we're wrong? Oh, God. She's going to hate me. She may not answer any of my questions simply out of spite. Shit! I hadn't considered how stubborn she is when she feels wronged. She might prefer torture than answer me!

The turmoil inside him was growing with each step leaving him feeling positively sick.

"What's up Capitan?"

David found his crew outside the medical bay talking with some off-duty nurses. He gestured for them to come over to him where he stood waiting, nearly fifty feet away.

The men double timed it over. "Sir? Orders to return to home base already?" Senior Airman Aaron Murphy asked looking weary.

"Actually, no. At ease boys. You did great today," David pushed out some false energy to try to hide behind. He was nearly suffocating by the choking dread squirming its way past his stomach and into his throat. "We have been ordered to stay put and get some rest before returning to home base. Twenty-four hours recoup." David glanced at his watch, "Report back here tomorrow at nineteen-hundred hours. Go report in to the Base Commander for your assigned barracks. Now off with ya. Go get some sleep, a shower and some chow. Whatever order you prefer."

"Sir, yes, Sir!" the crew answered in unison, a new energy in them at the thought of getting twenty-four hours of downtime.

They jogged off as one back toward the waiting nurses. One nurse blew a kiss in David's direction at receiving the news from Staff Sargent Callahan that he was off duty. The two of them hurried off together, the thrill of school kids apparent from David's vantage point. David watched as the rest of his men disbursed, heading in the general direction of the Base Commander headquarters. An odd sensation swept over him. One of sadness and regret.

This was our last mission together.

The thought swept through him quietly. Like a whisper caught in the current of the emotions surging through him. David recognized the gentle impression of the Holy Spirit speaking to him. It wasn't just what could come but what *was* to come.

Last? This isn't going to end well is it Lord?

"Not this time. Be alert."

David entered the medical facility through the emergency entrance taking care to walk unhurriedly and to try to appear as tired and worn out as he was. He didn't want to give away an ulterior motive by showing any strange behavior, though he doubted anyone would even notice him. Every medical personnel he passed was rushing here to there, looking worn out and overstretched.

No wonder Danielle had been getting away with whatever she was up to; no one had the energy to notice anything different.

As he went further into the emergency room, he scanned for Danielle, spotting her immediately in the far left corner next to one of the prisoner's beds with her back to him. All the wounded, including the prisoners, had already been moved off the gurneys and onto the emergency room beds.

The Taliban soldiers were cuffed securely by both wrists and both ankles to the metal bars running along the sides of the bed. The doctors and other nurses were tending to the American soldiers first on the other side of the room. The MPs who were supposed to be keeping guard over the prisoners were gone. David scanned the room, wondering where they were. No one was watching Danielle and the prisoners. No one except David.

Danielle was leaned over the prisoner speaking in a hushed hurried manner. She glanced up at the doctors and nurses working feverishly across the room on the American soldiers, their actions heroic and practiced as they worked in unison, tending to their wounds, their rhythms in sync, everyone knowing exactly what they were doing.

What was she saying to the prisoners? She didn't speak Arabic. David watched, his suspicions growing as he saw one of the prisoners answering her. She nodded, clearly understanding him perfectly. Maybe he was speaking English?

Danielle reached back and patted her back pocket, and he saw the prisoner visibly relax.

What the hell?

David snuck in closer, his training kicking in making his steps silent and his approach from an angle the prisoners wouldn't see until he was well within earshot. He crept up the left back wall, carefully maneuvering around three occupied hospital beds. Thank God the soldiers in them didn't utter a sound. They were too drugged up with pain killers or asleep so no one responded to David as he floated by.

David approached the bed closest to Danielle and the prisoners, slipping quietly behind the curtain that separated the beds. They never saw him coming. He waited silently listening to their hushed whispers. It was *not* English.

What are you saying?

He suddenly felt eyes on him and he looked over his shoulder, a nurse just entering the room had spotted him. Thinking he was about to sneak up to surprise a nurse, she giggled loudly. Danielle's conversation ended abruptly and he heard movement, Danielle must have looked over to the woman and seen her watching David. The woman smiled at Danielle and pointed at him, giggling even more.

The bed curtain ripped back in a flurry, Danielle stood there, shock all over her face at being discovered.

Instantly David grew angry, betrayal filling him and spilling over into something close to hatred. He glowered down at her and she stiffened taking a step back. The nosy nurse abruptly stopped giggling.

"It's against protocol to speak to a prisoner of war. That is *not* your duty. What did he say? What did you say to him?" David said loudly, breaking through the rhythm of the room and drawing everyone's attention. All plans to charm her quietly away so she could be apprehended unnoticed was rewritten by the red pen of his fury.

"I don't know what you mean," Danielle spat, defiance making her bold, despite having been caught.

"Don't give me that shit Danielle. I just heard you! What did he say? And where are the guards?"

Danielle started walking slowly backwards and rounded the end of the prisoner's bed, putting herself between the two prisoners, as if to shield herself from him between her true allies. Their eyes were wide and they both started speaking rapidly to her, demands and commands clear in their voices. She glanced at them, shaking her head and shushed them.

"Step away from the prisoners Danielle," David ordered.

"What's going on here?" asked one of the doctors on the other side of the room, confused and walking toward them but keeping a safe distance. The energy from their corner of the room growing dangerous to any astute soldier, and military doctors are soldiers too.

"I think maybe she did something wrong," said the same nurse who had given his position away, her high-pitched innocent little girl's impression infuriating David even more.

"Where are the guards?" David demanded of Danielle again.

"I sent them away," Danielle replied snottily. "They're cuffed," she gestured to the prisoners. "I don't need them."

"You mean you didn't want the MPs witnessing you can speak Arabic to these prisoners," David accused.

"You're a idiot David. It isn't Arabic. It's *Pashto*," she said with a superior air.

"Pashto? Well, aren't you one for secrets," David said coldly, advancing on Danielle.

"I'd stop if I were you," Danielle said, swiftly pulling a syringe out of her pocket and stabbing it into the shoulder of the prisoner closest to her, making him jump a little in surprise.

"What are you doing?" David proclaimed alarmed. He had orders to secure the prisoners for questioning. They were a prize catch. Top-ranking Taliban soldiers with hard to gather intel. He couldn't let her destroy them! They were mission priority.

"I said don't come any closer!" Danielle growled.

The prisoner nodded fervently to Danielle and began shouting something again and again at her in Pashto.

"Do it! Kill me! Kill me! You know you must!" The Lord gave David the interpretation to the man's foreign tongue.

"Nurse!" the doctor who had come toward them shouted in disbelief. "What is that?"

"One more step and I push it," her voice was growing uncertain now, her thumb ready on the plunger.

"Why? Why exactly would you kill them rather than let them be questioned? What intelligence have you been giving them that they can testify to?" David said, taking another step, his hands out. He didn't want to pull his weapon on his wife, even if she wasn't who he thought she was.

Danielle smiled, a glint of humor in her eyes that she knew something he didn't. Typical Danielle. Always wanted to one up someone else.

"Nurse, release your hand from that syringe right this instant!" The doctor ordered. "Beverly," he shouted to the nosy giggling nurse, "get security back in here now!"

Danielle stiffened. Fear finally showing on her arrogant face. She must have thought David incapable of doing anything to harm her, even as angry as he was. She thought she had him still, completely enchanted by her. But the MPs, they were an unknown.

"David, you haven't known me *that* long. You still don't know much about me. How do you know Pashto isn't one of the languages I speak? How do you know it hasn't been on my military record since I enlisted? How do you know that isn't exactly why I got this assignment?" Danielle spoke in a matter-of-fact tone. She tilted an eyebrow and looked at David haughtily.

"You didn't, and it isn't," David's tone wasn't just matter-of-fact, it was certain. "Now step away."

David heard footsteps running; the MPs who had been assigned to guard the prisoners were coming back. They were going to be in so much trouble.

Danielle glanced at the door as they stormed in, "No!" she shouted and she pushed the plunger. She grabbed a second syringe from her pocket and rushed to stab it into the other prisoner.

POP! POP! – POP! POP! POP!

Danielle spun around to face David as the shots fired, the force of the first two shots hitting her in the shoulder. Her eyes were wide and disbelieving. The syringe fell from her hand as her body jerked and convulsed. The last three shots hitting her square in the chest. Her heart exploded into shreds as the bullets ripped through it.

A couple of the nurses were screaming. The doctor was shouting. The MPs were rushing forward.

David looked at the gun gripped in his steady hand. He didn't even remember drawing it. His mouth opened in shock and he dropped his gun. It clattered to the floor, the echoes of the metal hitting the cold sterile tile piercing his reality. Everything that had held up his courage and fortified his heart throughout this war shattered.

David dropped to his knees, all of his strength stripped from him. His will and power gone. The world was silent now except for a buzzing that filled his head. His eyes no longer making sense of what he was seeing. The world in front of him was a blur of color, lines and fog.

The MPs rushed to Danielle and to him. More soldiers poured into the ER having heard the gun shots. The MPs closest were speaking urgently to him but the words meant nothing. The doctor and two of the nurses had hurried over to check on the prisoner Danielle had poisoned. They checked his pulse, administered CPR, even pulled the syringe from his shoulder and examined it, hoping to determine what she had given him. David saw them shake their heads. The prisoner was dead.

The other prisoner still alive was shouting, spit flying from his mouth. He struggled against his bonds wildly, fury and hatred on his face. It was all in slow motion and silent to David. He was still encased in a moment of time where nothing mattered anymore, nothing. The unbelievable had become believable, the undoable had been done. All was lost. Even him.

Someone was still talking urgently to David, shaking him. He slowly turned his head, his eyes unfocused. All his effort went into studying the mouth as it moved. What was he saying?

"Captain! Captain are you alright?" It was one of the MPs. He knew this soldier. What was his name again? How did he know him?

Without resistance, David let them help him up but once he was on his feet he stumbled away from them, fighting their pawing hands on him. Fighting, pushing, trying to get to Danielle.

"No, no leave her!" The soldier was trying to stop him. "You don't want to see her like this!"

David shouted something inhuman and animal, his ability to form words forgotten.

"She's gone. She's gone man!"

"No!" David shouted, finding a word. He pushed through the barrier of soldiers and nurses and scrambled over to Danielle. She was sprawled out, disbelief still frozen on her face, blood pooling around her body. Her shoulder was a shattered, bloody mess. Her chest was a hole of gory ruin.

"No!" David cried, collapsing beside her, his knees seeping into her warm blood on the ground. "Why?" he screamed at her, his body trembling. "Why?" he demanded in a whisper.

The emergency room was silent, all witnesses engrossed in his grief, and lost as to how to help him, all except the prisoner who now watched with wide fearful eyes, mumbling and pleading, thinking he was next to die.

David ignored them all. He reached out and gently closed her eyes, a desire to give her peace and also, a deep remorse and self-disgust consuming him that he didn't want her to see. A part of him knew she couldn't see him anymore with her physical eyes but even her empty shell shouldn't have to look at him - her killer.

David let out a strangled sob as he touched the side of her face tentatively with his fingertips. Then he stroked it softly with the back of his hand feeling her soft skin and beautiful face one last time.

He remembered suddenly that she had put something in her pocket out at the landing zone. Something he thought she had taken from one of the prisoners.

"I need a minute... with my...my wife," David croaked out.

"Oh my God, she was your *wife?*" the stupid giggling nurse exclaimed.

"Beverly, shut up," the doctor rebuked her.

"Of course, Captain. Of course," the doctor agreed. "People, give him a minute."

David waited until they had walked away before he gently picked up Danielle, cradling her upper body in his arms. Blood from her shoulder and back continued to ooze out of her body and onto him. He didn't care. Nothing mattered anymore except to try and salvage his last mission.

David glanced at the doctors, nurses, and soldiers. They had given him their backs, trying to give some kind of privacy to say good-bye to his wife. The prisoner who had been pleading and mumbling had grown silent, his heavy breathing the only sign he lay on the bed above, unable to see David clutching Danielle on the floor beneath.

David reached down and dug carefully in her back pocket and found the slip of paper. He couldn't read it. It was in Arabic, Pashto or some other language of the region. He quietly slipped it into one of his many cargo pants pockets.

Leaning his head down next to hers, he whispered in her ear, "I'm sorry you made me do this to you, Danielle. I'm sorry I wasn't enough for you. I'm sorry I failed you," David was weeping now.

He held her and wept, his body shaking and rocking as he held her one last time. Her betrayal was secondary to his grief.

When he felt he had no tears left to shed, he very carefully lay her back down and he stood. He looked down at this woman he had once thought he loved. This woman who had lied to him. Betrayed him. Betrayed his country. This woman who had tried to kill off important prisoners of war to protect their cause. It was her cause too or she would never have betrayed them.

David felt his face harden a little. Who was she really? How much had she told them? He would never get answers now. He would never know why.

"Good-bye," David whispered to her. He turned and left. He saw nurse nosy try to intercept him, but he heard the doctor order her to stay back.

"Don't worry. I'm not going anywhere. I just need to report in to my superior officer what just happened." He stopped in front of the MPs. "Come with me if you want. But you still have one prisoner of war left here to guard that I think you need to secure him more than me. I'm not going anywhere."

They let him pass, their faces showing a mix of sympathy for him and also trusting him. It surprised him. They had just watched him shoot a woman armed with a syringe and they trusted him to walk outside alone? Then it dawned on him, they knew him as *The Sentinel.* That was how David knew them, he'd saved their lives before on a mission he'd flow right before he met Danielle. Names Braum and Pierce.

Full circle meeting them here.

Full circle...I blew a circle right through Danielle's chest.

"We saw everything we needed to see, Captain. We know you had no choice. You have permission to step outside to make your call. Come in when you're done," MP Pierce said.

"I'll go with him," the other MP decided suddenly, rushing over to David's side to accompany him out.

David nodded mechanically. MP Braum was right to not let him out of his sight. He shouldn't be given any special treatment just because he was *The Sentinel*. What did that even mean anymore?

He exited the emergency room, his gait slow and labored; his limbs felt like they were made of lead.

David found an empty corner by the parked Hummers nearby. The MP stayed about twenty feet away, mindful and respectful of David's rank and superior clearance level. He pulled out his encrypted radio phone and called Colonel Lewis. He robotically recounted what had just happened and advised him one prisoner was left. He also told him he secured the note from Danielle to make sure no one else got hold of it. Colonel Lewis ordered David to wait for the CIA operatives and deliver the message to them. Most likely, they would still want Danielle's body for some kind of investigation, if only to ensure no one would know what she had done or what he had done.

"I expect they will want to interrogate me. They can lock me up too for all I care," David muttered, no desire to fight or prove himself innocent flickering in his soul.

"No, I won't allow that, Sentinel. You stay strong, you hear? I'll catch a bird and be there in a few hours. Hang on until I arrive. I'm coming." The colonel had never come to meet David at another camp before. David had always been ordered to go to him.

"Red Hawk, thank you but—"

"Nonsense. You need me and I need them to know we need you! I won't let them spin this in the wrong direction. Not after everything you've done for us, for our country, for this war! I'll be there soon," the colonel said in a non-negotiating tone.

"Roger," David conceded. "I have one request Red Hawk," David ventured.

"What's that, soldier?"

"I want to be the one to call her father. I should be the one. I was her husband. And I am— her killer," David's voice broke.

"Auh, yes. Her father," the colonel sounded concerned. "I had forgotten who her father was. This could get uglier still."

"Let me do it. Please," David implored.

"Alright. But no later than tomorrow night; we can't withhold news like this from someone like him."

"I'm more worried about breaking his heart as her father than upsetting a man of his influence or connections." David's voice held accusation and he didn't care.

"Admirable soldier. But it's my job to look at all the angles of every situation we encounter and anticipate the potential outcomes. And this...this could go very badly," the colonel said with true concern in his voice, taking no offense to David's accusatory tone this time.

"I'll try to help contain the situation. But I won't lie to him. No matter what orders you give me."

"I'm not asking you lie to him. He has the clearance to read the full report. If there is to be one," Colonel Lewis sounded pensive at the end.

"Once this is over...I'm...I'm out. I'm done. I can't do this anymore," David's heart was breaking more and more with each word. His men. These soldiers. The fallen ones in need of the PJ's. How many wouldn't make it home if he left? But he *had* to. He couldn't hold himself together anymore, not here. He didn't have anything left in him to fight with. Danielle had taken everything from him.

"If you feel you must, I can arrange that Sentinel. But before you set your mind too firmly on that course of action, let's talk about that when I arrive. Just...just wait. I'll be there soon." The colonel had never sounded so sincere or as worried.

The radio went silent and David put it back in it's pocket. He dropped his head into his hands and rubbed his face vigorously.

This isn't happening. Lord, this isn't happening to me!

"Be strong my son. I am with you."

David drew in a big breath and lifted his head. MP Pierce was coming with three other men in camo pants and T-shirts striding purposefully toward him. They had black sunglasses on and weapons on their hips. It was a military base; the guns were standard uniform, but the three other men with the MP had a different feel to them, a different training coursing through their veins. These men were the spooks, the onsite CIA.

They approached him, slowing to a cautious stroll as they neared. One directly in front of him, the other two splitting up to come around behind him on each flank. MP Braum who had accompanied David outside, looked apologetic as they ushered David forward.

"Captain, mind coming with us? These fellas need to talk with you," MP Pierce asked, rather than ordered.

"I know. Don't worry. It's okay," David said softly. He opened his hands, spreading his fingers wide to show empty palms and opened his arms out to the sides. He spread his feet and nodded. "Go ahead," he offered himself willing for search and arrest.

"Um, no, Sir, that won't be necessary, Sir," the MP soldier said embarrassed. "They already know what happened. They just got an ear full from the doctor. We aren't here to arrest you, Sir. They just need to debrief you." He smiled reassuringly at David.

"Alright," David answered, lowing his hands. He walked between them back toward the command base headquarters. They may not be putting cuffs on him, but he felt the uneasiness of the three CIA agents surrounding him. He was careful not to make any sudden gestures or change his speed or direction in any way that might make them overreact.

Then again, if I did, they'd probably shoot me. Maybe that would be best. I don't want to live like this.

The remorse and betrayal were strangling him, building up within him, consuming him.

I think I'd rather be dead.

"And, um, Sir?" MP Braum said, glancing over at him as they walked, looking him over head to toe. "You may want to change your clothes and wash your hands, Sir," the soldiers voice was cracking a little, having known the blood covering David belonged to his wife.

David stopped mid-stride and looked down. The CIA agents bristled in response, unsure as to his intentions. David didn't care. He was covered in Danielle's blood. Covered in the last of her life force. He held his trembling hands out and examined them. Blood already drying and starting to crack in the creases of his palms.

"Jesus," David whispered.

"Sir...let's get you cleaned up, Sir," MP Braum suggested compassionately.

"No," one of the CIA agents denied sharply. "Not until we're done debriefing him," the man's voice was full of authority; there was to be no more discussion.

"It may draw attention," MP Pierce protested, in spite of the other man's inflamed response. "He just landed clean as a whistle."

"Do I need to remind you that we're in charge? No stops. No cleanup," the CIA agent challenged.

"Technically, you are on *our* base at the invitation of our commander. You don't have authority here," the MP stepped up into the CIA agent's face.

Both men bristled.

"Hey, hey," David said, trying to bring peace. "It's okay, man," David said hoarsely, lowering his trembling bloody hands.

"It's...this won't wash off anyway. There's too much blood on my hands," David probably wasn't making much sense to them but he wasn't thinking only about the physical blood itself.

I should have known what she was up to. I should have stopped her sooner!

The CIA agent studied him hard for a moment as if trying to assess his soul. David didn't squirm or look away. He didn't care what the man saw in his eyes. Defeat? Despair? Guilt? What did it matter anyway?

They continued on and led David onward, closing in a little tighter around him as other soldiers on the base began to notice and watch as they had anticipated. Whispers and speculation were already starting to circulate. David was sure they would all know he shot and killed his wife by tomorrow. And they would all know she had been a traitor. The giggling nosy nurse in the ER would make sure everyone knew.

God, what will my own team think of me?

David was relieved they weren't still hanging around outside, but were most likely sleeping or eating in the mess hall right now. David would do almost anything in this moment to be with them or anywhere else but here.

"They won't ever trust me again," David couldn't help but whisper out loud, his voice dripping with regret.

"They won't ever know the truth," one CIA agent said quietly. It was the one who had studied David face moments ago. "No good would come of it. Everyone present in the ER has been ordered not to speak of it. If they do, they face a dishonorable discharge and imprisonment.

"How will you explain her...her *disappearance*? She isn't easy to miss. Her absence will be noticed. People will ask questions," David choked back tears. He didn't want them to take her body and try to erase her like she never existed.

"It will be said that one of the prisoners brought in today got loose, grabbed a gun, took her hostage, and in the course of events, she was killed."

David nodded. That was a logical coverup story. He swallowed hard, "I see."

"It's being classified," one of the other CIA agents clarified.

"Aren't you wondering what we will say about you, *Sentinel?*" the third CIA agent poked at him. His voice was condescending and mocking.

These men know about me? Interesting.

David looked at the man in the eyes, "Something classified and creative, I'm sure," David's voice was dry and uncaring, his lack of insulted pride at being mocked and not rising to the bait must have surprised the agent, because he dropped the posturing and frowned a little. He looked away and started ignoring David as they continued on.

David lowered his head back down and watched the ground as they escorted him to the command center. He felt utterly lost and alone. He suddenly felt like he didn't even know who he was anymore. How had he gotten here? Why hadn't he seen this all sooner to prevent this from ever happening. Why did it have to be him who was destined to kill Danielle?

He felt his soul fill with anguish and he stifled a sob. He would have to try to keep it together for this interrogation.

Just keep it together a little longer.

After a moment, David felt a familiar warmth nearby, a presence. He looked up and over to his left. He saw the faintest glimmering shape and essence of Jesus walking beside them, his eyes full of hope and love, locked onto David.

"I am with you. *Always,*" Jesus said, his words and his voice penetrating David's mind and his broken heart, coating it in warmth and peace. "It will be alright."

David didn't answer out loud. He swallowed back the tears and closed his eyes for a couple steps, letting the peace and hope sink into him, giving him back his will to live and fight for a tomorrow.

When he opened his eyes, Jesus was still there, walking beside them. Keeping pace with their purposeful gait to determine David's fate. David lifted his chin and squared his shoulders. He had followed his orders, though the outcome had been unpredictable. He had intercepted the traitor's message and stopped her from eliminating both their prisoners of war. He had managed to save at least one of them, and hopefully, the intel the last Taliban prisoner possessed, would prove to be worth killing her for. David had done his duty. He was a soldier. He had proven his loyalty to his country. Let them question him. Let them accuse him. He would stand tall and strong and know he was in the right, no matter how wrong it felt.

He glanced over at Jesus who smiled knowingly at him, his eyes full of compassion and love.

I will fear no evil, for you are with me.

Mark My Words

Chapter Twelve

*D*avid and I were still laughing as we left, arm in arm, though the front door of Picard's Bounty Hunting Academy. David turned to lock the door when I saw them; a small news crew rushing across the street from behind a conspicuous, color splashed, advertisement riddled van with it's tinted windows, mounted with antennas and their communication microwave satellite dishes on top.

I recognized the reporter immediately. Mark Jerseyman was smiling broadly, his glossy black and white wingtip shoes nearly sparkling as he jogged across the street, his cameraman at his heels.

"Miss Bishop!" Mark called as he approached us with a wave, his normally polished news anchor's voice lit with excitement. "Miss Bishop! May I have a moment?" He stopped in front of David and I, his eyes bright and attentive. He smiled broader as he recognized David.

"I, um," I stuttered. How had they known I was here? David came up and stood next to me protectively, unwilling to leave me at the mercy of the media.

I had three conflicting trains of thought colliding within me all at once which left me feeling dread, regret, and relief all in an instance.

Oh no! No, no! Now everyone will wonder what I'm learning about and know where to look for me! Crap! David—David's going to be caught up in this! But thank God it's Mark Jerseyman and not one of those other vultures!

"Ten o'clock," David whispered into my ear discreetly.

It took me a millisecond to put together what he was saying and I glanced in the direction he'd indicated. Tristina was crouching behind her Crown Victoria, smirking triumphantly. She had come back!

So, she had recognized me! She called them? But why!

Her eyes locked on David and expanded in surprise. She stood up straight taking a step toward the hood of her car, her face instantly hardening into something close to hatred.

Oh no. David.

Mark was aware of everything. His sharp eyes darting to follow where mine and David's had gone, not one to miss a thing. "Do you know her?" Mark asked me, his eyes squinting to make out the face of the woman glaring at us from across the street.

It registered on Tristina's face that the reporter and camera had now turned toward her, she retreated slightly as if trying to hide, alarmed at being discovered. She hadn't expected her spiteful trick to backfire on her and expose her unprofessionalism.

So, she must have called in anonymously and came back to watch! Serves her right to be caught!

"Who is that Melanie? Do you know her?" Mark probed, poking his microphone into my face. "What's troubling you?"

I took an automatic step back away from the mic. David stood his ground, ready to become a barrier if I needed him to. I'd learned over the past six weeks that when the media found me, to tell them with my body language that I was uncomfortable with their proximity to me. It was something Elisabeth had coached me on since they'd been hunting me down for an easy story to make their deadlines, headlines and keep the curiosity of the public at bay.

"If you get cornered, show them you're weary of their presence," Liz had instructed. "Remember, you were the *victim* of a vicious crime, so they are going to look like a school of piranhas if they come on too strong to you. The public will speak up against them if they treat you insensitively. You know how networks are about ratings and tweets. They can twist anything you say, so don't answer anything right away. Take a moment to think of an answer that is both as honest as possible, but as concise as possible. Don't give them anything else to spring off of. Don't reveal too much. Don't elaborate and don't fabricate. You can always just say, 'no comment', if you don't feel their questions are friendly. And you can continue to walk away, to show them you aren't interested in continuing. If they insist, keep walking silently until they give up or can't follow you."

Liz had been so ticked off the first time a news crew snuck into the hospital and somehow bypassed the restricted areas of the ward I was in. They had tried to infiltrate my ICU room for pictures of me after the attack was made public by some nosy cops and pissed off neighbors. She'd nearly gotten herself arrested when she'd yanked the camera right off a cameraman's shoulder and tossed it down the hall after the reporter and him had sweet-talked their way up to the ICU and refused to leave.

The reporter was some up-and-coming petite brunette who, prior to that, wasn't memorable enough to remember her name. She'd refused to leave when Liz caught them checking the other rooms looking for me again. In fact, she'd been out taking care of them when David had snuck into my room to check on me. I hadn't found out until I was home what had happened outside the room. Liz hadn't wanted to upset me.

When I was released, three network news' crews had been waiting outside the hospital and had shoved their mics in my face as Liz rolled me past in my wheel chair to her Lexus, loaded me inside and sped away. Later, they came by our home, waiting outside for a chance to ambush me and interrogate me about the assault.

News of a felon being released without his ankle monitor, a huge mistake by the Department of Corrections, and the immediate attempted rape of the felon's own daughter, was too juicy of a story for them to let go of. Dogs with bones. I was the bone. Something to be chewed on and sucked dry. Not caring that I was trying to enter my own home, barely able to walk because of the broken ribs and bruising!

They had shouting a stream of intrusive and insensitive questions at me like, "How often had he raped you before you left home?"

Eventually, the neighbors complained about their noise and disruption, their vans always blocking driveways and other vehicles from coming or going. The local police got tired of the calls and asked the news crews to leave.

It didn't take them long to find out that I attended classes at Cosumnes River College and started harassing me there instead. One time, David appeared out of nowhere and blocked them, giving me just enough time to escape into the Administration Building where they weren't permitted to go without prior clearance. I'd never thanked him for helping me that day since I had still been too humiliated at the time to look him in the eye, and had been avoiding him as much as possible.

By blocking their pathway to me, he'd virtually become their next target. Excited, no thrilled, that my knight in shining armor had again, swooped in to save me, they drilled him. Question after question. He'd handled himself well. He stood straight and commanding, his hands locked in a military "at ease" position and when asked his name at the start of their improv interview, he addressed them as Retired Air Force Captain David Abramson. In doing so, he clued them in that he was a man of action, integrity and honor. They changed their tone immediately to one of gratitude and respect for the obvious service he provided to me by saving me that night and of course, his service to our country. They had practically been eating out of his hand by the end of it.

When Liz and I watched it later on the five o'clock news, she said that he would have been an amazing public relations specialist or even a natural negotiator by how he'd handled them. They'd never chased him down again; he satisfied them in that one interview. Me, however, they couldn't seem to get enough of, and my elusive, cautious answers didn't sate them.

Now, as I looked at the hatred on Tristina's face toward David, and her alarm at being caught red handed, I felt my belly burn inside with anger at her hostility toward me and the man I loved. She had called them! She told them I was here and wanted to stay long enough to see me squirm. But she hadn't expected to see David. Oh no. He'd caught her off guard. I was glad! But now that she knew her daughter's husband was with me today, I could see she was barely holding herself together across the street. She had wrapped her arms around herself, her body rigid. Emotions played across her face at the sight of him.

She blames him. She never had all her questions about her daughter's death answered nor had she come to terms with it. And since she had suspected David had been involved in some way, but had never been able to have those questions answered about him either, she blames him for Danielle's death.

The understanding struck me, hard, chasing back the anger to one of compassion and sympathy. Grace for her flooded into me with more insights into her soul, popping in as God gave me words of knowledge about her.

She was angry and bitter because she'd lost her daughter. She distrusted her ex-husband because of wrongs done to her by other men before she'd met him, and by the example her own father had set in their home; one of betrayal, infidelity and lies. She didn't trust most people. How could she? She'd always been lied to, used, cheated on, or been betrayed by those closest in her life, even jealous and petty friends. And her mixed heritage had left her feeling rejected from each side of her family. I just *knew* it to be true.

She had sabotaged her marriage and every positive relationship left in her life, all to protect herself from the possibility of more pain and loss. It was counterproductive and created that which she'd feared. But she didn't know how to move past it and let it go. She didn't know how to forgive. Forgive herself. Forgive Doc. Forgive David. And she didn't even know how to forgive her dead daughter Danielle. She too had seen the coldness in Danielle, and her instincts told her, she had become something unspeakable, and had died because of it.

I felt my face soften as Tristina looked at me, her hard face turning smug again, then losing its edge as the pity I felt for her probably showed on my face from across the street. I was so easy to read.

I looked at Mark and his cameraman, still waiting for an answer, and suddenly knew what I needed to do.

"Hi Mark," I said genially, and took a step back toward his outstretched microphone. "Yes, that's an agent with the Department of Justice. We were briefly introduced a short while ago. I believe she's just keeping a friendly eye on me. You know, for my safety," I added with meaning. I glanced over at Tristina and gave a quick wave of acknowledgement. Mark did too, as if saying hello with a friendly smile to my protection duty. He probably thought now that her hateful glare was at their presence, not ours. I just hoped he hadn't noticed mine.

"She's a close friend with the owner of this establishment," I said, pointing to the *Picard's Bounty Hunting Academy* sign behind me. "I think she wanted to help ensure my safety today." I smiled at Tristina, and I saw her frown, distrustful of whatever I was saying over here, far out of earshot.

Maybe by offering Tristina an olive branch and giving her a publicized reason for being here, she wouldn't get in trouble with her boss for harassing me. She might even get a pat on the back for making their agency look good and for taking the initiative. I knew I could have reported her now. What she'd done was so unprofessional, acting on a misguided sense of revenge over her own jealousy and insecurity. I'd have every right to file a complaint about this, let alone how she'd treated me inside. But now that the Lord had let me see into her damaged heart, I had a desire to do something nice for her instead of pay her back in kind out of spite.

"So, she's guarding you? From your father?" Mark asked, his tone light to keep me talking. I was sure he'd seen the other failed attempts to get an interview out of me over the past six weeks, my reluctance to answer any questions, and my attempts to flee. He was probably thrilled that I was actually talking to *him*.

I knew of one instance that he'd been present and had actually helped me evade the other news crews. It had been the week the dean of the college had finally stepped in to formally request all reporters and news vehicles cease and desist. Their constant presence and harassing of the students to try to find me or get a story about me out of them was disrupting their academic activities, and blocking parking which was always tight to begin with. Since they weren't reporting on anything that brought a positive light or attention to the college, they had had enough.

Some of the reporters started getting sneaky after that. Waiting to surprise me going to my car and pop out to badger me with questions. Mark had been quietly waiting by one end of the business complex where I'd been seen once before sneaking out to the south parking lot to my car. He'd taken one look at my red puffy eyes and grim expression and stopped mid stride, his hand out to stop his cameraman, catching him in the chest to make him stop. Then he lowered the lens of his partner's camera and said something to him, causing him to lower it all the way.

I stopped, unsure as to his angle. But then he'd tipped his head to the left and pointed silently, indicating that I should go that way instead. I believed him and rushed off the way he'd hinted. As I crept back around the other side of the building, I saw them. Two other reporters approaching Mark, gesturing agitatedly.

I heard him say, "No. That wasn't her. My sources told me she wasn't in class today. Come on guys. Let's go before the dean bans us from the sport matches too."

Mark Jerseyman had spared me the humiliation of being ambushed, even though his own intentions moments before had been just that. He'd seen my distress, the evidence of my recent tears, and had shown me compassion. What he hadn't known, was I had just come from my Sociology class where the professor had been giving examples of different social norms in various cultures and how they were viewed by the American perspective as being a highly dysfunctional family life. Someone pointed out that mine was dysfunctional in any culture. What kind of father would rape his own daughter? The whole class looked at me, waiting for me to respond, even after the professor rebuked them. I'd simply gotten my things and left to cry my humiliated tears in the bathroom.

Now, as I stood in front of the same reporter who had shown me mercy, I knew he was the one to use to get *my* message out. He, and only him, would get the exclusive.

"Has she been protecting you long?" Mark asked me.

"I'm not exactly sure, Mark," I answered.

"They don't tell you who's assigned as a protective detail?" Mark asked me, surprised.

"Well, I haven't really had one in a while. Not that I've been told anyway. I think they're afraid of scaring me," I shrugged.

"Because of your father?" Mark led gently.

"Yeah. But that isn't what I meant. I don't know if she's here to keep an eye out for my father or those other people determined to hurt me," I said, my face showing him a grimace at the words.

"Others?" Mark pounced, just as I knew he would.

"Yes. You may not know this yet, but I was held against my will and...and things done to me by a group of older kids when I was fifteen," I began, and bit my lower lip. I knew now was my chance to do this, but I hadn't rehearsed anything. I wasn't sure how to say it.

Lord help me!

David tensed slightly next to me, unsure as to where I was going with this. It certainly wasn't the angle he would have anticipated.

"Really? No, I wasn't aware. Please, go on," Mark asked, his face interested and struggling to hide the glee as I gave him more than he'd hoped for. I saw the cameraman leaning in too and I felt encouraged.

"Well, a couple senior girls at my high school had made friends with me. They convinced me to go out with them and showed up with a van full of guys and another girl. It was pretty clear right off they were up to no good. I tried to leave but they shoved me inside the van. The boys intended to rape me. I found out later they had also intended to experiment with torturing me too. But they never got the chance...when they were starting to...hurt me, someone had heard my cries and intervened." My voice cracked and Mark's eyes grew large.

"I didn't see that in any of our research," Mark remarked aghast, not disbelieving me, but anxious for the facts. I could tell he was going to go dig around later to validate my claims before this aired, so I gave him some facts as reassurance.

"I was a minor, so if you were just looking me up you wouldn't find much. *My* file was sealed. A couple of my attackers were seventeen though and they were tried as adults. Their records aren't sealed. And the others were eighteen or older already. This took place on Friday, July 19th 2002 in Redding, California, in Shasta County. The ring leader was Jill Zeller. Her gang included Sarah Robinson, Pablo Gutierrez, Damian Durante, Jake O'Neill, and Leslie Rehl.

Mark's eyes flickered with excitement at the names and date I recited and the potential he saw for a follow up piece to this unexpected background story.

I pressed on. "I recently ran into Jill. She told me the others were all out of prison now too and that she'd tell them where to find me," I swallowed hard, not even having to lather on the anxiety because it was right there under the surface at the thought of seeing them again. "To find me...and finish what they started," I clarified once I'd put moisture back in my mouth.

Mark's face greyed a little, starting to see the world through my eyes and realizing that my fear of being following by the media wasn't only out of privacy but out of concern that my whereabouts would be easier to track not only by my father but by these other miscreants as well.

"Did you tell the police?" Mark questioned, logic dictating his next response, again as I knew it would.

"Yes, but Sacramento Police Chief Christopher Wales wasn't interested and told me to drop it," I said, my eyes large and unbelieving.

"Why? How could he do that?" Mark said, his tone conspiratorial.

"I didn't know at first! He even accused me of lying and trying to create more drama or attention for myself. He even threatened to arrest me if I pursued it further or asked them for help again. And this all happened a few days *before* my father was released from prison and came to my home to..." I broke off, my voice box squeezing tight, strangling the words. I felt real emotion hit me, heartache for Jill, a flashback of the terror that had crashed into me as my father burst through my door, the memory of what he had done to Vivian and my mother. I cleared my throat.

"Please, take your time," Mark said softly, his hand reaching out as if to comfort me, then retracting as he remembered it wasn't just he and I talking privately, but potentially hundreds of thousands or possibly millions of viewers if his story was replayed.

I tried again, clearing my throat and glancing at David for strength. He nodded and I plowed onward. "This encounter with Jill Zeller was a couple days before my father got out of prison and tried to, to rape me. So it's not like I could have planned any of it to get...to get attention like Chief Wales accused me of."

"But you've done nothing but try to avoid media attention. You haven't even tweeted a peep about this! You don't even have a Facebook or Instagram page that we could find," Mark defended my honor without a second thought and I could have hugged him.

"I—I know. It didn't make sense. I didn't understand at first," I repeated, leading him back to ask me the obvious.

"You didn't know at first?" Mark repeated. "Do you know why now?"

"Yes," I hesitated as if it was difficult to admit, "I didn't know it at the time, but I recently discovered, that the girl I ran into, the ringleader, Jill Zeller, is the Chief's *niece*," I said, shaking my head in despair.

"Really?" Mark said shocked. "You think he railroaded you to protect her for some reason? To protect his family?"

"I do. In fact," I wavered again, but for real this time. I wasn't sure if I should tell him about Jill's confession that the Chief had raped her for sport with his brother, her own step-father, for a few years before I met her. I decided I didn't want to open that can of worms yet. Not until we loosen the ground first. And not until we had more proof. But what could be proven with a little research by Mark was their connection.

"Maybe it's because he's protecting a secret of his own," I volunteered, keeping it close to the truth but not specific, like Liz had taught me. "Or maybe it's because...because she admitted to me that my father had beat and raped her too, shortly before she made it her mission in life to get to know me and trick me into going with them that night when I was fifteen. As payback," I rushed.

"Your father? He raped this Jill Zeller girl?" Mark said, frowning. I could tell he was unsure how this all linked together. I decided to help him out.

"You see, my father has raped *many* people," I said with emphasis. "I know of several in fact. I mean, he was arrested in 2006 after attacking that young girl. I wasn't his first attempt," I cleared my throat, growing uncomfortable but not letting my public humiliation choke me into silence. It was now or never. Everyone already knew what my father had done to me. I couldn't un-ring that bell. But I could ring other bells and bring more attention to his crimes. Hopefully, someone out there was watching and would ring one back.

"Jill was *his* victim. She was brutalized by him too. And...maybe, since she hasn't hurt me again yet, other than make some verbal threats, the agents that are currently investigating her and the others in wake of Chief Wales refusal, will be open to what she has to say about my father. You know, as a witness and a victim to his brutality and sadism," I hedged.

I purposely left out that she'd claimed that she and the others had killed other people already. I was starting to wonder if that was even true. I think I'd been their first attempt. They had planned it out, but their tactics for kidnapping and getting away with me hadn't been well polished. They hadn't even left my street when they'd started to assault me in Sarah's van and I lived at the end of the court. They couldn't even wait to begin. They hadn't been smart enough to leave first.

I also wanted Chief Wales to know that I wasn't afraid of him and I knew what he was. I wanted him to know that I had other agents looking into him *and* his niece. He needed to know that I could play his game and I had no intention of losing. But what made me even more hopeful, was that by outing Jill, the media would undoubtedly dig into her life. They might even try to find her and the others *for* me. Putting them in the spotlight like this would make it nearly impossible for them to come after me. Everyone would suspect them or my father of course, if anything ended up happening to me. Maybe they would be too afraid to come back for me and finally let it go. Hopefully, this would protect me and Liz from any retaliation.

"Are you asking Jill Zeller to come forward?" Mark interpreted, his sharp mind picking up her name easily and repeating it back for dramatic affect.

"Well, yes. I guess I am." I looked straight into the camera now, "Jill, I know my father hurt you. He hurt me too. We *both* have suffered so much at his hands. We both want justice! Please—" I swallowed hard, a real knot blocking my throat as the relevance of this moment sunk in further. "Please, come forward and tell the FBI what you know," I implored. "We need to make sure that once they catch him, he never gets out of jail again. Your testimony will add to the charges against him and the length of his sentence once convicted. Please, *please* help me lock him up for good," I was urgent and sincere, but not desperate. I would never show her desperation again. Not even for this.

"You said you know he's raped others. Can you clarify on that? Who?" Mark asked, making sure he explored every detail of my words.

"I could, but I'm not ready to say the other names at this time," I glanced down, feeling shame and embarrassment for the sake of my beloved mother and sister. I wasn't going to dishonor them and expose their darkest secrets until we had proof and it was officially listed with the charges against my father. Murder wasn't something you just said out loud without proof. Besides, I didn't want to hurt the ongoing investigation. I wanted to help it. And I didn't want to tip my hand to my father that I knew what he'd done or that I had witnessed both murders.

"What else can you tell us?" Mark pressed gently.

"I can say this," I volunteered. "My father was a long-haul truck driver on and off for over thirty years. He drove all over the United States. I have serious doubts that he kept his...his appetites centralized to California. I would ask," I looked back into the camera now, "I would ask that anyone out there who knew my father, survived an assault by him, got in a fight with him, or even saw something that has stuck with them throughout these years because it just felt so wrong or disturbing that they couldn't shake it, to *please, please* call the FBI to report what you know!" I had stepped up to the camera unconsciously, my urgency driving me further forward only two feet away from the lens.

Mark was eating this up, his face elated. "Is there anything else you'd like to share with the community or to those watching in other states?" Mark said, testing the conversation to see if we could keep going and also offer himself an option to wind down the conversation if he had to.

"Only that...I want to thank my friends who have stood by me and looked out for me during this difficult time," I reached over and grabbed David's hand. He'd been so quiet, letting me do all the talking and simply being a comforting presence at my side.

David smiled down at me encouragingly, his eyes telling me he approved of what I'd done here. "David was my hero that night," I said back at Mark. "He was just a friend at the time, but since then," I paused and glanced at David asking his permission to out us. He gave me an almost imperceptible nod. "We're dating now. I honestly couldn't have found a better man. Or rather, he found me," I smiled now, and felt my face turn beet red for the first time during this ambush-interview. "Dating" might be a stretch technically since we had yet to have one traditional date together, but the point was, we were seeing each other.

"A budding romance out of the ashes," Mark said pleased. "Mr. Abramson, I saw your interview a few weeks back. Thank you for your service, Sir." Mark sounded very respectful and even offered David his hand.

That isn't normal for these sorts of things, is it?

David shook Mark's hand firmly and nodded. "It was my pleasure," David said, and couldn't help but glance toward Tristina who was now leaning against the front of her car, her arms crossed, watching us curiously. She still couldn't hear a single thing we were saying from there but had decided to stick around to see how it'd end.

"I was so impressed with you, Sir, that I did a little independent research of my own on you," Mark said with a friendly tone.

Oh God, what was he going to say about David? I hope he doesn't mention him killing his wife. Oh Lord!

"Have you?" David said, cautiously. He seemed to stiffen next to me.

"Much of your record is classified. I wasn't even able to obtain any sneak peeks," Mark said with humor, rather than disappointment. "But what was perfectly clear to me, Sir, from what they did put on your public record, was what an *exemplarily* example of the model American Soldier you are. And what an example of humanity you are to us all. I read that you were an Air Force Pararescue Recovery Specialist helicopter pilot, is that right?" Mark asked excited again, stating the long title with precision.

"Yes, Sir," David nodded.

"You received the Defense Superior Service medal, Distinguished Flying Cross, three Medals of Honor—"

"Yes, but this really isn't about me," David cut in, polite enough but his hint to leave his record out of this news report obvious.

"Yes, yes. I just think the public may have been wondering about the hero who saved Melanie Bishop. As she said, you were her hero that night. Her guardian angel. The PJs are called the Angels of Mercy, are they not? Did you ever get used to being a hero in the war?" Mark pressed on. He seemed genuinely curious.

"I was only doing my job, my duty to my fellow soldiers and to the souls we were sent to save," David answered, glancing down at me.

"But it is in your instincts, Sir? To rush toward danger instead of away from it? To help those in need?" Mark asked with a look of admiration on his face.

"I do as my morals and my conscience dictates," David replied. "I'm not a hero. I'm just a man who wants to do what's right. Doing what's right and standing up for what's right, that's what a soldier fights for. That's all a soldier wants."

"Not fame and glory?" Mark stated more than asked.

"Some might. But I don't," David said flatly.

"I did learn in my research, that the pilot isn't usually trained as a PJ. They go to flight school as an officer, not a Pararescue crew member. But you, you did *both*. That is highly irregular, Sir. I also discovered that a PJ's training is among the toughest in the United States military's special units, including that of the Marine Force Recon units, Green Berets, SEALs, and DELTA Force." Mark said enthusiastically. He paused waiting for David to respond in some way. David stayed quiet, neither confirming, denying or adding anything to Mark's discoveries.

Mark pressed on, encouraged by the silence to get to the point. "Is it true ninety percent of soldiers who try to become a PJ won't even make it through the selection process? Out of those ten percent that do make it, eighty-five percent wash out. Why do you think that is, Sir? And how is it that you managed to not only complete the flight school and officer training, but complete the Pararescue Jumper program as well?" Mark asked, further expanding his mini-story into David to satisfy the public's curiosity.

David remained silent a moment longer, taking his time to consider the comments and questions as they had been presented. He looked up, out toward nothing before answering as if weighing what would be the best response that wouldn't put down those soldiers who had tried and failed to become a pararescue jumper, and how that might make him look all the more remarkable, not wanting to be a braggadocio. His brow creased as he thought, no other physical tells exposing his internal emotions or thought processes. Mark waited patiently for the answer, as did I.

"Being a pararescue jumper is a calling, not a choice. When a civilian becomes a soldier, it's either because their national pride and sense of honor burns within their veins and compels them to enlist, or, they are simply looking for a purpose in life and do not want to feel lost anymore. I believe that every soldier has heart and commitment. But some try to focus their hearts in areas they aren't destined to be a part of. They each have a place, a purpose. And the military will work with each soldier to help them find theirs.

"As a PJ, we train in a variety of disciplines and quite honestly sir, not all are cut out for it. Each area is harder than the next. Parachuting, underwater combat, wilderness survival, trauma paramedic training, hand to hand combat, weapons and tactical maneuvering, combat diving, ropes and mountaineering, extrications, and on, and on. And there is *no* room for error. If a soldier doesn't get good marks in one area, they're out. There are no exceptions. It *has* to be this way. They must be an expert in all areas of training because it could be the difference between life and death on every single mission they're sent out on. Not just their life, but their comrades' lives and the lives of the men and women they are sent in to save. It is a calling. It *has* to be *who* you are," David spoke clearly and with conviction, his eyes boring into Mark's. The cameraman had stepped up a little, pulled by David's passion and chosen career path and toward his defensiveness for his fellow soldiers.

Mark smiled at him. "And *that* is exactly *why* you are a hero, Sir. Honorable and humble. A true soldier at that."

"I couldn't agree more," I added, smiling up at David and gripping his arm.

"How is it you managed to be both a pilot and PJ?" Mark slipped his other question back in smoothly with a charming smile.

"I've been either in helicopters or flying them since I was a kid. My dad has been an aeromedical EMS helicopter pilot for forty years now," David replied.

"EMS?" Mark asked casually for the sake of his viewers ignorant to the term.

"Emergency medical services," David answered patiently. "When he got back from the Vietnam War, he wanted to use his helicopter skills to save lives instead of take them. He volunteered to be a part of the aeromedical trials being done at the time that later, proved to revolutionize the response capabilities of critical life-and-death medical emergencies on freeways or wilderness search and rescue."

"Your father was your hero?" Mark cut in, his eyes shining, loving every word coming out of David's mouth.

"Still is," David corrected wholeheartedly. "I begged to go with him to work as soon as I was old enough to say the word, *helicopter*. He took me out to teach me to fly, but never to work. Finally, when I was thirteen, I'd worn him down enough that he said yes. He said I was old enough to understand that sometimes, no matter what we do, we can't save them all. That it was up to God. He flew the helo, but God created the air that lifts it, and determines the destination of the passengers. He said God was the real pilot, we just had to do our best to get them wherever he'd already planned them to land.

"Sounds like you father wanted you to know the reality of our limitations. We are not gods," I said, forgetting for a moment that Mark and the cameraman were engaged in the conversation, and these revelations about David and his father weren't a private discussion. They were being recorded. An audience might watch this on the news later, unless they edited out all the dialog about God and our human reality.

David looked at me and smiled kindly. "Yes, he did. He wanted me to know that sometimes, despite using all your resources, and doing everything you could, a person might still die in flight." David looked back at Mark now, "After he made sure I understood the reality, he asked me if I still wanted to go. I assured him, I did. I thought I was ready."

"The first call of the morning was an assignment out to a horrendous car crash on Interstate 5. The driver of a Ford F-250 was headed southbound and had a heart attack. He lost control of his truck and the loaded horse trailer he was hauling, right into oncoming traffic just past Twin Cities Road. He crashed into a station wagon with a mother and her two kids. The little girl was my age at the time, and her son, about fifteen.

"We landed in the field nearby, my father and I stayed in the helicopter as the medical crew brought the mother and daughter back for transport. The boy was DOA. I remember watching the whole thing as if I wasn't really there. The flight there was charged with energy and anxiety, we couldn't seem to get there fast enough. Watching the medical crew working with the emergency crews already on the ground was captivating. They were heroes. All of them, including my father. It felt surreal watching my dad, my super hero, exemplify the courage it took to face that kind of carnage day after day, simply to help others.

"But the euphoria vanished shortly after we took off. The mother and daughter were strapped in and the medical crew worked to save them. I wasn't captivated anymore. I was scared. I was scared that they were going to lose them. Afraid of watching death take them right in front of me. Afraid to see that other side my father had warned me about," David's words were even and factual, a clear account of his first experience witnessing terrible carnage and gore. There was no sign that only two and or three hours before he was weeping on his knees, baring his secrets and his soul to me. Letting me see the brokenness war had inflicted upon him.

"Did they make it?" Mark almost whispered, completely engrossed in the story.

"We lost the mother and daughter mid-flight to the hospital. Once the commotion and desperation to save them was over, silence filled the helicopter among the crew. A reverent silence. My father said a prayer for them. The doctor on board just turned away, and glared out the window. He seemed angry they'd lost them," David said in a tone just over Mark's whisper.

"And how did that affect you at thirteen years old?" Mark wondered, plucking the thoughts right from my mind.

"I cried. I pulled my knees up to my chest and cried like a baby. My father didn't scold me. He didn't tell me to stop or say, 'I told you so.' He just patted my knee and let me see the sorrow he felt too. We shared that moment together. We'd tried to save them. We'd lost," David shrugged and wet his lips, emotion finally playing across his face.

"You said we? You felt like you were part of the rescue crew that day?" Mark smiled sadly.

"I was. I was there start to finish. I realized that day that for every life that didn't make it to the hospital alive, others did, it was better to try, than to do nothing. I wanted to be like my father. I wanted to save lives. Even if it meant sometimes you'd lose them," David took in a breath and pulled back in on his control.

"I can't wait to meet him," I said to David not thinking about the camera again.

Oops. Crap! I didn't mean to say that out loud.

Mark's eyes lit up. "So, how long have you two known each other?" Mark asked excitedly, pulling his interview back to the development of our mysterious relationship. "If you haven't met the parents yet, this relationship must be pretty new?" He switched his tone to that of a conversational talk show host now. He knew his viewers wanted to know too and were going to eat this up. He was asking for them as much as he was for ratings.

"Well, we didn't start seeing each other until recently but we met nearly two and a half years ago at Kate's Café," David wrapped his arm around my shoulder. To the viewers, it would look both protective, possessive, and of course, comforting.

"You don't say? The same Kate's Café down in Elk Grove that was hit with an unknown chemical attack last month which caused people to attack one another?" Mark was looking at us like we were gold. "Do you both still work there?"

"Yes," I confirmed. "I saw your news coverage that night. It was quite good," I smiled at Mark who beamed back. Pride in his work and pleasure at having been praised on camera making him overjoyed. He pulled back into his professional pose and continued.

"It's been closed for some time now. I believe this happened the night before your attack. Is that correct?" Mark asked kindly, not losing sight of both stories, his incredible memory of dates and times impressing me.

"You know your dates," I commented, letting him see how impressed I was.

Mark nodded in assent. "That was an eventful week for you, Miss Bishop," Mark said delicately. It was my turn to nod, not hearing a direct question in his statement.

"Any news on when the restaurant is going to open back up?" he asked, bringing the conversation forward again.

"We're actually heading there now to help with some final details. The owner, Frank Gable, will be running an advertisement soon announcing the grand reopening. We don't have the official date yet," David replied for us.

"Well, please let me know! I'd love to be there the night of the reopening to help support the event!" Mark sounded excited to see us love birds together in action.

"We will," I agreed quickly.

Maybe if Mark was invited, his presence would keep the returning patrons of the café and new lollygaggers from behaving too badly toward me. Maybe they would just come, eat, have a good time, and leave. Maybe with him there, they wouldn't ask me stupid questions or try to get a picture with me like I was some sort of Entertainment Tonight celebrity. Unfortunately, I had already run into those kinds of people.

I was almost dreading going back to work because now, everyone would know me! I had two choices, buck up and take it, or move to an uninhabited island with no televisions or internet. There wasn't any point getting a different job because right now, my life was still fresh news and I would still be recognized. No point going somewhere else if the same troubles were going to follow me. Besides, Frank was great about letting me change my work schedule around my classes each semester. I never had to worry that I couldn't sign up for a class because it would conflict with a shift.

"I'm sorry to ask a delicate question to you, Sir," Mark stated carefully, his tone indicating he was about to get us back into heavier topics, "but David, did you have any idea, the night you went over to visit your friend, that the man assaulting her was her father? Had she ever mentioned him to you before?" Mark glanced at me to see if I was going to get squirmy to this line of questioning and didn't want to push his luck too far.

I could sense he didn't want to stir up negative emotions between he and I. I knew he'd want a follow-up interview and didn't want to blow his chances by pushing us away or not get invited to do a follow-up piece on Kate's Café. I didn't vocalize any objections so after a pause and a glance at me, David answered him.

"No, we never discussed him up until that point. Melanie is very private by nature. And who can blame her given the kind of life she had under Dwayne Bishop's thumb." There was a warning to Mark in David's voice. It was clear, though I hadn't objected to the question, he did, and wanted Mark to be cautious moving forward.

"Of course," Mark nodded in agreement, giving a sympathetic expression toward me. "It must have been quite a shock. A man of your moral stature, confronting a man as vile as Dwayne Bishop, trying to do what he was doing," Mark said in a delicate tone.

"Actually, the violence or violation of any human being, is enough to upset me, Mark. No matter how they may or may not be related to someone I love," David said boldly, aggression seeping into his face.

Mark nodded again in assent, then said for the viewers benefit, "Anyone can see you love her very much. Melanie, are your feelings as defined as his?" Mark wondered.

I blanched. I hadn't expected to be asked *that*. I didn't think anyone would care to know about my love life to that degree. I hadn't even verbalized it to David yet! Mark looked at me expectedly and I opened my mouth but before I could formulate a tactful response, David saved me yet again.

"I don't expect Melanie to answer that, for you, or for me. It's too soon to put that kind of expectation on her. She knows how I feel about her, and that's good enough for me. I had hoped that the media and the public would have respected her privacy given the brutality of the assault and how badly she'd been hurt, let alone traumatized," David's voice had dropped dangerously low, "But her physical and emotional wellbeing seems irrelevant compared to their curiosity," David leaned slightly toward Mark meaningfully, "The reporters keep coming at her, only concerned with beating out the competition, and being the one to get the story." He finished his words clipped, a challenging look on his face. He had pulled away from me, his shoulder moving slightly in front of me, his posture showing how capable of aggression he was yet carefully in control of his protective impulses.

I could see Mark squirming a little, worrying, looking to soften the direction of the conversation again and befriend David into not thinking he was one of the reporters who had been unfeeling toward my situation.

I wanted to keep the line of communication open between Mark and I as well. I might need him later to help my cause and reach the public. Having him as an ally could help me gather evidence or witnesses against my father.

"I can understand why," I chimed in, placing my hand on David's arm to calm him and to show we were a united couple. "It's human nature. We're fascinated by the strange, the different, and true, even the horrible," I shrugged not having to pretend this truth made me feel sad inside.

I straightened back up to show I still had faith in people, "I believe it's also human nature to want to protect the innocent, the underdogs. There are those who thrive on picking on the little guy and don't care who they hurt. People like my father. But there are others who want to keep people like him off the streets and locked up where they can't hurt anyone else.

"So, I ask all those who believe in justice and want to protect the innocent to please, please don't dismiss this and tell yourself that it's not your problem! If anyone out there can help, please try. Call the FBI and tell them what you know. Make a difference. Thank you," I finished, effectively ending the interview before it got any more uncomfortable with tension.

"And thank you Mark, for your delicacy and discretion. We do appreciate you haven't lost sight of the fact that I'm a human being with fears and feelings. You'll be my first choice if I ever want to speak to the media again. Is that okay with you, Mark?" I asked with a friendly smile.

"Absolutely, my lady. Thank you! Thank you both for your time," Mark reached out his hand and I took it. He placed his other hand on top of mine, a warm gesture as if we were good friends. He offered his hand to David and they pumped each other's hand twice, a sincere smile of friendly terms present on both of their faces.

"My card," Mark said quickly, digging in his pocket and retrieving a glossy two-sided business card. "Please call me when you get word of the reopening, or...if you ever want to talk. Day or night, I'll answer. Well, as long as I'm not on the air," he chuckled.

I took the card and nodded. "Thank you. I will." I started to lead David away, his hand held tightly again in mine.

I glanced back at Mark Jerseyman and his cameraman, the little red light from the camera was still trailing us. Mark looked pleased. I think he thought it had gone well. I thought so too. Mark gave me a thankful smile and single wave from his lifted hand. I gave him a tightlipped smile back as David unlocked his Jeep and helped me inside. Before he walked around to the driver's side, he went back to Mark and the cameraman and said something to them. Mark patted his cameraman on the shoulder and he lowered the camera and headed back across the street toward the station's news van, giving them a minute to speak alone.

They talked for a good three or four minutes and Mark seemed to relax after the first few seconds. By the time David turned to come back to the Jeep, Mark was positively beaming and waved good-bye at me again. He almost skipped across the street to the van. They sped away, no doubt to go edit the footage for tonight's special report. Maybe even start digging into my background to get a bigger story started with the details and names I'd given him.

David climbed into the Jeep, a little smile on his face. He leaned over and planted a big kiss on my lips. "What was that for?" I asked with a smile. "And what did you tell him?" I looked at him suspiciously.

"I told him the angry boyfriend act was just to make sure that anyone else watching would think twice before bothering you again and wasn't necessarily directed at him," David said.

"Oh! Oh, good! 'Cause he was one of the ones who was always nice to me," I replied relieved.

"I'd noticed that from the first news reports that aired. Out of all the news stations that came after you, he was the only one in the crowd who tried to divert the questions away from the intrusive ones that crossed the line and seemed genuinely bothered by the conduct of the others."

"You sound a lot like Liz," I praised him.

"Well, whenever there's something that concerns you, I pay attention," David said so seriously.

I blushed. I still wasn't used to someone caring for me so much. Liz was all I'd had for so long; it was so strange to have another person love me and look out for me.

"Mark also warned me about a group of them that had snuck back on campus a few weeks back, giving me time to outsmart them and make it to my car unnoticed," I told him.

"Had he?" David seemed doubly pleased.

"Yes. That's one of the reasons I wanted to use him to get my message out," I said conspiratorially.

"Mark asked for my number so he can call and let us know when the story is about to run. Said he needs to do his due diligence first but it might run tonight or tomorrow if he gets the all clear," David's eyebrows were high with anticipation.

"Glad he asked for yours and not mine," I confessed. "And I'm glad he plans on fact checking. It'll make him even more interested in seeing his story through once he realizes who all the players are in all this. I wonder if his producers will get cold feet and have him hold the story?"

"Naw, I think they'll want it on the air A.S.A.P. It has everything they'd need for a lead story. Crime, mystery, violence, conspiracy, a beautiful woman in distress, a man hunt lead by the FBI. They won't be able to help him fact check quick enough," David surmised.

"And, don't forget! A devilishly handsome hero!" I added teasingly.

"Devilish?" David laughed.

"And an unexpected security detail," I looked over to where the Crown Vic had been and saw that it had gone as well. Apparently Tristina had left right after the news van. Was she worried about what David might say or do to her for calling the media after she saw him get all upset at the reporter? She'd find out later that I actually helped her. I still hoped somehow, that my kindness would show her there was still good inside of people, and not everyone wanted to repay evil with evil.

"Oh, she left," David said, drawing my eyes back to him.

"She—"

"Called Mark's news station, I know," David said annoyed.

"I was going to say, she's really hurting David. It isn't just losing her daughter. It's her. She's broken inside," my voice was sad. "I feel bad for her."

"I'm so proud of you Melanie," David said, true admiration in his voice.

"Me? Why?" I said taken aback.

"You have compassion for Tristina." He stated it like it was a miracle. "Who no one can stand by the way," he added at seeing my confusion. "You gave her a reason to be here, which probably saved her job since I'm pretty sure Doc was going to call her boss anyway once he's back. Now, he probably won't. You took that leverage away from him this time." David laughed. "Oh, that was classic." He laughed again.

"Why are you laughing at me?" I grumbled, even more confused.

"That was genius, Melanie! Don't you see? Once Tristina sees the news tonight, you not only defused a possible ongoing hindrance to your continued training here, but you put her in the light that she was doing something good, trying to protect you. She can't be seen as trying to harass you now. She'd really look bad if she suddenly turned hostile toward a victim she was supposed to be protecting. It might even lead to stronger disciplinary action or her instant termination from the DOJ at that point if she has a history of misconduct."

"I wasn't trying to play her; I was trying to help her," I said, getting a little annoyed.

"I know you were. That's the beauty of it. Your heart was pure, but your kindness had more benefits than you realized." David started the Jeep and let it warm up, not pulling out to leave quite yet.

"Do you think that I did okay? With the rest, I mean?" I was suddenly worried. Had my perception been off in that too? David had seen another angle to how I'd handled Tristina, would he have a different interpretation of the rest? Had I missed something important or sent the wrong messages somehow?

"You did great! That's the other reason I'm proud of you," David patted my leg right above the knee. "That might really help us. Someone might come forward."

"I hope Jill comes forward. Maybe she'll see it as her way out of all this or a way to atone. If she even cares about sins," I wondered out loud.

"Well, with any luck, the spotlight can turn to her and the others in the meantime. Maybe it will occupy them and you won't have to worry about them coming after you for a while," David put on his seat belt and I did the same, then he checked his mirrors and pulled out.

"I didn't think about it at the time, but I hope it doesn't have the opposite effect and piss her off. Make her want to get me even more for telling the world her secrets."

"I doubt it. Your message wasn't antagonistic. It was imploring. Asking her to do the right thing and help you take down your own father," David said reassuringly.

I sighed and flipped down the sun visor as we traveled into the winter afternoon's overcast light. The puffy gray clouds failed to darken the day against the raze of the determined sun. My own reflection in the side mirror caught my eye and I quickly slid the visor's mirror open for a better look.

"Oh no," I mumbled.

"What?" David asked?

"I look like crap. Absolute crap! You have a busted nose. And there is blood all over my sweats," I said, looking down at my legs, horrified.

"Okay. So?" David asked, obviously not following why I was suddenly horrified. "You don't look like crap."

I burst out laughing. I laughed and laughed and laughed. David shot me a couple confused glances as he drove. Finally, he started smiling and then started chuckling as my belly-laugh turned into a fit of hysterical giggles.

"I-I look a-about as haggard and sweaty as white trash ran over by a two-ton bucket of Crisco," I said between giggles, tugging on my tank top to indicate my winning wardrobe, the mismatched sports bra t-strap was visible on my shoulders. I hadn't even put my sweatshirt on before we'd left and I'd been so distracted with the news crew showing up I hadn't thought about how I'd looked, or how chilly it was.

I quickly looked down at my chest. *Oh thank God! I don't have nipple perk! God, I believe even more in miracles now!*

"Umm, well—" I knew David was going to try to say something to make me feel not so ugly so I cut him off before he dug himself into a hole.

"You tried to act all aggressive to ward people off and you look like you just got in a fight," I pointed to his nose and tussled hair. "And here we were, making an honest attempt at asking the viewers for help to build a case against my father. If the potential threat of my father doesn't scare them off, our looks sure will!" I was doubled over laughing again. What else could I do? It was too late to ask for "take two". It was probably going to air tonight, with or without our permission.

"We're done for," I chuckled and looked at David. He was thinking hard about everything I'd just said. "I'm sorry," I sighed, and the last of the laughter drained away in defeat.

"It's okay," he said quietly. "I don't think this will hurt us," David said pensively.

"You don't? Seriously? Have you seen this frizzy floppy bun of hair?" I said pointing to my head. "I look run over." I laughed again.

"No. Not at all. I think it shows them how human we are. Vulnerable even. Well, you anyway. I think it might make us relatable." David shot me an encouraging smile.

"Not many people can relate to *me*," I corrected him.

"But his victims would. And you looking all polished and beautiful would just show them you have it all together and are stronger than they are. Who knows how badly some of them are still hurting inside by what he's done to them. How he's disrupted their lives. Them seeing you look...well, tired and slightly unkempt—"

"Slightly unkempt?" I muttered.

David chuckled. "Yes, *unkempt* and not worried about your hair, or nails, or the latest BCBG sweats outfit, or something fancy, just shows them you're more interested in capturing Dwayne Bishop and stopping him from hurting anyone else than about how beautiful you are on camera. Which by the way, even now, I think you're lovely."

"Charmer," I shot back, but couldn't stop the silly grin he'd coaxed out of me.

"And as far as me looking roughed up. Good! I hadn't even thought of that! It will make me look like I can back up my bad attitude," He laughed, the hearty sound warming my heart.

"But you *can*," I corrected him.

David shrugged with a humble smile.

"And the blood?" I pointed down at my splattered sweat bottoms.

"I don't think Mark or his cameraman even noticed. It was trained on your face the whole time. And the wide shot from when they were crossing the street was when you weren't facing them all the way, so maybe it won't even be noticeable. If it is, from that distance, it could look like gutter splatter from the wet street."

"Okay, that makes me feel a *little* better," I leaned against the window for a second, replaying the entire interview in my head.

"Don't worry," David said after a few minutes. "God can turn any evil around for good, and any harm back into a cause for rejoicing. I don't think you spoke those words all on your own. I think God was leading you. Have faith Melanie. Wait and see what he does. Our God is faithful," David offered me his hand, and I took it. He brought my hand to his lips and kissed my knuckles lightly. "It will all work out," he promised.

I looked into his loving eyes and felt at home with him. I trusted him. And, I believed him. It would all work out.

Pop Quiz

Chapter Thirteen

e pulled up to Kate's Café and parked by the back door. Frank's old grey Mercedes was the only other car parked in the parking lot. It was in its usual spot but parked haphazardly almost crossing the line to the next parking space as if he'd arrived in a hurry. Guess it didn't matter since there were no cars nearby and no one but us was expected to arrive.

Hmm, he has a broken taillight. I wondered how that happened?

David let the engine run, keeping us warm a moment longer. I felt like he was waiting for something and I sat quietly, content with the silence and his company. And also grateful for a moment to ready myself to reenter the scene of the crime. Well, according to police it may have been an undetermined chemical attack of some kind that had caused everyone to lose their minds. At least they had given up the ridiculous idea that the crew had formed some sort of mutiny to take over the joint. It wasn't a pirate ship for gosh sakes.

I played with my necklace absentmindedly as I looked the restaurant over. You'd never know anything strange or extraordinary had happened here only six weeks ago.

"From what Frank mentioned we're in for a surprise," David finally said casually, breaking the silence.

"Think the renovations are going to look just like the old interior design, like new old stock or completely different?" I wondered.

David smiled at me, his face a little mischievous.

"What?" I said almost sniggering at the naughty childlike expression on his face. "What are you thinking Mr. Abramson?"

"I think Frank wants to surprise us with it. He's refused to tell me when I've asked. But that wasn't what I was thinking *just* now."

"And that was?" I leaned in like he was about to tell me a secret.

"I was just remembering the night this place got trashed," David rubbed his chin stubble with his hand. It was getting that slightly scratchy length that makes a man look rugged and more brute-like in the best possible way.

God, he's gorgeous.

"A-ha," I agreed, more focused on David's perfectly handsome profile than the restaurant. "It really got tore up didn't it?"

"I was actually remembering what happened right *before* it all went south," David shot me a raised eyebrow glance.

"Oh. *That*," I squirmed and felt my face turning red. "You know I wasn't...I didn't mean to...I just got...um," I stammered. I didn't even know how to explain to David that Jared had somehow projected his spirit of lust at me and had literally attacked me in the spiritual realm. An intense spiritual battle had commenced I had not been prepared for, and due to my own bad attitude and my anger that night, I had been even weaker to the assault, having no idea how to combat it at the time.

"Melanie," David chuckled. "No, not *that*." He threw his head back and laughed, a deep belly laugh that split his mouth into a wide smile. I loved his smile. His teeth were perfectly straight and white. Model perfect. "I know that wasn't *you*. It was something else entirely."

"You got that?" I said, thankful that he was spiritually aware.

"Yes, oh yes I do. I told you that night the difference in your eyes alone before and after was like turning on a switch. Your reaction to me that night, the tempers and irrational fights that broke out. It all started with that guy," David explained.

"I was so worried you wouldn't have understood that," I confessed. "It surprised me how quickly you seemed to put it together. I didn't want you to think I was...that I was usually so...seductive," I puffed out a big breath of nerves and embarrassment. The idea of talking about this topic with David still made me anxious. I was still learning how it all worked and wasn't sure how to have an intelligent conversation about it.

"Being consumed by a spirit of lust and domination would be how I would describe it. Don't forget, I was married to Danielle, a woman who drew out the lust and rebellion in others and always exhibited a need to dominate and control. She seduced me, ensnared me, manipulated me, and used me," David had stopped laughing and was frowning, his harsh memories and painful regrets resurfacing for a moment, making his voice cold.

"I could never forget that," I said dryly. I hadn't meant to sound bitter, but I guess I was still working out the details he'd shared with me and wrapping my head around it all.

"Oh, of course not. I'm sorry to bring it up again so soon. I just meant that—" David tried to apologize.

"I know you were trying to reassure me that you knew what the spirit of lust and domination were," I sounded awkward and uncomfortable and I hated that I wasn't able to talk about Danielle and him in an objective neutral way yet. But hey, it had only been a couple hours since I found out the man I was falling head over heels for had been married and had be forced to kill his seductive, lying, traitorous wife. Not exactly a first date conversation to have. Oh wait. We've never had a first date yet.

We need a date like a normal couple!

But... we aren't even close to normal. Nothing about our relationship has happened normally.

"I didn't mean to make you feel bad Melanie," David reached over and took my hand and brought it up to his lips and kissed it.

I love it when you do that. I looked at his mouth on my hand wishing he'd move his mouth further down my arm. *Kiss my wrist? My shoulder maybe?*

No. Bad Melanie. No more hanky-panky tonight! Chill woman!

I smiled at him. "I know."

"My point was, I recognized the spirit of lust and domination as soon as they manifested in the walk-in cooler with us," David explained.

"Oh," I nodded. "Interesting way to describe it but I think you're right. That makes sense. 'Cause now that I've experienced it, I know what it feels like too and I don't want anything to do with it!"

David sighed, taking a moment to think about how to articulate his thoughts. "During the war, it was one thing to be thousands of miles from home, thinking you could die any moment having never really broken out and lived dangerously," David continued.

"Being in special ops and a PJ pilot in the *War on Terror* wasn't dangerous enough for you, huh?" I almost laughed.

"It was dangerous, yes. But it was my duty, what I had signed up for. I didn't think of it as living on the edge, it had become my new normal in a way. So when a beautiful mysterious woman showed interest in me and made me feel a certain way, played with my emotions and deceived me into thinking she loved me, and convinced me we should break rules and have fun, it was easy to accept all that lust and recklessness and justify the behavior away. I had a right to have fun, right? I had a right to put myself first for a change? But I learned the hard way it wasn't worth it and that kind of selfishness comes with a price," David squeezed my hand.

"And then there you were, Melanie. Coming at me, wanting me, practically ripping my shirt off to touch me. Teasing me, trying to trick me, and me seeing right through it all. And even though I knew you weren't yourself and were being attacked by lust and a dominating spirit, I couldn't help but let it play out just a little. I told you before, I'm not *that* good," David drew in a breath and let it out.

I didn't say anything for a moment. What could I say? I'd been naughty and given into lust and had wanted to master him and make him surrender to me. David had been the common sense for both of us and not let it happen. Though his body had been screaming yes and had been responding to me, he had mastered himself and cried out to Jesus to help him.

"David, you still showed me respect and didn't take advantage. You told me you didn't want me to hate you afterwards because you knew you would be taking advantage of me if you gave in. *Thank you* for being strong enough to say no to me. Thank you for not making me hate *myself* more," I patted his hand. "But if that wasn't what you were remembering, what is it?"

"I was thinking about when I met Lust and Dominance face to face. Jared. Jared Kallis, wasn't it?" David asked me.

"Oh. Um, yes. His name was Jared Kallis," I bit my lip.

So David knew Jared somehow housed Lust? And he identified him as Dominance too. I hadn't thought of that. But it made sense! Seduction was all about domination of another person's will. Getting them to willingly surrender to your desires. Taking from them what wasn't to be given or shouldn't be given.

Please don't ask me how I know him. I can't tell you about Italy and my secret missions yet!

"That man was a physical manifestation of lust," David shook his head and glowered out the front window. "And he was also intensely dominate. Melanie, he was—" David broke off thinking.

"You called him evil before," I remembered the conversation David and I had had in the restaurant that night.

"Yes. He was entirely demonic," David looked over at me and made eye contact. I met his eyes and didn't look away. He was right. He was so right and I didn't even know if he understood just how right he was.

"I completely agree," I answered safely.

"He was very interested in *you*. Asked for you by name. Knew where you worked. Seemed to know you when he saw you. He knew what you looked like," David stated certainly.

"All true," I answered honestly. "I told you I had literally ran into him once. That was it." I didn't want to lie to David but how could I just come out and say it? There was no other way to explain Jared showing up asking for me.

"My first thought was crazy ex-boyfriend turned stalker. You seemed afraid to go talk to him. I saw you clinging to the wall around the corner. I was making my way back to you when you went out to confront him. I thought if someone like that was your ex, maybe that was why you were so cautious with men. With me. But then I remembered who you are and I don't think you would have ever dated a man as...as dark as him. And, I don't think you have ever had a long-term boyfriend. Am I right?" David asked conversationally, though his question was direct and intimate.

Geesh. Well, guess he has a right to know about my past love life. Or lack of love life.

Melanie, virgin.

Melanie, zero kissing experience before David.

Melanie, strictly-dickly but never had her hand on one. Or seen one other than...ugh. My father's.

Ewwie. Oh, go away image!

Oh God. He knows I was forced to witness my sister being raped. He's going to realize what I've had to see over and over again, even when I tried and begged not to.

"Melanie? Did I make you uncomfortable again?" David asked kindly. "Am I—"

"It's okay David. Yes. You're right again. Never had any boyfriend actually," my voice was soft and I felt embarrassed so I looked down. "I never trusted anyone enough to say yes," I risked a glance.

David's face was open and non-judgmental, even understanding. "That is nothing to be ashamed of Melanie. I think you've been wise not to rush into anything after what you've been through."

"You're as good as they get David and look how long it took me to give into you," I added.

"Exactly. You slapped Jared in the face hard. Twice! And he told me he wasn't going to leave until he got what he came for. So, if he's not an ex-boyfriend, then who was he?" David finally asked me matter-of-factly.

"Not an easy question to answer," I admitted.

I hope he didn't think I was trying to hide anything from him. I just didn't know how to answer a question that didn't have a reasonable answer. The truth was, I didn't know Jared at all. I'd bumped into him once, saw him a little while later through a window, and again a few days later when he showed up demanding the book in exchange for unimaginable sexual pleasures of my choosing. Now how was I supposed to explain that without sounding delusional?

"Harder than the questions and answers we're asking and looking for together now about your family?" David guessed, a deep crease in his brow made him look pensive rather than accusatory. He wasn't being snarky. He was just trying to gauge what could be worse or harder than that to answer.

"In a way. Because with my family, there is a physical explanation and sequence of events that will make it all make sense someday. Details and evidence that can be mapped and identified. There is tangible evidence out there yet to be found. But with Jared...it's not like that. It's—," I broke off.

Lord, how on Earth am I going to explain Jared to David? What do I say?

"Were *you* what he had come for?" David tried another angle.

"In a way," I repeated unhelpfully and glanced away, not wanting to reveal that I had secrets to keep, but I was sure he could see it in my tell-all face. I was so easy to read. But it didn't matter! I couldn't tell him about the book I had been chosen to find and keep safe. I couldn't even tell Elisabeth about the book!

"You rebuked him using Jesus's name. You commanded him to leave, you didn't ask," David was very serious.

He had seen me engage in the spiritual warfare that night. I had to! Jared's demonic presence and influence had been nearly overwhelming as he'd attacked me with lust. His voice had nearly crippled me, making my flesh feel the seeking tickling fingers of his lust touch my skin and slither their way into the intimate corners of my body. Only through righteous indignation and a Holy Spirit boldness had I walked out to confront him and rebuked him.

How could I explain any of that to David? Would he even understand the depth of the struggle I had had? I knew he had discernment and seemed to understand biblical spirituality. But was the warfare and battle he was used to fighting as a human special ops soldier equal to that of a spiritual warrior? Was he just as aware of the spiritual as he was of the physical?

Yes. Yes, I believe he is.

He had taken authority and prayed in the Hope Box today. He had known exactly how to pray through the battle he was having. He would understand this if I was brave enough to tell him the truth.

"Let's try something instead," David offered helpfully, sparing me from having to decide if he could or should know the truth. His face shifted to show me he was open to possibilities without expectation.

"Okay," I said, a slight unsure lilt to my voice.

"I'll say one word and you say the first word that pops into your head. I'll center my words around impressions or ideas I have regarding Jared or us. I'll start off with some general basic words to just warm you up, okay? You say the first thought that pops into your head after I say each word. Deal?"

"What will that accomplish?" I sounded skeptical. I didn't know what I'd say if the rule was to divulge my first thought. My brain was unpredictable and dripped in sarcasm. Why would I want him to see into my feeble mind without the protection of a filter? Was he wanting trouble and disappointment?

"I don't know if you *want* to hear what's bouncing around in here," I said warningly, tapping the side of my head with a crinkled nose. "Might scare you away," I joked, but inside I half-meant it. Now that I had him, I didn't want to scare him off.

"I want to know everything about you Melanie. Nothing you could say or do or share will change that," David's voice was soft and he looked into my eyes penetrating my apprehension with the rawness of his passion. My breath caught for a moment as I felt heat creep up my face and I bit my lip.

David smiled at my reaction to his gaze, his mouth turning up on one side just the way I loved. "Don't worry Melanie. This is just an exercise to help you put into words what you can't figure out how to explain. And it helps me know if my thoughts are on target with the truth or way off base."

"Did they teach you this in one of your psychology classes?" I asked teasingly, trying to derail the conversation and distract him from his own unknown power over me. Whenever he looked at me like that he made my soul quiver and my stomach flutter with butterflies.

"Nope. Not yet. It's just an exercise I know. It helped me break through my own barriers when I started confronting my PTSD. It kind of warms you up to cracking through the tougher emotional walls. Lets the pressure off before uncorking it all. It's a gentle way to start to pull forward and up what gets pushed down deep," David smiled at me warmly and I couldn't help but return the smile. I was like putty in his hands. Not because he was manipulative, but because I trusted him.

"Want to give it a try?"

"Okay. Why not. Sure," I mumbled and shot him a playful irritated look so he didn't think I was *that* easy to talk into awkward stuff.

"Great! Here we go," David sat a little straighter and grew serious.

"Hit me," I leaned in, hands posed out defensively and narrowed my eyes, pretending we were about to wrestle. I smiled mischievously at him, my humor kicking in as an automatic self-defense mechanism to what would likely be embarrassing and difficult. I wasn't sure what to expect.

"Sex."

"Really?" I said flatly, dropping my hands into my lap with a thud. "Didn't even bury the lead there man."

"Just go with it," David laughed, a deep masculine sound filling the jeep.

"Is this word about Jared or us?" I accused lightheartedly with a frown.

"Mel," David gave me a "stop stalling" look.

"Tsk. Fine." I pursed my lips and wrinkle my nose at him.

"Sex," David tried again, smiling broadly at me now.

Why did that word sound so naughty on his beautiful heart-shaped lips?

"For-bid-den," I said deliberately, purposefully narrowing my eyes more and more at him again with each syllable.

David smiled good naturedly back. "Friend."

"Trust." I returned his smile now, glad we had moved off of the "sex" word.

"Desire." David was watching my face closely.

And we're back.

"Scary." I glanced down and then back up at him, forcing myself to be bold and honest.

"Ocean."

"Rocking."

"Wilderness."

"Isaac." I felt a rush of fear hit me for a moment. *Don't ask me about Isaac,* I begged David in my thoughts.

"Dream." David continued without hesitation.

"Nightmares." I shuttered.

"Childhood."

"Sorrow."

"Children."

"Afraid."

"Family." His voice was warm and his face relaxed.

"Broken." My voice was sad and I felt my face drop at the images I'd seen in the case files of my mother and sister's broken bodies dumped in their unnatural graves.

David paused, concern showing in his face as he saw the pain that one little word had caused me.

"Longing," he said quietly.

I realized I had closed my eyes and I looked up at him to answer, but I couldn't help but pause. That word held so much for me. Too many words rushed into my mind at once. I didn't know which I should say. "I—" I broke off.

"First impression, remember," David coached.

"I know, but there is so much there." I tilted my head, biting my lip, the confusion to my own feelings around that one word making me almost paralyzed, unsure as to how to answer.

"Okay, try this," David reached over and took my chilly hands in both of his warm strong ones. He looked into my eyes searching, his eyes touching upon my mouth. "Close your eyes Melanie."

"Okay." I did as he asked.

"Now, think about the word longing. Don't worry about finding the one perfect word it brings to mind. Say whatever train of words want to spill out. Just let them come. Don't think. Just speak. No matter how many words there are, no matter what they are. Okay?" David's voice sounded very reasonable and calm.

God, he's going to make a great psychologist someday. I was so proud of him.

"Ready?" He asked.

"Yes."

"Keep your eyes closed," he said to me as I began to open them and I closed them. "Now, relax. Empty your thoughts. Just hear my voice. Feel my hands in yours. You're here with me. Safe. Cared for. You're not alone," he said slowly, his voice was so gentle.

I felt my shoulders relax and I took in a slow deep breath. I loved his voice. The deep masculine yet boyish tones were ear candy for me. I felt a small smile of satisfaction come.

"Longing," David repeated.

In that moment I just let go. I said every word that filled my mind when longing entered my ears. I rattled them out quickly, afraid my conscious mind would stop them and try to filter them. I wanted to know as much as David why this one word was so hard for me. "Desperation. Closeness. Passion. Understanding. Acceptance. Independence. Freedom. Joy. Validation. Justice. Retribution. Victory. Resolution. I want it all to end!" I was breathing heavy by the end of my rant, my eyes shot open.

"That was good," David said proudly. He was nodding, his hands gripping mine. "Really good," he said again.

I let out a big breath. "This is kind of hard you know. You said it was easy," I complained.

"You're doing well. Keep going?" He asked my permission, studying my face again, determining my mood.

"Yes. Keep going," I swallowed. *I could use a Dr. Pepper right about now.*

"Secrets."

"Silence. Too many," I couldn't help but give him more than one word again. Both were there in my mind fighting to be heard.

"Keeper."

"Protector. Chosen." Again, two words presented themselves and I felt both to be equally true and important.

"Stranger."

"Danger," I giggled. "Think I heard that in kindergarten."

David laughed. "I heard that one too. Want to try the word again?"

"No, strangers do represent possible danger for me. Unknown variables. So that still kind of fits," I admitted.

"Okay. Next word," David paused to think before continuing. "Touch."

"Warmth. Need." My eyes roamed over David of their own accord and I snapped them back this face. Heat and desire were quickly creeping into his face at my confession and my physical response to the word but he mastered it and puckered out his bottom lip as he thought about his next lead word.

"Controlled."

"Never." My voice had dropped low in defiance at the thought of being controlled. I suspected however, he had said "controlled" to remind himself to keep in control of his own passions with me.

Hmm, this exercise can give me insights into him as well. Interesting. Me likes.

"Intimidation."

"Bullied. Defiant. Resistance." I spouted off the words that came.

"Surprise."

"Unpredictable."

"Jared."

"Evil. Seducer. Molester. Thief. Demon. Dubious. Monster. Liar," I rattled on.

"Demon." David said, selecting his next word from one I had provided.

"Sent. Fight."

"Lust."

"Trap. Dirty."

"Temptation."

"Deception."

"Fear."

"Power."

"Enemy."

"Blood."

"Death."

"Destination."

"Holy Spirit."

"Liberty. Revealer of truth. Lion." I smiled at the memory of the lion on my hand and resisted the urge to rub my left palm.

When is the lion coming back to me? The Archangel Gabriel had said it would return to me.

"Grace."

"Hope. Forgiveness."

"Cleansed."

"Beginning. Redemption."

"Love."

"David." My breath caught.

David paused at my answer, a soft smile lifting the corner of his mouth again, his eyes twinkling with happiness.

"Life," he pressed forward rather than lingering on the association of him to my idea of love. I appreciated it! I hadn't intended for that to just slip out, but the sneaky man had us on a roll and that word had been trying to escape my lips all day.

Guess this word association thingy works a little.

"Life," David repeated, pulling me away from my thoughts.

"Uncertain."

"Hunt."

"Hide. Capture. Defend."

"Marriage," David had a little glint in his eye this time.

"Pass," I gawked at him.

"Oh no, you can't pass. What's your answer?"

"To marriage?" I laughed.

"Yes."

"To the *word* marriage?" I clarified, making sure he didn't mean anything else.

"The word, yes." David's eyes lit up at my uncertainty. He was loving this.

"Um."

"Hey now, don't think. Just answer," David reminded me. "Marriage."

"Years away," I said chuckling.

"Okay, got what I need," David concluded.

"How? You hardly asked me anything!"

"Actually, I got quite a bit from this."

"Mind explaining it to me?" I probed him back.

"You believe Jared is evil incarnate. Sent to deceive you, steal from you, and to destroy you," David said without hesitation.

"Um... yeah. Something like that. And what else?" I blinked, his accuracy shocking me. At the same time, I was kind of relieved I wouldn't have to lie.

"I'll explain the rest of what I got out that pop quiz later. Once I think about it and pray about it."

"Well, that doesn't seem fair," I grumbled. "I want my psychoanalysis, Doctor Abramson," I pretended to give him a stern face.

"I will later. I promise," David laughed.

"Well, just so you know, I have an analysis of my own about *you*." I pointed at him and looked away haughtily, trying not to laugh. "Didn't think I'd use this to my advantage either did ya?" I teased.

David laughed. "Not surprised at all actually! You're a smart one, Miss Bishop. I wouldn't have expected anything less."

"Sure," I snuck a glance back at him and winked. David was grinning ear to ear, a twinkle in his eyes.

A-huh. What are you up to Mr. Abramson?

Family Tries

Chapter Fourteen

"*S*o, you ready?" David made to open his door but stopped to wait for my response, ever the gentleman.

"Ready?" I questioned. David tilted his head toward the back door of the restaurant. *Oh! To go inside. Duh.* I'd almost forgotten why we were sitting here. "Yes, but suddenly, I'm kind of nervous," I confessed, my voice growing small.

A pang of anxiety had hit my insides unexpectedly and I gripped the door handle, biting my lip. *I'm going to end up biting a hole right through this bottom lip of mine today.*

I knew for sure that Frank was my great uncle now. The lineage from my mother, Helena, to her mother, Gloria, had been linked irrefutably to Katherine, Gloria's sister. Frank was my great uncle through marriage, and from what Liz and I were able to determine, that made me his only living relative and him mine since I didn't count my father as any kind of family.

I had decided it would be best to wait and let him bring it up when he felt brave enough to do it. He'd kept it from me for this long. Was he keeping it quiet because he didn't *want* to be related to me and wished I'd been someone else? Was I a disappointment to him? Or was he just afraid to tell me and scare me away because he thought I would wish *he* was someone else and he would lose a chance to have family?

Hmm. Maybe he is just as insecure about it as I am?

Frank had put those pictures of his wife in his office the night this place fell apart. Had he been trying to tell me? Created an opportunity for me to see them, hoping I'd ask?

"What's put that frown on that gorgeous face of yours?" David asked me quietly from right beside my ear.

I startled and looked over, finding his perfectly beautiful face inches from mine. I felt my frown vanish in a wash of delight finding him there. I mean, I knew he was there obviously. We hadn't gotten out of the car yet. But I hadn't felt him shift or move over, lean across the center console, or breathe.

Sneaky soldier.

"Hi," I replied, almost sounding drunk with love for him.

David smile widened into one of delight. "Hi." He studied my mouth.

Oh no dude. Nope. No smooches for you. We'll never leave this car.

"I was just thinking that Frank doesn't know. You know, that I know he's my great uncle I mean," I shrugged. "What do you think? Do you think I should tell him I figured it out?"

David leaned back a little and rested his elbow on the steering wheel, arm draping over to display his long strong hand and muscular forearm. He looked relaxed and casual, and boy did he look good. There was something incredibly sexy about his hands and forearms.

Huh. I never knew I was attracted to forearms. That's random.

Or is it? Is that normal? I'll have to ask Liz.

"In my opinion," David answered thoughtfully, "I think you might want to give yourself time to digest it a little first. You only *just* found out yourself. It's a lot to adjust to. He's known a lot longer than you and he hasn't been ready to say anything yet. So, he might be in a place where you shouldn't try to intrude until he brings it up," David tapped the side of his temple.

"Oh. Huh. Right, I don't know where his mind is at," I said considering this.

"Maybe give it some time. Pray about it. Try to understand why he might have kept if from you so when you do talk to him about it, you won't get upset with him for his reasons. It could simply be out of fear of rejection. Or, it could be he's afraid you might want to try to use him. We just don't know him well enough to be able to predict his reasons. But I do know he respects your opinion of him more than anyone else here. In fact, yours is the only one he seems to care about at all."

"He asked me once to keep telling him when he crosses a line. Told me Katherine used to do it to him and he missed that. Said she kept him honest," I recalled the first time I yelled at him. I had been harsh and hurtful. Instead of firing me, he had asked me not to quit. It had been the last thing I'd expected.

"Makes sense. He hasn't been able to stop telling you since he met you how much you're like his wife, even your fire." David smiled approvingly at me. "To him, maybe that is his way of telling you. Maybe he's hoping you'll remember him and be the one to say something. But I do know this; You're both the only family either of you really has left," David said warmly.

"Thank you," I sighed and nodded. I felt the knot in my stomach unclench and I relaxed into the back of my seat.

"For what?"

"For being honest with me and giving me good reasonable advice. And for not trying to preach at me that I'm obligated to count my father as a relative," I added with a grimace.

"I'd never do that. He lost the privilege to call you 'daughter' when he treated you and your family the way he has. The fact that you don't talk about wanting to kill him yourself is remarkable to me. You amaze me, Melanie Bishop," David's voice held pride.

"Who says I don't?" I teased in a mock serious tone. A small smile creeping onto my mouth to give me away.

David smiled at me. "If I told you I did, would you think me a bad man?" David confessed.

"Did what?"

"Wanted to kill him," David grew serious, his wasn't an act.

"I don't think that would make you a bad man. It's actually understandable. You were a soldier trained to take out the enemy and eliminate the threats, right?"

"Yes," David answered simply.

"Well, you'd just be taking out my enemy. Blood relative or not," I shrugged again. "But I know you would never do it unless it was a matter of life or death. I trust you. You aren't a murderer David," I leaned over and touched my hand to the side of his face. He melted into my hand and he raised his own hand up to hold it there longer. His eyes closed and I felt his body relax under my touch.

"What is it?" I asked quietly.

"Melanie," David said my name almost reverently. "You are so kind to me. So forgiving and...and incredible." He took my hand and brought it to his lips, kissing the top passionately, his eyes closing, and his mouth lingering for several moments as he pressed his love into my hand from the depth of his heart.

"Why do—"

"I confessed to you earlier today the decision I was forced to make at the base hospital." David looked at me now, true regret deep within his soul-filled honey brown eyes.

"I'm glad you told me. You didn't need to carry that alone anymore." I made sure he heard me tell him this again. It had been hard to hear, but it had been a necessary uncomfortable truth that needed to be released from it's hiding place within him. It had caused him enough pain and torment. I could relate to that.

"Had you kept that from me deeper into our relationship, it might have caused irrevocable damage. I appreciate you telling me now. Even if it was hard to hear, and I'm sure it was even harder for you to say," I whispered understandingly. "I trust you David."

"You know what I've done in my past. And here you are, telling me you trust me. Reassuring me I'm not a murderer. You are so full of love and grace." David's eyes were boring into mine and I felt once again as if I was falling down into the depth of his soul, touching the essence of his innermost being with mine.

"David, I—" I couldn't get the word out! I couldn't get the word "love" to squeeze past my fear-locked lips.

"Come on. Let's get in there before Frank thinks we aren't coming tonight," David graciously didn't try to force me to say it. He'd known what had stuck like peanut butter in a dog's mouth behind my lips.

"Right!" My exuberance was a wee bit forced but that was alright. I wasn't really up for a time-consuming detailed clean up work in the restaurant tonight. But we'd promised Frank we'd come and help and the poor old man didn't have anyone else he trusted to ask.

I would have thought Susan and Lucy would have offered by now. They'd both worked there almost fifteen years before I'd come along. They'd even been friends with my Aunt Katherine. It had been one of the reasons they'd stayed. They both felt Katherine would have wanted them to keep an eye on Frank.

They had told me stories about Frank and Katherine's love affair. It sounded too good to be true. Like a fairytale or fantasy. Apparently, he'd been quite the romantic in his day. He sang opera to her in the restaurant as the customers watched with awe, romance filling the hearts of all who'd witness him adorn her with his music. He had sounded like Pavarotti, bringing the customers, the waitresses and Katherine to tears. He was always bringing her flowers and whisking her away to unexpected nights on the town, mini-honeymoons and dancing. I couldn't even imagine Frank dancing or singing.

I wish I'd known *that* Frank. All I knew of him personally was that the man loved his wife so deeply that without her he had become a miserable grumpy poop-head, insulting staff, throwing out distrustful accusations, and hardly ever laughing or smiling. I'd only seen a smile on him a few times, and it had only been directed at me.

I suddenly felt overwhelmingly sad for Frank. He must be so lonely. He must feel so unlovable. He probably was incredibly miserable, living his golden years without his wife, the love of his life. Was the sight of me hurting him more since I looked so very much like her? Did I cause him pain?

I felt my eyes starting to bristle with tears as David opened my door and offered me his hand to help me out. He looked at my eyes as I climbed down, a question starting on his face and his mouth opening as if to ask me what was wrong, but as soon as my feet hit the ground, I rushed off instead, heading straight to the back door.

I rang the buzzer three times in a row, anxious for it to open. I heard loud uneven steps approaching. I recognized Frank's limp. I backed up to give room for the large heavy metal door to swing out and open. David had caught up to me and was standing a little behind me at a respectful distance. I guess he didn't want to out our relationship to Frank unless I wanted to. We hadn't actually talked about that. I was glad he was letting me decide. Afterall, they news interview with Mark Jerseyman hadn't aired yet.

The door swung open and Frank stood there, a frown on his face as normal, his expression inconvenienced. He had lost more weight. Maybe even another fifteen pounds these last six weeks. Over the past two and a half years since I'd started, he'd lost forty pounds and had whispered privately to me that he wanted to lose another hundred. This last fifteen pounds showed the stress the last six weeks had caused him while his restaurant had been under reconstruction. I realized it had been his life. The only thing that kept him waking up in the morning. His last connection to Katherine. It had been their life, their dream, their everything. My heart broke even deeper for him, crushing me from the inside. The ache and sorrow, enormous.

"'Bout time! My God. You two get lost?" Frank barked briskly in his New Orleans accent. "Forgot how to tell time the last month or so?"

I didn't answer him. I couldn't speak under the weight of sorrow breaking my heart.

"What the hell happened to you David? She cold-cocked ya?" Frank pointed at David's busted nose.

"Actually—" David started to say.

Instead of answering, I rushed at Frank and hugged him fiercely, tears bursting from me as my arms landed around his girthy waist. I'd caught him off guard and he staggered backward half a step, his arms straightened out to the sides in shock, not sure if he should hug me back or why I'd even hugged him at all. I'd never hugged him before. Most I'd ever done is pat his shoulder consolingly when he had teared up once talking about how much he missed Katherine.

"Umm," Frank grumbled.

I didn't say a word. I just cried harder, unable to keep my heart from breaking all the more as I seemed to feel every ounce of sorrow and loneliness he held within his heart. My crying was becoming a sob, and rested my head on his large puffy chest, squeezing him harder. It didn't matter to me that he smelled like sweat, bourbon and bacon grease. To me it was the smell of sadness and desperation to forget a life he would never have again.

"She okay?" Frank asked nervously, looking over my head at David who was standing back silently, a look of surprise on his face.

"She was," David answered honestly, his voice unsure.

"I...I...I'm—" I tried, stuttering in between sobbing breaths.

"Did you say somethin' mean to her?" Frank accused David, his voice growing protective and challenging.

"No Sir," David answered honestly again.

"Well, why the hell is she crying all over me?" Frank growl-hissed to David.

"Um, well—" was David's only articulation.

I peeled myself away from Frank's gut and stepped back, wiping my eyes. Oh, how much I wanted to tell him I understood him. How much I wanted to let him know he wasn't alone anymore, he had me. His niece. I looked into Frank Gable's shocked, almost scared face, and my mouth dried of any saliva. I couldn't say anything.

"Your father really did a number on you, huh kid?" Frank's voice was the most tender I'd ever heard it. His face had turned from shocked to worried.

He's worried about me? Aww.

At his kindness, I started sobbing again. Inside him was still a man capable of gentleness and love. He was just lost underneath all the pain, loneliness, anger and sorrow.

"Un...Uncle Frank," I stuttered, the secret we had both been keeping slipping out while my defenses were down.

Frank's eyes grew large and his mouth opened. I think he'd stopped breathing. He shot David a look, fear in his eyes. Why was he afraid? Frank stepped back, a whistling of air escaping him. The fear was turning into an expression of guilt.

"How'd you—" he tried to ask.

"A lot about my father and mother has been coming out since he...since the—"

Oh God.

"Since he hurt you," Frank helped.

"Yes."

"Saw it all on the news ya know. I'm so sorry that happened. He should have been stopped years ago. Wanted to come check in on you, but...um. But I didn't think you'd want me hanging around," Frank bit the inside of his cheek and looked down ashamed.

"Why not?" I asked. "It wasn't your fault."

"'Cause I'm a miserable old goat. Last thing you'd want butting in is someone like me. I was surprised when David said you was still comin' to help." Frank shifted his feet uncomfortably.

"Why?" I asked again.

"'Cause I haven't tried hard enough to...to be good to you," Frank almost apologized.

"For being a grumpy boss with a temper?" I clarified for him.

"Yeah, but for being...for being family and not trying harder to make you want *me* as your family. I'm nothing like Katherine would have wanted. She would be ashamed of me," Frank's voice was vulnerable and his eyes tearing up.

"Uncle Frank," I stated it as fact now. He nodded in acknowledgment, looking pitifully ashamed. "You saw the news and what they said about my father. Trust me, you're a work of art compared to him," I smiled and wiped the last of my tears away with my hand again. I sniffed my running nose.

"Here," David said kindly, handing me a handkerchief from his pocket.

"Thanks," I said a little embarrassed. His eyes were warm and encouraging me to continue.

"Why didn't you ever say anything?" I asked Frank, pressing him while the conversation was open. Now was my chance.

"I didn't want to freak you out. You might have left! I hoped you might have heard about your great aunt and uncle before your mom died. The day you walked in here and asked Lucy for an application, I nearly had a heart attack. I was standing over by the bar. Felt I'd seen a ghost. You were Katherine at twenty. I knew immediately who you had to be. I prayed for the first time in years once I got over the shock. Begged God to let you come back with that application so I'd know. And when you did, I knew. Soon as I saw your name. Melanie Olivia Bishop. I hadn't seen you since you was about six months old." Frank shook his head. He spoke quickly, ready to tell me his story and make me understand. His eyes were wide and eager.

"You saw me when I was a baby?" I said in wonder. "You met my mom!" I was thrilled. Finally! Someone who had known my mother. Someone who could tell me about her!

"Yeah," Frank nodded looking quite sad. I felt my excitement disappear in a puff of dread.

"I met her," his voice held true regret.

We both stood there silently looking at the other, our stories and secrets colliding. Our paths having crossed two and a half years ago finally being defined.

"Wanna come in? We can talk about it inside if you want," Frank held out his hand to usher us inside.

"Yes, let's get inside. I don't want to leave Melanie out here any longer," David said glancing around behind us. Frank looked around too, his eyes narrowing.

"Come on in," Frank waved his hand to speed me along.

"Good idea," I agreed and passed by. The smell of new construction, paint and glue filling my nose within inches of the doorway.

"So much for giving it time," David chuckled quietly in my ear from beside me.

I glanced at him giving a small smile. I felt so many things right now. Happiness that Frank hadn't rejected me. Sadness that he felt so alone all these years. Relieved it was finally out in the open. Thrilled to know someone who knew my mother. Trepidation to hear the story that brought him so much shame and regret.

But here we were. We had to try to understand each other. We were all each other had left. Well, I was all he had left. I had Elisabeth, David, and, in a way, I had Bradley like an annoying older brother, and grandpa Billy, Elisabeth's grandfather.

"Family tries David. We have to try," I said softly.

Five's Company

Chapter Fifteen

ome on in here kids." Frank led us in toward his office. I glanced around as we went to try to identify all the changes back here. I couldn't wait to see what he'd done to the kitchen and the front of the place.

The old tile floor had been replaced with a decoratively textured non-slip coating. Black, white, red, metallic-grey, and blue flakes littered the surface. The walls were no longer a dingy dirty white. They were a tasteful dark grey. Black baseboards ran along the floor. The doorframes of the walk-in cooler, freezer, mop closet and office were a bright red. The lockers against the back wall were a shiny black powder-coated steel. It all tied back into the floor. The ceiling was a bright white to reflect the light and keep you from feeling closed in on.

"Oh, Uncle Frank! I love it!" I praised him, my face lifting with delight.

Had he picked out the colors on his own or had he left it up to the construction company's designers? It was so clean and tasteful. It looked so modern. Frank was a lot of things but he wasn't modern.

Frank turned around and puffed out his chest and belly with pride. He smiled, pleased he'd received my approval and my praise.

"She's right," David added. "Looks great Frank."

"Who cares what you think," Frank said bluntly. David and I looked at him surprised and he chuckled. "Well, she does I suppose," he gestured to me and winked.

"What do you mean?" I asked a tad defensively.

"Aw now, don't pretend. I can see how you two look at each other. And something's changed with both of you. Love is the only thing I know of that is powerful enough to do that." He looked a little sad.

I smiled at Frank but said nothing. He glowered at me and David, a pretend mask void of any real anger.

"Not going to admit it, huh?" he shot at David whose growing masculine smile of contentment was answer enough.

"A gentleman doesn't kiss and tell." He winked at Frank.

Frank let out a booming laugh and I startled. I'd never heard him laugh so good naturedly before. He had a good laugh! A rich deep sound full of warmth and cheer.

Oh, he should be Santa Clause this year at the restaurant! Ooh, that'd be so fun for the kids!

"So you admit you've kissed her!" Frank teased.

"How'd you pick out the new colors and design?" I asked, changing the subject immediately.

"Susan and Lucy," Frank mumbled annoyed.

I was so pleased to hear this. They hadn't abandoned him after all. *Oh, thank you God!*

"They've been pestering me for weeks now. On my ass. Took over the whole damn thing. The wrinkly ol' witches," he complained.

David and I laughed. "Oh, come on now," David said genially. "I'm sure you appreciated the help."

"Well, maybe," Frank grumbled sarcastically with a roll of his beady eyes.

"I'm sorry I wasn't here to help," I said solemnly.

"Nonsense," Frank said sternly. "You—" His voice broke unexpectedly and he cleared his throat. "You were mending up." He nodded, his eyes connecting with mine and I could see how deeply he had been afraid for me.

"Uncle Frank," my voice was tender. "I'm okay now." I reassured him, nodding back and maintaining our intense eye contact.

He blew out a big breath full of emotion and cleared his throat again. Then he pulled up his pants as if readying himself and squared off his chunky shoulders. He took off his driver's cap and passed his hand over his balding grey head as he looked down. The sight reminded me of his age, and how many years he'd been alone and hurting.

"I'm okay now," I repeated and stepped up, embracing him in a light hug. He patted my back awkwardly and I felt his hands trembling a little, his emotions running higher than he could admit.

"Okay, come on in you two love birds, and I'll tell you a story." He opened his office door and went inside, his shrinking body made passing through the door frame easier than it used to be. The door itself was new. Solid metal with a long narrow window in the center about eight inches wide and twenty inches long.

We entered and I sat down in one of the new dark grey high-backed leather office chairs he had inside. A new silver Scandinavian style desk was in the corner of the small office with a flat screen computer monitor sitting on top next to the old fashion bookkeeper's books and pile of mail. The office was just as small as it had been but seemed bigger with the bright white ceiling and new creamy tones of the walls. It was only big enough to fit the new desk, two chairs, metal locking filing cabinet, the two rows of shelves above the desk lined with framed photos, and a small combination safe which was placed underneath the desk, bolted securely to the floor.

"David, mind if I sit in my own chair?" Frank asked flatly.

"It's yours Sir, by all means," David said sardonically.

"Rump kisser," Frank mouthed off. A playful humor rallying between them. I realized it was how the two of them had always behaved and communicated together. It was probably the reason Frank respected David more than anyone else who worked here.

"Haven't made it that far yet," David said flatly back.

"Good," Frank jabbed, a twinkle in his eye.

"Don't let him, okay?" Frank ordered me.

"Wha—" my mouth was hanging open and Frank laughed again as I shot David a scolding look.

"As Assistant Manager, the chair's mine when you're not here. Deal?" David changed the subject, making up for his bad choice of joke.

"Whatever," Frank said dismissively.

Oh yeah. Frank had asked David to be his Assistant Manager. How had I forgotten that?

David propped the door open with the kick stand and I noticed a new golden kick plate along the bottom. He positioned himself between us against the wall next to the door where he could see both of us.

"Um," Frank looked up at David, his face very serious again. "Thank you, David, for stepping in and, um—" Frank cleared his throat.

"It's nothing sir. Anything I can do to help," David replied respectfully, he too growing serious.

"No, not that you moron," Frank complained, waving to the place. "For stepping in and stopping that bastard from finishing his...from...If Melanie had been...I...thank you, you bastard," Frank grumbled.

"I appreciate that Frank, but you don't owe me a thank you. No one does. I'm just glad I finally listened to God trying to send me there," David looked at me. He knew this topic was humiliating for me and he gave me a concerned look, asking if I was okay. I nodded.

"Thank God for you then," Frank all but whispered. "Never thought I'd be thanking God for you," he half shouted now, his need to remain a grumpy old man always rushing to the surface.

"How about that story," I suggested, sitting back in the new chair. It was quite comfortable, squishy and cushy.

"Yep. Good idea," Frank swallowed. "I'll start with what I know from her childhood. Sound good?" Frank asked me, eyes widening in anticipation.

"Sounds perfect," I said, my voice eager. I felt hungry to know more about her through his stories.

Over the next half-hour Frank recounted everything he could remember about the night my mother had driven from Redding to Elk Grove in the old blue pickup truck. Finding Vivian and I sleeping in the truck had been a complete surprise. My mother had been badly beaten, nearly passing out from exhaustion upon arrival. They'd taken us in.

"It was the first time I'd been around babies so young. Vivian was so small for her age. She stole my heart away when she'd sing to me. Every day she was there, she'd come up and make up a song for me," Frank choked up and so did I, our eyes both swimming with tears.

"You were so little, I was afraid to hold you. Thought I'd drop you. Katherine made me the last night you were there. I never felt something so powerful crash over me. I realized what we'd missed out on. Your little eyes were like magnets and you wouldn't let go of my finger. You hardly ever cried. Never fussy. Just quiet. So quiet," He looked away into his memory, his eyes haunted. "Course, we didn't know it was going to be the last night we'd have you all there. It had only been about four days when he came," Frank cleared his throat.

"Showed up all cleaned, shaved and shirt pressed driving a rental car. Helena was hiding with you both in the back. Course, his truck was out front. He knew y'all was in there. I didn't let him in. I wanted to kill 'im and Katherine nearly clawed his eyes out soon as she opened the door. I had grabbed her and pulled her back inside but he wouldn't leave so I stepped out to talk to him, man to man," Frank shifted uncomfortably in his chair, seeking comfort but finding none.

"He made some rational argument about it having been the first time he had lost his temper like that with her. Said women can be so emotional and unreasonable. Explained he'd always seen his dad hit his mother and he didn't know what had happened. He never wanted to be that kind of man. He had just gotten so angry, she'd been nagging him. Pushed him too far," Frank said with a shrug, his voice carrying doubts.

"You see, Helena hadn't told us what had happened past him just loosin' his temper that time!" I could hear the pleading in his voice to make me understand. "She wouldn't talk about it. Just...just wouldn't. Refused to talk to the police and press charges. I'd always thought she was too afraid to get him in trouble 'cause she still loved him. Or maybe something worse like he had threatened to kill her if she did. She would never say!" Frank stood up suddenly and turned around to hide his face, his head hung down.

"I...I believed him. He convinced me she'd pushed him too far. He sounded so reasonable and so remorseful. He promised never to harm her again. I made him swear it to me and he did. He looked me in the eye, grabbed my hand like a man, and swore he'd never hurt his wife again. And I chose to believe him. In my heart I knew it was all a lie. But...but I wanted our life back. I wanted Katherine back to myself. I was scared I was falling in love with you two girls and could feel it already breaking my heart at the thought of you leaving. I wanted to protect myself and protect my safe, comfortable life. I was a selfish, foolish, old man. Even then." Frank turned around with tears streaming down his cheeks. He had a look of trepidation and fear written all over his face.

I could tell he was expecting me to lash out at him but instead I sat there silently, pondering all he'd shared. His story was filtering through my emotions and trickling into me slowly so I could make sense of it. Frank waited, his silent tears bubbling into a tremble in his hands. His chest stuttering as he tried to hold back his sobs.

I felt David beside me, he had shifted over to be closer to me as Frank had recounted his story, his hand a soothing presence on my shoulder. I felt his calm reassurance that he was here to support me in any way he could, and I was grateful to have him by my side.

"I understand," I looked up at Frank, tears starting to stream down my face.

"How could you understand something so selfish," Frank whispered in disbelief.

"You were deceived by him. You weren't the first Uncle Frank. He was...he *is* a master deceiver. He's so much more vile than you could ever know," I offered him the truth.

"I made you all go back with him!" Frank's sob burst from him along with his confession. "I sent you home!" Frank's self-loathing was tangible. "God punished me for it. I know he did. He took my Katherine to punish me. She was all I wanted, all that mattered to me. And he took her from me for my selfishness," Frank sobbed, his hands covering his purple-red patchy face.

"Frank, that isn't true," David interjected. "God does not take what we love out of punishment. He doesn't do that. Satan does that. Satan is the primary source of evil and pain in this world. We can cause our own suffering too of course, made with our own choices. Cause and effect. Action and consequence. But sometimes, it isn't anything we can control. It's just the human experience of unexpected sickness, misfortune, poverty, even death that we find ourselves a victim of. A world ran by evil, under the domination of evil, produces evil," David explained.

The truth he spoke reminded me of what Archangels Michael and Gabriel had explained to me.

"I was being punished," Frank denied. "I deserved it. But she didn't," Frank sobbed. "She begged me not to make them leave." He looked imploringly at David. "She hated me for weeks after that. Wouldn't talk to me. Wouldn't touch me. Wouldn't look at me." His eyes held so much regret. "It hurt so badly to have her mad at me. But losing her to cancer was more devastating than I could have ever imagined."

"Uncle Frank," I whispered. He looked back at me, his eyes barely able to hold mine. "I don't blame you. Would my life have turned out differently if we'd stayed? Possibly. Maybe my father would have eventually let us go. But you know what?" I paused, realizing a very frightening truth.

"He never would have taken no for an answer. He'd rather us all be dead than give away what he felt *belonged* to him. No one takes from Dwayne Bishop. No one." I shook my head, a deep frown lining my face with disgusted certainty.

"Dead?" Frank whispered, eyes growing wide.

"You very well may have saved Katherine's life by sending us away and probably your own. And you probably saved our life too at that point. As twisted and wrong as that seems, I feel it in my heart to likely be true," I stood now to look at my Uncle Frank eye to eye. He stayed where he stood, looking broken and defeated.

"My father isn't just a rapist Uncle Frank. He's a murderer. And it's only a matter of time before we have the evidence we need to lock him away forever." Frank's eyes grew larger. "Please believe me when I tell you, you did the right thing. We all would be dead right now if you hadn't had your moment of...of fear and selfishness." I had stopped crying and felt every ounce of truth resonate in my spirit. The Lord was giving me insights into what the outcome would have been. It wasn't a guess. It was the unwritten path our destiny had nearly traveled down.

"God used your fear of relationship and losing your life as you knew it, to save all of ours. Frank, stop blaming yourself. Stop feeling punished. Stop believing the lies of the enemy." I gripped his thick sweaty hands. They were shaking.

"You think that's true?" He glanced helplessly between me and David.

"I do," I said.

"I know truth when I hear it Frank. This is truth in it's most insightful form. Trust it," David encouraged Frank.

"Oh," Frank breathed out, a huge burden being lifting from him. He collapsed into this chair and hid his face into his hands once more. He sobbed in relief and release. I placed my hand on his shoulder and patted him gently.

Frank looked up at me, eyes showing a deep regret once more. "I should have known what he was," Frank's voice cracked and he swallowed down his emotions. "I'd met him once before," he nodded, his eyes beseeching.

"At their wedding?" I guessed.

"Oh no. None of us ever got to go to that. Dwayne and Helena had eloped," Frank shrugged.

Well that explains the absence of wedding photos or stories about wedding crashers growing up.

"Every year Katherine would throw a little Fourth of July barbeque at the house. Her sister Gloria would come, your grandmother. Helena would always come too. That was about all the family we all had around these parts. My parents were still living at the time in New Orleans and never wanted to come to Cali. Katherine and Gloria's parents had passed away a year or two before. Some freak accident. Anyway, the last time I saw your mama before she showed up with you girls was at our family get together. She showed up with Dwayne and all hell broke loose."

I walked backwards to my chair, sensing a story I'd rather be sitting down for.

"Oop!" I exclaimed, accidentally sitting on David's lap. "I didn't see you sit down!" I laughed.

David was chuckling and shifted me to his left leg, placing a hand around my waist to steady me, his mouth a slanted smile.

"Sorry to take your seat. I can move if you'd like," David offered.

"It's okay," I smiled at him. It was nice to be held right now. *Oh God, I hope Frank is okay with it.* I glanced at Frank nervously. He was smiling a little sad smile watching us. His face was nostalgic.

"So, she came with *him*," I continued for Frank.

"Yup. Declared they were married, she was dropping out of school, and moving to Redding. Gloria flipped out. Accused Dwayne of being a bad man like her ex-husband. Said she could see it in him. That didn't go over well. Helena never knew her mom had been married. She'd always been told it was a one-night stand. Things really got heated. Dwayne didn't even seem phased by any of it. Kind of just smiled and watched the show. I didn't get involved. I didn't know the story about Gloria's ex. Katherine never told me. I don't even know if she really knew much about him either. But anyway, they stormed off and left. None of us ever saw her again until that night she showed up with you two," Frank ran his hand over his face, sitting back in his chair. He threw up his left ankle to cross his right knee, this time it went up without the extra help. That weight loss was really starting to pay off.

"I didn't care enough to pay close attention to the man. I thought Gloria was just a crazy wingnut. The only thing that really bothered me was seeing Katherine so upset. Gloria and Katherine dug around and found out where they'd moved to up in Redding and wrote letters, ya know. Lots of letters. Tried calling too. Even went up there once but Helena refused to open the door. It was really hard on both of them." Frank looked down sadden by the memory.

"No way you could have known what he was, even back then," I said consolingly.

"If I'd bothered to listen to the ladies, I might have tried to see it for myself. I could have gone with them to try and see her. Maybe having a man with them would have given her the courage to come out and leave him. Ya know, for protection or somethin'," Frank sighed and blew the air out of his cheeks.

"Do you have any fun stories about my mother?" I asked, ready to lighten up story telling time and hungry to hear more about her life. I'd never had anyone I could ask before.

"Sure do! She and Gloria came over all the time when she was growing up. I didn't really participate much, usually left the ladies to do their girlie stuff, ya know? But I remember quite a bit of the stories Katherine came home and told me after their trips. Wanta hear some?" Frank's voice was pepping up and his eyes were starting to sparkle.

"Yes, please!" I leaned forward in anticipation, David's arms around me like a warm comforting blanket. I hugged his arms to me, a rare moment of complete happiness filling me as I listened to stories about my mother's adventures and learned more about my grandmother Gloria and great Aunt Katherine.

David leaned forward to rest his chin on my shoulder, his head close to mine as he listened intently with me. I relaxed into him, his chest at my back. I was so happy he was here to "meet" my family through Frank's stories and share this moment with me. I wouldn't forget a thing I learned today for the rest of my life. The bad and the good.

Hide and Seek

Chapter Sixteen

"*I* don't know what to tell you Picard. He isn't here! Get out of my face!" Auburn Sheriff Miles Dundee yelled.

"If you want to give up, then fine! Be a quitter! But I don't give up! He's here, you lazy son of a bitch," Doc stepped up into Dundee's face, matching his hostility with some of his own.

"It's been six hours! It's getting dark out!" Dundee threw his hands into the air.

"Big flippin' deal! We have flashlights and choppers with spot lights. Afraid to hunt in the dark now, are we?" Doc mocked.

FBI Special Agent Nichols rushed over, hands out to separate the two men. "Eugene, give it a rest," he ordered. "Sheriff Dundee is just following my orders."

"Your what?" Doc rounded on Agent Nichols, his hands on his hips, his face furious.

"Hey now," Nichols backed up a step. "Mind your manners. You can be banned from this man hunt as easily as you were invited."

"You wouldn't. You owe me!" Doc hissed.

"You got paid for those bounties. You aren't owed anything past a professional courtesy, Eugene."

Doc blew out an angry breath and heaved a big inhale back in, his chest expanding to stretch the Velcro of his Kevlar vest into making an involuntary ripping sound.

"The dogs haven't found his scent anywhere around past that two-mile marker. It's like he got beamed up or just turned around and came right back out the way he'd come. The drones haven't found any new life signs. All the heat signatures were checked out and the hikers escorted off the trails. There is no one left out here to find. We're spinning our wheels and wasting our man power. He's gone," Agent Nichols argued coolly.

"Ya know, before your day we did things the old-fashioned way. Hands and feet. Instinct and grit. Intelligence and profiling. We followed our gut! All you boys these days know how to do is rely on your damn technology! We're missing something, I'm telling ya!" Doc fumed, starting to pace again, his footsteps hard, his face heated, the cold winter air doing little to cool his nerves.

"I don't think Dwayne even came out here. It was probably a misidentification. And the dogs might have just latched onto the smell of is deodorant or something and followed some other poor hiker's sent," Dwayne's parole agent, Agent Redford, said dismissively. "How do we know that damn jogger didn't just freak out over some backwoods fella? Lot of people hike out here alone. I bet it wasn't even him. Why would Dwayne Bishop even come out here? There ain't nothing in his file about him knowing anything about Auburn," Redford scoffed.

"And there's nothing in it that says he don't either," Doc snapped. "We should keep looking. Talk to that jogger again. Anyone get his name?" Doc looked around for the missing jogger. Seeing only law enforcement left in the parking lot, he added,

"Anyone else talk to him besides the park ranger who he reported the sighting to?" Doc scowled.

"Um, no. No, I didn't have a chance," Sheriff Dundee admitted.

"Why the hell not?" Doc scowled at him. "You were the first responder."

"'Cause I was too busy getting the FBI here and calling your stupid ass!"

"Hey now, you better—"

"Enough!" Agent Nichols hushed them both. "I was told the jogger reported it to the ranger and left right afterwards. Told the ranger he was too scared to stay."

"Hey Jerry! Come here, will ya?" Doc yelled over the crowd of Sheriffs and FBI Agents' heads. Doc was taller than all of them so spotting Jerry, the park ranger, had been easy. He was still lingering awkwardly by his truck, hanging out in case they needed him again.

Jerry jogged over, almost elated to be included in the discussion with the superior law enforcement officers. "What's up, Doc," Jerry said, his smile large and inviting.

"Funny. Never heard that one before," Doc replied dryly. Jerry's smile vanished and he grew sullen. "Now listen. What was that witness's name again?"

"Who?" Jerry asked, his expression void of intelligence.

Doc closed his eyes and took in a slow breath to control himself. "The witness that reported seeing the FBI's most wanted fugitive. The *trail jogger* who said he saw Dwayne Randal Bishop. The man who told you he was afraid for his life and left before giving any of us an official statement!" Doc's voice had started out calm but had grown with intensity and aggression with each sentence, until he was nearly yelling in poor Jerry's shocked face.

Jerry blanched, unable to think under such verbal assault and pressure. Doc was grievously annoyed. No wonder Jerry was a park ranger. He never would have made it through the police academy.

Or even the military. The Army would have broken this poor useless soul.

"What was his name?" Agent Nichols repeated, shooting Doc an unfriendly look.

"Um…um… it was… I have it written down!" Jerry sputtered, searching his pockets frantically. "Here it is! His name was Shawn Piebody!"

"And did you get Shawn's phone number so we can follow up with him?" Doc asked.

"Um, no." Jerry's face fell even further.

"Address?" Agent Redford asked, his tone wasn't hopeful.

"I thought you guys can just look him up!" Jerry was looking at the group of irritated officers pleadingly.

"We can, but there might be more than one…Shawn Piebody." Agent Nichols crossed his arms over his suited chest.

"Any word back on the rancher that thought someone was living in their barn?" Doc asked Agents Nichols and Redford, willing something good to come of his wasted afternoon.

"Agent Riker reported in a few hours ago. They investigated the barn and took some samples to run for DNA but she wasn't hopeful. Said if someone was sleeping there, they were careful not to make too much of a mess and they cleaned up after themselves pretty good." Agent Nichols gave Doc a warning look that clearly said he needed to simmer down and not get upset about his answer.

"Course. Nothing again," Doc mumbled. "Whelp, gentlemen, it's been real great spending the day with y'all. Hope we get a real lead soon. In the meantime, who wants to run Shawn Piebody's information and let me know when we can go talk to him?"

"I'll do it," Redford offered.

"Thanks Jerry. You can go now." Doc turned his back on Jerry who was still lingering like a dog waiting for a bone.

"Oh. Okay fellas. Um, night," Jerry said sheepishly and wandered off toward his truck.

"Sleep well," Doc said sarcastically. "Stupid little shit."

"I'll call you Eugene, once we have Shawn's info. I wish to God we had cameras around this park, some footage we could pull! What a joke," Agent Nichols's own frustration was seeping out past his professionalism.

"K, let's go!" Sheriff Dundee shouted to the crowd and put his hand in the air making circle gestures. The other Sheriffs present started walking to their cars in packs, talking excitedly. The FBI just stood there giving Dundee challenging expressions. They didn't answer to him. He wasn't even in charge out here. Special Agent Nichols was.

"It's fine. Head out. We're done here," Nichols confirmed. His agents began to break apart, heading to their unmarked SUVs and Forensic Vehicles.

"Skylight One, you can return home," An FBI agent near them spoke into the radio to the chopper still hovering in the air a couple hundred yards away. It immediately took off in a southwest direction.

"Thomas," Doc skooched over, speaking quietly now. He hardly ever addressed Special Agent Nichols by his first name. Nichols sidled over while the rest of their circle disbursed, heading to their vehicles.

"Eugene," Nichols said, his eyes serious.

"I don't have a good feeling about this. We've missed something. I think he's playing with us."

"Maybe. Or maybe it was just all a big mistake by an overly zealous jogger, spooked by his own shadow," Nichols raised a shoulder in a shrug. "We'll be in touch."

"Roger that." Doc walked off in a purposeful gait toward his Hummer, pulling out his phone as he went. "So much for finding a fugitive in *Hidden* Falls Regional Park," Doc mumbled to himself.

Taste Test

Chapter Seventeen

rank was laughing, a rare moment of humor tickling him as he recalled Helena, my mother, sneaking into their bedroom in the middle of the night when she was seven years old and putting her hamster in their bed. She was having her first ever sleepover at Auntie Kate's house. Frank had been indifferent to the idea, but agreed to appease Katherine who wanted time with her niece. Frank always felt compelled to oblige given it was because of him she didn't have kids. He had never wanted any.

"I never heard Katherine scream so loud in all my life!" Frank roared, rocking backwards holding his jiggling gut. "It had crawled up her nightdress. Think it was looking for a hidey-hole." Frank couldn't breathe he was laughing so hard.

He really needs to be Santa for the kids this year!

David and I were laughing too, the sound of all three of us roaring filled the small office space and bounced around the room, the sounds foreign. Well, from the restaurant's perspective.

I was holding my stomach from the stitches ripping across my ribcage, trying not to cry, my eyes little squints of uncontrollable contractions from mirth.

"We both shot out of that bed! That fuzzy little creature peed all over the sheets we scared it so bad," He boomed between laughs. "The look on Katherine's face!"

"Me too! I'm going to pee!" I confessed, laughing harder at the images his story invoked.

"I grabbed my pillow, ready to beat the little stinker to death. Helena started bawling! No! No! She cried, panicked that I was going to kill Harry, her hamster," Frank shook his head.

"Harry?" David asked, his wonderfully deep laugh vibrating against my back. "Or Hairy?"

"Ooh, good one!" Frank retorted.

"Oh, wait," David said suddenly, his voice growing somber as the sounds of his cell phone ringing interrupted our laughter. "Give me one minute please. It's Doc. Excuse me," David said patting my hip.

I stood, letting him up and he squeezed around me, his body warm and inviting as he slipped past me. I had to remind myself not to smile given why Doc was most likely calling.

"Who the hell is Doc? Somebody sick?" Frank asked, growing only slightly more serious between chuckles.

"Oh, um. Doc is my CCW instructor, and a bounty hunter. He's helping the FBI hunt down and apprehend my father," I answered, humor draining from me at the distasteful mention of my present circumstances.

"Wow. Glad you're doing that. He keeping you in the loop?" Frank asked, completely solemn now.

"Yes. So is Special Agent Nichols from the FBI. He's been updating us regularly on their progress, or lack thereof," I shared. "Well, I better get out there too. I want to know what's happening.

They were following a lead today that might take them to him." I smiled bashfully at Frank as he got up to walk me out the office. "Thanks for sharing these stories with me Uncle Frank. I can't tell you how good it feels to hear them."

"It feels pretty damn good to share them with you – Finally," Frank added with a sheepish smile of his own.

I hugged him and he patted my back carefully. I pulled away, both our smiles growing to match each other's, a silly joy filling both of us at having found family, even a far from perfect family, and both with heaps of messed up issues in toe.

We left the office and found David deeper inside the kitchen. He was leaning his back against the salad bar prep station, looking up at the ceiling, listening intently. Hearing us coming, he glanced over, his face showing frustration. I asked him with my eyes if they had caught Dwayne though I could already tell what the answer would be. The small shake of his head and crease in his brow was a perfect "no".

"Shoot," I sighed, my hopeful shoulders drooping down to make me feel saggy.

"Didn't get him, huh?" Frank guessed, his voice a rumbling grumble, though he was making an effort to try and be quiet.

"Not today," I whispered, feeling disappointed.

"Want me to call Professor Elisabeth Becker or did you want to take lead on that?" David asked Doc, his voice clear, holding a hint of that mind-in-mission-mode tone I was starting to recognize. David listened to Doc's answer, nodding.

"Yeah, I don't like that either," he replied, listening again.

"Strange name—" David cut off, his frown deepening and his mouth thinning.

"Do me a favor, give that name to Professor Becker to have it ran. Don't wait for the FBI to get back to you on it. Something about it doesn't feel right to me." David had that look of concentration and know-how on his face. I think he was sensing something in his spirit about whoever they were talking about.

"Yes, I have a *feeling*," David said carefully, glancing over at Frank who was busying himself in the pots and pans cabinet, his attempt at being quiet forgotten along with his attention span.

"Roger that. We'll connect later." David ended the call and straightened back up, his hands fisting around his phone.

"He escaped again," I stated.

"Yes. And the witness disappeared. Name he gave doesn't feel right to me. In fact, the entire thing doesn't feel right to me," David quietly said, walking up toward me to place his hands on my shoulders, making sure I was okay.

"Hey you two love birds! You two ever taste my Beef Stroganoff?" Frank shouted, his head down almost inside the cabinet now looking for something, banging and clanging echoing up from around his buried head.

"Um, no. Not yet," I answered, confusion in my voice. What was this man up to?

"Well, you're gonna! Go find yourselves a table out front. You'll be my first customers in the newly decorated joint!" Frank ordered cheerfully.

"I am kind of hungry," David admitted, giving me a happy face. "Nothing more we can do tonight anyway," he leaned over into my ear, "Unless you want to get to work and start—"

"Sounds wonderful Uncle Frank," I said with a giggle in my voice.

Frank popped his head up, his face shiny red from the downward pressure. "You won't regret it!" He started bustling around the kitchen grabbing his skillets and snatching up an apron from a hook on the wall.

I looked around the kitchen, seeing the bright sparkle of all the new stainless-steel surfaces and LED lights with a new appreciation. The kitchen had been entirely redone as well. The cleanliness was breathtaking. "Wow, George and Francisco are really going to love their new kitchen!" I remarked admirably.

"More than they deserve, the lazy sons-of-bitches," Frank grumbled.

I laughed, throwing back my head. "Aw, come on. They've been loyal to you."

"So was my dog before he crapped on my couch and ate up my slippers. Kicked him out too," Frank remarked snidely, a twinkle in his eyes.

"Do you need any help?" David offered, leaning his hands on the food counter and peering through the hot lamp opening at Frank.

"You cook?" Frank spun around, an accusatory glare in his eyes.

"Master Chef," David winked.

"At what? Grilling a hot dog?"

David grinned, "My mother and sister and I used to attend cooking lessons when I was in middle school. It was something to do together. Mom said every man needs to know how to cook for his lady and be self-reliant. And she told my sister a good meal was the key to a man's heart. She insisted we both learn. Said it was investing in the longevity of our future relationships. It was either that or dance lessons. I opted for the cooking."

"You've been holding out on me boy!" Frank barked good-naturedly.

"Yup!" David lifted his chin in mock challenge. "Sure have."

"Bastard," Frank jested.

"Old goat," David poked back.

"I'm hungry!" I announced. "And I want to go see the rest of the restaurant. Come on!" I grabbed David's hand and hauled him off with me, having to lean forward and tug just to budge him, he was so much heavier and stronger than me. I might as well have been trying to pull a stubborn pony.

"Fine. Didn't need your useless help anyway. I've got this! Go make out or something. Try the walk-in cooler again. I know you know what I'm talking about!" Frank shouted after us. I blanched and glanced up at David who looked about as mortified as I felt. His eyes darted quickly away from mine. I thought I could see a slight blush making it's way into his cheeks.

David blushes?

David risked a glance down at me as we rounded the corner into the cashier's station and stopped us at the counter. The heat radiating off of my face told me I was already beet red but I tried to smile past it. I felt my face grimace instead.

Crap. I thought I had let this shame go already? Double crap.

We had *just* made out rather intensely during training earlier today but the thought of what I had almost made David do in that damn walk-in cooler made me feel dirtier than a blown-out baby's diaper.

"It's not a bad idea actually," David said surprising me. My words caught in my throat and a slightly nervous chuckle escaped David. "I'm kidding. Totally kidding. Just trying to flip the shame we're both feeling with some inappropriate humor."

"Umm...I don't think it's working," I confessed. "I—"

"Naw, don't worry about it. Remember. I could have left at any time. Do you really think a buck twenty could stop me?" David gestured to himself and my eyes couldn't help but roam over his muscular physique.

"Buck thirty-five actually," I corrected him with a shy smile.

Leave it up to Uncle Frank to not let us forget he caught us in a state of heated passion in the walk-in once, and not too long ago at that.

Thanks a lot uncle.

"Whoa," David breathed, his eyes lifted over my head to search the restaurant behind me.

348

"Oh, wow!" I agreed, turning around, relieved to have a distraction. "Everything looks so modern. I did not expect this!"

The old fashion Café had been stripped of the old oak counters and wood panels and replaced with stainless-steel. There was newly installed chair rim molding and light grey paint on new rectangular beveled-textured walls. The wide baseboards and even wider crown molding were black and added an elegant touch. The outdated curtain fabrics were gone and replaced with bright white vertical shutters that elongated the ceiling to floor presence and welcomed in light from the parking lot lights outside. During the day, it would be spectacular. I couldn't wait to see it in daylight.

The crusty booths were all replaced and redesigned so the new booths faced outward toward the room, the backs stretching up five-feet high against the walls in a dark silver, grey and black, striped fabric. The dimly lit hanging lamps had been torn out and were replaced with strategically placed light bars, scattered across the entire ceiling, shining like starts in the night. Their chrome shells and bright blue-light filling the room with a surreal atmosphere full of unknown potential and class. This chic new design made the café elegant and modern. And I absolutely loved it.

"Frank outdid himself," David said with wonder, walking out into the lobby and running his hand over the stainless-steel host podium, its little calla lily shaped lamp cover curving up and over the top to alight on a digital panel. David tapped the screen and it came to life and showed the restaurant's new floor plan. Each booth and chair and even the stools at the bar, were numbered. The computers at the cashier station were new along with their flat screens.

The bar was still the same bar but it had been cleaned, sanded and stained, the polished surface a brilliant shine, making the dark oak wood underneath look wet, the grains of wood and carvings, beautiful. The bottles of wine and beer were dusted and gleaming. The taps polished and the brass sparkling like new again.

"Um, David?" I said, a flickering catching my eyes over to the left just past the bar. I headed over to the lights. Four candles flickered, half melted, atop a small table draped in a crisp white cloth. A bottle of champagne laid at a slant in an ice bucket, the outside sweating. Two place settings with a full spread of silverware, folded cloth napkins, champagne and water glasses sat in front of each of the two chairs.

"That sneaky devil," David said softly coming up next to me, placing his arm around my shoulder.

"You didn't know?" I asked suspiciously.

"No! I swear," David looked down at me with humor sparkling in his eyes. "I would have dressed up for our first date," David said, a small smile growing on his face, his eyebrows going up to wiggle.

I looked down myself and sighed. "Great. Just great." I glanced at David embarrassed. "Yeah, me too."

David laughed. "Well, we can't waste this opportunity. I think you look breathtaking. Your sweats are quite becoming." He took me in his arms, pulling me slowly to him. I felt my pulse speed up and my face growing red at the look of desire growing in his eyes.

Suddenly music kicked on and I jumped, looking up to find the nearly invisible speakers hidden up on the ceiling, embedded as smooth disks to saturate the room with the pleasant sound. Frank Sinatra's *Love is a many Splendored Thing* started playing and I glanced back to see Frank trying to tip-toe unnoticed back toward the kitchen.

"Oh, Frank," I said humorously to myself. I smiled and looked back up at David, about to comment on Frank's scheming abilities, but my words died in my throat at the passion on David's face.

He drew me back into his arms, tightening them around me to press me into him so I wouldn't jump out of them again, a hand going to the back of my head to lead me gently forward, lowering his mouth to mine. My hands were on his waist, gripping his shirt. I was trying not to be naughty. All I kept seeing in my head was how beautiful he was earlier today warming up in the matted room, his shirt having gone up to expose his deep tanned washboard stomach and perfect happy trail.

David brushed his lips on mine, softly, tenderly, slowly, moving them from side to side as if feeling their softness and warmth on his for the first time. His eyes were closed and mine seemed to flutter to a close as well, my body almost draping into his arms.

He slowly moved his face around to rub his cheek along mine, breathing me in deeply. Chills ran down my neck and back, and along my arms as his nose found my jawline, the tip tracing down my neck and into my hair. My neck arched back to give him the full line of my throat. It was as if all thinking had stopped and all that was left of me in this moment was wanting to know him. He planted a gentle kiss along the center of my neck, his lips pressing tenderly but lingering with each kiss as he made his way across to the other side. I had never had my neck kissed before, it felt wonderful.

I was completely helpless in his arms, once again my body surrendering to the warmth and feel of his hands on me, his mouth on me, his body against mine. "David," I whispered unconsciously, melting more into him.

He didn't answer, he just slowly began to move us, swaying us to the music as the next song started. Nat King Cole's *Unforgettable* filled the air and David suddenly and unexpectedly spun me into a dip across his arm. I let out a, "Whoop!" of surprise, my eyes flying open to see David smiling very knowingly down at me, his mouth open in a half-smile half-charming slant of flirtatiousness.

He lifted me back up easily, my weight insignificant to him. Seeing this beautiful man holding me with so much love and longing in his face, I felt overwhelmed with delight. A deep yearning was also there that brought with it a slight trembling of fear in my stomach of the unknown, iced with an exhilarated anticipation of what our future could hold.

David kept us dancing, in the slow swaying language of love. If he were to say what his eyes were telling me, I don't know if I could have remained standing. My knees were already weak, and I felt tingly all over like I was being deprived of oxygen. David was consuming my world.

I rested my head on his chest and clung to him as we danced so that I didn't have to gaze into that heated passionate look burning in his eyes any longer, lest I break. His heart beat was strong and reassuring against my ear. I closed my eyes, feeling so safe and peaceful in his arms. I thanked God for a man like David in my life. I never thought I'd ever have love. I never thought this world held someone who could possibly love *me*.

We danced until a timid, "A-hum," broke through the music and Frank emerged, two steaming plates of Beef Stroganoff on one hand and arm, the other carrying a fresh roll of bread on a wooden platter with a knife and whipped butter.

David and I pulled apart slowly and faced Frank.

"Bon appétit." Frank said happily. "Let me grab your salads!" He hurried off, a little pep in his step.

"Smells amazing," David grinned. "God, I'm starving." He walked over to the table and pulled out a chair for me, smiling warmly at me as I approached. I glanced at him a little shyly, a man had never pulled a chair out for me before. It made me feel all delicate and special inside. A new feeling altogether.

"Thank you, Mr. Abramson," I said formally, and giggled.

"It is entirely my pleasure, Miss Bishop," David pushed the chair in and then joined me, sitting across from me, the candle light flickering in his honey-brown eyes, making golden flames within them.

"That's more like it," Frank said conspiratorially, dimming the overhead LED lights so that the candles were practically the brightest source of luminescence in the front of the restaurant. "Enjoy kids," he said as he set the Caesar salads down on our table.

"Aren't you going to eat with us?" I asked, suddenly feeling incredibly rude.

"Naw, I'll eat back here out of the way. You two enjoy. Don't wanta be a third wheel." Frank winked at us. "Besides, I need to be heading home soon. I wasn't kidding about the dog. Got a new puppy. Little shit been destroying the house when I'm gone. Pooped on the couch, the bed. Ready to skin him alive."

"But—" I glanced at David, suddenly nervous to be left in a romantic setting with him. I didn't trust myself. I didn't trust myself to say no or stop things if we got carried away again.

"Got your keys?" Frank asked David.

"Sure do," David confirmed. "Security system code the same or did you change that?"

"Changed. 6-3-5-2-6-4-3," Frank rattled off.

"Okay," David nodded.

"Don't need to write it down?" Frank said skeptically.

"Nope. I got it," David tapped the side of his head and winked back at Frank. They shared a moment of understanding that skipped right over me. Why would David be able to remember those numbers so easily? I'd already forgotten most of them.

"Lock up after yourself, will ya love birds?" Frank smiled warmly at me. "And don't stay here all night!" Frank shot at David, a warning look glinting in his eyes. David burst out laughing.

"No intention of it, Sir," David reassured him. It reassured me too.

Oh, thank God.

"And careful with those plates, they're hot! Don't drink more than that bottle of champagne 'cause I'll know. And no taste tests from the desserts in the freezer!" Frank barked, his brow furrowed, but lacking any real misgiving. "I expect that meringue to be free of finger dents in the mornin'."

"No taste tests. No touching. Got it," David agreed, looking at me a little too long, making me blush.

Oh gawd.

"Especially taste tests," Frank boomed, hands on his hips, growing playfully protective of me.

"You have my word as a gentleman, Sir," David bowed his head to Frank with a mischievous smile.

"Right. Like I believe you. Gentleman? Ha!" Frank turned to leave.

"Frank!" I yelled after him, getting up and walking quickly to him. Frank smiled at me as I approached him. I gave him one more quick hug and a small peck on the cheek. "Thank you for everything." I gestured to the candle lit table and the delicious food he'd made for us. "I thought we were coming to work with you tonight."

"Eh, I got it all done days ago," Frank said dismissively, waving a hand as though it was nothing. "Thought you and your hero here might deserve a meal in a classy place like this all to yourselves. And besides, it needs to be christened with the blessing of a new blooming love again before she reopens. Katie would have wanted it. And she'd be so pleased it was you." Frank's voice broke and he sniffed conspicuously, clearing his throat. "Not sure about you though," he added dryly at David, who smiled in reply to his constant teasing. Frank spun on his heel and rushed away.

I watched him disappear around the corner and I sighed. He had done all this for me and for Katherine. He still loved her so much.

He was still a romantic! My heart squeezed as Nat King Cole came back on singing *A Blossom Fell*.

"Unbelievable," I quietly said, lost in my thought.

"This smells unbelievable. Come here, baby. Have some dinner," David spoke to me softly.

Oh, baby. I like how his voice sounds saying that to me.

I turned smiling in delight. I was smiling like a fool and I didn't care.

"Time to taste test this Beef Stroganoff!" I laughed, coming to my seat, but David jumped up and angled it out for me again, ever the gentleman. I sat down and he skooched me in again, helping me to get settled.

I waited for David to walk back around to his chair, but felt him touching my hair instead. His hands carefully wove into it, unknotting the loose bun I'd thrown it up into. My long strawberry blonde hair fell down, descending to my butt. I felt David run his hands through my long silky hair, stroking it, letting it pour through his fingers. Then his fingertips tickled my neck as he moved my hair aside. I felt his warm breath on the back of my neck moments before his lips connected, pressing a hot kiss at the nape of my neck. I shivered and screwed up my shoulders to my ears, a nearly silent giggle coming out I hadn't expected.

"Hmm," David said as if he'd just tasted something wonderful. "Shall we?" He came back around and sat down, offering me his hand from across the table. I gave him my hand, not sure what he was about to do. David closed his eyes and then I got it. He was going to pray for our meal.

"Oh!" I said out loud, closing my eyes. *Hope God doesn't mind I was just thinking naughty before this prayer. Well, probably David was too.*

David spoke softly and reverently. His prayer coming out comfortably and honest.

"Father God, we thank you for this meal. Bless the hands that prepared it. Bless Frank with peace and healing. I ask that you remind him in his moments of loneliness that he isn't alone, that he has family. And Father, I ask that you place your hand of protection over us all as we pursue these hidden truths and seek justice. Lord, you are the bringer of justice. You said revenge is yours. We give it back to you and place it at your feet. We surrender our right to be angry, our right to inflict revenge, and we trust that *your* justice, which is beyond compare, be served.

"Cover us with the blood of your son Jesus, and send your angels to camp around about us, to guard us, and keep us from harm. Give us ears to hear your Holy Spirit speaking and guiding us, Lord. And open our eyes to see others through your eyes and with a heart of love, Father. Oh, and give me control Lord. Help me not to grieve your heart. Help me to treat Melanie as a daughter of the King, to be good to her, to respect her, to honor her, to guard her virtue and her life, and help protect her. In Jesus's name I pray. Amen."

"Amen," I repeated, feeling peaceful and content. David brought my hand up to his mouth and kissed my knuckles delicately.

"Let's eat!" He declared excitedly, grabbing his fork, his eyebrows lifting with the thrill of a hot meal cooked by the famous Chef, otherwise known as our grumpy old boss, and newly found great uncle, Frank Gable.

Not so grumpy anymore. Getting happier.

I smiled and took at bite. My eyes closed, my chewing slow to taste it all. "Oh, my Gawd," I said around my bite. "So goowd."

David nodded, eyes wide in full agreement. "Champagne?" He reached for the bottle.

"Sure. Half a glass please."

David stood and gripped the bottle, setting it on the table as he peeled off the foil. He untwisted the bonnet and removed it before resting the bottle on his right leg, knee slightly bent to tilt the bottle away from us as he pressed along the side of the cork. It erupted in a foaming gush, David grabbed the towel conveniently hanging from the handle of the ice bucket and caught the dribbles.

I swallowed. There was something extremely sexy about David holding a gushing bottle of champagne on his thigh. His defined forearms and strong hands gripping the bottle expertly. I watched his hands, fascinated again by how attractive they were. I felt a hot blush creep up the side of my neck and across my reddening face.

David reached for my glass and I handed it to him, hoping he wasn't reading my thoughts. He poured the champagne, a small smile playing on his lips. I think he knew he was having some kind of effect on me.

For the love of God, Melanie. We just prayed for control for heaven's sake! Cool it! Just focus on your food. Your cooked food!

David reached for his own glass and served it before he sat back down. He held the glass up to me, "To us," David announced.

"To us!" I tapped my glass to his and was about to take a sip.

"To you Melanie. The love of my life." His voice was soft and sincere, his eyes bore into mine, driving his words deep into the pit of my stomach to make the butterflies dance on fluttering wings. My breath caught.

"Now, before I make you any more nervous about being trapped in here alone with me," David said teasingly, "Let's eat!" And he took a bite, closing his eyes again, telling me with his expression how amazing it was.

I brought the warm loaf of bread closer and cut it, serving us both a piece before I started in on my beef stroganoff and salad. The rest of the hour we talked, laughed, and shared. It was wonderful. The romantic music played, filling the air with an ambient ease to nurture the love growing between us. When we'd finished our dinner, we sat a bit longer just talking. It felt so easy and natural, unforced and as if we'd known each other our whole lives.

"I'll clean the dishes. Wanta help me take these to the back?" David suggested finally, getting up and walking to my chair before I could stand up.

"Sure." He helped my chair out and gave me his hand to help me up. I half expected him to pull me into a hug or a kiss, but he released me with a smile and reached for our plates and silverware. I followed his lead. Together we bussed the table with our dormant waiter and waitress skills, the rest picked up and piled in our arms on one trip.

"Why don't you call Liz while I clean up. She's probably ready for a check-in," David reminded me casually.

"Oh! Good idea! Thanks!" I wandered away to call Liz, a huge smile spreading on my face at all the things I wanted to tell her, but I'd wait until I was home.

My gosh, I haven't even told her about my travel back in time yet to Mount Moriah! I remembered suddenly. I was so behind. My life was happening too fast, I could hardly keep up with sharing the details.

The phone rang and Liz picked up on the second ring. "Hey Melanie."

"Hi Liz. Boy do I have a lot to tell you. But first thing, I'm still at the restaurant with David. He's cleaning up."

"Cleaning up?" Liz asked, her voice telling me she sensed something new in my voice and wasn't sure what kind of "cleaning up" I was referring to.

"Dishes Liz. Dishes. We ate dinner. Frank cooked it!" I said in amazement.

"Wow, that's unexpectedly random," Liz laughed. "How'd that happen?"

"Long story, but basically, he planned the whole thing. Tricked us. Gave us our first date," the smile in my voice was audible.

"Oh how sweet!" Liz's romantic side bubbling out in gooey delight for me. "He left you two there alone?" Liz asked. I could almost feel her looking at the clock.

"Only about an hour and a half ago. We were talking with him up until then."

"No set up needed at the Café?" Liz wondered.

"Nope. It is amazing, Liz. So stylish and modern. Classy! Totally not what I had expected. I *love* it!"

"Ooh, I can't wait to see it!" Liz sounded genuinely pleased. "Um, is that Tony Bennett I hear?"

I laughed. "Yes. Frank put in a sound system. Great isn't it?" I said swaying to the music and closing my eyes for a moment, remembering my first dance with David.

"You. Are. Happy." Liz stated. "Any particular reason?"

"Um...I got a little taste of luv," I said quietly, and giggled. "I'll tell you tonight. You home?"

"Just got in a little bit ago. I will expect to hear *everything* from you," she added for good measure.

"Oh, yes. Most definitely. See you soon," I hung up, the smile on my face starting to hurt my cheeks.

Oh crap! I forgot to tell Liz my father got away! Damn.

Oh well, Doc was going to call her anyway. She probably already knows.

I walked back over to David who had already washed the dishes by hand and was drying them with a towel, placing them back on the stack of china. He had wrapped up the rest of the bread in a little to-go bag. He looked so handsome whipping that towel around in his all-terrain tiger camos and a solid tan V-neck T-shirt. To see such a strong man so willing to help with domestic kinds of chores just turned me on.

What the hell is wrong with me? Is this mother nature's opinion or mine?

David caught me watching him and slowed his movements, placing the last wine glass on the hanging rack without looking. He seemed to take me all in; my mood, my expression, my body, all in that one visual pass with his eyes, his masculine instincts in full alert of this "in-heat" female. His face grew serious. Not the "I have something serious to tell you" kind of face, but the "I know what you're thinking and I want the same thing" kind of face.

I remembered the last time we had been the last ones here. It had been like peeling two magnets apart just getting into my car to leave. The desire to be near him, and chemistry had been intense. Now, we had to find a way to somehow make it all the way back to my house – together – before separating for the night. Could we endure that kind of chemical sexual tension and physical torture? We'd have to.

Oh, God. Help us go straight home and make it there without pawing at each other.

"All done here," David said quietly. His eyes starting to burn with heat as he looked me over. "We really need to go," he warned me.

"Yup," was all that I could think of to say.

He walked up to me and stopped, his body about eight inches away. I could almost feel the heat radiating off of him as his passions tried to overtake him. He seemed to be warring with himself. I felt the same way. Almost unable to move, afraid I'd move toward him instead of away, toward the door. His breathing was growing heavier and I realized my heartrate had spiked, I felt my pulse in the side of my neck, almost kicking its way out of my skin.

God help me.

I took a deliberate step back, adding more than a foot of additional distance between us. "I'm ready to go home," I said, my voice small, asking for him to take me somewhere we'd both be safe from making mistakes.

"Right," he said, and flexed his jaw. His eyes seemed to flex as well as the battle of his thoughts intensified. He gazed at me, considering something. Then he wet his lips and pressed them together, keeping his thoughts to himself. "Yeah, let's get going," he said softly. "I need to get you home so I won't...so I won't try to rush us into things too fast." He gave me an apologetic look.

"A-huh," I agreed.

"Give me a sec while I turn off the lights and set the alarm. Be right back." He jogged off, powered down the restaurant lights up front, turned off the music, and came around to the stoves to make sure they were all turned off again. He marched up to me, clicked his heels together, head high and offered me his elbow to slip my arm through to escort me out, never looking down, choosing to be the gentleman once more.

Guess our taste test is over for the night. Good thing. I think I need to go on a David diet.

Pickers

Chapter Eighteen

texted Elisabeth on the way home asking her to come meet us in the entrance to say good night to David. I didn't want to tell her I was afraid that if she didn't, I may not be able to send him home because I'd want to sneak him upstairs to my room and make passionate love to him all night. I needed her to help me maintain my self-control and self-respect. I didn't want to make an impulsive decision based upon hormones, chemistry and sex drive. I knew logically those instincts were the temporary superficial aspects of relationships designed to draw people together. But they weren't the ones that truly mattered like unconditional love, emotional intimacy, earned trust, and mutual respect. I felt sure that somewhere between the two spectrums, a deep passion could thrive when nurtured into becoming a healthy balance of all those things.

Our drive home was full of small talk. Nothing too deep or too revealing. I think we both were afraid to get any more intimate right now, even if it was only through communicating personal things about ourselves. We resigned to talking about our latest show addictions in between the madness of studying for our college finals we'd just finished up. Now that the semester was over, he was hooked on *American Pickers* as was I. It turned out to be a great small talk topic. Light, fun, and interesting.

What I didn't tell him was that my interest in the show had been birthed out of finding myself in an antique shop in Italy where I roamed through the ultimate assortment of collectables and historical artifacts. It had been the most remarkable antique shop I'd ever been in. In fact, it had been interdimensional, existing in a moment within space-time, never aging or deteriorating, just like Angelica and Obadiah, the shop owners. It had also been where I'd discovered a concealed door behind wall tapestries, revealing a deeper room within. A room that stretched into unfathomable dimensions and held a book of secrets, hidden there, waiting for me to come extract it.

By the time we pulled up to the house and David checked all the mirrors – ever the watchful protector – we were playfully arguing over if Frank from the show would lose to Frank from Kate's Café, if they were ever locked in a negotiation over an antique.

"Come on now," David said laughing. "You can't possibly think that Frank would give in! He's too stubborn!"

"Yes, but all he'd have to do is wave some grilled franks in front of Frank's nose, and he'd be done for! He would give into any price if it meant he was getting fed," I argued, laughing at the absurdity of the visual I was getting.

"Wait, wait. Which Frank are you referring to again? Gable or Fritz?" David chuckled, giving me a confused expression.

"You know what I was sayin'. Frank Fritz!" I laughed, smacking him on the shoulder. It was the first time I'd touched him the whole way home, playing it safe and keeping my paws to myself.

"Weenie lover or feeder?" David snickered.

"David!" I bust out laughing. "He's the one wanting to eat the hotdog!"

"Oh, then you might be right," David surrendered, his lopsided grin ever so charming.

"Hey, you coming inside to say hi to Liz?" I asked, making sure my tone was light and expectation free.

"Naw, not tonight. I don't want to wear out my welcome," David said casually. "Tell her hi for me, okay?" David requested.

"Sure thing. Will do." I reached for my door handle but David lightly placed his hand on my arm, stopping me.

"Allow me," David smiled and got out of the Jeep on his side first. He looked around, taking his time to study the shadows, the bushes alongside the neighbors' houses, and the parked cars on the street before walking around to my side of the Jeep. He opened my door for me, offering me his hand to help me out.

"Thanks," I took his hand and climbed out, biting my lip, unsure if I should risk kissing him or just hug him. What was safe? What does he expect me to do?

"I'll walk you to the door." David offered me his elbow again and I slid my hand through it. We walked in silence to my front door. I saw the camera light blinking red; our motion having activated it. David pointed to the camera and nodded. "I like the upgraded security by the way. I meant to tell Elisabeth I was impressed when I spotted it yesterday."

"How do you know I didn't pick it out?" I pretended to be annoyed by his accurate assumption.

David chuckled and glanced down at me, his eyebrows raised. "Well, she's been trained for safety and security. It was just a guess."

"Whelp, you're right again," I shrugged and stopped at my door, pulling my arm out from his and swaying my shoulders from side to side a little, still unsure if I should kiss him or not.

"Sleep well Melanie," David's voice was low and he leaned down. I lifted my face up thinking he was going to kiss my lips, but he dodged my mouth and kissed my cheek. He smiled and tapped my chin with the knuckle of his index finger before turning away to walk back down the sidewalk and around to his side of the Jeep.

"Um, David!" I called after him. He stopped to look at me, a little hope in his eyes. "Thank you for all your help today. For everything you shared with me. For instructing me, and for a perfectly wonderful dinner. I can't even begin to tell you how much it means to me," I gushed, my words coming out urgently. I needed him to know how much I appreciated him before our day and night together was officially over.

"It is my honor, Melanie Olivia Bishop," His voice was warm and he smiled at me, pausing for a moment to look at me standing under the light of the door. Then he reluctantly climbed back in the Jeep and nodded, waiting to see me enter the house before he'd leave.

I unlocked the door and waved at him once I was in the threshold. He waved back and I leaned against the open door, feeling my heart ache as he put the Jeep in gear and drove away, the silhouette of his hand still raised in good-bye imprinting my mind with a desperate desire to run after him.

Instead, I watched him leave, finding this new array of emotions an intriguing experience.

"I love you," I whispered almost silently, afraid the world would hear me.

"I knew you did," Elisabeth's voice said clearly from behind me.

"Auh!" I spun, startled at her silent approach. "Will you *stop* scaring the living turds out of me!" I yelled, nearly laughing at my own ridiculous shriek.

Liz was jogging backwards laughing, hands out. "Down girl. Be nice."

"I'll show you nice!" I closed the door and locked it then spun, hopping on one foot to take off my tennis shoe. I chucked it at her, laughing harder as it whizzed by and skittered across the kitchen floor behind her. Dexter howled and dashed away, his tail a fluff of scared frizz.

"Oh no! Dexter! Aw, come here baby. Come here," I called after my terrorized cat. I heard him tell me off with a growling meow. "Fine. You'll forgive me later when I have treaties. You'll see."

"So, how'd it go?" Liz asked, her eyes alight with excitement and lingering laughter.

"Which part?" I returned her excited look with one of my own.

"Start with...all of it!" Liz demanded, plopping herself on the couch and crossing her legs under her, hands in her lap expectantly.

"Oh, is that all?" I chuckled. "Can't I shower first? Please?" I looked down at myself and signed. "I'm a sticky sweaty mess." I looked up at the sound of Liz roaring. She was rocking backwards and forwards holding her gut. "What?" I whined, narrowing my eyes at her.

"How sticky?" Liz said tauntingly.

"Liz!" I whispered horrified! "We didn't!" I burst out defensively.

"But you *almost* did." She pressed her lips together, trying to contain her outbursts.

"How in the world did you know that?" I threw my hands in the air.

Liz just smiled mischievously at me.

"Elisabeth Becker?" I walked around the couch to stand in front of her, hands on my hips, with a mother-make-child-tell-truth look on my face.

"Well, would you like the clinical answer or the friend answer?" Liz smart mouthed, straightening up and grinning like she was a cat who just ate the puppy. Um, yes, I said *puppy*. Liz never was one to do the "normal" thing and act predictably, like a cat eating a guppy instead of a puppy.

"I'm going to kick you into the middle of next week if you don't spit it out," I threatened uselessly.

"With one shoe?" Liz glanced down at my socked foot and back up at me, her expression frisky.

"Yes! With one shoe!" I burst out laughing.

"Okay then, hold your shoestrings. Well, I heard you tell the back of David's head that you love him after he drove away."

"You were eavesdropping, you sneaky little spy."

"You're glowing."

"No, I'm not! It's perspiration!"

"You're voice on the phone was all dreamy."

"I was relaxed! It had been a big meal!"

"You look all tussled."

"We were practicing self-defense moves, remember?"

"Your hair has been fingerpicked."

"How can you *possibly* know that?"

"You smell like his cologne."

"We were wrestling!"

"You said you got a little taste of *luv*," Liz mimicked my voice on the phone earlier.

"I was referring to our first date! He danced with me!"

"He didn't walk you inside."

"He wanted to give us some *space* so we wouldn't keep—"

"He didn't walk you inside because he didn't want to have to look *me* in the eyes. He knows I'd know. And he feels guilty about how far he almost took things with you tonight," Liz sounded one-hundred percent sure of herself.

"How can you possibly know that? You didn't even see him when he dropped me off," I questioned her, amazed and bewildered.

"Sure, I did," Liz pointed to the digital display on the wall next to the door. "I watched the whole thing. Don't forget, we have perimeter warnings we can turn on."

"Oh. My. God." I sat down next to Liz and glared at her.

"I bet he noticed the security system when he was over here yesterday. He's observant. He probably saw where all the visible cameras were too and the digital display panel. Did he mention them?" Liz asked knowingly.

"I hate you sometimes," I growled, crossing my arms like a pouting child.

"He did, didn't he?"

"Yes. He said he liked the upgraded security system." I sighed. "I hate it that you're almost always right."

"Almost?" Liz asked.

"Fine! Always!" I laughed and smacked her shoulder. "So, what did you *see*," I exaggerated the word "see", dragging out the "e" as I waved my hand at her.

"He looked tempted, even longingly at you. But already guilty as hell. He knows I'd read him. He didn't want to embarrass you by having me question him in front of you." Liz patted my leg.

"Poor guy," I sighed.

"Tell me. Did you call me on your own the second time or did he have to remind you to call?" Liz asked, her left eyebrow going up in inquisition.

"He said you were probably ready for a check-in," I frowned at her, puffing out my bottom lip as I saw where she was headed.

"He was already considering my pending reaction to your...physical expression or affection toward one another," Liz sat back against her cushion, a small smile on her mouth.

"I feel bad he has to worry about upsetting you. But wait! Liz, why would he be worried about you being upset?" I questioned, shifting to face her on the couch.

"I assume it's because he sees me like your adoptive big sister and in a way, like an emotional mother to you. He wants to be respectful and make a good impression since he knows I already looked into him. And I'd bet, when he is ready to ask you to marry him, he'll come ask me first, too," Liz smiled approvingly at me.

"Married!" I shot up off the couch. "Why would you say that Liz?" I asked, a suspicion forming in my gut that sent the butterflies into a tumbling frenzy.

"Don't worry. He hasn't asked me, *yet!*" Liz chortled.

"Oh, thank God," I breathed, and plopped back down.

Liz looked at me carefully, reading my tells and all my unspoken thoughts. "Mel, why? What did he say?"

I snuck a peek at her and looked back down and away. Did I want to tell her right now that he was married before? No, I needed a shower first. That was going to be an awkward conversation. Still part of the story of my day with David, but a delicate and sensitive part. It dawned on me suddenly that I hadn't asked him if I needed to keep it a secret. After all, the manner in which Danielle had died and her treachery had all been classified. Or was that something Liz would have read in her research into him? Would she have dug deeper and accessed classified files if she thought it was necessary to vet him before giving him her blessing?

I stood up and stretched. "Later. I need to shower first, Liz," I said casually.

I didn't know how to bring it up or how to ask her if she had known. If she had, she'd kept it from me. Had she known that the man I was falling in love with had killed his first wife in a horrible situation of unforeseeable circumstances that included, treachery, espionage, and coverups? If she had known, what difference would it have made? She wouldn't have been able to tell me. It was classified! She'd have to just wait to see if he would ever tell me on his own. Had that been what they'd been talking about outside for so long last night? Or was it the silly fantasy I'd had about what my favorite flowers were? Somehow, I doubted it had been anything too mundane.

"Okay, take your time." Liz gave me her nonthreatening, easygoing face, her eyes roaming over my expression like she was reading a book. She probably was. The open-faced book of Mel.

"See ya in a few," I wandered off, careful not to rush or run. I suddenly wanted to hide my face from her so I could think things through. How was I going to tell her about everything David had shared? Had David broken any kind of military law by telling me? Would I be, if I told her? Had he been allowed to pick who he'd tell being that he was a key player in the classified story? Could I tell her? It was classified, but would her clearance level allow her to know? I didn't know. I needed to ask David.

I headed upstairs to my bedroom, pulling out my phone as I went. I entered my room and went to my dresser, opening my drawer to grab my pajamas and clean underwear while the phone rang. On the third ring David picked up.

"Hi Melanie. Everything okay?" He sounded relaxed and I heard the Jeep engine downshifting.

"Yep. Sorry to bug you," I said quietly, not wanting Elisabeth to hear me.

"You never have to apologize for calling me Melanie. You're never in the way or a bother."

David, I love your voice when you say nice things to me.

"Thanks David," I could hear the dreaminess in my own voice and I blanched. Liz was right! "Um, I wanted to ask...Danielle...am I allowed...to talk to Liz about...*it*? Or is that bad 'cause it's...ya know?" I tried to be cryptic. I wasn't sure if the NSA or CIA or who knows what, screened calls for certain words and phrases, but I was pretty sure Liz had hinted to me once or twice that they did.

David paused, nearly silent on the other end of the phone.

"David?" I asked quietly.

"Yes. You can talk to her about my marriage, but not about *how* it ended exactly," David sounded distant and careful.

"So, she passed...in war."

"The official report that I shared with you, the non-classified one, that would be what you should tell her." David sounded apologetic.

"Okay." I got quiet. I could sense the struggle going on in him and wanted to be respectful. He'd been through a lot today.

"You're quiet, Mel. Does it upset you that you can't share it all with her?" David's concern was tangible.

"No, it isn't because I'm mad or anything," I reassured him. "I'm just not used to keeping things from her. I share everything with her. It's a new experience for me to separate secrets from people I lo—ah, people I care about. I never had more than one before." I admitted.

"I'm sorry I put you in that position Melanie. It's just—" David stopped talking.

I waited, wanting to give him time to think this through if he had reservations.

"You know, go ahead and tell her everything. The full story," David said suddenly.

"What? No, it's okay David. Don't feel—"

"Really, it's okay. Tell her," David said confidently.

"You sure?"

"Yes, I'm sure. Go ahead," David added, his voice sounding a little odd but certain.

"You don't sound too sure. I don't have to talk to her about it at all, I just didn't know if I could or *should*, given that it's—"

"No, really, Melanie. I don't mind you telling your best friend. I understand that it will help you to have someone other than me or Doc to talk to about it. I *want* that for you, for your own sake. It's just that, I think she already knows," David said carefully.

"Why do you think that?" I sat down on my bed, squeezing my pink underwear and pajamas in my other hand. Dexter waddled up to my legs and started rubbing on them, purring excessively. I ignored him.

"She's made comments here and there to me about certain truths are best spoken from their keeper, and the way she looked at me when she asked me if I've ever loved anyone before, the night you were in the hospital—her eyes told me she knew things, and my instincts told me she would see through a lie," David answered honestly, his voice thoughtful.

"That sounds like Elisabeth," I whispered softly. "Thanks, David, for letting me share your story. I wouldn't if you had said no. I hope you know that."

"I know. And I really appreciate that Melanie. I trust you," David said warmly.

"I'll try to find out if she already knew. Just so you know, okay?"

"That'd be great. Good night."

"Night," I whispered and hung up the phone.

I leaned down and petted Dexter who had stopped rubbing on my legs and had sat down to peer up at me with his predator's glare.

"Back off bub. I can talk to another man," I said testily, scratching him behind the ears. It instantly changed his little furry expression from "I want to eat you for ignoring me" to "I love you so much". Yes, cats do have expressions. Oh yes, they do.

Jacked Up Jill

Chapter Nineteen

"*I* feel so much better!" I declared as I bounded down the stairs in my clean pajamas and fuzzy slippers. I was wearing my granny-style panties. You know what I'm talking about ladies. Those full butt cheek covering, hip wrapping, non-wedgie, extra soft cotton underwear we all keep hidden in the back of our drawer when we're desperate for complete relaxation and there is absolutely zero chance of them being seen by any other living soul. Men, you have those too, I know it! But I suspect yours have holes to give airflow to the *boys*. Anyway...

I heard Elisabeth's voice answer but she wasn't responding to my proclamation.

"You're kidding me Bradley," Liz sounded aggravated. "So basic. How did I miss that?" She was pacing in front of the television, a commercial about wet cat food was playing in the background with three fluffy white Persian cats delicately eating the oversized portions of moist food nibblettes on their fine china dishes. Dexter sat in front of the TV, his tail twitching. I could almost sense his envy.

"What is it?" I whispered as I came into the room. Liz was too aggravated for it not to be about my father.

"Okay, thanks Bradley. Soon as Doc told me, something felt off." She paused, looking at me with the residue of frustration still covering her face.

"Of course. Thanks. Talk to you later." Liz hung up and let out a huge sigh. "That witness named Shawn Piebody," Liz paused, flexing her jaw.

"Yeah?" I asked, coming around the couch and sitting down. Liz joined me with an aggressive thrust of her legs wrapping under her.

"He gave a false name. There are no Shawn Piebodys in the state of California. It was a ruse. A basic cryptogram letter scramble. Bradley figured it out. At least his cryptology skills get used for something these days."

"What does that mean?"

"It means the letters that make up the name, Shawn Piebody, can be unscrambled and rearranged to spell the name, Dwayne Bishop," Liz explained dryly.

"What the hell," I blew out a breath of disbelief. "It was him! That jogger dude was my father!" I jumped up off the couch.

Liz looked at me calmly. A little too calmly. "Yes. He was playing with them. With all of us. It's like he wanted to rub it in our faces. *Pie-body.* Pie in the face. Serves himself whatever *body* he wants. He believes he's entitled and superior. It's like he's leaving us the crumbs to follow. Literally." I saw Liz stir, her hands clenching around her folded knees to keep herself seated. I guess she wasn't as calm as she was trying to act.

I sat back down, lowering myself gently, trying to use my own self-control like my strong, well controlled friend. "He could have been caught playing a game like that. He went right up to a ranger and claimed to have seen the fugitive. He *was* the fugitive. Why didn't this ranger recognize him?" I was floored. How stupid did my father think they were? Oh wait, he already proved his point. He had gotten away – again.

"I don't know Melanie, but he's getting bolder. More confident. He's escalating. I don't like it. It could mean..." Liz shut her mouth and looking away from me.

"What could it mean Liz?" I reached out and grabbed her wrist. "What could it mean?" I repeated, anxiety starting to build within me, knotting my stomach up, and making me feel jittery like I wanted to run or hide or scream.

"It could mean he wanted them diverted or distracted so he could go do something else. Or, it could mean he wanted them centralized, where he could watch them from afar, take inventory of the opposition, the collection of force he is up against, so he can plan his next move." Liz was looking off into nothing, her thoughts going places I couldn't even begin to predict as she readjusted her profile of him.

"Do you think he's really that smart? Couldn't he just have wanted to screw with them? Simple as that?" I asked, unable to think of my father as a super evil genius or criminal chess player.

"Maybe. But it's what I would have done." Liz looked at me finally. She tried to mask the worry she felt and conceal it behind a pondering expression.

My cell phone rang and I snatched it up off the coffee table where I'd dropped it. It was David. "David." I showed Liz the screen.

"Go ahead," Liz approved.

"Hi David. Guess what, that jogger—"

"Sorry to interrupt you Melanie, but Mark Jerseyman just called me. Said his entire team spent the rest of the afternoon digging, researching and calling in favors. They had enough solid details and documentation to confirm everything you said so his producer gave them the green light to get the story on the ten o'clock news

– tonight! He said he has a little surprise in it for us at the end but refused to tell me what he was talking about. Said it would spoil it if he told us. You in front of the TV?" David said hurriedly.

"Yes," I reached for the remote, my fingers wagging for it as I overstretched.

Liz, being closer to the remote, grabbed it and handed it to me. "Here ya go."

"Turn to channel thirty-one," David advised. "It should be coming on in a few minutes. He said it was going to take most of the allotted time for the evening report."

"Oh my gosh, I have butterflies," I said nervously.

"You did beautifully today Melanie. As long as they didn't edit the interview in a way that will retract or imply things you didn't say or mean, it should be fine."

"I forgot to mention this to Liz!" I glanced at her. "Actually, I haven't had a chance to tell her much of anything yet. Been in the shower." I admitted.

"What am I missing?" Liz asked skeptically.

"A lot." My tone was apologetic. "But you're about to get caught up on part of it anyway. We're about to be on the news." I gave her a grimace.

"The news?" Liz's eyebrows went up and her mouth opened in shock. "You did an interview?"

"Actually, *we* did. It just kinda happened. I'll explain later. Or actually, you might even be able to put the pieces together on your own if they show Tristina," I said unhelpfully.

"Who is Tristina?" Liz said confused.

"Um, Melanie," David cut in. "I'm going to let you go, okay? I need to call Doc and let him know to watch. Got about sixty seconds until the news starts. I'll let him be the one to call Tristina and let her know to watch so she isn't caught off guard at work tomorrow with questions," David said, a little humor lifting his voice. "This is going to be interesting."

"Amen to that."

David hung up the phone and I did the same.

Liz was leaning forward, her eyebrows furrowed now in question. "What was that about?"

"Well, um...well, just watch." I flipped the channels until I saw the Channel 31 News at Ten programing advertisement on the screen.

"Melanie?" Liz sounded like a distrusting mother asking for her daughter to explain why she ate all the chocolate chips and left the empty bag in the back of the pantry.

"Just watch," I pleaded, and gave her a sorry excuse of a smile.

The music started and the news logo waved across the screen, zooming into focus with bright colors and booming sound. The friendly familiar face of Mark Jerseyman faded in, filling the screen, a warm neighborly smile on his face.

"Good evening. Tonight, we bring you an exclusive interview with recent assault victim Melanie Bishop, and her hero, David Abramson. If you've been following this story, you know that up until now, Ms. Bishop has refrained from commenting on the tragedy that befell her the night of November 9th at the hands of her father, one of the FBI's most wanted fugitives, Dwayne Randal Bishop. A warning to any parents out there, the details and images you are about to see may be disturbing to younger audiences." Mark's tone was professional and rhythmic, practiced to capture the audience's attention and tell a story with factual ease and an unbiased delivery.

"Here it goes," I patted Liz's hand next to me.

"At least you picked the lessor of all evils," Liz said under her breath, commenting on Mark. She knew he had helped me out and let me escape the clambering news crews at the college a few weeks ago.

"It felt like the right thing to do since they came up on us unexpectedly when we were leaving Doc's," I said quietly, cluing Liz in.

"How the hell did he know to find you there?"

"You'll see," I pointed to the television.

"Later today, I met up with Ms. Bishop and Mr. Abramson leaving Picard's Bounty Hunting Academy," Mark continued, setting the stage for the interview to run. "I'd like to extend a special thank you to both Ms. Bishop and Mr. Abramson for their cooperation in today's discussion—"

"Discussion? It was an unplanned interview assault!" Liz hissed at the TV.

"Listen Elisabeth," I shushed her. She shot me a look and then glowered at the screen.

"God help us," she mouthed.

The interview began, you could see our surprised faces as the camera approached us, our disheveled appearance and defensive posturing, a reaction to the ambushed interview. I felt Liz getting tense next to me, seeing my unease on camera making her defensive, pushing her protective buttons to the max. The camera zipped to Tristina, a look of satisfied aggression on her face, then an undeniable "oh shit" expression as she realized the camera had caught sight of her.

"Tristina?" Liz asked abruptly, her tone indicating she had read more in those four seconds than I'd ever have to explain.

"Yep!"

I felt Liz tense more, her body going completely still, her face growing harder, her eyes colder, as she watched, intent on memorizing every nuance, gesture, expression and word.

Then as I stepped forward, toward the camera instead of away, and started working Mark, confidently and smoothly, being led by the Holy Spirit with what to say and how to say it, I saw Liz's shoulders drop and her body lean forward, captivated. Her mouth was open, her eyes absorbing everything I was saying, analyzing the potential impact of my words, the possibilities and options they were creating for us, and for our case.

Liz looked at me, surprise and then pride on her face. I smiled shyly at her and she gripped my hand, squeezing it tightly in relief.

"Um, owe," I winced.

"Sorry." She let go of my hand and turned to watch the TV again. She watched as David stepped up protectively beside me. She sat up straighter, watching him bristle at Mark, playing his size, military experience, and power to the camera's audience. His non-verbal threat clear to anyone watching who may wish to do me harm. Liz was smiling now, shaking her head back and forth in amazement, humor playing in her eyes.

"And thank you Mark, for your delicacy and discretion," I was saying on the TV screen to Mark. "We do appreciate you haven't lost sight of the fact that I'm a human being with fears and feelings. You'll be my first choice if I ever want to speak to the media again. Is that okay with you, Mark?" My friendly smile was honest and inviting. If I was watching someone else and not myself, I would have thought I looked sincere, and even a little delicate, despite my unkept appearance.

"Absolutely, my lady. Thank you! Thank you both for your time." The cameraman had captured it all, even Mark reaching out to take my hand and placing his other hand on top of mine in a warm offering to be a thoughtful host once again, if I'd allow it.

The next scene was us walking away together, victim and hero, a new couple emerging from the ashes of a tragedy. And then it cut back to the studio.

"Wow, Melanie!" Liz said to me, thrilled and delighted.

"We did okay?" I asked, needing reassurance she was okay with everything we had said.

"Okay? That was genius!" Liz praised me.

I laughed. "That's what David said."

Mark was smiling proudly at his co-anchor now back in the studio. Donna was sitting upright, stretched tall and thin in her too-tight blue and black dress, eyes aglow, makeup and blonde hair perfect.

"Mark, what an amazing couple. Beautiful to see something so pure come out of something so tragic. And what an incredibly brave young lady. She's gone through so much and has been treated so unfairly by other reporters these past six weeks. What made her change her mind and open up to *you* this afternoon?" Donna purred, affectively coaxing another compliment out of Mark, who beamed at their writer's strategy.

"I guess she was just ready to tell her side of the story and trusted me to let her tell it her way. Sometimes, that's all a good reporter can hope for," Mark said tactfully, avoiding the chance to spit on the other news station's reporters, but marking his territory nonetheless.

"For those of you watching at home, Dwayne Randal Bishop is still at large." A picture of my father's mug shot filled a quarter of the screen. His cold-demonic eyes seemed to leap out of the TV screen at me and I jumped, feeling chills race down my body. Liz reached over and placed her arm around my shoulder, soothing me but saying nothing as she listened intently.

"We warn the public, if you see this man, call 9-1-1 immediately. Do not attempt to apprehend him or corner him on your own. He is extremely violent and dangerous. Also, if you have any tips that could help the investigation into his *other* crimes, or could lead to his whereabouts, please call the designated FBI tip line at—"

"This is great Mel," Liz commented. "I am just...what a great idea."

"How was your afternoon after that intriguing discussion with Ms. Bishop and Mr. Abramson today, Mark?" Donna asked, purposefully leading Mark further into his own story of investigation and discovery.

"Eventful, Donna!" Mark looked right at the camera now. "After Ms. Bishop divulged the distant traumas of her past to me, I began to investigate the six individuals who allegedly assaulted her when she was fifteen. My team and I obtained the arrest records and the court transcripts, all of which revealed that Ms. Bishop was completely factual with her description of the events."

Donna just listened and shook her head in dismay. "What a shame. This girl has been plagued by violence."

"My investigation also uncovered that Ms. Bishop had experienced other terrible sorrows prior to the gang rape attempt, with the murder of her mother when she was only four years old, and the murder of her sister when she was just twelve years old."

Donna gasped, acting as if she had not heard this before the airing of tonight's news program. "How has she survived so much? So much violence and loss, and with a father so abusive. Oh Mark..." Donna's voice seemed to lose power and trailed off. She had started full of sympathy and let her voice drag down to the depths of despair, an Oscar winning performance.

"She should have said it sounded like too much of a coincidence and leapt to speculate that Dwayne had killed them," Liz grumbled. "She's such a puppet. Says what they write and doesn't think for herself."

"Liz, shh," I patted her leg. "Let's just see how this goes."

"You had it right Donna. Ms. Bishop is as brave as they come," Mark sounded sincere, the tone to his voice said he truly respected me. I didn't think he was acting.

"Did your investigation lead you to the other criminals in her life today?" Donna asked a tone that clearly said she was leading him further into the next big angle of tonight's story.

"Yes, it sure did Donna. I caught up with Jill Zeller and a few of her friends this evening, at Ms. Zeller's residence in Wilton," Mark continued onward. "Again, Jill Zeller was the ring leader of the gang that assaulted Ms. Bishop when she was fifteen," Mark was saying.

"What?" I yelled. "He went to talk to her!"

"Oh wow," Liz breathed. "This ought to be good."

"This must be the surprise he didn't want to spoil when he called David to tell him the interview was airing tonight. Holy crap, Liz." I leaned forward, my hands wringing in my lap, my mouth going dry.

The scene switched to a very "all American" looking, white with yellow trimmed country-style home. The bright porch lights and outdoor London-style post lights lit up the driveway and the country house, giving it the false appearance of a warm and sweet home away from home. A set of wicker chairs and a wicker table sat on the right side of the porch. A porch swing rocked gently in the mild later evening breeze, dangling on the left corner of the wrap around porch.

"How can she live there? It looks too cozy and happy to house someone like her." I wondered out loud, shifting with unease, waiting to see Jill open the door.

"The numbers match the address I saw in her file," Liz confirmed with a shrug.

The camera followed Mark as he approached the steps to the porch and went up, jogging with purpose, his trench coat flapping behind him to look like an old fashion Private Dick. He rang the doorbell and waited, glancing around from side to side in case of movement at the front windows. He rang the doorbell again. His breath coming out in a fog from the cold night air.

Jill opened the door, a deep annoyed frown on her face. She saw the camera and took a step back, her face transformed into shock and fear.

"Miss Zeller!" Mark exclaimed. "Mark Jerseyman, channel thirty-one news. Can I speak to you for a moment, please," Mark asked with a polite tone of voice.

"No! Go away," Jill snapped, her face contorting into a nasty snarl, the valley girl voice she had had six weeks ago gone, leaving her new raspy tense voice. It's the tired voice you get when you spend too much time screaming at something or someone, like after going to a concert.

"It's regarding the night you and your friends were arrested for kidnap, unlawful detainment and attempted rape of Ms. Melanie Bishop. Please, I'd like too—"

"Get off my property!" Jill yelled, her voice rising in pitch to give away just how scared she was.

"Get the _____ out of here!" A male voice shouted from behind Jill, the face of the speaker blocked by the door. The news had "bleeped" over his original curse.

"Oh my God. I think that was—" I began, but Mark confirmed the identity for me.

"Mr. Damian Durante!" Mark said enthusiastically. "I hadn't expected to find you here. Oh! And Mr. Pablo Gutierrez, what a surprise. Hooking back up the ol' gang now that you're all out of prison?" Mark asked boldly. "Are the others here?"

"You'll get the _____ out of here if you know what's good for you," Damian said, pressing past Jill and stopping inches from Mark's face. His dark completion and unshaved face made him look eerily demented, like the darkness in his soul had saturated the outer epidermis of his skin with its toxins.

The camera zoomed in to catch Mark's growing smile at the threat. He didn't seem intimidated at all.

"Um, live feed to the station kid," Mark remarked confidently pointing over his shoulder toward the camera. "I don't think you want to hurt us on film, do you? Go back to prison?"

Damian glared at him and shot the camera a look of pure hatred.

"Ms. Zeller. Obviously, you like hanging with the rougher crowd still. But come now. Surely you have some regrets about how you and your gang treated Ms. Bishop in July of 2002. Wouldn't you like a chance to show the world there's more to you than that?"

"My only regret is we didn't get to finish what we—"

"Shut your mouth, you stupid bitch," Pablo swore, coming into sight to grab Jill's arm, pulling her backwards off balance.

"Let go of me!" Jill hissed at him, yanking her arm to get away. He released her, his hardened face looking much older than it should at twenty-six years old. Jill turned to Mark, her eyes narrowing. "I have nothing to say to you." She grabbed the door handle and made to close it but Damian halted it with a loud *smash* as his big booted foot shot out to catch the door. He shot her an unfriendly look and snapped the door further open as he pushed her out of the way with his shoulder to get back into the house first. She looked pissed and yet nervous at his open aggression toward her, but she rearranged her face and reached for the door again, meaning to close it.

"God, she looks awful," I whispered to Liz. Jill's face was paler than I'd ever seen it. Dark circles sunk in around thickly lined light hazel eyes, making her look anemic. Her thick black hair was now streaked with grey tints and cut at irregular angles around her shoulders. If she had been going for the chic, gothic look, someone had really jacked it up. Her tight black pants and braless black and pink striped tank top made her really look trashy.

"Ms. Zeller. Ms. Bishop is hoping you'll tell the police about the night her father raped you. She's hoping you'll come forward and tell them what you know—to help ensure he is locked up much longer, once he is apprehended. She claims you were a victim of Dwayne Bishop and fears there may be many others. Being that you aren't friends, you have no reason to lie for her, making your word in this instance, believable. That may mean something to you. So, what say you? Will you help her? Will you help the police? You owe her that much, don't you think?" Mark implored, his face serious, void of any humor or bravado now.

"What?" Jill's eyes were wide. Whatever she had expected him to say or ask her, it hadn't been this. "She told you what he did to me?"

I saw real shock and sadness in her eyes but watched with dread as it all turned to anger. Her face hardened into a cold mask as she blinked her eyes lids rapidly, fighting back tears of rage. "That wasn't her story to tell!" She growled.

"But *you* told her. You told a girl you attempted to kidnap and rape. You told someone who you knew would understand, and someone you once intended to treat the same way Dwayne Bishop treated you. Why would you have confessed this to her if you hadn't been asking her, in some way, to help *you*? This is your chance Ms. Zeller! Your chance at redemption!"

"I...but I—"

"I ask you again Ms. Zeller. Don't you have regrets? Prove to the world, to yourself, there's more to you than acting like a criminal. Be brave. Be brave like Ms. Bishop." Mark powered through. His eyes were locked on Jill's eyes, and they both fell silent. She seemed torn. The rage that had infiltrated her eyes was battling with the fearful and broken little girl inside.

"Oh Liz," I whispered, gripping her hand. "Liz, look at her." I said, my heart pounding in my chest. Not of fear or anger, but with compassion. "She's so broken Liz."

"I...I can't," Jill said nearly silently through clinched teeth, her eyes nearly panicked.

"You can," Mark said gently, extending his hand out toward her. "You can come with me right now. We'll drive you." He continued to hold his hand out. He looked past her at the two men behind her, lingering just out of the bright porch light, hiding inside the threshold in the shadows.

"Jill, come inside," Damian commanded.

She remained still, eyes jumping between Mark and the camera, the pulse visibly jumping in the side of her neck as well. "I can't," she said firmly, trying for resolved, but looking cornered instead.

"But we—"

"I won't!" She shouted now. "Go away! Get off my property or I'll call my...I'll call the police to have you arrested for trespassing!"

"Ms. Zeller, please. Let's just talk a little—"

Jill went to step inside when Mark tried one more trick to get her to stay. "Why is the Sacramento Police Chief Christopher Wales, protecting you? Why would he threaten to arrest Ms. Bishop if she asked the police to protect her from you?"

"What?" Jill's voice was pitched high in panic.

"What's your relationship like with Chief Wales? He's your uncle, is he not? Are you close? Is that why he's protecting you?"

Jill's eyes went wild with panic, her mouth opening as if wanting to scream. Two hands appeared from the shadows behind her, one on each arm. Damian and Pablo dragged her backward into the house.

"Ms. Zeller? Ms. Zeller? Are you alright?" Marked called out to her in concern.

"Yes!" Jill hissed. "Go away! Just go away!"

She stepped back up into the light of the porch to take hold of the door. She glared at Mark. True hatred and fear shone within her eyes. "Get the _____ off my property!" She slammed the door.

Jill turned off the porchlight to make sure her rejection of their presence was clear. The light on the camera was still on and kept Mark bathed in light as he sighed, and gave the camera a look that said it was sad to see her being bullied and controlled by men all over again. He shook his head and gestured to the camera to follow him as they left.

The camera panned the driveway as they walked to the news van parked out by the white gated entrance. Five cars were parked there. Jill's red Corvette, a beat-up green Dodge pickup, a white Toyota Camry, a black Mustang, and a large white Chevy GM cargo van with blacked out front windows and big dents and scrapes along the side and along the two center-closing rear doors. There were no other windows except the front windshield and front side windows.

I wondered who drove which car and why they had such a large van. I felt dread hit me as I studied the van and had an image popped in my head of ghosts and horrors clawing at the inside of its walls, and feet kicking at the outside of the doors trying not to be forced inside, trying to escape.

"You catching those plates?" I asked Liz as I glanced around for a note pad to write down the numbers and descriptions.

"On it," Liz tapped the side of her temple. "I'll run them all."

"I have a horrible feeling I can't explain Liz," I said, my voice quivering.

The driveway scene faded out and Mark sat with Donna once more inside the studio, both their faces grave and disturbed. "As you could see, Ms. Zeller seemed to struggle with doing the right thing. A conflict her *friends* seemed determined to decide *for* her.

And even more interestingly, she appeared deeply distressed at the mention of her uncle, Sacramento Police Chief Christopher Wales, possibly protecting her. It may be beyond my duty as a reporter to infer, but I fear for Ms. Zeller's safety with those two men. What I witnessed is clearly the behavior of a woman still being victimized. Or at the very least, she is in an abusive and misguided relationship once more."

"And how is it she's living on such a splendid property? She was just released from prison earlier this year. Being from Redding, is there any explanation for how she can afford such a home?" Donna prodded, taking the time to appear conspiratorial and ask the questions she knew their audience would be asking at home.

She has to know the answer already. That look is so telling.

"Yes, Donna. Research on Ms. Zeller revealed she recently moved into that house after becoming the primary agent, power of attorney, for her grandfather. She was also appointed to be his health advocate. Strangely, he was sent to live in an elderly care center just last month with a sudden onset of severe dementia." Mark's cool reporter's tone was wavering, as if he didn't believe the cause of the old man's commitment to the care facility any more than he expected the viewer to.

"Seems she's been given a fairytale comeback out of prison," Donna remarked snidely, a hint of jealousy in her voice and playing across her face, which she quickly rearranged.

"Well, that is one way to look at it Donna. But for all intents and purposes, you are correct. She seems to have an opportunity here to start fresh. Unfortunately, the present company she's keeping would indicate she's not taking it seriously. It's so sad to see young adults fall back into such circumstances after having another opportunity at life literally handed to them." Mark sounded genuinely disappointed.

"It really is Mark," Donna said with a sad nod of her head, her theatrical mask back in place. "What a waste. Tsk, tsk." Donna pursed her lips and straightened back up. "Any parting thoughts Mark?"

"Donna, I just hope that someone out there *will* listen to their conscience tonight and call the FBI. Dwayne Bishop is a *monster* who needs to be kept off our streets and away from young women. There seems to be no line he won't cross. He was arrested in 2006 for molestation and rape of a minor. He attempted to rape his own daughter in her home only hours after being released several weeks ago, after savagely beating her. And now, Jill Zeller has confirmed, that she was in fact, raped by Dwayne Bishop when she was a young girl as well. I believe Melanie Bishop's fears are founded. There are other victims out there." Mark leaned into the camera, hands clasped imploringly in front of him. "Please, don't hesitate to call and share your story if you fell victim to Dwayne Bishop as well. It's time to speak out and break the silence," Mark finished triumphantly.

Phone numbers to the dedicated FBI line and local police department flashed on the screen once more.

"When we come back, the week ahead! Will we get more rain in the valley and perhaps some snow in the Sierras?" Donna said cheerfully, her eyes bright, mood switched as quick as flipping the channel. A commercial about soap started and Liz flipped off the television.

"I don't even know what to think right now," I confessed. "I'm glad he ran our interview and encouraged the public to call in if they know anything. But Liz, I'm nervous about Jill. Did you see how they treated her?"

"She is allowing it Melanie. And frankly, as sad as it is to see how openly they control her, she deserves much worse," Elisabeth condemned her coldly.

"But they seemed keen to keep her from telling the FBI what she *knows*. We need her help!"

"We don't *need* her. We can do this without her. If she wants to do the right thing for once in her life, she will. But I'm not going to hold my breath or leave the case in suspense, reliant upon someone like her." Liz looked up at the ceiling, hands going to the back of her head as she thought.

I sighed. "Me either. I wasn't suggesting that. I just hope she comes forward," I stretched my arms up and my legs out, my spine extending to arch my back in a long stretch. I yawned, a loud drawn-out sound coming out of me as I felt all the energy I used up today finally hit empty, completely drained.

"Oh, no you don't," Liz laughed, nudging me. "You have days' worth of adventures to tell me!"

I laughed and sat back up. "I know. I know."

"Jill did look pretty bad though. Seems afraid of Damian and Pablo, but somehow empowered to give them orders too. It's an odd relationship. Almost repulsed by each other but possessive too. Like they are forced to be together. I think it is complex and drastically unhealthy. What I wouldn't do to be fly on the wall in that house," Liz commented with a frown.

"Yeah. She looked pretty jacked up. And she looked so old for being in her mid-twenties. Think she's on drugs?" I asked.

"Definitely. But it's also hard living, an abusive past and present, living in darkness, doing hard time, lack of sleep and proper nutrition, living multiple lives. All those things wear on you. Break you down," Liz's voice was softening a little toward Jill now as her better nature of thoughtfulness and empathy overrode her own desires for revenge.

"That's just sad," I said with a sigh, propping my feet up on the coffee table.

We both sat silently for a couple minutes, contemplating what we had just watched. Both of us analyzing Jill and her companions' actions, how they looked, what they said, how Mark had handled them.

"Do you think Mark did good?" I finally asked Liz, curious what she thought about his tact and approach to both our interview and Jill's.

"Surprisingly, I do. I think he was highly professional and respectful to all of you, even when he could have been vicious to Jill, Damian and Pablo. You know he was lying right? The camera wasn't sending a live signal to his headquarters. Didn't you see their news van? The dishes on the top weren't rotated to the correct angle to project signal to their satellite."

"How on earth or space do you know that?" I gasped. "Really."

"Yup. He was bluffing. That took some major balls."

"Wonder if he ever goes armed. I would if I was about to surprise a felon."

"Don't worry Mel. You're working on it. You need to finish your sixteen hours of CCW training first. Wish Doc would buckle down more uninterrupted time so you could get those done," Liz replied, a slight tightness to her voice.

"Oh yeah. I need to do that. I'll call him tomorrow about scheduling the rest of the hours. I don't think self-defense training counts towards that right? Just the CCW stuff?"

"Correct." Liz nodded.

"Hey, what was your impression of Tristina?" I asked slyly, perking up a little to see her expression. I wanted to know if she had read the situation right.

Liz looked at me knowingly. "Testing my observation skills are ya?" she teased.

"Yup!" I smiled mischievously.

"Had she been at the Academy earlier in the day?" Liz asked on point.

"Yup," I tried to hide my smile but failed miserably.

"Is she a past fling of Doc's? Or do you know if she was in a relationship with him?"

"Yup."

"Did she see David with you prior to the camera crew showing up?"

"Nope."

"She misinterpreted your presence there," Liz stated rather than asked.

"Yup."

"Hmmm," Liz tapped the tips of her fingers together in thought. "So, Tristina must have called the news to out you once she realized who you were. She's a possessive, spiteful and bitter sort of woman and wanted to hang out to see you caught off guard for her own satisfaction. But, she wasn't expecting to get caught. And it was obvious from the long hateful look on her face, she knew who David was too and despises him, though I don't know why. Maybe for being Doc's best friend and being a possessive bitch, she despises him for intruding upon the relationship she once had with Doc. Or could be something else. But I do know she hadn't know he had been there. Her expression was too shocked for that. Am I right?"

"Yup. Mostly." My smile broadened.

"Mostly?" Liz asked. "Which part am I getting wrong?" Liz took extremely interested. She wasn't used to being wrong or guessing far off the mark.

I started to answer, then paused, my thoughts spinning. I knew David had given me permission to tell her all about Danielle, but I still felt like it was a betrayal of his secrets and his story. I felt as though the classified circumstances weren't mine to share. I knew he and Doc had clearance to know. But I didn't have any such official clearance and it wasn't my story to tell. It was David's. Maybe someday, when I invited him over for dinner at our house, he could share it with her if he wanted to. But I shouldn't be the one to tell Liz. Danielle's own mother didn't even know how she really died. It didn't feel right to me.

"That's a lot of emotions and a lot of heaviness for what I thought was a light-hearted question," Liz observed, a tender tone in her voice. "Are you okay Melanie?" Liz reached over and took my hand.

I smiled at her, "God, I love you Elisabeth Becker. Yes, I'm alright. Just remembering a few things David shared with me today."

Liz released my hand and sat back, her head tilting in contemplation and assessment of my unspoken words. "Must be some story."

I nodded. "Oh yes. Tristina is—" My phone chirped and I snatched it up. "Oh, text from David. Wonder what he thought about Mark's story!"

I read it to myself, not sure if he was going to say something playful like mention our make out sessions today or something more serious. I wanted Elisabeth to hear it all from me first.

Hi baby. God, I like calling you that, Melanie. Doc couldn't believe it. Boy was he pissed Tristina called them. Said he would call Tristina so she would watch it. Make her wonder if she had a job in the morning. I told him you actually covered for her, but he didn't want to give that away. Wanted to make her sweat. Just got a call back from him. Said she called him after watching the news, wants to talk to me tomorrow. She's going to meet Doc and I at the Academy tomorrow morning. He said she seemed meeker than he ever heard before. I'll let you know how it goes. And

I hope you don't take this wrong, but I may not be able to meet up with you tomorrow. I have a few other appointments I need to keep and promised my mom I'd come over for a dinner. Call me if you need me or want to talk. I'll always pick up for you. Love you. David.

I smiled to myself and started texting him back.
"What does he want?" Liz asked me nonchalantly.
"Oh, just wanted me to know Doc and Tristina saw the news and he has some things to do tomorrow so we probably can't meet up." I rattled off as I texted him back.

I love it when you call me baby, baby. Hahaha :) Hope it all goes well with Tristina. Maybe she'll even apologize for being such a crab to us. Hopefully NOW she believes I wasn't anything but Doc's student. Geez. How insulting was that? Anyway. Sleep well my handsome man. I'll be up for a bit longer talking to Liz. THANK YOU for telling us about Mark's call. Let's keep praying Jill comes around. XOXO Your, Melanie.

"So, where do you want to start?" Liz prodded, an anticipatory smile on her face. "I want to hear everything! Including who Tristina is." Liz winked at me.
"Ooh, tough question. You tell me. Would you prefer to hear about the four days I spent four-thousand years in the past surrounded by angels, demons and biblical legends? Or all the revelations and training I received today at Doc's? Including who Tristina is." I winked and smiled at her teasingly.
Right. How do you choose between those choices?
Liz let out a tremendous laugh, clapping her hands together, her eyes alight with joy. "Oh, my, Melanie! Talk about a tough

question!" She threw her head back and laughed again, holding her stomach, kicking her socked feet out. She composed herself and swiveled her head back in my direction lazily, looking amused.

"Start at the very beginning. A very good place to start," she sang the classical lyrics and the tune to the *Sound of Music* song and we both laughed.

"Right! Coffee?" I said, standing up with a flourish and gesturing toward the kitchen.

"Why, yes please!" Liz said excitedly. "What? You're drinking coffee?"

"I do now!" I smiled. "David's fault. Brought me Peet's this morning. Damn it was good."

"In that case, extra shots for us both. Think this will be a long night, am I right?"

"For once," I smart-mouthed.

"Melanie, your new spiritual life is so interesting. You're like my own entertainment and real life historical and scholastic research resource!" Liz's face was bright and expectant, sitting up posed for anything.

"Oh, you just wait! It was amazing!" I said as I walked into the kitchen and grabbed the filtered water pitcher from the fridge. I poured fresh water into the coffee pot machine and started getting out the *Don Francisco's Butterscotch* coffee grounds.

"Hurry up! I can hardly stand it!" Liz chuckled.

"You can't hurry perfection. It won't taste right," I said sarcastically.

"Not the coffee silly," Liz laughed. "Your adventure! When did you get transported to the past? You said you were there four days but it was only a matter of a few minutes here. At what point in *our* time did you get pulled out and placed in the past? Did you know it was happening when it happened? What did you see? What did it feel like? Was there a strange sound? How can you—"

"Whoa! Slow down girl!" I burst out laughing. "I'll get there. I'll get there. Right after the coffee's done," I raised my eyebrows in challenge to her and snickered. "Wait for it."

"I am waiting," Liz huffed, crossing her arms to look sullen, a small smirk playing across her mouth. "I've been waiting. I'm tired of waiting."

"Ah, thou shall only wait but a moment longer, and in so doing, reap an abundance of knowledge and scholastic insights to feast thy tremendously large brain upon," I giggled.

Liz looked at me dryly and we both burst out laughing.

Forbidden Knowledge

Chapter Twenty

"Sorry I'm late but a call came into the FBI around 2 a.m. from a woman named Betsy Martinez. I had to follow up this morning," Bradley reported, as he entered the front door, excitement in his voice.

"Who's Betsy Martinez?" Liz called from the kitchen. "And it's nine thirty Bradley. Sorry, but I started breakfast without you. Never keep two hungry ladies waiting," Liz teased.

I was sitting at the breakfast counter waiting for her to serve me her famous Colorado omelet for breakfast. I literally had a fork and knife in my hands, plate ready, mouth salivating appropriately to the delicious smell filling our great room.

We had been up nearly half the night talking. I'd told her as much as I could remember of the last few days in the past and about my training session with Doc and David yesterday. I'd left out *how* Danielle had died and simply said she was killed in the course of an attempted prison break on base, keeping the official story intact, and my conscience clear from spilling government secrets, but more importantly, David's secrets. They weren't mine to share.

I did feel guilty about not telling her, but sadly, I was kind of getting used to leaving out details. When I filled her in over a month ago, I hadn't told her about the book I'd found. Nor had I told her about all the contents of the hidden back room I'd discovered at Angelica's Antiquities.

I also didn't tell her about the ram horns I saved from the hands of Mastema and Verin and how the angels had taken them from me to be crafted into the weapons of musical warfare they are meant to be. Gabrielle said that God himself was going to mold them into his shofars. He had called them *Keren Yeshuah*, horns of salvation.

I had told her everything else about my adventure four-thousand years ago. I even told her about the giants turning into demons. Elisabeth had been gobsmacked, her mind blown by the details and accuracy of my adventure from an archeological and anthropological standpoint. Her excitement was barely containable as her eyes had enlarged and her mouth hung open for nearly two hours as I recounted it all for her. She said she couldn't wait to dig into her theological research and archives to show me just how accurate it was. But she was also fascinated by how much it explained things scholars like herself had been unable to fully connect or uncover in her own research. She insisted I was the luckiest person on Earth. Being in the past was so much better than reading about it in ancient scrolls and artifacts. She said she envied me.

In my account of yesterday with Doc and David, I had confided in her about David flipping out on Doc and how we had gone into the Hope Box where David could feel safe enough to explain why his PTSD had kicked in just then. I told her that he had gone through some really tough missions that required him to make horrible decisions. I had left out everything about how David had been helping the military uncover a traitor when he was in serving in Afghanistan and that ultimately, he had been forced to kill his own wife. But I did tell her that his wife was a surgical nurse on base that had died.

I saw her recognize my intentional shifts and stutters as I paused to select my words carefully around those issues. She didn't dig or insist on more information than what I was giving her. She almost looked proud, making me wonder if she already knew the full story and appreciated that I was keeping the secret. It was after all, a U.S. Military classified incident. She should appreciate my discretion as that was what she lived with every day.

"I know. I know. But like I said, I was interviewing—" Bradley started to say, hanging his head in mocked shame.

"Betsy Martinez?" I interrupted, taking a sip of my cocoa-coffee Liz had made me.

"And she was?" Liz added, eyebrows high as she peered at Bradley, spatula tapping her other hand in a playful threat.

"*Well,*" Bradley said significantly, "Betsy Martinez was a bartender at the Broken Heart Saloon in Redding from 1972 to 1999. She recognized your father's picture on the news when your interview with Mark Jerseyman aired." Bradley said to me, coming in to lean on the back of the stool next to me.

"Really?" I exclaimed.

"I just finished interviewing her." Brad looked please with himself.

"What did she say?" This was important. I could feel it!

"Really?" Liz repeated, turning off the stove and rushing around the counter to Brad. "What did she say? Did she have a lead?"

What about my breakfast? My stomach growled and I placed a hand on it to shut it up. *Shh, this is more important! It isn't like you've never eaten before.*

"Hold your ponies woman, I'm getting there," Bradley smirked.

"Well, giddyap cowboy! You're making me stir crazy."

"Okay, okay. I know what happens when you get all stirred up." He laughed.

Liz glared at him, "No, you don't really. When have you ever stirred me?" Liz mouthed off.

"Can you two *please* stop flirting for one minute and just tell me!" I blurted out jumping to my feet in angst.

Oh my gosh. Play later! This is important!

Brad and Liz looked at me, a little taken aback. "Sure thing. Facts before flirting. Copy that," Bradley teased.

I glared at him and cocked a hip. He laughed and winked at me. I waved my hand for him to go on already.

"Right then. So, Miss Betsy the beer babe, called and said she remembers Dwayne when he was in his twenties. Never did strike her as being a young man, like the dark soul of an old man lived in him. Those were her words. Anyway, she said he was way too serious and way too intimidating. He felt dangerous so she tried her best to avoid him as much as she could in that bar. That's where she knew him. Said he used to just come hang out in the corner of the bar and watch everyone. Studied the men real hard like he was trying to recognize an old friend he hadn't seen in years. But the way he'd look at the women who came in, especially those who came in alone, just made her anxious inside. Like he hated them all but wanted to screw them at the same time. Really gave her the creeps. The kind that made the hair on the back of her neck stand on end. And this coming from a woman who served beer to drunk pawing losers for almost thirty years. I mean, can you imagine? What woman chooses bartending as a career choice?" Bradley digressed.

"The point?" I redirected, hands gesturing then springing back to my hips.

"Oh right! Well the *point* is, he's been stuck in her mind all these years. It wasn't just his creepiness that made her remember him either. She said that after he hung out in the corner of the bar for a few months, never talking to anyone, just glaring, one day he went up to some old guy sitting at the bar and struck up a conversation with him. She said she'd seen him watching the guy for a few weeks before he ever talked to him. Said your father went up to the guy all friendly, funny, fun like. Nothing she had ever seen from him before. It was like he was a whole new person. Your father, not the other guy," Bradley clarified.

"Yes, I follow. Go on please," I said a little annoyed. I wasn't *that* dumb.

"After that they were inseparable. Like Bert and Ernie," Brad smiled mischievously.

"I doubt those were her words," even Liz sounded exasperated.

"Right. No. But well, they'd come to the bar together, leave together. Started dressing more alike. She even spotted them fueling up their truck once, all packed up for a fishing trip or something together. And you know what they used to say about Bert and Ernie," Brad winked.

"Brad! Be serious! For once, please!" I implored, afraid I was going to explode inside with mounting anticipation and aggravation.

Brad gave me the hurt face of a misunderstood child and I gawked back at him blandly.

"Okay, fine. You're such a kill joy Bishop. Anyway, so, what else was weird was that old guy had once been a cop. A detective from what she could recall. She'd heard him whining about being fired for some bullshit indiscretion. That was a couple years before he and Dwayne became friends. The other guy was a lot older than Dwayne too. Probably in his early sixties back then. She couldn't remember his name. She thought it was something like Rick, Richard, or maybe Roger.

"Anyway, sometimes that old man would come in alone, hit on women, play some pool, pinch her ass when she would walk by. He always creeped her out too, in the same way Dwayne did. He and Dwayne were friends for only a couple years because one night when Dwayne wasn't with him, that guy got arrested right in the bar for drugs or something like that. She remembers the cops saying they got a tip and searched him. Found more in his truck too. They searched his house later and found loads more. And she remembered that not too long after he got arrested for the drugs, the police connected him to a recent rape right out back in the bar's alley. When they put him in a line up, the victim identified him. But shortly after the man got arrested, he committed suicide in the jail before it ever made it to trial. She never heard anything else about him again.

"The old guy died in June 1978. She remembers because days later, Dwayne nearly beat some young guy to death in the bar after he made a cheap joke about his dead friend. Said your father was really scary. In a crazy fit of rage over it. He didn't get arrested cause everyone was too afraid of him to call the cops. Even the guy he nearly killed. They just asked him to leave and not to come back to the bar, ever. And he never did.

"She said sometimes she dreams about the two of them. Like she escaped some kind of horrible fate of her own just by crossing paths with them time and time again. She wakes up in cold sweats sometimes, still feeling their eyes on her. Like evil was watching her from the shadows.

"When she saw your interview, Melanie, and you asked people to call in who remember your father, she felt like you were talking only to her. She couldn't sleep. She couldn't shake off the feeling that she *had* to call. She doesn't know if any of this helps, but maybe it will mean something to those leading the investigation," Brad looked significantly at Elisabeth.

"Brad," Liz spoke his name quietly, almost trance like, as revelation dawned across her face.

"I know," Bradley replied, his thoughts in line with hers.

"What? What do you know?" I asked eagerly.

"Remember I theorized that Dwayne may have teamed up with a partner or a mentor at some point?" Liz's voice was still distant, like she was still catching up with reality of her revelation.

"Yes," I frowned, still finding it hard to believe my father would have ever shared his "sport" with anyone, let alone agree to have someone else teach him anything, which would mean admitting he didn't know everything already.

"Maybe this other guy was *him*. It fits. Ex-cop. Ex-detective. Trained in the standard crime scene investigative techniques of the day. He would know how to evade police capture, cover his tracks, hide in plain sight. Dwayne approaching him and becoming his friend for no apparent reason? It was almost like—" Liz broke off, her face going blank and her eyes glazing over.

"What?" I breathed, my voice losing volume. Whatever was going through her head was transforming her face into one of horror.

"What?" I asked louder, anxiety building with every increasing moment of silence she made me wait.

"Name?" Liz demanded, turning to Bradley, snapping her fingers for an immediate response.

"Whose?" I asked confused.

"Roger Richman," Brad answered on queue.

"Date," she asked, their shorthand kicking in for efficiency.

"I looked it up on my way over here," he said, all the humor finally gone from his face and his eyes serious, locked onto Elisabeth.

"Date?" Liz repeated urgently.

"June 13th 1978."

"Deceased?"

"June 22nd 1978."

"File?"

This must be what it's like when the two of them are working alone on a case together. I felt obsolete.

"Right here," Bradley opened his satchel and pulled out a file and handed it to her. "I haven't had a chance to read it yet," he confessed. "I was driving," he justified.

"That's fine," Liz snatched it and ran to the counter. She set it down hastily and started reading, cover to cover digested in less than five minutes.

She looked up at me and Brad, her eyes wide and her face grave.

"Brad? Did Stewart get you the rest of the information on Dwayne I wanted?" Liz asked abruptly.

"Yeah, well, sort of. I have a lot of it right here. He's still working on tracking down the old trucking routes and—"

"Pass it to me," Liz held out her hand, eyes insistent.

Brad shut up and handed her the additional fat file on Dwayne from his bag. She placed it next to the other file, reading it in its entirety at top speed, before flipping pages between the two files and comparing things with her index fingers, one on each file. Her eyes were everywhere. I was almost dizzy trying to keep up with their zipping from side to side.

Liz took in a breath and slammed the files shut, a new edgy energy in her.

"Melanie, I need to go."

"Where? Why?" I asked coming up to her. "What did it say?"

"I need to get to one of *our* computers," Liz answered briskly. The "our computer" meant one of the local command center terminals. Which branch of the government exactly, I still didn't know. But I knew better than to ask.

"You have your laptop!" I said confused. Why couldn't she just stay here and use that? "I promise I won't try to peek this time."

"Melanie," Liz said patiently, "It isn't that. There are too many restrictions and encryption protocols that block my ability to access certain kinds of records off site. I have to go in." Liz shrugged.

"But why?"

"Remember the two women I told you about?" Liz answer, appeasing my need for answers. "Maggie White and Jamie Schwartz?"

"Um, yeah. Bodies dumped in the same places as my mom and sister, right?"

"Both of those victims were blonde, blue eyes, about five foot four, and around a hundred and twenty pounds."

"Okay. How does that matter? My mother had auburn hair and my sister had black hair," I wasn't tracking with Liz.

"I know. That isn't the point I was going to make. The point is, there were other victims who matched the description of Maggie and Jamie who were murdered throughout the state of California for decades *before* your mother and sister died. The largest clusters in Shasta County and Sacramento County.

"I need to do some digging before I know if I'm right, but I think we have a bigger case here than we ever suspected, Melanie. If I'm right, we'll be solving hundreds of rape-murders, not just the ones by your father. I think there is a link here that connects Roger Richman to decades of murders before your father ever started.

"It was theorized that a serial killer was traveling throughout California murdering blondes. They nicknamed him the Goldilocks Killer. He terrorized California for about thirty years, ranging from 1948 to 1978 when suddenly, the murders finally stopped," Liz said with certainty. Her eidetic memory allowing her to recall details about things she'd read, heard or witnessed with precise accuracy.

"If we can get our hands on the other suspected Goldilocks rape-murder cases, we might see a pattern."

"What pattern?" I said bewildered. I looked at Brad, he didn't seem confused at all.

Great. Must just be me. The only non-PhD person here.

I sighed, giving Liz a look of apology for my lameness. Liz smiled reassuringly at me and continued.

"Per this file, we know that in 1978 Roger Richman was arrested at Broken Heart Saloon for possession of illegal drugs with the intent to sell, but hey, it was the 70's. A lot of guys did drugs. It wasn't seen as really that big of a deal and would have come with only about five years slapped on his wrist.

"He was an ex-cop. I suspected that they would have known that it would be safer for him to be released than to await his trial locked up with the real criminals. I was right, they were pretty much about to release him on bail. But it got stopped at the last minute. A certain detective made a connection to the unique tattoo he had on the inside of his left forearm. A description of that tattoo had been recently given by a young girl who had been raped in the alleyway behind Broken Heart Saloon.

"She'd escaped before he could bludgeon her to death with the liquor bottle he'd brought with him. If it hadn't been for a mysterious man who suddenly walked up behind Richman and hit him over the head, knocking him out, she probably would have been killed. Her mysterious hero ran off as soon as he'd hit Richman. Leaving her to struggle out from underneath Richman's unconscious body and she ran.

"She was absolutely convinced she would have been killed by her attacker and insisted that while he was raping her he bragged about having gotten away with it before. She never knew who had knocked Richman out and saved her life but she could remember vividly the face of her attacker and his tattoo. The cop who made the connection went to his Chief with his theory and asked to postpone Richman's release so he could be placed in a lineup for his assault victim. The Chief agreed, and she identified him immediately as the assailant," Liz's eyes were starting to light up a bit, but her face was still grave.

"And how is that related to my father?" I asked, not following the significance of the story she was telling me.

"In this file," Liz tapped my father's file next to her, "Is a list of all police encounters your father had thus far in his lifetime worthy of notation that could be located, by whatever agency or department that had made them, whether through his own arrest record, being a person of interest, or simply being present when police were called and noted as a witness. Our friend at headquarters compiled them for us. A tedious task I assure you given the extent of his criminal history and traveling as a long-haul trucker on and off across the entire United States for five years."

"Okay," I nodded, trying to track with her.

"The list includes the stuff we know such as his arrest in 2006 for child molestation and rape, as well as his recent release and the FBI's most wanted status. But it also has stuff we *didn't* know. Such as a record of every parking ticket he ever received, even a wellness check to his home in the early 80's brought on from a domestic violence call by a concerned local pastor."

"And?" I prompted, lack of sleep from our long talk last night and feeling ill imagining all these rapes and murders, making me impatient and anxious.

"*And*, it also lists him present when a patrol car was dispatched to Broken Heart Saloon in 1977. Roger Richman had gotten into an altercation with another patron at the bar and Dwayne stepped in to break it up. According to the report, Dwayne told police his *friend* Roger had just had too much to drink and hadn't meant anything by it. He even promised to drive his friend home. He knew him Melanie! His own words can link him to Richman!"

"But we still don't know *if* Richman really *is* the Goldilocks Killer," I wanted to make sure we didn't jump too far ahead of ourselves. Hadn't she told me before we shouldn't rush into anything?

God, I need more coffee for something this complex in the morning.

Or my omelet. I really want my...nope. No, I don't. Rape. Murder. Who can eat after this?

"When I flipped to Richman's file for the details of the call that got him arrested, it contains a transcript of the statement the unknown good Samaritan made to police tipping them off to Richman's stash of illegal drugs! The man who called never identified himself and never used Richman's name or indicated he knew him personally but instead, gave them the address where he claimed to have seen a few drug deals go down. And he gave them the license plate number and description of the truck the dealer was driving. It was Richman's truck and Richman's house!"

"I thought you said in the '70's everyone was doing drugs so why would they have bothered," I shook my head.

"I'm with you there," Brad said to me. "Lizzie?"

"The caller said he had seen the man dealing the drugs to young teenage girls and seemed to be trying to lure them into his house. That got the police's attention enough to check it out. When they found enough drugs in his truck to sell to a small school, he was arrested."

"Ooh." My brain was clicking over and starting to keep up.

"On Tuesday, June 13th, 1978 at two forty-five p.m. I deduce that your father told police about a crime that would get Richman arrested, mentioned his fascination with young girls, two weeks *after* a victim escaped his grasp," Liz paused expecting to see the dawn of understanding cross my face. She must have been disappointed because she pressed on after a brief pause.

"From that arrest they were able to make the connection. I think your father planned it all! I think your father figured out Roger Richman was the serial killer no one had been able to identify for decades." She looked at Brad whose eyebrows had gone up, amazed by the revelations and still able to be impressed by her after all their years of working together.

"Didn't the bartender lady, Betsy, say she thought he had committed suicide?" I had a horrible sinking feeling in my stomach that even if we could prove that Roger Richman was the elusive Goldilocks Killer he would never see justice.

"Yes, Mel. Richman never saw a trial for the rape of the young girl or for the drug charges. He killed himself while in police custody shortly after he was officially charged by the DA. The file says that the police suspected that an arsonist or possibly an angry relative of the victim had set his house on fire. But they didn't stop there. They broke into the tow yard and blew up his truck too. They thought it was just some kind of retaliation. No one ever suspected he had a partner trying to destroy evidence." Liz paused looking worried.

"I see," I nodded, trying to encourage her to keep talking.

"If I'm right about your father figuring out who the Goldilocks Killer was, that *alone* is remarkable," Liz was starting to look dishearten. "He did what the police and the FBI couldn't do, Bradley. He's much smarter than any of us have been giving him credit for. I may have seriously underestimated him," she looked pained admitting it.

"You've never profiled someone inaccurately before Elisabeth Becker," Brad defended her. "Don't assume that—"

"I'm afraid I have," her admittance was strangled. "Melanie, I need to know. I have to go. If I'm right, I need to let the FBI know as soon as possible so we can reevaluate our strategy to apprehend him and change how we try to get into his head. Obviously, he outsmarted all of them at Hidden Falls Regional Park yesterday. He was probably way ahead of them the whole time." She was growing angry.

"Liz, you couldn't have known any of this. As it is, you were the only one smart enough so far to even theorize that he might have had a partner! How could you have known that he was some kind of evil genius teaming up with—"

"I should have known!" Her disappointment in herself was growing by the second.

"Oh get over it!" I rebuked her. "I lived with that evil son-of-a-bitch for eighteen years of my life Elisabeth and I didn't even know he was *that* smart. So ya didn't know what ya didn't know. Welcome to my world Elisabeth!" I glared at her, challenging her to keep pouting.

"Melanie is right," Brad said, "But now you know. So, go connect the dots and push this investigation back on track before the FBI gets even further behind him," Brad told Liz as he came up beside her and kissed her cheek. "Go on."

"I'm sorry I missed this," Liz couldn't help but apologize.

"I'm sorry you feel you have to say you're sorry to us at all Liz," I rebuked her again. "You should know us better than that," I added, trying to remind her we loved her no matter what.

"I'm just missing a lot of stuff lately, aren't I?" Liz further degraded herself.

"Shit, that's not what I was saying," I replied surprised. "I hadn't meant it that way."

"I should have known," Liz repeated shaking her head.

"Why? Because you're superwoman? Because you should know everything? Even stuff you've never heard or read before?" I said disbelievingly.

"But I did, Melanie."

"What?"

"The officer who connected Roger Richman to the raped girl in the first place was my grandfather, Melanie. That's why this rang such a loud bell in my head as Brad was recounting the woman's testimony. The events sounded too familiar to be a coincidence. It was the case that turned grandpa's career from street cop to Detective overnight. And from there, he worked his way to become the Chief of the Redding Police Department," Liz rebutted.

"Really?" I couldn't keep the wonder out of my voice.

"I told you when I was a girl my grandfather tried to inspire me and encourage my analytical mind by letting me read up on his old solved cases," Liz said with a shrug.

"Yeah."

"That was one I read Melanie. He had the girl's case file. He wasn't a detective yet but his Chief had given him the case to see how'd he'd do. The Chief didn't think he'd ever find a thing, so gave him a losing case on a whim. In the file, it showed that he'd been searching for her rapist for a couple weeks but was coming up with nothing. He started checking recent arrests hoping to get lucky, in case the perp had gotten unlucky, simply to be thorough. When he came across a picture of Richman's tattoo, he had a thrill go through him. It matched the one she had described in complete detail. A tiger eating a dragon who was eating an eagle.

"He had the perp brought in for a line-up and she identified him through the one-way glass. He never showed me Roger Richman's file though, probably because it ended with him committing suicide and all. But even if he had, it wouldn't have listed your father anywhere," Liz held up the file Brad had given her, "This file doesn't even mention Richman's known acquaintances or relationships," She closed her eyes, pulling up the case file in her mind again rather than read it. "Known associations – Former Stockton Police Department Detective. Relationship status – Divorced—"

"Elisabeth, why were you reading cold case files about that poor rape victim when you were just a young girl yourself? I still can't wrap my head around that Liz! What was Grandpa Billy thinking! I am so mad at him right now," I couldn't keep the disgust out of my voice. I was growing outraged at the thought of a young Elisabeth Becker reading such horrible things.

"He thought—"

"They weren't some fictional crime novels Liz! They were real life! About *real* women who had been raped and murdered. How could he expose you to that?" I felt sick and protective of my best friend. The idea of Elisabeth's grandfather exposing her to so much, too soon, was just nauseating to me.

"It wasn't like that Mel. When I was about thirteen, I'd asked him how he moved through the ranks so quickly. So he told me all about the case that had launched his career to new heights," Liz admitted shyly. "I wanted to see the case file but he refused. Adamantly refused me in fact. For over three months! But I was stubborn and pleaded with him. I was relentless! And I worked tirelessly at convincing him I could handle it, until he finally, reluctantly, gave into me."

"But still, he was the adult and you—"

"You know how persistent I can be Melanie. And you know I've always been a little too curious and compulsive in my need for details. As a child, well, you can imagine how bored I was reading children's books or watching kids cartoons. I didn't even have many friends my own age. They were...uninteresting to me. He had let me look over the tame and mundane cases with him sometimes to satisfy my brain's need for data input and puzzles of sorts. It was kind of our hobby, like a game we'd play when I'd visit. I'd see what I could find that he missed. He didn't usually miss anything significant. In this case, which was way before my time, he had made the connection between the rape victim and Richman all on his own.

"It was one of the biggest cases he'd ever cracked and it streamlined his career. Making a nearly impossible ID of someone who had raped a young girl, based on a tattoo from someone arrested on a different charge. This was before DNA evidence was a crucial part of the forensic process. DNA wasn't actually used until 1987 to convict anyone of rape. And there weren't the instant high-tech data bases we have today."

"I see," I said relenting. "So, this was the first time he'd ever shown you something that violent?"

"Yes, Melanie. I swear it. And only after I pushed him into it."

"So, Grandpa Billy might have found out more about Richman if he hadn't committed suicide? And you feel from that small bit you read about him when you were thirteen, that you should have known Richman was the Goldilocks Killer?" I pressed, disbelief in my voice that she could expect the impossible from herself at thirteen years old.

"I never knew who had tipped off the police about Richman. I never had that information to connect. I didn't know about your father's murders and that he reused previous dump sites. It wasn't until *now* that I figured it out!" Liz defended herself.

"Exactly Liz. You couldn't have known. So please. Stop being so damn hard on yourself," I scolded her, my voice softening.

Liz's self-loathing seemed to fizzle out and she started pacing, thinking hard again. Her hands in tight fists, one hand gripping the other as she wrestled with articulating the ideas and connections her mind had made into common English so that Brad and I could understand.

Well, Brad probably gets all this. I'm the one she had to break it down into kindergarten reading level for.

"It couldn't have been a coincidence that the Goldilocks Killer stopped when Richman got arrested," Liz declared. "Dwayne *knew* him! He made sure a victim got away who could identify him later. *He* had a *teacher* and wanted to become the master," Liz said the last words with significance.

"Oh crap," I exhaled miserably, the possibility that maybe he had sought out a mentor starting to sound more believable.

"If he had a teacher, he was taught a certain set of rules. Probably not unlike being trained in the military. It becomes ingrained, a part of your habits, almost like a compulsion, or a ritual," Brad interjected confidently as he paced left then right in thought, glancing at me and Liz.

"Exactly. And from what I remembered of the Goldilocks murders, his killing spree spanned thirty years. He'd been able to elude capture for decades. It seems he may have brought on an apprentice, someone to pass along his knowledge too, to feel even more like a god and able to continue his work even if he was caught or ended up dead someday. He was sixty-seven when he committed suicide."

"How does any of this help us?" Brad questioned.

"Once my brain made the connection from Dwayne to Richman, it kind of exploded. Like turning on a light switch in a warehouse and seeing the inventory stacked up the walls and down the aisles. I started seeing the details line up in my mind. I'll have to get the unsolved Goldilocks Killer cold case files again to be sure my memory is accurate. I haven't laid eyes on those since I was fifteen. My criminal justice class at college had shown some old news coverage from the 70's. My grandfather brought some home for me. I had been so fixated with the stories from the news that I begged him—"

"Liz, stick to the point babe," Brad cut in, eager for the explanation but wanting her to cut to the chase.

"Right. Well, you see, I started looking at cold cases and missing persons reports with my grandfather. People across the state had been terrorized for years. Families destroyed and heartbroken by this Goldilocks Killer. They wanted closure. It was tough. My grandfather couldn't get copies of all the files. It wasn't like they had department computers linked up through the internet or could even email them over back then.

"There was a working theory already that the Goldilocks Killer took trophies from his kills. I'm sure some of the cold cases they tried to pin on this elusive criminal legend weren't associated to him at all and just easy outs, but they were able to confirm at least one-hundred and nine of the victims had trophies taken from them. Earrings, necklaces, bracelets, watches, even underwear. It was clear that robbery wasn't the motive. He always left the purse and cash. He would just take something intimate from each victim.

"Remember what we put together the other day Mel? The ditch off Gas Point Road where they found your mother had previously been used as the dump site for Maggie White in 1973. And your sister's body was found in nearly the exact spot as Jamie Schwartz's in 1977? In a field later rezoned for the Cottonwood High School."

"Yes," I breathed nearly silently.

"I'm betting that Dwayne knew of these locations from Richman. It's possible he's been reusing his dump sites for years. All we need to do is get the Goldilocks files, travel records for Richman if we can, and a list of the suspected Goldilocks Killer victims."

"Wait," I said suddenly, doubts flooding my mind. "Were the White and Schwartz cases included in the one-hundred and nine linked to the Goldilocks Killer because they had trophies taken? Or is that just something you are putting together now that the other detectives didn't?"

"I don't know for sure if they were or not, Mel. I'll need to get their files and they full list of the suspected Goldilocks Killer victims to know for sure. But the victimology matches up. And of course, again, some of the victims on the list might be conjecture so we should only focus on the one-hundred and nine who had trophies taken to narrow our search. We'll need to identify where each body was found and cross reference that with other crime scene locations that followed *after* Richman's arrest between 1978 and before 2006 when your father was sent to prison."

"That's going to take some time," Brad said, rubbing his hand over his mouth in thought. "Records are a lot harder to dig up the older they get. They aren't all digitized yet, Elisabeth. As it is, Stewart pulled an all-nighter just for these and –"

"I know, I know," Liz looked pained but pressed on. "As far as I know the Goldilocks Killer didn't commit crimes out of his home state of California. That's where I'm sure Dwayne and he are different along with their victim type. Your father had thirty years of truck driving and ample opportunity along the way. He most likely didn't keep his hunting ground isolated to California. And the women we know he's raped, all had different hair color, body types and heights." Liz's voice was rushed and excited.

"That's going to be a lot of files, Liz," Brad said again, sitting up straighter and running his fingers through his hair.

"I know, but if we can link Bishop to Richman, and prove they knew each other *beyond* the bartender's testimony and *beyond* the police report when Dwayne defends Roger Richman as his beer buddy, we might even be able to find a connection between

Richman's crimes and Dwayne's! And if we can prove Dwayne was at or near several of the reused homicide locations in California, or had opportunity due to his trucking routes, and we can link him to victims of other crimes dumped at those same sites, it's more than enough legal precedence to take it to the DA and have additional charges pressed. If we find murders that cross state lines, it's a guaranteed FBI case, and we can let them have it! But we'll have to build a rock-solid foundation," Liz finished, her eyes gleaming with determination and a hunger for justice.

"But we'll need more evidence than just his whereabouts lining up with homicide victims or knowing Richman, don't we?" I asked.

"Eventually, yes. But it's a place to start. If he used more than these two sites Richman used, it establishes a pattern. A pattern that shows he had inside information into the Goldilocks Killer dump sites since the details of where the bodies of White and Schwartz were found were never released as public knowledge. It gives us clear tracks to follow. We aren't hunting blind anymore for Dwayne's victim trail with nowhere to start looking. He may have even participated with Richman *during* his training. If we can establish the links, the FBI *just* might be willing to have the old evidence tested for DNA. Assuming they still have it stored somewhere after all these years! We have a real lead here," Liz said urgently.

"I just can't imagine him doing what someone else told him. Following around another man like a puppy? Not the Dwayne Bishop I grew up with. And why would he be stupid enough to use the same sites!" My voice was cracking with fatigue and panic. "It feels so thin!"

What if we can't nail any of this on him!

"It's possible he only did it to get what he wanted like David was saying the other day," Bradley chimed in. "Maybe he needed someone to show him how to get away with it. Clue him in before he perfected his craft."

"We know Richman used to be a cop. In fact, he had an impressive record until he suddenly took an early *retirement* about six years before he was arrested. According to his file he was actually fired for inappropriate conduct toward an unwilling female officer. Her husband complained to the Mayor, a family friend, who finally did something about it.

"It wouldn't surprise me if Dwayne sought Richman out just like Betsy said. Not the other way around. Dwayne wouldn't have wanted to stay an obedient pup for long. Perhaps just long enough to learn the ropes. Then he would have wanted Richman out of his way. It's even probable he was the man who knocked Richman out so that girl could escape and made the call to get Richman arrested. He was done being the follower. Like you said, he was no one to be led around by a collar." Liz stretched and closed her eyes for a moment.

"This is it. This is the lead we needed," she sighed, relief on her face at having found something significant. "I just can't believe I never connected it until now." She shook her head, looking disappointed in herself and she started pacing again. I watched her as her temperature began to rise.

I didn't know what to say. It all sounded possible. Maybe even too convenient to be true. But maybe that's what investigations were always like. Find a loose thread and keep pulling to see what comes undone and when you run out of string, start looking for another thread.

"I really missed this one, didn't I? Why didn't I see it sooner!" Liz fumed.

"Liz, that doesn't matter right now," Bradley said trying to soothe her again.

"He played Richman and he played the police. He played with the correctional officers at the prison and they forgot to put the GPS tracker on him when they released him! He played with the entire search party yesterday and won! And he's still playing with us! This has all been one big game to him! And I missed the clues! They were in my face years ago and I—"

"You were a kid yourself Liz. You should have been out playing hide-and-seek, not reading cold case files," Bradley cut her off, pulling her back to the present.

"It's just so infuriating!" she stormed.

"Liz, you figured it out now—" I tried.

"Lazy! The detectives didn't even finish their basic investigation into Roger Richman after he committed suicide! Even with the brutal rape of Linda Hatfield being connected to him by my grandfather! They just stopped looking! They told him to drop it and move on. What was he going to do? Defy them as soon as he became a Detective? *God*, I wish he had! They could have found more victims!" Liz was furiously marching across the living room. Her fists balled into tight knots at her sides.

"It doesn't change anything. We still have to find proof and connect the dots ourselves to make this stick. Go," Brad insisted.

"He's right, Liz," I said, my mind spinning. "Wait...did you say Linda Hatfield?" I knew that name. "Linda...Oh Jesus! The young girl Richman raped was Linda?" I exclaimed.

Liz turned to me, a sorrowful look in her eyes. "Yes, it was Linda."

"*Officer* Linda Hatfield? One of the officers who answered the call the night you called your grandfather about Jill and the gang throwing me in the van?" I felt disconnected from my body. This was unbelievable.

"Yes. That Linda." Liz came up to me, moisture touching her eyes.

"She was the one raped by Roger Richman? Oh Liz!" I felt a sob start to grip my chest and strangle my throat.

"I know."

"So when your grandfather dispatched her to respond to the call...he knew about her past. She grew up to work for him?"

"Yes," Liz said with a small smile. "My grandfather kept in contact with her and her family for a couple years after she was raped to make sure she was making it through and encouraged her to seek out a counselor. They lost touch when she left for college. But years later when she applied for a job in his precinct, he snatched her up. He knew she'd have the kind of insight and heart a good beat cop needs to serve and protect citizens."

"Wow, poor Linda. But I'm so grateful he looked out for her. I'm going to have to give Grandpa Billy an extra long hug when I see him again."

"You wanted to smack him around a little bit ago," Liz teased me.

"Only because I thought he had been showing you horrible things when you were too young. I got protective!" I pouted.

"Um, Liz, honey. Let's go. Go do what you have to do at...at the office," Brad interrupted, waving his hand to remind us he was still here.

"Yeah, right. Go!" I insisted. "We'll talk more later!"

"Right. You're both right, of course. I'll be back in a bit," Liz dashed past us and snatched her purse off the living room couch. "Bradley, you coming with?" Liz asked.

"Oh, yeah. Sure," Brad agreed.

"Mel, you good to stay here until I get back?" Liz confirmed, the fury she had been feeling toward herself transforming into deadlocked determination.

"Of course. I'm just going to stay here and relax today. Yesterday drained me dry," I went and joined her in the living room and plopped down on the couch. "And I'm a bit sore," I admitted, rubbing my puny arm muscles and the big bruise on my shoulder.

"Okay, see you later. Lock up after us okay?"

"Yup," I said, still sitting there, letting my legs flop out into the ultimate relaxed position.

She shot me a look and I lazily got back up and meandered over to the front door where I knew Brad was going to exit through. His very sensible dark-grey Honda Accord was sitting in the driveway. Liz would take her own car so Brad could go where ever he needed to after they were done.

"Meet you there," Brad told Liz and exited the house.

I had stopped asking Liz where "there" was years ago. I'd figured it was somewhere they had access to classified information and government resources and computers. Maybe even a local secret office for the CIA or NSA.

I locked the door behind him and turned around to find Liz standing right behind me. "Oh geez!" I exclaimed. "You startled the poopoodos out of me! Stop doing that!"

"Mel, do you recall your father ever talking about an old friend named Roger Richman or any reference to his life before your mother? Ever talked about a mentor or someone he looked up to?" Liz asked me, ignoring my startled reaction.

"Um, no. He hardly ever shared anything personal about himself with us. Most I know about my father's past is that his parents died in a car crash when he was nineteen, he inherited their house, played baseball in college where he met my mom, he moved her back into the house he grew up in and started driving trucks to pay the bills after his inheritance ran out. That's all I really know. I don't even know my grandparent's names or what they looked like. He never allowed any pictures of them to be put up. I don't even know what college he and my mother went to, Liz," I finished with a shrug. "Why? Do you think this Roger guy might have taught him more than how to hunt women and get away with murder?"

"Maybe. I just don't know enough yet. It's like, I don't know. I have this feeling...I think I need to get more details about Richman's personal life. It's just a feeling," Liz repeated.

"I think I know what you mean. Kind of like a tickle to the back of the brain that won't go away?"

"Yeah. I need to go now Mel. I'll let you know what I find out, okay?" Liz embraced me in a tight hug and hurried away, exiting through the garage where her car was parked.

I locked the door behind her then set the house alarm to *stay*.

So he had a beer buddy huh? Beer, blood and babes. Some male bonding time.

Beer Buddies

Chapter Twenty-One

My insides were already twisting into knots as I went back to the couch, once again plopping down gracelessly. No one was there to see me sprawled out unladylike. Well, Dexter was around here somewhere, but he didn't care. He'd sit there and lick his butt spread eagle in front of me.

Guess now we're even.

My fingers were tapping the cushion and I tried to make myself relax.

"Lord, I pray you guide Bradley and Elisabeth to the truth. Let them find the connections and reveal to them whatever they need to know to build an irrefutable case against my father, leaving no shadow of a doubt of his guilt."

He was already being charged with several felonies: Violating his probation on several accounts by refusing to check in with his probation officer as directed and providing an address of residence. Neglecting to have his GPS installed, a fact he knew was a condition of his parole. Breaking the no contact order I had filed against him. He had committed crimes within hours of his release! Not something minor like stealing a pack of gum either, but a violent premeditated hate crime of rape and battery against his own daughter. His altercation with David and running over his motorcycle, which technically was a hit and run, though it was all intentional. Could they call that attempted murder? All that was going to come with quite a bit of jail time, but we wanted to make sure we tacked on time and got justice for his most heinous crimes: thirty years of serial rape-murders.

Evidence. They need evidence! Where can we find more evidence? We need more witnesses to come forward! Oh Lord. There has to be someone else who remembers him or survived.

I knew it had only been less than a day since my interview with Mark Jerseyman had hit the ten o'clock news last night. The National News stations hadn't picked up the story yet but once they did, *if* they did, chances were a victim or two out there might see it and hopefully, they'd come forward like Betsy Martinez, the old bartender. But even when they did, we'd need evidence to go along with their testimony. What if they didn't have any of their own evidence to provide? We'd need to show physical evidence, old video footage or DNA. It couldn't all be hearsay.

We didn't even have Jill's official testimony yet. I had the recording of what she had said to me, but she could claim it had all be an elaborate lie. And since I hadn't informed her I was recording, I didn't think it would be admissible in that regard either. We needed her to come forward on her own. Mark had found her and tried to convince her to speak up but she had been too afraid of either my father or Damian and Pablo. Hell, she might ever be afraid of Chief Wales based upon her reaction. She might never talk to the FBI now!

I have to help gather more evidence somehow! But how? Where?

I shot upward suddenly, compelled by a restless desire to find and seize evidence. I started pacing, my plan to lay low and lazy today puffed out with an adrenaline rush of purpose.

I racked my brain for every little memory that existed of my father making references to his past. Of course, there had been many snide remarks about my mother and her useless family. I quickly dismissed those. They would hold no clues. He had only said cruel things to be hurtful and abusive. He had also talked about how great he had been at baseball, his home runs in high school and college. How remarkable he had been and how far he could have gone if my mother hadn't gotten pregnant. We had all ruined his life. Again, he would go off like that to be cruel and usually before he'd start hitting her or one of us. He didn't even have to be drunk to lose his temper. His anger and hate made him drunk with power.

I pushed those thoughts away too. Nothing good would come from reliving those memories. I needed something else. He had to have said something else!

Your house.

The words swept through my mind with a vivid image of the front of my house coming crystal clear into focus.

"Lord?" I asked out loud. "Is that you?"

What did my father used to say about our house?

Most of his comments about that house had been orders to keep it clean and don't break anything or he'd break us. That horribly old, dark, frightening prison I had been forced to call my home had been like a castle to him. He was master and ruler of the home and we were his servants, slaves and concubines.

The memory of witnessing him rape and murder my mother crashed through my thoughts. I saw him in my mind beating her, blood splattering across the light green comforter and pillows and onto the antique brass bed frame. Then it was as if I was being pushed from the room and their bedroom door slammed in my face.

I shook my head, dislodging the images, my breathing heavy.

My father had always been adamant that we stay out of their bedroom. And after my mother died, if we even tried to peek inside or asked if we could go smell mom's clothes and look at her things, we saw the back of his hand and the belt unbuckling in threat.

Once when he was gone for three days on a long-haul trip, Vivian and I snuck in there to do just that. Somehow, he had known we had gone in there and beat the shit out of us. That time, I had really thought he was going to kill me, the belt had just kept coming and coming. I had lost consciousness from the pain and had woken up in the hall outside of our bedroom where I had been trying to run to hide, right where he had been beating me.

When I was twelve, after Vivian died, he added a lock to the bedroom door to make sure I didn't go in there. It wasn't like I would have ever tried again after being beaten unconscious. I always thought he had added the lock because he was afraid I'd go in there when he was away on a long-haul or off on camping or fishing trips with his beer drinking Nazi buddies. But what if there was more to it? Was that where he hid his trophies? Or had he hidden them near places he would go camping and fishing with his buddies?

Buddies? Oh my God! That's right! He had other *friends!*

I ran to the kitchen and grabbed the phone, it was closer than my cell phone still upstairs on the charger. I had to redial Elisabeth's cell phone number three times in my haste because I kept screwing it up. My fingers were clumsy with adrenaline. Liz answered on the second ring.

"Mel—"

"He had *other* friends Liz! Other fishing buddies when I was a kid! Mike...Um...no, um, Michael Schmidt and Bobby Mueller! They were the ones he'd talk that Nazi crap with and go fishing with! Maybe they know something. Maybe they can—"

"They FBI already talked to them weeks ago Mel," Liz cut in.

"They did?" I asked, my zest fizzing out.

"Yeah. The two of them still hang out together but want nothing to do with your father. They seemed very truthful. They cut ties with him as soon as he got arrested for raping that young girl in 2006. Both of them are dads of daughters and still really upset about it. Said they hope he goes out with a bullet to the head. They were just relieved they never left him alone with one of their kids."

"How did they feel about what he tried to do to me?" I couldn't help but ask.

"They were disgusted and horrified Melanie. They said they wish they would have bothered to pay attention to you a little more when they used to come over to drink with your dad because they had no idea he was that kind of a monster. They both seem to feel really bad about that Melanie."

"Humph," I snorted. "Right. Didn't know Nazi lovers could feel bad about anything," I judged with disdain.

"Well, people who hate can still be capable of love," Liz said wisely. "But I can understand why you'd feel that way."

"I suppose. Oh, hey, maybe they can tell you where they—"

"Where they used to fish and camp with your father?" Liz answered quickly, knowing already where my mind was going.

"Did you—"

"Yes, those areas were already partially searched with dogs and drones but they are too big to be fully monitored. That's what the police and FBI tell me. I thought it was a mistake not to pour more resources into it in case he heads back up to familiar territory but given the fact he was spotted down here in a park he was never known to frequent, means I wasn't right about that either. Now I think he's smart enough to avoid going places he knows. So again,

I was wrong wanting to redirect resources," her disappointment in herself was growing again.

"Where did—" I began, ignoring her self-degradation.

"Up near Lake Shasta, Castle Crags State Park, Mount Lassen National Park, even Whiskeytown National—"

"So too many places and too many acres to search. I get it," I interrupted this time, feeling defeated.

"Don't worry Mel, we'll get him," Liz tried to console me.

"It isn't that. It's when we *do* get him, and I believe we will, we need evidence of his crimes. I was thinking maybe he hid something at the house or somewhere he used to go camping. You know, like trophies or mementos. If we can—"

"Melanie you're a genius!" Liz shouted into the phone.

I pulled the phone away from my ear, cringing. "No, I'm pretty sure I'm not," I frowned even though she couldn't see me.

"Trophies! If Dwayne was an apprentice of Roger Richman, he probably knew where he kept his trophies. It would have been one more show of power and dominance by Richman to show him all his past victories. A way to remind Dwayne of his superior power and superior knowledge. To remind him he was the master. Serial killers are extremely possessive and territorial. Bringing on a pupil would be a point of pride for them, feeding into their self-deluded ideas of being a god. Taking life, giving life, transferring their forbidden knowledge to the select chosen. It wouldn't be because they were lonely but because he wanted acknowledgment and praise," Liz rattled off excitedly.

"You think Dwayne kept them for himself after Richman died?" I asked, catching on to why she was so excited.

"Most likely, yes Melanie. If he knew they existed and where Richman had hid them, he wouldn't be able to resist taking them as his own," Liz was almost running out of breath. I didn't think she had breathed since she stopped speaking a moment before.

"Holy smokes," I whispered.

"You thought of it, Mel. You!" Liz was so proud.

"Well...actually," I confessed, "I had only thought about where he might have hidden his *own* trophies. I never considered he may have kept Roger Richman's."

"If you think of anything else, call me Mel. This was great!"

"I want to drive to the house." I called it 'the' not 'my' because I never felt at home there. Only trapped and imprisoned.

"What? Today?" Liz sounded concerned.

"Well, yeah. It's only ten o'clock. I can make it there by one. I want to...well, not really *want* to, but I think I *need* to go to the house and see if I can find whatever he hid there." I was speaking my plans out loud as I made them, having not really formulated the idea yet in my mind past the impression of what I needed to do.

"The FBI already searched the house."

"But *I* haven't Liz. I know that house better than anyone. I can do this!"

"Not alone, no," Liz stated.

"You're busy, I'm bored. Come on! I can do this. He isn't up there Liz. He's probably still somewhere around Auburn, opposite direction."

"Ask David to go with you," Liz countered, tired of having to tell me no and trying to compromise past her own protective feelings and fear of losing me at my father's hands.

"Can't. He's got something to do today, remember?" I answered quickly, hoping she wouldn't dig in and ask what. It wasn't my place to tell David's secrets or about his pain. That was his story to tell, not mine.

"What is he doing?" She asked.

Damn it.

"Um, well, he has to go talk to someone about something that happened sometime during the war," I said evasively. That was about as specific as I could get. "And he is supposed to go visit his parents."

Damn, this double talk Liz has done with me for years is tough!

I had a new-found respect for the difficulty she must have keeping secrets about classified information and trying to talk around them to me.

Liz was silent. I could almost literally hear her brain gears turning. I heard her take a breath as if to say something, then let it go.

"Okay, but if he can't go with you, can you at least wait for me to get back later? Can it wait until tonight or tomorrow and we'll head up there together? One of us has to be with you. Please Melanie," Liz asked.

Hmm, she let that go pretty easy about David. Does she know something she isn't telling me? Or did she recognize I couldn't talk about it?

"Tonight or tomorrow will be fine. But it has to be soon. I feel it Liz. I need to go up there."

"Thanks Mel. I'll call you when I'm on my way home."

"I'll be here," I agreed.

"Do me a favor?" Liz asked.

"Sure thing," I agreed.

Hope I didn't agree too quickly.

"Can you pack an overnight bag for both of us? It'll be faster to get on the road if all I have to do is grab-and-go once I'm home," Liz asked. I heard a beep and some kind of electronic interference static over the phone connection.

Where are you Liz? You already at your secret office? That was fast.

"I shall pack the perfect get-away bag," I said lightly.

"Thanks Mel! Call you in a bit."

Liz hung up and I put the phone back on the charger before coming back to the living room and plopping back down on the couch. I let out a huge sigh and immediately my knee started bouncing impatiently again.

I glanced at the grandfather clock.

"Ten-eleven," I read out loud. "Ahh," I sunk down deeper into the couch, resting my head against the back. I closed my eyes.

I heard little padded paws making their way across the kitchen tile and I smiled to myself as I heard Dexter advance. I kept my eyes closed pretending to be asleep. Whenever I played asleep, he'd come up and climb onto my lap, reach up with a paw as if to poke me, then smell my face, his nose and whiskers tickling my eyes. He'd purr louder and louder until I'd wake up to pet him. It was one of our sweet little traditions.

Dex didn't disappoint. He jumped up onto the couch and into my lap. Kneading my thighs for a minute before he stepping up onto my chest to rub my chin with the top of his head, purring softly, demanding my attention and that I pet him. I ignored him, pretending to be asleep. His purr grew louder and began sniffing my face.

I giggled, losing the battle of silence to his whiskery attack and insistence for love.

"Aw, I love you so much buddy," I said, opening my eyes and scratching his neck and behind his ears. "Now why can I tell you that so easily but I can't seem to get the words out of my mouth when speaking to David?"

Dexter meowed as if answering me and nibbled the fleshy side of my hand.

"'Cause you give better kisses, you say?" I chuckled. "Sorry little dude, but he's an *amazing* kisser. Yours are kind of rough and scratchy," I giggled, as he licked the end of my nose on queue.

My stomach gave a loud growl and we both looked down at it.

"Guess I can finish cooking that omelet now," I said to Dexter. He meowed and jumped down, heading for the kitchen, tail high and pointed straight up in anticipation.

"Fine, I'll give you some eggs too you little rascal."

Gutted

Chapter Twenty-Two

I was almost finished packing our duffle bags for our trip to Redding. I had been looking for my bathroom travel bag in my closet unsuccessfully for the last few minutes. I'd pulled out almost everything that wasn't on a hanger or on the shoe rack, trying to find the little green and white polka dot bag.

I had left the green suitcase in the back of the closet where the celestial book was hidden. Now would be a perfect time to try and open it again, but with the embossed lion head gone and unable to emerge from my hand, I didn't know how I'd ever open it. There was no other animated key that I knew of. I really hoped the lion would come back to me soon. The archangel Gabrielle had promised he would return to me. It had only been gone a couple days, but it already felt like forever.

"Come on! You have to be in here!" I grumbled, my arms reaching for the last box of stuff in the upper righthand corner of the closet.

That darn bathroom bag had all my miniature travel goodies inside. Last time I used it was when Elisabeth and I spent the night at a little bed and breakfast on the ocean for the weekend at the end of the summer. We had gone hiking for the day in Purisima Creek Redwood Forest near Half Moon Bay. It had been a splendid little getaway.

I pulled down my box of memories and peered down, all the bits of stuff I had managed to save from my childhood were in here. The bright pink shirt Liz had given me to cover myself up with the night she'd saved me from Jill and the gang was folded carefully on top of the box. I went to my bed, my mission to find the lost travel bag feeling unimportant now.

I lifted out Elisabeth's shirt and carefully set it on my bed. I ran my hand over it silently, feeling the rush of comfort and protection cover me all over again just as it had the night I'd met her. I looked back down into the box and pulled out the crinkled blue folder where I saved drawings my mom had made for me before she died. I set it aside, apprehensive about opening it to look at them again.

"Later mom. I promise," I whispered to her, my heart squeezing with a deep ache.

I pulled out my flute music book, flipping the pages and seeing my chicken scratch notes on the sides of the sheet music recreating my own version of the songs.

"Wow, I was good once," I said, humming the notes to myself. I missed my flute. It was still up at my dad's house unless he had thrown it away and gutted my room. Maybe I could see what else I'd left behind and take back what was mine and Vivian's, if anything was left.

I glanced down in the box and kept removing the little treasures. A broken jewelry box of cheap jewelry Vivian and I had shared looked smaller than I remembered. We almost always shared everything pretty or decorative. Being poor, we choose to share whatever we could with one another. The idea of being possessive of personal belongings wasn't a part of our sisterhood relationship and just hadn't crossed our minds.

I pulled out the little Precious Moments Bible my mother used to read to me. I cracked it open and found a little dried daisy inside. I remembered plucking it out of the crack in the sidewalk in front of our house and giving it to my mom when I was three. She had kept it in this little bible, our favorite nighttime reading.

I picked up the dried flower and cradled it in my hand, it seemed too frail and brittle, but priceless.

Just like my memories of my mother.

I glanced down at the page in the Bible it had been pressed in. A slight discoloration of the page reflected the impression of the flower, the dye of the yellow daisy petals and the green of the steam nearly imperceptible but present nonetheless.

"And they overcame him by the blood of the Lamb, and by the word of their testimony; and they loved not their lives unto the death. Revelation 12:11," I read out loud where the impression of the flower had begun on the page. "Wow, cool verse. But kind of foreboding, isn't it Dexter?"

I read the verse again, it seemed to resonate within my spirit. We would overcome my father and Satan with the blood of the Lamb. We would!

When I had told Elisabeth about seeing Jesus as a younger man, no beard grown in yet, kneeling down at the altar and reaching out to rest his hand on the slaughtered ram and wept, her eyes had filled with tears and she had let them fall, wiping them with the back of her hand only after they had run down her face for several minutes. I had been overcome as well, feeling all the reverence and gratitude I had felt that day fill me up again.

I had shared with her the feeling of all his love pouring into me as Jesus smiled and whispered, "I love you more," after I had cried out to him that I loved him. It had almost made her break into a sob. His words had been carried upon the air like a gentle kiss that touched my soul and filled me and as I shared that with Elisabeth, she too felt the depth of that love come rest upon her.

God's presence had filled the living room last night, confirmation that Elisabeth and I were meant to support one another in whatever it was we were both being called to do. Both in the physical world and in the spiritual world. It seemed as if the veil that had separated the two worlds only a couple months before was thinning, ripping and being torn asunder. It was as though the lines between the two were blurring. I was caught in the middle and my friends caught in the current of my struggles.

I pulled my thought back to my box of memories, a smile on my face at having a friend like Elisabeth to share this new chapter of my life with. It was remarkable how God had set us up to be friends. We were exactly what each other had needed at the time. Maybe she more than I, but a blessing to us both just the same.

I looked down into the box and saw a little stack of notes bundled together with a purple ribbon. Vivian had left these under my pillow instead of money when I'd lose a tooth. Since she didn't have any money to give me, it was her way of keeping mom's traditions alive in her absence. The notes were all signed, *The Tooth Fairy*, and written in her most swirly and fanciest cursive. She had drawn flowers and butterflies on the outside and had folded them into complicated little triangles that I'd have to open like presents to read. I'd always known she had put them there but pretended I didn't, just to see her giggle at my excitement.

"Oh, hey you."

I pulled the chubby stuffed yellow bunny out of the box. I used to squeeze it and pretend I was pouring all my *too big* emotions into it when I was a kid. I had always felt so small and powerless and my emotions had always felt bigger than my body, as if I was constantly spilling outside of myself. Bunny, yes, I had named him Bunny. He had been my secret keeper and emotional reservoir.

I sat down on the bed and held Bunny tightly in my arms once more. I closed my eyes and just remembered how it had felt to pour my heart and tears into him. Bunny had once been Vivian's. I had claimed him as my own the night she didn't come home. It was another way to keep her feeling close to me. Her scent was nearly gone now and I strained to breathe in the last of her soft perfume.

"Oh Vi," I sighed, sorrow and longing to be with her threatening to overcome me. I felt tears prick my eyes and I opened them, resting my head on the top of Bunny's head and rubbed my cheek across him just like I used to do when I was little. I squeezed him harder and heard a small crunch.

"What the—"

I sat up and turned Bunny to face me. He looked a little mangled and matted from age and obsessive snuggling when I was a kid, but didn't look like he should be making a crunching sound. He was full of stuffing and fake fur, wasn't he? I felt a thrill go through me and I bolted upright.

"Bunny? Have you been holding out on me?" I set him down on the bed and glared at him as if he should start spilling his guts in confession to me.

"Guts?" I exhaled, transfixed. If I was right, Vivian might have hidden something inside of him she didn't want my father to find. If I was wrong, I would be desecrating one of the last memories I had of Vivian and destroying my *old friend*, Bunny, in the process. But I had to know.

I ran to my bathroom, rapidly opening the drawers, frantically looking for my little manicure scissors. If I was going to gut Bunny, I could at least try to be surgical about it so I could try to repair him again later.

The damn scissors weren't in the drawers. I opened the cabinet doors under the sink and saw my green and white polka dotted travel bag stuffed into the back.

"Aha!" I exclaimed triumphantly and yanked it out. I unzipped it and found the scissors at the bottom clipped inside the manicure set pouch. That was right. Liz and I had given each other manicures the first night at the bed and breakfast.

I rushed to my bedroom, tossing the bag on the bed next to our duffle bags and snatched up Bunny.

"Sorry Bunny. Don't look okay?" I turned his little furry face away from me and held my breath as I parted the matted fur on his back to look for the stitch line. Dexter wandered into my room and plopped down next to my feet, licking his paw and cleaning his face. Apparently, he'd just had his afternoon snack.

"No, don't watch Dexter. I don't want you getting any crazy ideas in that little fur brain of yours."

Dexter stopped cleaning and eyeballed me. Sometimes I thought he actually understood English.

I found the stitch line and carefully began clipping the old treads. As they snapped, Bunny's back began to part, the white cotton stuffing inside starting to spill out as the hole grew wider. I finished cutting a five-inch incision and readied myself for extraction. Carefully, I began pulling out the cotton setting it into a little fluffy pile above Bunny's body on the bed.

"Holy crap!" I saw a little shiny plastic casing corner emerge.

"Phone. I need my phone," I said excitedly to Dexter. I grabbed my cell phone off the nightstand, ripping it away from the charging cord. I turned Bunny around and snapped a picture, then flipped him over and took a picture of his exposed cotton innards spilling out the back of him and the plastic poking through. The pile of removed cotton was visible at the top of the shot.

"Have to preserve the evidence. Show discovery. At least, I think I should," I informed Dexter who was watching with his head tilted, managing to look both confused and intrigued.

I set the phone aside and gently began to finish uncovering the plastic object and recognized it instantly. It was a plastic cassette tape.

"Holy crap!" I exclaimed again as the source of the crunching was revealed. I took another picture then pulled the cassette out of Bunny's back, carefully holding it only by the pointed corners.

"Dexter! What if Vivian's fingerprints are on this?" Dexter crouched down, the unexpected volume of my voice startling him.

The clear outer plastic casing was cracked and fissuring into a spiderweb like pattern. Inside, a perfectly preserved cassette tape remained. I flipped it over. It had no labels on either side. I took a picture of both sides then carefully opened the case and froze. A little scrap of paper about an inch long and a quarter of an inch wide slipped out that had been hidden under the bottom of the cassette, obscured by the spiderlike fissures of the casing.

Vivian's handwriting was scrolled in tiny ballpoint pen inked letters. It had a date written on it, "Sunday June 6, 1999. Dad raping me." I read in ragged breaths. "Oh Jesus."

This was only a few weeks before he had killed her. She had recorded him assaulting her? How? How had she done it? I never knew!

I nearly forgot to take a picture as I bolted to the door, cassette tape in my hand. "Crap!" I rushed back, grabbing up my cell phone again and took pictures of the note from close up and then a foot above it next to the tape and the case on the bed. I carefully put the note back in the case and closed it, worried I would lose it or tear it.

Snatching up the cassette tape again, I rushed down the stairs to the living room. Inside the stereo cabinet beneath the TV was a cassette deck. We had been putting off purchasing a new sound system, having clung to the idea that old was retro and cool. Though admittedly, I was just too poor to pitch in half the cost for the new one, and Liz was too busy to really care about upgrading to the latest surround sound technology anyway.

I turned on the power and opened the cassette deck. I carefully put in the tape on side one, still touching only the edges. I paused, suddenly afraid of what I was going to hear.

"Lord...Lord I don't know if I can do this again," I whispered to God. I had spent half my childhood listening to my father rape my sister. I never wanted to hear those sounds again. I never thought I would have to live through that again either.

I closed my eyes, emotions so strong I thought I was drowning as they came flooding up, my heart physically hurting at the intensity of them. My breathing was shaky and my hands were trembling.

"Jesus help me. Help me." I sat down on the floor in front of the stereo, hardly feeling anything as I thumped onto my butt. I had no strength, my legs loose and my body tingling with weakness, as though I would pass out.

"Pull yourself together Melanie. You can do this. You can do this. You lived through it before and it didn't break you. It won't break you now. Come on. Come on." I coached myself. "Come on," I repeated again, tears swimming in my eyes.

"And they overcame him by the blood of the Lamb, and by the word of their testimony; and they loved not their lives unto the death." I heard the Lord's voice whisper through my thoughts and peace surrounded me, warm and safe. The atmosphere in the room shifted and I felt the Lord's presence fill the house, a hope and light penetrating the darkness in my thoughts and lifting the heaviness of my heart.

Tears of relief began to pour from my eyes and I opened them, expecting to see Jesus or his angels, my friends, standing guard nearby. Instead the room was empty, but his presence was still thick in the room.

"Thank you for coming to comfort me Lord. Thank you for always being with me."

Then I heard a low rumbling and the house began to tremble as if from a small earthquake. The rumbling grew into a deep rolling thunder traveling forward, as if rushing from a great distance. The trembling of the house became a quaking shutter and the walls rattled as a bright light split the air like a veil, right inside of the entertainment center as if the light was opening up into another dimension and the solid objects in my living room were all but imaginary.

A blindingly gold mane and fire amber eyes emerged, the Great Lion roaring in triumph and power as he entered my living room, stepping through the light. His massive paws pressed down into the carpet, his translucent body both solid and unsolid, being both present and elsewhere, in my time and beyond it's borders.

He went silent as our eyes connected and yet, no fear resided within me as the pureness of his light and fire grabbed my soul and filled me with a sense of hot oil burning through me. It wasn't painful, it was strength and joy and hope, swelling within my heart and soul. I smiled, a desire to laugh breaking through my every emotion.

He approached me slowly where I sat, the breath from his massive nostrils blowing my hair back from my face the closer he came. He was still huge, his back nearly five feet tall, his head closer to six, but fear still had no place within me in his presence. He was my friend, a protector and my comforter.

"Are you...are you the Holy Spirit?" I asked him, wondering for the first time if this was so.

Rather than answer me, he lowered his head and rubbed his forehead on mine, as Dexter often did. He purred, and in his purr, I felt love and peace.

"*I am that I am,*" his voice spoke into my thoughts, a deep rumbling voice. "*I am the comforter, the revealer of truth and of all mysteries. I am God's power and anointing that rests upon his chosen. I am the seal, the proof of purchase given to all who call upon the name of the Lord, through Christ's blood. I hold the blood of the Lamb. I am that I am.*"

"Oh, wow," I whispered in reverence, a shudder going through me at the power and truth of his words.

Then without warning, he rushed forward, his massive form filling my body as he entered me. It was both gentle and powerful. I felt fire and ice burning through my entire body and my spine arched backwards, my head upward, my eyes open but unseeing. I felt an increase of the hot oil covering me, filling me up and running over, tingling as it raced across my body. The necklace of truth and mercy around on my neck flared to life, it's brightness blinding me as it floated in the air as if it too was being filled with electrical power and supernatural anointing.

"Oh Lord Jesus," I uttered, air finally filling my lungs as I gasped, bowing forward as the burning and tingling began to subside and slowly stopped.

I blinked rapidly and drew in another long deep breath. Reminding myself how to breathe.

I looked around the room. All was quiet. No trace of an earthquake or room rattling anywhere. It had all transpired in the supernatural realm. I looked down at my left hand and traced my palm with my right fingers. I felt my palm tingle. I knew the lion was there, ready to emerge again when it was near the book. And I knew the Holy Spirit had never left me. He was more than one lion.

He was everywhere all the time, throughout all of time. He was a part of God. And I was filled with his spirit.

I looked up at the little red power light on the stereo. The cassette tape sat waiting to be played. All fear to listen to it was gone, but the dread was still there. I knew it would be hard to hear. I knew it would hurt my heart to listen to her cry out for mercy and beg my father to stop. I knew it would break my heart all over again. And I knew I would grow angry at hearing him hit her and rip her clothes and laugh in her face.

"But she will overcome you by the blood of the Lamb and the word of her testimony. She loved not her life unto the death. She will still beat you," I said with certainty to the image of my father I saw in my mind. "We will take you down."

I stood up and prayed out loud with authority this time. "Thank you, Father God, for your gift of life. Thank you for your Holy Spirit that reveals all truth. I ask in Jesus name that you lead us and guide us. That you lead the investigators and this investigation to *see* all hidden truths, to expose all lies, and to uncover all that Satan and my father wanted to keep secret. I ask that your Holy Spirit will begin to stir the hearts and minds of all those who have knowledge or experiences with Dwayne Randal Bishop that we need to hear. Let them feel compelled to come forward Lord and not hold back. Give us favor and Mark Jerseyman's story favor so it reaches nationwide and all those who need to hear it are made aware of it. Thank you, Lord Jesus, that we will overcome by the word of our testimony!"

I felt strong. I felt ready. I reached out and turned up the volume and before I could think twice, I hit play.

Parental PTSD

Chapter Twenty-Three

*D*avid was lounging in the same chair Melanie had been sitting in yesterday in the lobby of Picard's Bounty Hunting Academy as he listened to Doc's impressions of the news cast last night. Doc had expressed both amazement and surprise at how well they'd handled it. And was absolutely thrilled Mark Jerseyman had tracked down Jill and confronted her at her home. But he was most impressed with Melanie.

"Damn boy, you two really surprised me. Who knew Strawberry was so sly and bold. She really handled that reporter like a pro," Doc commended.

"She surprised me too. I didn't know what she was going to say when he came jogging across the street. Tristina really tried to screw her over," David agreed, resting his arms across his chest and shaking his head.

"Stupid bitch. She's crossed one too many lines this time. Just wait until she gets here. I'm gonna rip her a new one," Doc seethed, picking up his pacing again in front of the lobby door. He looked out the windows for Tristina and then checked his watch for the fifth time in the past ten minutes.

"Chill, my friend. She'll get here when she gets here."

"Always makes people wait. Wants to control the conversation before it even starts. I swear—"

"I don't know Doc. Maybe she just hit traffic like I did. It's still rush hour."

"You're too nice, you know that?" Doc complained, his face softening.

"Just trying to be fair. And don't lay into her just yet Doc. Let's hear what she has to say first. You said she sounded humble on the phone. Maybe she's actually going to apologize," David said with a shrug.

"Not likely." Doc finally walked away from the front windows and went to lean against the receptionist counter. He had left the closed sign on the door and kept it locked pending Tristina's arrival. He didn't want wanderers or walk-ins coming by this morning. Not when Tristina was expected to arrive any moment, and only God knew how long she'd be here yapping. He didn't have a class scheduled today and had called Monique, his receptionist, to give her the day off, paid.

"Hey kid, how was the rest of your training with Strawberry yesterday? You both looked pretty beat up in front of that camera," Doc laughed heartily. "She nailed you good, huh?" Doc gestured to the black bruise across David's nose that was trailing under his eyes.

"Sure did! I was so proud of her!" David proclaimed happily. "She kicked me solid too, forgot it was all pretend."

"You pushed her pretty hard, eh?" Doc guessed.

"Yeah, I did. Didn't let up. I thought for sure she'd hate me. But she's a smart girl, knew it was for her own good," David said thoughtfully, a slight frown shifting his face at recalling his roleplaying as Dwayne and how it had affected her.

"That must have been hard?" Doc half stated, half asked.

"I felt pretty horrible pretending to be her father to force her to push through the paralyzing effects of her fear of him. It took some really harsh words to break her vision of *me* and see *him* in the role I was playing. But once she did," David pointed to his nose and then lifted his shirt to show Doc the dark bruises on his ribcage where she had kicked him.

Doc whistled. "Damn boy. Remind me to wear my body armor when it's my turn to teach her some new moves. She'll jack this old man up," Doc laughed. "Unless you just got soft being a regular civvie and all."

"Hey now, be nice," David laughed good naturedly.

"You two have any *play* time?" Doc raised his eyebrows with a teasing wiggle and whistled again.

"Hey, hey! None of that. I don't kiss and tell," David laughed.

"So! There was kissing, huh?" Doc said in a deep chuckle.

David shrugged with a smirk. "Maybe."

"I knew it! Can't leave you two alone, can I?" Doc asked, his laugh growing deeper at the thought of kissing a woman again, his own masculine desires showing.

David smiled, watching him, choosing not to take the bait.

"And how you feeling today anyway kid?" Doc asked, studying David more seriously now. "You good?"

"Yeah man, I'm good. Got a lot worked out yesterday. Thanks for being there for me like always and pulling me back from the edge," David answered with sincerity.

"I wasn't really sure how our roughhousing triggered your flashback of Danielle. But the mind can play all sorts of tricks on us when emotions are strong and pinned down too deep. They can seep out or erupt with the slightest bit of pressure or change in force. Were you able to think on what might have triggered your PTSD relapse?" Doc asked in a gentle unthreatening voice.

"I did," David shifted in his chair, growing uncomfortable.

"Anything you want to share?" Doc prodded, seeing his unease as a sign he needed to say it out loud.

"Yeah. But it's a tough one," David admitted.

"Shoot kid. We've got time. Who knows when that crazy bitch will get here."

"It was a twisted mix of a lot of things Doc. Honestly, I'm still praying it through. I'm not used to feeling...umm. Feeling insecure," David confessed, taking in a big breath and looking Doc in the eyes.

"About?" Doc pushed for more.

"Myself. And...us man. Us," David maintained eye contact with Doc, refusing to let the uncomfortable admission keep him from voicing his concerns.

"Us?" Doc frowned. "Why *us*?"

"See, this is where the whole twisted mix of thoughts and feelings come in," David stood up and started to pace, working out his nerves, helping himself to process his thoughts.

"On the one hand, I finally won over the girl of my dreams," David held out one hand and stopped pacing to turn and face Doc. "On the other hand, I feel as though at any moment, she can be snatched away from me and lost forever. Remember, I stopped her father from raping her. He could have killed her and he was well on his way. Her concussion and broken ribs. He had already beat her so badly before I got there, she was nearly unconscious."

"That wasn't your fault kid. You still saved her!"

"I didn't act fast *enough*. I didn't obey as soon as I heard the Holy Spirit tell me to go to her house. I hesitated and it was almost too late. In the case of Danielle, I didn't listen right away either. My deafness meant we lost soldiers, secrets, missions were compromised, and in the end, she even lost her life at my hand. Something I have to live with the rest of my life.

"Doc, I worry I will lose Melanie too. I don't know. It could purely be my own fear of losing the only woman I've ever truly loved. Or it could be, I'm concerned her own fears of being hurt and betrayed by men will separate us in the end, something I am desperately trying to prove to her I would *never* do. Or, I could lose her to the violence of her father! If he gets his hands on her again, he'll kill her, Doc. He won't stop until she's dead. I can feel it in my gut. He has to be stopped."

"We're looking for him kid. We'll get him!"

"But...but I also feel like I could lose her to...to you," David glanced away then back at Doc. David shrugged and rubbed his hands together. There. He said it. He admitted it. He was feeling threatened by Doc.

"To me?" Doc asked, his voice growing slightly cold with offense. "Why the hell would you think that?" Doc pushed away from the desk, hands going to his hips.

David held out his hands in a peaceful gesture. "I see how much she respects you. The way she looks at you. I can see that she's seeking something from you. Approval maybe, understanding? I'm not sure," David admitted, no evidence of threat or accusation in his voice.

"Maybe she's just afraid I won't pass her or approve of her CCW?" Doc tossed out flippantly, voicing the first thought he had.

"But it's more than that. She's drawn to you. I can see it. It makes me...feel insecure," David further admitted with a 'well, there you go' expression on his face. "I haven't ever felt this way about anyone, Doc. I can't even articulate into a coherent sentence how much I love this girl."

"Not that I'm not a hunk-a-hunk of burnin' love," Doc cracked a smile, making David laugh. "But I would never take a girl away from you boy. I respect you too much. You should know that by now. Besides, now that I think about it, I think it has more to do with her needing a father, a daddy, rather than wanting *me*," Doc gestured to himself.

"You're probably right. But then..." David paused, scratching his chin. "You look at her in a way I've never seen you look at a female student before." David studied Doc's unspoken tells now, looking for any sign of untruthfulness.

Doc's wide smile faced and became sorrowful. "You got it all wrong kid. All wrong." Doc went and sat down in a chair by the right-hand wall, slouching back to look tired.

"Then what is it man, tell me," David sat back down again in Melanie's chair, leaning forward, hands clasped out in front of him, elbows on his knees, poised to listen and read Doc's body language.

"I see a broken kid, kid. A broken young woman. She's hurting, scared, been terrorized her entire life, and she has too many creeps to count out to get her. She breaks my heart and makes me angry knowing what she's been through. Hell! What she's still going through! No daddy should ever treat his wife and daughters the way they were treated. It's disgraceful, repulsive! When I look at Strawberry—" Doc sat straighter. He cleared his throat and swallowed a lump. He tried again.

"When I look at Strawberry, I feel very protective of her. She done crawled into my heart the day she came in here, all timid and afraid, eyes wide as can be, so locked up inside. Afraid of me too. I could see it in her face. I scared her. Not big black me. Just the big *man* me." Doc pounded his chest to emphasize his six foot eight inch frame.

"I just wanted to hide her and protect her from the monsters. I feel like...like a foster dad or something. Does that make any sense? It's like you said. I never looked at a student like that before. I feel like it's my personal duty to hunt down that bastard, Dwayne

Bishop, and make sure he pays handsomely for what he's done. I feel...it feels personal to me," Doc finished, eyes narrow and jaw set.

David understood exactly what he was saying and knew his words were nothing but the truth. He could feel it in his soul. "I can understand that."

"David, I lost my stepdaughter to her own wild, immoral, twisted ways. I feel like Dwayne is wild and twisted, but more sadistic and devious than my Danielle ever was. Danielle hurt you somethin' awful. She nearly broke you, and you only were with her six months. Dwayne's been terrorizing that little Strawberry her whole life and the son-of-a-bitch is still goin' at it!

"I look at Strawberry and I have this fear inside my gut too. Like, if I don't keep my eye on this one, she's gone. That dread, ya know? A feeling of being this close to losing her," Doc held up his pinched fingers. "It's like a rock in the pit of my stomach just like you got." Doc tried to explain himself, a question in his voice. "It's like...an instinct when you're out in the field, on a mission, to go left instead of right like the compass says. And if you don't listen, bad things are waiting for you just around the bend."

"Sounds like we both have an instinct to watch over her," David agreed. They met each other's eyes, a deeper understanding fastening between them.

"What is it about this little Strawberry of yours? It's more than just feeling protective of her for both of us, isn't it?" Doc leaned forward. "Big Man got his hand in this?" Doc pointed to the ceiling.

"Most definitely."

"I want you to know, my intentions are honorable kid."

"I know. I hear you my friend. I hear you."

"So, we're good?" Doc asked David, making sure.

"Yeah man, we're good." David nodded. "When you snatched her right from my arms yesterday, I felt all those things flare up in me, all at once. It triggered everything. Danielle, all the betrayal, killing her, fear of losing Melanie. I almost went blind for a moment with these intensely powerful and twisted up emotions. It had been a long time since that's happened to me."

"You did good son. You really did. Don't you worry on it no more. You're good. We're good. You're going to make it through this. And for some strange reason, I think Strawberry really cares about you. If she's still speaking to you after yesterday, then I don't think you have to worry about her running away from your relationship neither. Now, all we gots to do is get that son-of-a-bitch and pin his ass to the ground," Doc smacked his fist into his palm and flexed unconsciously, picturing breaking Dwayne's face with his fist.

"Can't wait," David agreed, picturing his own confrontation with Dwayne, his face growing aggressive.

"Speaking of being honorable," Doc changed his tone to a mischievous one. "You better have honorable intentions yourself with our little Strawberry."

"I do," David smiled a little too mischievously back.

"No, seriously boy. You walk the line with this one. She's a good girl and pretty innocent if you don't mind me saying. She's gonna need a special kind of handling and consideration now. You feel me?" Doc raised an eyebrow, and pointed to David. The big man's protective grid up front for David to see without pretense now.

"I know Sir. I will. I'm holding back. Don't worry," David nodded, not taking any offense to Doc's warnings.

"She's got me and that friend Elisabeth of hers watching out for her now. So, you just mind your p's and q's."

"Don't I know it," David chuckled. "Elisabeth doesn't miss a thing. I couldn't even walk Melanie to the door last night. I didn't have the guts to look Elisabeth in the eye," David confessed, looking rightfully ashamed.

"So, you did get frisky with Strawberry? I knew it!" Doc shot up indignantly, his finger pointing to David again in accusation, but a broad smile broke across his face at David's wide-eyed reaction.

"Calm down," David laughed. "I only got frisky a little. It's been a *while*, man. I got a little carried away, but nothing she wasn't okay with or encouraging. Give me some credit. I reeled it back in. Her honor is intact, man. I swear it!" David held up his hand in a boy scout salute.

"You better watch it boy. I know where you live," Doc said with a teasing threat to his voice. "I told ya. I feel like her foster daddy. Don't make me whoop ya ass."

David laughed and held up both hands this time in surrender. "I'll be a gentleman, *daddy*!"

"Promise me!" Doc demanded.

"I promise. Oh, hey," David said, pointing toward the street outside.

Doc looked to the left. Tristina's Crown Victoria pulled up to the curb out front just behind David's Jeep. Tristina adjusted her hair in the rearview mirror and put on her red lipstick before climbing out of her car and sauntering up to the door.

"She still wants to look good for you man. Huh," David whispered to Doc. "Guess you still got it."

"You shut up," Doc scolded him, a crooked smile on his face.

Tristina walked up to the one-way glass and straighten her tight olive green, figure-accentuating top, before pulling on the locked door handle. She frowned and tried again.

"Aren't you going to let her in?" David teased Doc quietly so Tristina wouldn't hear them through the door.

"Yes, fine. Damn it," Doc walked slowly and lazily, almost meandering to the door. He swiftly unlocked it and then pulled it open in a sudden burst. Tristina's eyes went wide as the door suddenly ripped out of her hand.

"You're so bad." David chuckled softly.

"Tristina." Doc stated, his tone annoyed. "You're late as always."

"Um, I know. I'm sorry about that," Tristina said in an unusually modest voice.

"Say what?" Doc acted shocked, placing a dramatic hand on his large chest, his mouth open in mocked surprise.

"Don't be an ass Eugene. I said I was sorry," she pushed past him and entered the lobby. Her smooth mocha-colored face was slightly red, real emotions playing across it.

David stood up, a small smile of greeting on his face. He nodded respectfully, "Hello Tristina, Ma'am."

"David freak'in Abramson," Tristina said sourly. "It's been almost three years."

"Yes Ma'am," David nodded. "I didn't think you'd want to talk to me again after—"

"After you arrived on my doorstep with this giant oaf, declared yourself a widower, husband to my daughter, who I didn't even know got married overseas, and informed me she had been killed? You mean, after you told me you watched it happen and didn't protect your wife? My oldest daughter, letting her get murdered by a prisoner of war trying to escape? You thought I wouldn't want to talk to you again after that?"

"Ma'am, I—"

"Or because after you told me about her death, and I fell to my knees crying for my baby girl, you turned and walked away, leaving me there in the doorway of my home to grieve alone?"

"Ma'am, I—"

"Or because you never once came back to tell me about my Danielle! About how the two of you met! About what her life was *really* like over there. You never once called me to say you were sorry for how you told me or asked me if I was okay. To see if I needed anything! How much could you really have loved my daughter if you couldn't even do that for her grieving mama?" Tristina was yelling now, angry tears streaming down her face, her finger poking David in the chest.

David's eyes were swimming with tears as he looked at the pain in her eyes and saw the love she held for her daughter fueling her sorrow and her hatred. A love he had never truly felt for Danielle. A truth he could never confess to this woman.

"Tristina, you listen here—" Doc started, stepping up to Tristina as if to hold her off from assaulting David.

"It's alright Doc. It's alright. She's right," David's voice broke. Tristina shot Doc a spiteful look.

"Fine," Doc growled and stepped back.

David looked down at Tristina's hand still poking him in the chest. He took her hand gently in his, placing it flat over his heart and held it there. She didn't pull away, she just gazed at him, eyes full of sorrow and hate.

"Ma'am. I couldn't just stand there and watch your heart break for Danielle. I just couldn't. It took all the strength and courage I had left in me to come to your door and give you such terrible news. I...I only knew Danielle about six months before she died. We'd met while I was on mission, delivering injured soldiers to the base hospital where she was stationed. We hit it off. Two months later, we asked the Chaplain to marry us. It was compulsive and way too fast. We barely knew each other. But in war...sometimes in war, Ma'am, you act first, think later.

"We didn't have enough time together to make a real marriage. Those foundational years full of thousands of moments and interaction together simply weren't available in that environment. It wasn't our reality. I would be lying to you Ma'am if I said I knew her like the back of my hand. I was still getting to know your daughter. I was still learning what love was with her.

"I'm truly sorry I didn't come calling on you again, Ma'am. I didn't know what else to say or how to help you. I could hardly help myself. I felt responsible. I blamed myself. I...I wasn't able to predict or prevent the outcome. And...and she died." David's voice broke, but he kept speaking. He sensed she needed to hear this to heal, to start to try to understand. "Losing her the way I did...It broke me Ma'am. They sent me home. I wasn't any good anymore. I was...I am still suffering from PTSD. Losing Danielle nearly broke me." David swallowed, a tear escaping him and sliding down his face.

"She never once mentioned you over the phone or in her emails or our Skype video calls. Never once!" Tristina sobbed. "Why? Why would she keep you from me?"

"She loved her secrets and, in some ways, she was a very private woman. I think she would have told you at some point. Maybe she was waiting to see if we would work out. She never wanted to admit failure, you know?" David gave her a small smile.

"Oh, God. Isn't that the truth!" Tristina acknowledged, almost laughing. "She was such a stubborn girl! Always so defiant!"

David released her hand. "Ma'am. I'd be happy to share with you every memory I can of her, if you want me to? I never meant to keep the last months of her life from you. I thought her letters and calls would have been better than my stories. She was so animated and articulate." David shrugged. "And honestly Ma'am, I thought you blamed me, like I blamed me.

"I did blame you for a while. You were an easy target to my grief and anger. So was this idiot," She pointed her thumb at Doc. "But I realized I was just angry she was gone. It was war. She knew what she signed up for. At least, that's what I tell myself."

"She did Ma'am. She always knew what she was doing and what risks came with her choices," David shot Doc a look. They knew his words held far more truth than Tristina would ever perceive. But it was truth nonetheless.

"I would like to hear your stories, if you have time?" Tristina asked David, wiping her eyes and looking around for a tissue.

"Here woman. Never in my life have I known you to have a handkerchief," Doc grumbled, handing her a handful of tissues from the receptionist's desk.

"Thank you." She took it and turned her back on them to blow her nose and wipe her eyes. "Damn," she complained, turning around to flip her tissue over to cover the smear of running mascara she had wiped on it.

"Don't worry woman. You're always the most beautiful without that paint on your face," Doc commented coolly to Tristina, a slight gleam in his eyes.

Tristina looked at him with appreciation in her expression. "You always did know how to make me feel a little better," she admitted.

Doc smiled at her. "What are giant oafs for?"

"And then you know how to make me feel worse, almost as quickly," she snapped, "Tsk."

Doc chuckled. "So, what did your boss think of the news last night?" Doc redirected, intentionally reminding Tristina of her recent transgressions and unwilling to let her forget it or pretend it didn't happen.

Tristina shot him an unfriendly look that melted into embarrassment when she glanced back at David. "About that. I'm...I'm really sorry I called them. I...I thought she and Doc were fooling around."

"Guess I can't get too mad at you. So did this moron," Doc gestured at David. David stayed silent and gave him a 'really?' look.

"I don't know why but I still get jealous sometimes Eugene! God help me, but it's the truth!" Tristina hissed. "I know I have no right anymore. You're not my husband any longer. But when you cheated on me with Monique, I nearly lost my mind!"

"Woman! How many times do I have to tell you? I never cheated on you! Damn it woman! Monique is *just* my receptionist. Her husband works three blocks down at the Capitol. When for the love of all that is holy will you listen to reason? After all the years of putting up with your shit and insecurities, doing everything I could possibly think of to prove to you I would never do to you what your daddy did to your mama, and you still can't accept the truth when you hear it! So hear me now because I will not say it again! I *never* cheated on you woman! Never! I'm not that kind of man!" Doc boomed, anger and indignation making him appear to grow another six inches.

"I *know*! At least, I want to know that. I just—" Tristina turned away again, hands on her hips, a sob escaping her. "I really screwed things up, didn't I?" Her shoulders shook and her head leaned forward as she buried her face in her tissues and tried not to cry.

Doc's shoulders sagged. He glanced at David, his face remorseful. David gestured for him to go to her. He knew the whole back story between the two of them. He knew Doc was just a hard ass with Tristina because he was still hurt and angry she had filed for divorce and left him. All because she had convinced herself to believe a lie written by her own insecurities and past hurts. David had never seen the big man cry so hard. He knew Doc still really loved that crazy woman. How had he ever thought he'd make a play for Melanie? It was so obvious now. Doc was still in love with Tristina. Maybe David was worried Melanie would bolt because he had seen Tristina do it to Doc. Huh? He hadn't considered that.

"Tristina, baby don't cry," Doc's deep baritone voice softening to a gentle rumble.

"I...I," Tristina tried.

"Now, now. Come here woman," Doc said tenderly, drawing Tristina into his arms and holding her. "I'm not mad at you no more. Come on now." He held her for a moment.

"I'm sorry for everything Eugene," Tristina's small voice was barely audible over a whisper.

"Me too baby. Me too," Doc soothed.

After another moment, she pulled away from Doc and wiped her eyes and nose. She cleared her throat and glanced up at Doc shyly and tried to give him a small smile, but instead, it showed how ashamed and insecure she was. Her heart was written all over her face today, her emotions close to the surface, making it hard for her to hide how badly she wished she was still with him and hadn't screwed up their marriage with her accusations and cruel words.

"David, please tell that young woman I am so, so sorry. I treated her with such cruelty yesterday. I was so rude. Tell her, won't you?" Tristina finally turned to look at David, her eyes pleading, real remorse in them. "I was...I mean, I don't think I could look her in the eye to do it myself yet."

"Of course. I'll tell her," David agreed without hesitation.

"And...thank her for covering for me in front of the camera. She probably saved my job," Tristina admitted, looking down in shame. "If she needs anything, have her call me, okay?"

"Thank you, Ma'am. I'll tell her," David said warmly.

"Lucky Strawberry isn't a vindictive bitch like you," Doc couldn't help but mouth off in a teasing tone for old time's sake.

Tristina shot him an unfriendly look until she saw him smiling, teasing her. "I said I was sorry," she said in a small voice, not quite ready to make light of it.

"Would you like to hear about Danielle now?" David asked Tristina gently, pulling her eyes back to him and off of Doc before he accidentally ruined what could be a good re-start for them.

"Yes, please," Tristina almost pleaded. "Everything. I want to know *everything*."

"Have a seat." David gestured to the cushioned chairs in the lobby. "I'll tell you everything I can."

"Thank you, David," Tristina replied sincerely. "Thank you so much."

Broken Promise

Chapter Twenty-Four

I closed my eyes to listen as the scratchy recording started, I heard a scraping muffle as the handheld recorder was being covered up by something light. I heard rustling and then accelerated breathing as Vivian's voice spoke in hushed whispered tones.

"My name is Vivian Katherine Bishop. I'm eighteen years old. Tonight, is Sunday, June 6, 1999. It's approximately seven-thirty at night. God, I hope this works." I heard an exclamation of fear from a small voice in the background and Vivian's voice cut off abruptly to listen.

The sounds of my own cries carrying in from the other room carried enough influence to nearly transport me into the past, my memories seared in vivid living color for the remainder of my existence.

Loud banging could be heard in the distance from another room. My father's voice yelling nonsense. His untamed rage without provocation or focus. His hatred of life and hatred of us, was all he needed to go insane with violent rage. Alcohol was rarely the cause or catalyst of his abuse though it was sometimes a primer.

"My father is Dwayne Randal Bishop. He's out of control again," Vivian's voice whispered hurriedly. "He's been shouting and throwing things around the living room for nearly ten minutes now. He'll probably be coming to find me next. Been raping me for years. Started when I was fourteen. I'm...I'm eighteen years old now. I can't leave or he'll start in on Melanie too. I can't let this happen to her too! I hope this tape will be enough to save us both. Please, whoever listens to this. *Please* help us. *Please*," she pleaded, desperation and despair clear in her voice.

I could hear her heavy breathing as she tried to gather herself and retain her courage. She was being incredibly brave and I loved her all the more for it. If my father had found out, he would have probably beaten her to death that same night.

Vivian inhaled deeply and rushed on, beseeching the listener of the tape. "Don't let him start hurting her like this. It's...it's," Vivian's voice broke and I could hear her ragged breathing almost consume her. "I'd rather be dead than let him touch me one more time. God knows I've fantasized about killing myself dozens of times. Sometimes, it's almost all I think about. But I can't leave Melanie behind. I couldn't do that to her. She'd think I didn't love her enough to stay. I couldn't bear this life without her. And I can't kidnap her! I'd go to jail! Then she won't have anyone left to watch out for her...no one to protect her. No one to take on the worst of his rages and sexual demands. Our mother is dead. Our father convinced the world he was a grieving husband. Makes me sick...he doesn't know how to grieve. He doesn't even know how to love. We have no other family that I know of! No one I can go to. We've been alone in this. I *can't* risk losing her. I *have* to save her. *Please. Please.* I'm begging you. Whoever is listening to this. Help us!"

Another loud bang from the living room and Vivian's breathing staggered, the fear escalating her panicked voice and rushing her recorded words all the more. "Melanie was taking her shower until a few minutes ago. Poor thing walked out to find him waiting, screaming at her for no reason. He ordered me away. He's throwing stuff at her, missing her on purpose until he's ready to really hurt her. It's part of his fun to scare us to death before he starts hitting us sometimes. He's likely going to be coming in here for me. He tends to work himself up like this, into a rage over nothing, before he...before he rapes me. It seems to...get him more excited. He...he likes violence with his sex," Vivian's voice held pure terror. "I hear Mel coming!"

The shuffling noise again. Paper! It was paper! She must have hidden the recorder under some school papers so it could still pick up the sounds.

Footsteps were heard stomping down the hall away from our bedroom at a quick pace. My father's shouts were carried away with it, growing distant as if he was pacing deeper into the living room or kitchen now. I could almost see it in my head.

"Vi!" I called for her as soon as I entered the room, my light footsteps drowned out by the sounds of his thundering footsteps in the distance. You could hear me close the door securely behind me, as if it could ever keep him out. "I didn't do anything wrong Vi! I swear. He just saw me and started yelling again. He—"

"I know. I know." Vivian soothed. I heard a muffled sound of my sobs being hidden against her body as she hugged me close. "Melanie, go on now. Go hide in your bed. Go on! You know he'll be coming for me any minute now. Hurry," Vivian's panicked voice ordered me urgently.

"No, not again," I begged. "We can fight him Vi!" I told her, my young twelve-year old girl's voice cracking with fear for her.

"No, we can't. He's too strong. You know we won't make it. Go on now. Do as I say!" she whispered more insistently.

I heard a shuffling and small creak as I jumped onto my rusty bed and buried myself in the corner. "I don't want him to hurt you anymore," I sobbed brokenheartedly.

"I know. Me neither. I'm going to take you away from all of this soon. You'll see. I'm working on something. Just be strong a little longer for me, okay Mel? I'll be strong too."

"But—"

"No, no buts. I promise. It will be over soon. After he fi-finishes with me this time, it will be his last. I swear it!" Her voice warbled.

I heard the flipping of bedsheets and blankets as Vivian covered me up, tucking me in tightly to shield me from watching what was to come. My father always knew I was there and thought it was funny that she tried to protect me this way from him. But it was all the protection she could offer me. There was nowhere else he would let me go. He insisted I stay in the bedroom with them. He loved an audience. He loved knowing we were powerless to defeat him. Vivian and I were both afraid that one day, he would switch our roles and make her listen or watch. It was my greatest fear. And I think, it was hers too.

Dwayne's heavy footsteps grew louder as he finally remembered his entertainment stuffed in the back bedroom. The door crashed open with a bang and I could hear his labored breathing as he entered the room, he had already torn up the living room, all that was missing for his rage to be sated was blood and forced sex, then he'd be calmer the rest of the night. With any luck, he'd go back, sink into his filthy recliner and drink himself to sleep.

And so, it began. I listened in helpless horror as every sound brought forth vivid images. It was as if I was a little girl again, hiding beneath the blankets, listening to it all and completely powerless to do anything to stop it.

I began to sob harder, my heart pounding in my chest and rushing through my veins as I listened to him brutally rape my sister once again. It was as if I was letting it happen to her, playing this tape and releasing the sounds of her misery and pain back into the atmosphere. But I knew I couldn't chicken out and end it. She had never had a choice. So I would endure it once more with her. I wouldn't let her be alone again.

As every muffled scream, cry of pain, thump, rattle, rhythmic creak, smacking of flesh into flesh and roar of outrage filled my living room, I hardly noticed that my jaw was locked so tight that I risked fracturing my teeth. The deep rumble of his laugh as he mocked her pain and despair set the hairs across my entire body to stand on end.

Finally, the sound of his zipper going back up and his footsteps carrying away his cruel laughter brought me a little relief. Hearing the bedroom door slam shut, meant it was over.

I heard sobbing and both of us crying. I heard Vivian spitting over and over again, trying to rid herself of his filth. He must have wanted to taste her mouth this time, or perhaps, forced her to taste him in other ways too.

"Vi?" I said in a trembling voice. "Vi?"

"I'm...I'm going to be okay," Vivian tried to comfort me.

"Here," my small voice whispered.

"Thanks Mel," Vivian said quietly. I heard her drinking something, swooshing sounds, then spitting in the wastebasket again.

"Your ear is bleeding." My fright was making my voice shake.

"He ripped my earring out this time. Damn it." Her voice was growing harder again. Her expertise at shielding her heart and mind from such repeated trauma and sexual abuse a terribly sad habit and skill learned from necessity to survive and remain sane.

"Your face is going to bruise bad this time," I said, my voice breaking and growing even smaller.

"I have coverup. They won't see it at school."

"But your graduation is this week!" I worried for her.

"I'll be fine," Vivian replied in a raspy voice. She hacked and cleared her throat again.

In my mind I saw it all as I remembered vividly the events as they unfolded exactly as the recording predicted. Vivian was leaning over the wastebasket again, spitting up anything else she could that may linger in her mouth, trying to feel clean and rid herself of him, but her efforts were useless. She knew better than to try to take a shower. If he saw her, he might attack her again. She would have to wait until he was asleep, if he fell asleep. She took another big swig of my water and swished it vigorously in her mouth, angry tears streaming from her eyes despite her resolve to remain strong and unaffected.

"I heard him on the phone on Friday when I got home from school Vi. I think he got fired again. He won't be leaving for another route tomorrow! What are we going to do Vi? What are—"

"Shh, don't worry. I'm taking care of it," Vivian hushed me. "Listen!"

More raging had erupted further in the house. In my spirit I saw that which I had never understood as a child, my father's angry shouts were at the demons and the unseen forces of hell that tormented him and taunted him, mocked him. They told him he wasn't a man and he was nothing if he didn't have complete control. They had led him into the darkest desires and evil that man was capable of; taking the free will of others, controlling their every thought and emotion. This was his only path to the euphoric rush of power and immortality they promised him. It drove him to prove himself strong and dominant. They stirred within him a blood lust for violence, domination, sadistic pleasure, feeding his hatred of goodness and purity, but even more, his utter loathing of women.

"Hide!" Vivian ordered me suddenly. I listened with renewed attention as I heard my younger self obey her immediately, the hurried rush of my small feet and the pouncing and squeak of my bed sent my pulse thundering even harder in my chest as I listened to the recording, transfixed and horrified.

Hard stomping footfalls were growing louder, coming back down the hall again, my father's roar of rage was thundering toward us in a fury, once again unprovoked except by his demons. He said no words this time as he burst through the door and rushed in. Vivian had risen to her feet to face him rather than being caught on her knees at the wastebasket. In the past, when he had come back like this, if she was on the floor or sitting, he'd deliberately knee her in the face. She had learned to stand up and be ready rather than be caught off guard like that again.

As I listened, I remembered. He had already stripped half his clothes off in the living room during his tormented rage and had come in half naked. His shirt was off and his belt was flopping open on each side of the unbuttoned and unzipped jeans, sagging off his hips. His shoes were also gone, and the smell of his sour feet permeated the room.

I screamed, my fear of his nakedness and the potential terror it held for me as well as Vivian making me forget to be silent. His eyes looked at me with wild, demonic rage and I gasped, throwing the blanket over myself to hide from him, to make him disappear.

He shoved her violently backwards, the force propelling her onto her bed. She couldn't help but yelp at the attack. Although it hadn't been a surprise, it was still a shock to her body to be shoved so violently. The loud thump of her headboard was heard on the tape, and Vivian shouting and screaming her hatred at him as hit after hit burst across her face and the thuds of his fists as they found other parts of her body to beat as well.

He never spoke any sensible words this time, but the growls and roars on the tape were unmistakably his. This time I could barely stand to listen as it seemed to go on forever. Then finally, the sounds of the beatings and his sadistic pleasure came to an end with my father's final grunts followed shortly by his stumbling footsteps leaving our bedroom.

I found myself sitting on my living room floor on my butt, knees curled up to my chest in a tight ball, my ears covered by my hands, jaw locked. I was rocking, eyes tight shut, holding myself, whimpering. I had become twelve years old again listening to that terrible moment in time. My blood was pounding through my ears and I was taking in fast shallow breaths.

"No, stop it Melanie. Stop. You're not there. This is the past. It's all in the past," I told myself, willing myself to stop whimpering. I pressed my lips together and squeezed my eyes even tighter to regain control as the sounds of Vivian and my sobbing still playing on the tape echoed and bounced around in my head. All else around us on the tape seemed quiet now. The sobbing continued for a couple minutes then slowly began to calm until we were both saying soothing words to one another in urgent, nearly silent hushed whispers.

"I'm going to take you away from all this Melanie. I promise you. He won't ever touch you like this, I swear it! I'll kill him first," Vivian whispered desperately to me, her words coming out funny from her busted lip.

"Oh Vi," I whimpered in a tremulous voice.

"Shh. Shh. I promise. I'll stop him."

"How?" I whimpered.

"Don't worry about that now. Just trust me. I promise you. He's going to pay," Vivian whispered urgently, her voice breaking into another strangled sob. I joined her. Together we cried and held each other until the tape clicked and the recording cut off abruptly.

I uncoiled my arms and legs and opened my eyes. Vivian had left the tape recording until it had run out of room on that side on its own. Or, had she just forgotten about it completely after what she had just endured?

I stood up, my legs slightly wobbly from reliving the trauma and squeezing the life out of them. I extracted the tape and carefully examined it. My hand trembled. *This* was real evidence. This could change everything.

I had always thought Vivian had broken her promise to me. I never hated her or blamed her for dying and leaving me alone with that monster we both called our father. But I had often wished she hadn't made me promises like that at all. It gave me hope at the time, yes. Strength to hang on and keep fighting to keep myself alive inside, yes. But once she was taken from me, all the hope I had clung to was left unfulfilled and only added to my devastation, torment and agony.

The dream and hope of running away and living our lives together, had lost all its power to give me strength. All I had left had been my own hopes and dreams of somehow escaping it all, and one day being rid of him completely.

"Well Vivian," I said to her, looking up at the ceiling. I truly felt as though she was watching me right now from Heaven, witnessing the discovery of her secret recording. "Perhaps your promise will be kept after all sister. This tape may finally make him pay for what he did to us!"

Blood Line

Chapter Twenty-Five

I stood at the front window looking blindly out into the world beyond. Somewhere out there my father was biding his time. Patiently waiting like a hunter for the doe, lying invisible in the thicket for her to happen by. She would be young and fresh and full of life. And he would feel absolute elation as he strikes her down with practiced perfection, his weapon aimed not to kill her instantly but only to maim her. He will come stand over her twitching body and soak in her suffering like a drug. As fear fills her eyes, he will crouch down beside her and stroke her almost tenderly, feeling the heat of her body and the pulse of her blood in her veins. He will watch in rapture as the life leaves her eyes. He will relish the moment of her death with a release of euphoric pleasure, the sight of her dead body bringing him to a sadistic climax.

I shuddered, raw fury at the twisted images in my mind. I turned from the window, my hands balled into fists, and screamed. I screamed out my rage and fear and helplessness. I felt overcome with rage and lost all sense of self-awareness and self-control as I gave in and screamed.

Suddenly, I snapped back into awareness of myself as if boomeranged back into my body. "Stop! Stop this screaming and get ahold of yourself!" I rebuked myself disdainfully for my weakness.

What am I doing? Don't give Satan the satisfaction of knowing he got to you this way. Stop freaking out Melanie! I rebuked myself again, ashamed of my outburst. *You're better than this!*

"God!" I called out. "God, don't let it be! Don't let him hurt me again! Don't let him hurt anyone else. Please!" I begged. Hot angry tears were spilling down my face.

He had come into my home! He had tried to violate me *here*. My sanctuary. What if he tried to come back again? I never wanted him in here ever again! I knew Elisabeth had an extremely sophisticated, state of the art security system put in, but my father was clever and resourceful. I didn't want to ever have to worry about him coming in here again.

"God, I want to feel safe in my home. I want my friends safe and...and the book safe. Oh Lord." I buried my face in my hands as I paced through the living room.

"Ouch!" I abruptly drew my hands away from my face and looked at my left palm. The skin was on fire. "Ouch!" I said again, shaking my hand to try and cool it.

The lion's head was emerging from my palm, the nose protruding out first, followed by the mouth and whiskers. Then the full face and mane, ears on top, the details of the fur and eyes lifelike. The lion's face glowed a golden white, my skin transformed into whatever it needed it to be.

"Pray. Pray over your home, claim it as territory for the King. Use the blood." The voice of the Holy Spirit instructed me within my heart, the mouth of the lion moving with it, his voice filling my mind in a clear deep rumble.

"The blood? How?" I fervently asked the Lord. I wasn't sure how to pray this way.

"*Open your mouth and I will fill it.*"

"Um. Okay," I agreed, in a small voice.

The lion's mouth on my palm opened further into a silent roar, the sharp teeth inside glistened like diamonds. As I watched, oil began to pour from its mouth, filling my palm with its hot, sparkly essence, dripping down the sides. The fragrance of roses and jasmine filled my nose and permeated the air.

"Oh!" I exclaimed in awe and wonder. I cupped my other hand under the other to catch the overflow.

"*You will place a blood line of protection over every entry to this house and along the exterior perimeter. This oil represents the blood that was shed for you by HaMashiach Yeshua, Jesus the Christ. Just as the blood of the lamb was used to stop the Angel of Death from entering the homes of the Israelites in Egypt, so shall the blood of the Lamb stop the forces of Hell from entering your home and the King's territory which he has given you authority and dominion over.*

"*It shall be secured both in the physical realm and spiritual. The breadth and length, and depth, and height, all sides shall be covered with the blood and impenetrable. From what is below and what is above, and all that lies in between, so shall it be.*"

"Yes Lord." My heart was pounding in my chest, and the fire in my hand was spreading along my arm deeper into my body.

"*May you be warned!*" His voice thundered now, audibly from all around me. "*Only God's anointed shall enter this place. But so shall those and that which you allow to pass, and all that you bring with you. Be not deceived! Guard your heart. Guard your mind. Abstain from sin and evil doing. Let your heart and mind and body remain pure. For sin is a doorway through which Satan and evil spirits and demons may enter. Snares he will lay to entrap you and temptation he will flaunt before you to bind you. Lust of the flesh, lust of the eyes, and the pride of life. All manner of sin and carnal living is found within these three. Be alert and be not deceived."*

I shuddered at the thought of inviting Satan or his evil ones into my home through sin. "Give me wisdom Lord to know the difference and not become deceived. Help me to remain pure."

"Now, open your mouth and pray."

I felt my hand lift of its own accord, the glistening oil began to shimmer, as if gold dust was swirling within it. Suddenly I just knew that not only did this oil hold the essence of the blood of Christ, but it was infused with the glory and power of God Almighty. It felt like electricity racing down my arm into my palm now and a sense of authority and security girding me up from within my spirit.

I walked to my front door, my hand reaching up, and I wiped the oil on the left, top and down round to the right side of the door frame. Then I swiped it along the bottom of the entryway, drawing a line along the front of the floor as if it was an iron gate.

"In the name of Jesus, I draw this blood line. I declare this home and the perimeter on which we live, the property and territory of Jesus Christ and God the Father. I am of *his* bloodline and I am *his* child, chosen and called. And this territory is off limits to Satan and all who follow him!" My declaration was loud and full of boldness and authority. I had no fear and felt no intimidation. I was a warrior in Christ who gave me strength.

I walked to the front windows and ran my oil-dripping hand along the four sides.

"With the authority of the King of kings, as his daughter, bought and paid for by his blood, I claim this home and this territory! Listen up Satan! You and your followers have no place here! You have no authority here! I expel you from this place!"

I continued on. Touching all sides of every window and door inside the house, both on the first floor and the second floor. I continued to pray as I went, the Holy Spirit filling my mouth just as he had said.

"No principality, powers, rulers of the darkness of this world, spiritual wickedness in high places, evil spirits, demons, or Satan himself shall pass! The blood of Jesus Christ is against you Satan! The blood of Jesus covers me, Elisabeth, David, Bradley, Doc, and all I call mine. We are bought and paid for and you will not have us!"

I finished inside the home and turned off the house alarm to go outside. I went into the backyard first, past the patio and straight for the back fence. I ran my hand along the top redwood slats of the fence that ran horizontal to the earth.

"Father God I thank you that your blood covers us and covers this home and this territory. The breadth, depth, length, and height are held in the palm of your hands and secured by the blood of your Son."

I walked to the entire length of the backyard fence and back, being sure the run the never ending oil pouring from my hand across the backyard gate before unlocking it and walking along the flower bed that separated our front yard with the neighbors on either side. There wasn't a fence or wall to touch, so I just let the oil drip from my hand onto the ground.

The oil in my hand increased in abundance, the dripping speeding up to match the gait of my walk. The physical world seemed to fade away, fogging as I began to see in the spirit what this oil, this blood of the Lamb was doing in the spiritual realm.

"Oh Jesus," I whispered as I walked, the ground beneath my feet was there, but not there. Translucent yet solid. "I thank you that your blood covers this home and this territory on all sides, below and above and every dimension in between."

I could see darkness and light clashing beneath my feet, the dimensions pulsating like waves, bending and flexing, stretching and pressing together. As the oil ran from my hand and landed on the earth, I could hear a rumbling of thunder and the crash of lightening. It seared the realms into place, closed the veils, inhibiting the motion and struggle between the dimensions. Along the line they held together, knitting and binding, locking and tightening. As the blood line connected to all sides of the property, the shimmering translucent ground vibrated with the unseen power of the Creator, the Almighty.

"I thank you Lord that your blood covers me, your angels surround me, and your army goes out before me! There are no forces of evil or hell that can or will penetrate your covering and none that try to stand before me shall defeat me!"

As I spoke the words and ended the walk of the perimeter, I saw the massive bodies of my friends, the angels of God, taking form and materializing in my reality. The Archangel Michael, Gabriel and Uriel stood tall upon unseen platforms in the air. They each had six wings three-times the size of their bodies. They were flexed outstretched in a wide powerful position. The top two were aimed toward the sky, the middle ones were held straight out, horizontal to the ground, and the bottom two wings were flexed, pointed toward the earth at 90-degree angles.

They were over twelve feet tall and light seemed to emanate from within them, their faces shrouded in a luminescent aurora. Their wings held pulses of light that zapped and snapped between the tips, connecting one angel with the next, until the three of them created an arching dome of electrical power that glowed like a multicolored aurora above me and over my entire property.

Their robes were brilliant white and came down to their ankles; the edges shimmered like diamonds and rainbows. Light refracted everywhere as if from prisms. Their swords were drawn, poised for battle, alight with flames of fire, just as mine had been at Mount Moriah.

Michael's silky platinum hair hung past his shoulders, fluttering in a breeze I could not feel or from the energy that pulsed around them. Gabriel's wavy golden-blonde hair was floating and fluttering as well and all of their robes rippled with whatever energy or breeze they stood in. The tips of Michael's wings matched his hair as did Gabriel's. And whereas Michael's skin was closer to a silvery-white, Gabriel's was a golden-tan.

Likewise, Uriel, stood tall and powerful beside them. His skin was that of a polished onyx stone, and his long silky black hair was so dark black that it shimmered blue in the bright morning sunlight. The feathers of his wings were both the deepest black I had ever seen, and laced with shimmering silver, bronze and bright white feathers. They were all glorious and fierce and magnificent.

Their swords all pointed to the ground behind me and I turned, looking down where they had gestured. I saw beneath my feet swarms of demons racing toward the surface of the ground beneath me. My breath caught but I held firm. I pointed with my lion-oiled hand and shook my head, no.

"Stop. You shall not pass! The blood of Jesus is against you. You have no claim here," I rebuked them, my voice strong and void of fear.

I didn't care if my neighbors saw me out here talking to the ground. I was sure I looked like a lunatic to them anyway, walking my yard line, my hand dripping with something shiny they wouldn't be able to figure out the source of.

The demons hit the barrier, clawing and writhing, their mouths opening in silent hisses. Their deformed grey and yellow-green faces and twisted blackened horns were a blurry mess beneath the shifting multidimensional ground.

At seeing the barrier holding, I turned my back on them, ignoring them. I nodded up at the angels in greeting. They nodded back, a smile of pleasure on all of their faces that I was being allowed to see them again. Uriel placed his right hand over his heart in a fist and bowed his head slightly. I think he was telling me he was proud of me. Michael had told me that Uriel was my guardian angel and had withstood more demons and battled on my behalf than I would ever know.

I waved to him and blew him a kiss. I felt as though I knew him already, though we had never spoken. Back in the past, I had seen him, but had not been permitted to talk to him. Michael didn't want me giving away to the enemy prematurely that he was my assigned guardian. Otherwise, they would hunt for him and every human he was ever assigned to guard and protect throughout time. All those he was seen guarding prior to my birth would have been doomed to unimaginable torment and pain in their life just as mine had.

I took a last look around; the air was calming and the shimmering light and ripples of the dimensions were fading out of sight. I looked back up at Michael, Gabriel and Uriel. Their bodies were fading into translucency, until I was no longer able to see them. The ground beneath my feet was once again solid and the world seemed even quieter than before.

I had already completed my walk of the perimeter so I made my way back up to the front door and reentered the house, locking the door as I had promised Elisabeth I always would. I went and reset the house alarm. I heard my phone ringing.

I jogged over to the living room and snatched it off the couch.

"Hey Liz," I said, my voice still strong, not sounding much like me at all.

"Melanie. Are you okay?" Liz said hurriedly.

"Yes, I'm okay," I answered, trying to tone down the sound of authority clinging steadfast to my spirit and coming out my mouth. I didn't want to alarm her in a different way.

"I got an alert on my phone that the house alarm was turned off and I was afraid you were leaving for Redding without me," Liz's voice sounded concerned. "I've been calling you for over ten minutes!"

"Sorry I worried you. I'm still here. Don't worry. I won't leave without you." I reassured her.

"But I couldn't access the house cameras. The system was on the fritz! All I could see was bright light and static from every camera! Did something happen?" Liz's voice was borderline panicked.

"Yes. Something terrible and wonderful. In that order," I confessed.

"What? What does that mean?" Liz insisted, I could feel her unease seeping through the phone.

"It means that right now I am just fine Elisabeth. So please don't worry. Finish what you're doing. I'll be here when you get back and I'll explain it all when I see you. The alarm and cameras are working again, correct?"

"Yes. It all seems to be back in working order now."

"All is well here. See you in a while?"

"Um, yes. Maybe another hour or so. You're sure you're okay?"

"I'm good. Drive safe."

"Always."

Liz hung up and I let out a big breath. So, the cameras had freaked out and she couldn't see or hear what I was doing or saying outside the house? That was interesting and unexpected.

I wonder if my neighbors couldn't see or hear me either?

Thank God if they couldn't. I didn't need more people thinking I was weird.

Blood Enemies

Chapter Twenty-Six

*T*he bitterly cold winter afternoon was cast in a grey hue by the clouds up above, pregnant with a heavy rain soon to come. An otherworldly darkness glided across the sidewalk crackling with malicious energy, unseen by the humans nestled ignorantly in their homes. It paused, lingering at the edges of the blood line, seeking entry. It lashed it's tongue out, tasting the atmosphere for any point of weakness through which to penetrate the blood line barrier, but it found none. A tall muscular figure stood across the street from Melanie Bishop's house waiting. His face intensely following the slithering darkness, hopeful that it would make it past the barrier.

The darkness pooled together and swirled, an angry red lava splitting the outer edges like living molten rock. It lashed out at the blood line, striking it, and was zapped backwards with a forceful *crack!* It convulsed and constricted in on itself, pulsating and trembling before slowly unwinding. It slithered slowly back across the street until it reached the man. It wound and coiled long tentacles around his feet. He glanced down at it, opening his hands in welcome, accepting the darkness back into himself.

The darkness slithered up his green and black snakeskin boots, wrapped around his muscular legs, and wound itself tightly about his torso. Then it seeped through his clothes and soaked into his body from which it had come. The man shuddered, a wicked smile lifting his perfectly heart shaped lips at the rejoining.

A ghost-like image of a snake fought to fit behind his perfectly gorgeous face and pressed beneath his skin. The last features to fade away into his humanoid face were the grey-blue slitted eyes. Black soot floated on the surface of the man's eyes until it slowly blended into the green-and-gold flakes that glittered like stunning specs of colored glass in his rich caramel eyes. His thick jet-black hair came to his shoulders to frame his long thick neck and chiseled jaw covered in a rugged stubble.

His perfectly straight nose lifted and his huge, barreled chest expanded as he breathed in the fresh cold winter air. He could taste the purity of the precious blood of the Lamb that sealed the blood line and could feel the impenetrable force drawn to keep them out and his prey safely within. His massive arms flexed and his eyes narrowed as he glared at the house, his hatred and an unquenchable blood lust burning a fiery hole through him.

She had no idea how long his master had been plotting against her causing her devastation and pain. Did she not know the importance of her destiny? Perhaps after recent events, she was finally beginning to realize the truth.

He did not yet know if she understood just how much they despised her or to what extent they would go to stop her. Not only had she been chosen as a vessel through which God was preparing for the beginning of the end to come by taking back the Book of Mysteries his master had stolen, but now he was sending her through time to collect those things his master had no understanding or knowledge of! How could it be? It had been clear when she took the horns off the ram on the altar God himself provided to Abraham for his sacrifice, that their destined purpose was significant. The angels had taken them immediately from her keeping. But for what? If only he had the answers!

"I *hate* you," he seethed under his breath as he glared at the house. "I shall destroy you."

God himself had declared it to be so when he said to his master in the beginning, "I will put enmity between thee and the woman, and between thy seed and her seed; it shall bruise thy head, and thou shalt bruise his heel." His bloodline was that of the Serpent. Hers was of God's creation, Eve. Now as a follower of Christ, she was also of God's spiritual bloodline. His hatred of her was innate, unquestionable. It simply was. His loathing of her purity and righteousness was all consuming. They were blood enemies because of their bloodlines, and would remain so for all eternity.

"Were you talking to me?" a sniveling demon hissed in a weak, high-pitched cracking voice, creeping up to stand beside the man. Its skin looked leathery and clammy, as if moisture clung to it. Its large orblike eyes were a deep empty black. It had no ears on its hairless head and the mouth that stretched from one side of the bumpy jawline to the other, was downcast like a crescent moon as if forever bowing to Hell.

"No," the man snapped harshly, his voice cold like razor sharp steel.

"Oh. Well, she is inside and we can't get in," the demon snapped back, his weak voice rising in pitch.

"I know that," the man growled.

"Then why did you have us try to penetrate the blood line to find out while your...other self did the same?"

Smack!

The man struck the demon with the back of his hand, his face contorted with rage. "Because I needed to be sure. If she's here, so is the book. I cannot fail again."

"Do not strike me! I am not one of your succubi, Jared!"

Smack!

"You were given to me to command at my will. To do with as I please!"

The small demon let out a long hiss, his forked tongue lashing out and his clawed hands pawing the air in front of him as if ripping the large man to shreds, his fury uncontainable. "You know nothing!"

"I know more than you think!"

"I asked for this commission to see to this female's destruction! It was *I* who stalked her dreams and plagued her with fear since her birth! *Me!*"

"Your commitment must have been halfhearted for she is stronger than ever and free of your influence!" Jared spat, a snarl on his face.

"Do not question me! No one wants to see her grovel and beg for mercy *more than me!* I will bring her to her knees as I destroy her. And no one can do it better!" The emaciated demon pounded his skeletal chest with both fists, the hollow sound reducing any impact of intimidation his boastful proclamations may have held.

"Ah, but I have been placed in charge, not you. And you are still subject to me. Do not forget that!"

"Perhaps, for now. But heed my words—You are still mortal and I immortal. Once you are like me, you will regret ever treating me so. Eternity is a long time to be subject to another's seniority or command. And I shall request you specifically for my legion."

Jared threw back his head and laughed. "Oh Mastema, you forget yourself. You have no legion. I know you were once a feared warrior among the Rephaim, but in the ranks of Satan, you are nothing. Whereas I being yet mortal, have already been given power as an incubus, and shall always outrank you as a son of Lilith!"

"Your bloodline is of no consequence! If you fail, you will be *my* servant. I will see to it!"

"After four millenniums, you have yet to prove your worth, Mastema. You have yet to destroy this mere human female. Do you really think our master will give *me* to the likes of *you*? Gremory and Verin have told me much of how you failed to eliminate this human female at Mount Moriah when you had the chance. Again and again you failed through the hands of her father!" Jared pointed at the house, his eyes fiercely locked onto Mastema.

"You know nothing! She always had help!"

"Excuses! You are pathetic!"

"Angels of the Most High God gave her weapons! And the spirit of God came upon her in the form of a—"

"Have you learned nothing? Do not speak the name!"

"I wasn't going to! I'm not a traitor—"

"You are worthless! That's what you are."

"Do not blame me for being unable to seduce her, *incubus*. You failed to deceive her into handing that book over to you! Twice you were in her presence and she mastered you! Given power?" Mastema mocked with scorn. "You are not powerful enough! You are angry at your own failure and afraid of your own fate!"

"Shut your mouth!" Jared roared.

"Why? Does the sight of me remind you of what is in store for you upon your death? I was once strong and tall and powerful like you, but even mightier! When you look upon me, do you see your fate? Do you fear an eternity amongst us?" Mastema opened his arms as if welcoming Jared home, a contemptuous smile on his face, his large orblike eyes blinking rapidly in feigned innocence.

"I said shut up!" Jared yelled, leaning down into the shorter demon's face.

Mastema laughed spitefully. He took three bouncing steps back on his double-jointed legs and long boney feet. He laughed harder, bowing over and rocking, the high screechy sound of his laughter piercing Jared's ears like metal nails scraping along a cold tile floor.

"Stop it!" Jared hissed.

"You...you are afraid! I see it now. Oh, this is priceless," Mastema howled, pointing and rocking. "I shall tell—"

"You shall not speak of it! You shall not spread your lies!"

"Lies? I am a demon, fool! Lies are sweet upon my lips and fill my belly with contentment. But lies I do not need to speak. Truth, as vile as it is in my mouth, will be your ruin."

Jared snatched for Mastema's neck but the scrawny little demon dodged him, dancing around him, taunting him.

"You cannot touch a demon if they don't wish to be touched. I thought you would have learned by now. Have you learned nothing?" Mastema mocked, throwing Jared's own words back at him with a malicious smile.

"Rraaar!" Jared roared, dashing out to grab him again. Mastema danced out of reach, giggling and wiggling. "I have hit you before!"

"Tsk, tsk. Naughty naughty, son of Lilith. Afraid to tell us what he fearith. Upon your death, you will arise. A demon with these orblike eyes." Mastema petted his own face and batted his lashless eyes at Jared.

"Stop it!" Jared roared.

"Your seductive looks you will not have, and these earthy women, you will not cleave. For at the sight of your mangled form, they will run, and scream, and heave!" Mastema sang and danced around Jared, delighted by his growing fury.

"Go! Just go! I need you not," Jared demanded.

"You cannot send me away," Mastema howled in delight, smiling broadly. "I am your charge, my master," he replied, facetiously lowering himself nearly to the ground in an exaggerated bow.

"Then I send you away as punishment for defying me! I banish you from my presence!" Jared growled, pointing to nothingness beyond them.

"No. You cannot! She is my prey!" Mastema shot straight up into the air, his giggling abruptly stopped. "She is mine!"

"No. She is *mine*. Your punishment for defying me and mocking me will be to never taste the sweet pleasure of her flesh or drink the blood of her ruin. I shall have her. I shall destroy her mind and her soul, all on my own. I need you not!"

"No!"

"Be gone or I shall call our Master and let him decide your fate."

"Fine! I shall leave. But you will regret it!" Mastema began to walk backwards, his insides quivering with dread and terror at the thought of their master, Satan, coming to place judgment upon him. Then he squared his boney shoulders and puffed out his ribbed chest in defiance of Jared's satisfied smile at his fear. "I shall be glad to leave! I will watch you fail from afar! Then there will be no one left to blame but yourself! But know this. I too was a son of Lilith! I too was favored among her and our master once. I failed and I was reduced to nearly nothing! So, enjoy your failure, Jared, *son of Lilith!*" Mastema pranced away with a look of triumph on his face, waving his knucklely hands in an overexaggerated farewell. "I am your future."

Jared was fuming as he watched him go, his fists clenched and his chest heaving. Mastema was one of his brothers? He hadn't known! But it can't be true! Was he lying? Was that really what he was to become at his rebirth? A sniveling writhing servant?

No. No, he couldn't let it become true. He must *not* fail. He would not! He would not be subject to their master's punishment. He knew his mother Lilith was only able to give him so much protection. But who was he kidding? He was one of a thousand sons! He was replaceable...just like Mastema.

Jared didn't have a choice. He'd have to succeed. He may have proven himself valuable in the assignments he'd had the last one-hundred and fifty years of his life, but he knew his status was only secure until he failed. If he lost favor with Lilith or their master, he would suffer worse than Mastema ever had. *That* was what he was truly afraid of.

If he were to fail an assignment of *this* much importance, they would torture his humanoid body until it gave out from the agony. He was stronger than a mortal human, so his body would endure ten-times longer than the average male. But once he succumbed to the death of his flesh, they would bind his reborn demonic form down in the pit for further torment. All who wished to partake of his flesh, through any method they chose, would be free to have their turn. Over and over again they would use him, torture him, assault him. Only after hundreds of years, would they tire of him and only then would he be pushed under the command of one who hated him the most. They would cast lots to purchase him and the winner would ensure his eternal damnation held nothing but suffering and misery.

Jared had seen it happen to Gremory, second son of Lilith. He had failed at Mount Moriah just as Mastema and Viren had. As the great commander of Satan's army over that region, the Angels of the Lord had delivered him back to the pit and handed him over to Satan, bound and stripped of his power. He had been punished in unspeakable ways for nearly a millennium for failing.

Jared *had* to succeed. He couldn't let the book be lost for another seventy generations! Rumors were circulating. They were saying the beginning of the end was near. It was foretold that the Messiah was coming back soon thereafter. And then, the great war would begin. None of them knew the day or the hour of the Messiah's return. Likewise, the year, decade or millennium was also a mystery to them. It was said not even the Messiah himself knew the precise time. Only the Almighty One knew.

Was it even going to be in this millennium? Nine-hundred and ninety more years seemed too long to wait. Too many prophecies had come to pass of late, and the Earth was travailing, calling out for vengeance for the shedding of the innocents' blood, and the corruption in men's hearts turning them toward evil. Wickedness was more accepted now than ever before in human history. As was the worship of idols, backed by demons claiming to be gods.

It was also written in the shifting of the stars and the thinning of the veils between the realms. They all felt something coming. Something their master said they would destroy and conquer. But would they? Or was his master delusional with his self-conceited proclamations of being equal to God?

I must never speak of these doubts! He must never know I feel this way! Jared thought, reminding himself to never express such doubts out loud. He was thankful his master could not read minds. However, his master's ability to read the unspoken language of the body and the almost imperceivable changes of the face, was nearly flawless. *I must never let my face say it either!*

Jared turned back to the house, his face lowered and his eyes fixed like a rabid dog, desperate to attack. He wanted Melanie's blood in his mouth, to taste her life force fill his throat as it left her body. He wanted to drain her dry.

Not until she hands over the book or until you take it from her. Not until then. Patience! Jared reminded himself. If he killed her before she handed him the book, or better yet, opened it for him, it would all be for not, and he would be punished anyway.

He saw movement by the front window and quickly pulled a black baseball hat out from his back pocket, slipping it onto his head and low over his eyes. He stepped back a few steps into the darkness of the shade in front of her neighbor's house. The darkness folded in around him, welcoming him into its depths. The branches and red-purple leaves of the large fruitless plum tree that provided the shade seemed to wilt in his presence, as if his very existence was saturating the ground he walked upon with toxic radiation.

He was not able to see the angels of the Lord that camped around about Melanie's home, but he knew they were there. Being not yet fully demon, he did not have the ability to see past the veils when the Angels of God did not wish to be seen. Otherwise, he had to wait for *the sight* to be granted to him by his master, his mother, or another demon in his presence in order to see them. And with Mastema gone, and no minion reassigned to him yet, he would not have access to *the sight* until one returned.

Amezarak, a Watcher and one of the leaders of Lucifer's fallen angels, had been the one to take Jared to Turin Italy and slip him in between the folds of space-time where he had first encountered Melanie. It had been Amezarak who had given him *the sight* that night. And Amezarak who had since been ordered to be Watcher over Jared's success or failures in this assignment. If Jared called him, he would come. But he must reserve his requests for only the direst of need. Otherwise, he would appear unequipped to handle the human female on his own.

Jared squatted down, looking left than right. The neighborhood was quiet today. If only there was a crack in her defenses. If only he could find a way in.

He looked down at his watch. Twelve-thirty. What was she doing inside? Eating lunch? Was she leaving soon? Was she staying? He hated the waiting and the not knowing. He couldn't get close enough for his lustful presence to affect her and draw her out to him. It couldn't slip past this damn protective blood line!

Jared was still humanoid, but also a demonic abomination, so the blood line Melanie had drawn through prayer and anointing of the home and the perimeter of her territory, though extremely painful and resistant to him, may be penetrated with a direct invitation past it's borders.

Several weeks back they almost succeeded in destroying her at the hands of her father. He and the demons that took residence within him had done their best, but the angels of the Lord had fought them, and the man of God had come, chasing their puppet away.

At the time, Jared had followed his instructions not to seek out Melanie himself. She and her friends would likely expect his return or recognize him from afar and flee. But look how things had turned out without him! And still his master had restrained him. Finally, he convinced his mother to speak to their master and ask on his behalf to trust her son and allow Jared to seek out the woman yet again. His master had been reluctant, but agreed.

Jared was ordered to find a loophole or other ways to trick them into letting him or one under his control into the home so he could steal the book. If that tactic failed, he was to find her weakness and would force her to hand it over. If she withstood him still, only then was he authorized to kill her himself.

It was his master's desire for her own father to be the one to do it. He saw it as a mockery to throw in God's face, her loving *heavenly father*. It would also ensure her humiliation and disgrace and cause the most psychological torment to her during her death. His master wanted her to despise God as he did and swore that she would even curse God before the end. This way, he could have her soul for all eternity, breaking God's heart all the more.

Likewise, her friends would suffer the greatest if her death was at her father's hands. Their weak attempts to stop him, fight him and protect her would all be for nothing, and they would lose all faith and belief in God's love. For it was not only Melanie's destruction they sought. All of them must pay for standing in his master's way *and* for following Christ.

Those deliciously wicked plans were already underway. Jared was not to associate with Dwayne or to assist him. He was to perform his own attacks on several different fronts. Together, they would exhaust she and her friends into giving up or denying their faith. And with any luck, she would walk away from her destiny before she was permitted to die.

Soon you will be begging for mercy at my hands. If I get to you before Dwayne, oh how I will enjoy you. You have no idea what true suffering is. And that book, whatever it is, will be mine to present to my master. He will love me and praise me. He will pronounce before the Kingdom of Hell that I am to be at his right hand. I will rule Hell beside him! I will be like a son to him and be worshiped like a god as he is.

He was a son of Lilith, mistress demon and succubus. Should he succeed in his task to destroy Melanie Bishop, as an incubus himself, his demonic powers would only grow stronger at his death. His rank in the army of his master, Satan, was almost guaranteed to be a significant one. Perhaps over a great territory.

Rome, he would ask to have Rome. His father had been human, a corrupt cardinal of the Roman Catholic Church, who sought the mystical powers and influence of a spirit guide. He had mated with Lilith during a sex ritual. After she had conceived, she killed him, drinking his blood and sacrificing him to her master, Satan. At Jared's birth, she anointed her son in the blood of the innocent, babies murdered by cold steel and fire, and consecrated him to Satan.

Jared was a Nephilim. There were many like him still walking among these filthy humans and they knew not of it. Well, most of them did not. Those that did either believed they were their brethren and had aided in their conception and birth through blood and sacrifice. While others knew the truth, that they were a threat.

The wise ones chose not to engage them until they understood more about them. Such as some world governments who consorted with 'specialists' who had much knowledge of the world religions and ancient practices, spoke the dead languages, and understood much about spiritual manners and mystical rituals. These few were also familiar with the abominable creation of the Nephilim and of their second birth after the death of their humanoid bodies, which turned them into demons. A few of these specialists consorted with demons themselves and sought after mystical powers through witchcraft.

Others saw them for what they were and knew them to be true evil, unyielding in their belief in God and his goodness. These few would report to their government the biblical and historical warnings written about their deceptive purposes and the destiny of these otherworldly beings. In essence, they were sounding a warning to all who would listen in their sphere of influence and in positions of power that the Nephilim were Satan's creation, designed to be weapons of warfare by adding to his legions of demonic armies.

Melanie's friend Elisabeth Becker was such a one. Satan had known from the day Melanie and she met that their friendship would be problematic. He knew not the full impact their relationship would have on Melanie's life and how much she would stand in the way of his plans. God had fooled him. God had strategically led their paths to intercept and interfered. He had turned the evil deeds of others into an opportunity to introduce Elisabeth into her life, someone full of wisdom, goodness and light. Elisabeth would have to be punished for her involvement. They all would.

Jared heard a car turning down the street. He glanced toward the sound and saw Elisabeth's silver Lexus RX 350 rolling slowly toward the house. She was looking left and right, carefully making mental notes of the neighborhood. Hatred swelled within Jared as he watched her. Maybe she was the answer? A way to get the Melanie.

I should go. I am without support.

"I summon thee whoever be near to take me. Now!" Jared ordered out loud. He knew a direct order to any demon of inferior rank within the territory would *have* to answer his call. A small cracking noise was the only warning that the veil's dimensional tear opened up behind him. He felt a clawed hand dig into his left shoulder and pull him backwards into the folds of the veil, just at Elisabeth's car pulled alongside her front yard, and she swiveled her head to the left toward their neighbor's fruitless plum tree.

To Be Continued In...

Grave Keys

Volume 5

ACKNOWLEDGMENT

I want to give a shout out to my editors, AJ and Ruth, for your straight forward feedback, direct honesty, and insights. Of course, helping me catch those spelling errors and "seeing" what I had left inside my mind and neglected to put onto the page, was also a tremendous help! This book would not have gotten released without you both. Thank you from the bottom of my heart!

Books By

R. J. Machado De Quevedo

The Deceiver Saga...

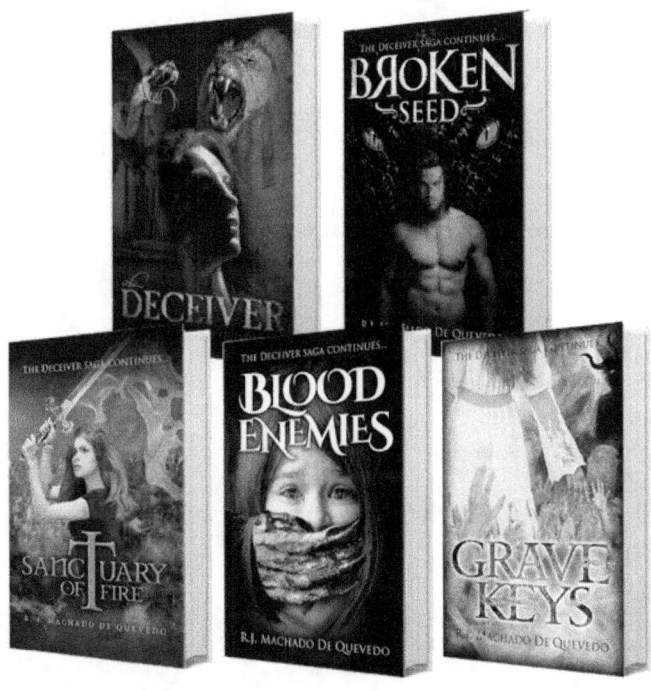

The Deceiver Saga Continues in **Grave Keys**!

Stay Tuned!

For Updates and Release Information Visit

www.TheDeceiverSaga.com

Follow Information

@TheDeceiverSaga

www.RJMachadoDeQuevedo.com

R. J. Machado De Quevedo
P.O. Box 1505
Elk Grove, CA 95759